New York Times and *USA TODAY* bestselling author **Katee Robert** learned to tell her stories at her grandpa's knee. Her 2015 title *The Marriage Contract* was a RITA® finalist, and *RT Book Reviews* named it 'a compulsively readable book with just the right amount of suspense and tension'. When not writing sexy contemporary and romantic suspense she spends her time playing imaginative games with her children, driving her husband batty with *what-if?* questions, and planning for the inevitable zombie apocalypse.

Nicola Marsh is a *USA TODAY* bestselling and multi-award-winning author who loves nothing better than losing herself in a story. A physiotherapist in a previous life, she now divides her time between raising two dashing heroes, whipping up delish meals, cheering on her footy team and writing—her dream job. And she chats on social media. A lot. Come say hi! Instagram, Twitter, Facebook—she's there! Also find her at nicolamarsh.com.

GW00643147

If you liked *Make Me Crave* and
Wild Thing, why not try

Destroyed by Jackie Ashenden
Best Laid Plans by Rebecca Hunter

Discover more at millsandboon.co.uk

MAKE ME CRAVE

KATEE ROBERT

WILD THING

NICOLA MARSH

MILLS & BOON

First Published in Great Britain 2018
by Mills & Boon, an imprint of HarperCollins*Publishers*
1 London Bridge Street, London, SE1 9GF

Make Me Crave © 2018 Katee Hird

Wild Thing © 2018 Nicola Marsh

ISBN: 978-0-263-26647-4

MIX
Paper from
responsible sources
FSC™ C007454

This book is produced from independently certified FSC™ paper
to ensure responsible forest management.
For more information visit www.harpercollins.co.uk/green.

Printed and bound in Spain
by CPI, Barcelona

MAKE ME CRAVE

KATEE ROBERT

MILLS & BOON

To Hunter McGrady.
You're an inspiration!

CHAPTER ONE

"I SHOULD CANCEL." Allie Landers threw another massive load of white towels into the washer and bumped the door closed with her hip. "Honestly, I shouldn't have let you talk me into this in the first place."

"It's cute that you think you let me do anything." Her best friend, Becka Baudin, laughed. She pulled another set of shoes out of the metal bin and paired them up with the appropriate-sized cubby. "And, besides, I already checked us in for our flight. It's too late to turn back now. Our classes are covered. Claudia is handling all the administrative work for the week—for both the gym *and* the shelter. If you stay, you'll just stand around and stress out because things are operating just fine without you." She slid another set of spin shoes back into their cubby. "When's the last time you took a day off, Allie?"

Allie sighed, because that was the one argument she couldn't win. She didn't take days off. Her gym, Transcend, and the women's shelter it helped support were her life. She even lived in the apartment above the building combining the two. When she wasn't filling in teaching a class for one of the girls she employed, she was handling administrative work or doing whatever was required for the shelter.

She preferred it that way. Being busy made her feel complete in a way that nothing else did. She was a vital cog in a perfectly operating machine.

Except little about it was perfect these days.

The few donors she'd had who helped keep the women's shelter afloat had dried up. The gym functioned just fine on its own, but she'd been using every bit of profit to keep the shelter going. Because of that, the gym was in jeopardy now, too. The result... She was in trouble. More trouble than she'd let on to anyone. Admitting it aloud was akin to making it real, and she couldn't do that. There was a way out. There had to be.

A way that didn't involve selling out to the vulture investors who'd been circling for months. Allie just needed *time* to figure it out.

The very last thing she needed was to jet off to the Caribbean to some private island for a week. But if she admitted as much to Becka, then she'd have to admit everything else.

She couldn't. Not yet.

Allie had just sunk what remained of her personal savings account into keeping the power bill paid at the shelter, which meant another month gone by without debt collectors calling. Or, worse in so many ways, without having to turn out any of the women currently living there.

"Hello? Earth to Allie." Becka waved a hand in front of her face, a frown marring her expression. "Where'd you go?"

"Nowhere important." She forced a smile and reached over to flick her friend's hair. "The blue suits you." It was just as bright as Becka's personality, several shades melded together to create something beautiful.

"Don't change the subject." Her friend frowned harder. "You aren't going to cancel, are you? If you try, I will hog-tie you to your suitcase and haul your ass to the airport myself. You're going to relax and enjoy yourself for a week even if it kills both of us."

Allie snorted. "If it kills both of us, that's hardly relaxing, is it?"

"Smart-ass." Becka's blue eyes were pleading. "I've already left our contact info with Claudia. I promise, if something happens and they need you, I'll pay for your flight back to New York without bitching about it once. And I'll never bully you into going on vacation again."

Allie raised her eyebrows. "How much did you have to pay Claudia to make sure she doesn't call me?" That was the only way Becka would make a promise like that. Her friend played to win, and she wasn't afraid to play dirty. Claudia was just as bad.

Becka all but confirmed it. "Claudia is on the

same page as I am. We both agree that you need to get the hell away from this place for a little bit."

She sighed again, but a small part of her looked forward to seven days with no email, no phone calls, no weight of the world on her shoulders. The island had no internet access except in the main lodge, so she'd have no choice but to relax. "I guess I have to go, then."

"Yes, you do!" Becka gave a little wiggle. "Now help me get the rest of these shoes put away before your class. I'm going to pop in if it doesn't fill up. Seven days of drinking and sunning myself are going to add up quick."

Allie laughed and moved to help. She pushed away the worry and stress that had plagued her for months. It would still be here when she got back. What would it hurt to just cut loose for once in her adult life? "I'm looking forward to it." And for the first time since she'd bought the tickets, she actually meant it.

Roman Bassani glared at the pretty Chinese woman behind the counter. "You've been giving me the run-around for weeks. I know for a fact that Allie Landers is in here daily and she's actively dodging my calls. I just need to talk to her." He couldn't tender her an offer to invest in her business if he couldn't pin her down, and he'd been having a hell of a time managing that since his initial call to propose the idea. Coaxing reluctant business owners into seeing things his way was something that usually came easily for him. But Allie Landers was a slipperier quarry than he'd expected.

Apparently she'd successfully dodged him. Again.

"I'm sorry, sir." Claudia didn't look the least bit sorry. "She's out of town for the next seven days. Any business you have with her will have to wait until then."

"Out of town? Where the hell did she go? There's got to be some way to get ahold of her." He didn't actually expect Claudia to answer, but apparently needling him was too much of a temptation.

She leaned forward with a small smile. "She's on a private island with no cell service or internet. If you want to contact her before she gets back, I suggest smoke signals."

Cheeky.

He could use this. Roman plastered a disbelieving look on his face. "That's bullshit. There isn't a damn place in the Western Hemisphere without cell service or Wi-Fi, let alone without both."

"There is on West Island."

Aha. He didn't let his expression shift. "If you say so. You tell Allie to call me when she gets back."

"I'm sure she'll have you at the top of her list," Claudia said sweetly.

Roman turned without another word and stalked out of the gym. He breathed an audible sigh of relief once the door closed behind him. Everything about that place was so feminine, he couldn't walk inside without feeling like a bull in a china shop. It was more than the tiny instructors that he seemed to argue with the second he asked after the owner. There wasn't a single pink thing in sight, but the place was always packed with women.

None of that was a bad thing, but the looks they gave him—as if they expected him to go on a rampage at any moment—and the subtle flinches they made if he moved too fast… It grated. It wasn't their fault, and he applauded what Allie Landers was doing there, but their behavior left him painfully aware of how big his body was by comparison to theirs, and of the fact that no matter how carefully he spoke or how expensively he dressed, he was still a goddamn animal beneath the suit.

He didn't let anyone see it, but those women sensed it all the same.

A predator.

It didn't matter that he'd chop off his hand before he raised it to a woman or child. To them, he was a threat.

Roman cursed and started down the street. He should hail a cab, but he needed to work off his aggression more. The long strides helped clear his mind and ease his agitation, leaving nothing but cold purpose in its wake.

This Allie thought she could skip town for a week and ignore the fact that his deadline was bearing down on them. Two weeks until she had to make a decision, or other investors would make the decision for her. Normally, Roman wouldn't hesitate to play dirty, but his client wanted Allie to agree to the contract without him putting on undue pressure. *An impossible task.* He had a healthy bonus waiting for him if he could pull it off, but that was secondary. His client wanted full acquisition of the business with the shelter intact—the women in the shelter would scatter if they thought it was a hostile takeover. They trusted Allie, and they sure as fuck wouldn't trust *him.*

All of it boiled down to his needing the damn woman to go along with this buyout and he couldn't convince her to get onboard if she wasn't here.

But he had a location.

Roman fished his phone out of his pocket and did some quick searching, his frustration growing when he realized that the resort was booked for the next year straight. The website promised a discreet paradise, which translated to the staff being unwilling to move things around to accommodate him. Since giving him guest names so he could offer his own incentive was against company policy, he'd hit a dead end.

Only one thing left to do. He called his best friend,

Gideon Novak. "Hey, don't suppose you have any connections with West Island in the Caribbean?"

"Hello, Roman, so nice to hear from you. I'm doing well, thank you for asking."

Roman rolled his eyes. "Yes, yes, I'm being a prick. We both know that's not going to change. The island. It's important."

The slightest of pauses on the other end wouldn't have been there if he hadn't fucked things up royally six months ago. He and Gideon were mending that bridge, but rebuilding the trust was slow going. It didn't matter that Gideon understood where Roman was coming from—Roman had still almost cost his friend the love of his life, Lucy.

Finally, clicking sounded on the other end of the phone. "I haven't dealt with the owner specifically, but I've placed two separate clients with his company and they're both still working there."

It was better than he could have hoped. "I need one of the villas."

Another pause, longer this time. "Roman, if you need a vacation, book it yourself. I'm not a goddamn travel agent."

"No shit. This isn't pleasure—it's business. I need to find a guest arriving today. And offer the owner of the reservation a truly outstanding amount of money to reschedule. The resort won't give out that information to me, but if you have an in, they'll give it out to you."

"This better be *really* important."

It wasn't a question, but Roman had nothing to lose at this point. "Vitally. One of the businesses I've been trying to court for months is coming down to the deadline. If my client doesn't invest first, the other wolves circling will. They'll damage the integrity of this place and do irreparable harm to people's lives as a result."

"Sounds like you're playing the hero. A new look for you."

"Fuck no. I'm in it for the bottom line, and the bottom line is that with the right spin, this place could be making a significant amount of money, and the good press that comes from it being connected with a women's shelter would go a long way to opening doors to me that have previously been closed."

Gideon snorted. "Whatever you have to tell yourself. Give me thirty."

"Thanks."

His friend hung up without saying goodbye. Gideon would come through for him. The man was an unstoppable force, and Roman counted himself lucky to have him on his side.

Sure enough, thirty minutes later, a text came through with the reservation details—and the significant amount of money to be wired to the owner of the reservation he was co-opting. Roman wasted no time sending the money and booking the first flight out of New York.

He had seven days to track down Allie Landers and convince her to see things his way. How hard could it be on an island with only ten villas on it?

CHAPTER TWO

ROMAN TOOK FIVE minutes to change and stalk through his villa, getting a feel for the place. It was all vacation luxury, heavy on the driftwood furniture and big open spaces to maximize the view of his private beach and the foliage that surrounded three quarters of the building.

And therein lay the problem.

He should have anticipated that an island with only ten villas would play heavily into privacy, but with the various activities open to all guests, he'd anticipated there would be plenty of time to find Allie and make his argument.

He hadn't figured on not knowing which part of the island she was on.

He strode onto the beach and looked around. The natural curve of the island created a miniature bay that blocked out the view of anyone else. There were bicycles and walking paths to get to the main buildings, where there was a restaurant, a bar, a yoga studio and a boutique gift shop. He could hang out there and hope like hell that Allie would venture in for a meal, but with the option to have dining brought to the villas, he didn't like his odds.

No, better to get the lay of the land and plan accordingly.

A quick examination of the storage unit right off the sand—designed to look like a weathered shack—gave him the answer. There was gear for a variety of water sports. He considered his options and went with the kayak. It was the fastest way to get where he needed to go and stay relatively dry in the process. He shucked his shoes off, paused and then dragged off his shirt, too. The summer sun should have made the heat unbearable, but as he pushed the kayak into the water, it was damn near pleasant.

Roman hadn't been on a kayak before, but it seemed easy enough. He experimented in paddling until he got a good rhythm, then set off, heading south around the island. He'd make a circuit and go from there.

The main problem lay in the fact that he didn't exactly know who he was looking for. He'd never managed to pin Allie Landers down into meeting him in person. The digging he'd done online had brought up precious little—both in details about her as an individual and pictures of her. Her social media accounts were both set to private, and the one photo he'd found of her was from ages ago. The Transcend website, which revealed more about the company's services and vision than its founder, didn't give more information than a contact email address. Considering it was linked with a women's shelter, *that* wasn't surprising, but it still irked him.

That said, Roman had secured deals in the past that began with even less information than he had now. He was confident he'd pull it off this time, too.

The first villa to the south had a family with two smallish children making sandcastles, so Roman kept going, starting to enjoy himself despite the fact that he much preferred the city to anything resembling nature. This didn't feel like *nature*, though.

It felt a whole lot like paradise.

He made his way around the island, surveying beach by beach. There were two with families, two with groups that seemed to consist solely of men, three empty and one with a group of four women who catcalled him as he paddled past. He filed that information away to check on later. There was no telling how many friends Allie had come down here with, but he knew she wasn't married and had no children, so at least he'd narrowed down the search.

By the time he came around the north point of the island, he was fucking exhausted. Roman spent time in the gym regularly, but the heat and the constant paddling wore on him. He steered around the outcropping of rocks and let his paddle rest across the kayak in front of him, taking a moment to roll his shoulders.

Which was right around the time he saw the woman.

She lay on her back, her arms stretched over her head, her long blond hair stark against the vivid red of her beach towel. But that wasn't what made his breath dry up in his lungs.

It was the fact she was topless.

Her golden skin glinted in the sunlight as if she'd oiled herself before coming out to the beach, and the only thing resembling clothing she wore was a tiny triangle of indeterminable color. Her long legs bent as she shifted, her large breasts rising and falling with a slow breath.

He forgot what he was there for. Forgot that his muscles were damn near shaking with exhaustion. Forgot everything but his sudden need to see what color her nipples were.

What the fuck are you doing?

He shook his head. Going closer was inappropriate. Fuck, sitting there and staring like a goddamn creep was the height of inappropriate. It didn't matter how mouthwatering her curves were or the fact that she'd propped herself up on her elbows to watch him.

Roman took a deep breath, and then another. It did nothing to quell his raging cockstand, but he managed to pick up the paddle and keep rowing. Whoever that woman was, no matter that he wanted to spend a whole lot of time up close and personal with her…she wasn't Allie. The one picture he'd managed to source of the woman alone was several years old. Her goddamn senior yearbook photo. She'd been skinny to the point of being unhealthy with her hair chopped short and dyed pitch-black.

He highly doubted she looked anything like that currently.

The one defining characteristic of the women who staffed Transcend was that they were all tiny and chiseled and didn't have a soft spot on their bodies. Beautiful, yes. Roman could appreciate all body types, but none of them had made his hands shake the same way that woman on the beach did. Soft and curvy and with breasts he ached to get his mouth on.

Knock that shit off. You aren't here to fuck anyone, no matter how sexy she is. You're here for business.

He'd go to dinner tonight and see if he could sniff out which of the women on the island was Allie and make his plan from there.

And if he saw the mystery woman once he'd gotten the rest of it figured out?

Roman grinned. Maybe he'd make an exception to his rule and indulge in some pleasure along with business.

He was in paradise, after all.

"How are you doing, sweetie?" Allie pulled on a sundress and headed over to check on Becka. Her friend had indulged a little too heavily on the vodka on the flight down from the city, and the short plane ride from Miami to West Island had made her sick. She'd spent the afternoon sleeping it off, but she still looked a bit green around the gills.

Becka managed a shaky smile. "I think vodka and I broke up."

"It's temporary." She hesitated. "Do you want me to stay? Nurse you back to health?" She was pleasantly tired, but the draw of tonight's menu was enough to have her itching to ride to the lodge and get a better lay of the land. Becka had been so out of sorts when they arrived, it had been a rush to get checked in and settled in the villa so she could sleep off the worst of it.

"God, no. It's bad enough that I've brought shame on my family for ruining the first day of your desperately needed vacation. I'm not going to let you spend any time paying for my bad decisions. Go. Eat delicious food. Drink."

Allie still didn't move for the door. "Why don't I see if the chef can make up some broth or something easy on your stomach?"

"Go, go, go. You're on vacation. You're not required to mother me." She softened the words with a smile, still looking queasy.

Allie went. Becka wouldn't thank her for staying and would only feel guilty if she did, which would distract her from resting. Tomorrow would be soon enough for them to go exploring and try out the stand-up paddleboards Allie had eyed when she'd checked out the beach.

Her face heated at the fact she'd been caught sun-bathing topless. Whoever that guy was, he'd been far off enough that she couldn't clearly see his face. Those shoulders, though... Allie shivered. Even at a distance, she'd seen the cut of his muscles and how purposefully he'd maneuvered the kayak through the turquoise waters. The island must have already gone to her head, because she'd spent a truly insane moment hoping he'd come to shore so she could get a better look at him.

Maybe more than a better look.

Allie laughed at her fanciful thoughts. Vacation hookups were all well and good, but if that was what she'd wanted, she'd chosen the wrong place to go. Isolation and relaxation were the name of the game on West Island, which was exactly what she'd craved when she let Becka talk her into booking the trip. It was the exact opposite of New York and her life there.

But now she found herself wondering if maybe something *slightly* more chaotic would have been a better choice. The sun and sea had soaked into her blood and the heady feeling had her convinced anything was possible. It was only a week. The perfect length of time for a fling...

If she wasn't on a private island in the middle of the ocean without a single man in sight.

She bypassed the little golf cart that was one of the main forms of transportation here. It felt good to walk after being cooped up on the plane and then lying prone while she sunned herself. She usually taught at least one class a day at Transcend—more if she needed to cover someone else's schedule—so being inactive wasn't natural for her. It was only a mile or two to the restaurant and the day had started to cool as the sun reached for the horizon. It'd be downright pleasant tonight.

She'd make sure to wake early and attend one of the yoga classes offered, and the rest of the day would be filled with activities that would keep restlessness from setting in. There was even scuba diving available, though Allie wasn't sure she was feeling *that* adventurous. Snorkeling? Sure. Going deeper with only a tank and a few tubes between her and drowning? That would take a whole lot more convincing.

The path was cleared and well maintained to allow the carts to drive without problems, so she let her mind wander as she fell into a natural stride that ate up the distance without tiring her out. Every once in a while, the path would branch off in different directions, some heading toward other villas, some heading deeper inland. There was a small selection of hiking trails that offered tours of the history of the island.

She made it to the restaurant easily and found it practically deserted. Allie paused in the doorway, wondering if she'd misunderstood the woman who'd checked them in. Maybe it was closed?

"Looks like it's just you and me."

She jumped and spun around. The man stood a respectable distance away, but his sheer size ate up the space and made her feel closed in. She froze. *I'd recognize those shoulders anywhere.* Confirming her suspicion, his gaze slid over her body as if he was reminding himself of what she looked like with nothing but what she'd worn on the beach. She tried to swallow past her suddenly dry throat. "You."

"Me." He finally looked her in the face, and she rocked back on her heels. The man was an Adonis. There was no other way to describe his blond perfection, from his hazel eyes to the square jaw to the cleft in his chin to the body that just wouldn't quit. He might be wearing a shirt now, but the button-down did nothing to hide his muscle definition.

He held out a wide hand with equally perfect square fingers. "Let me buy you a drink?"

"We're at an all-inclusive resort."

His lips twitched, eyes twinkling. "Have a drink with me."

Oh, he was good. Charm practically colored the air between them, and she had the inexplicable impulse to close the distance and stroke a finger along his jawline. To flick that cleft chin with her tongue.

Allie gave herself a shake. "Since we're the only ones here, it'd be silly to sit apart."

The look he gave her said he saw right through the excuse, and why not when it was pathetically flimsy? The truth was that this man was magnetic and she suspected she'd be drawn to him even in a room full of people. He waved a hand at the empty place. "Lady's choice."

"How magnanimous of you."

"I try."

She laughed and headed for the table in the middle of the small patio. There were half a dozen tables, and she picked a spot that put her back to the building and presented the best view of the ocean through a carefully curated gap in the foliage.

He eyed the view and then the chair on the other side of the table, and then he picked it up and set it adjacent to hers so they were sitting on a diagonal, rather than directly across from each other. "Nice view."

She turned to agree—and found him staring at *her*.

Allie wasn't falsely modest. Life was too short to play games with body shaming and pretending she didn't have access to a mirror. She was pretty— beautiful when she put some effort into it—but she'd given up being skinny or petite after the agony of high school, and she wasn't athletically built like some of the women at her gym. Sure, she had muscle beneath her softness, and she could keep up with the best of them in her spin classes, but she loved food just as much as she loved to sweat, and her curves reflected that. Some guys had a problem with that, though she didn't keep them around as soon as comments like "Should you really be eating that?" started.

This guy looked at her like he wanted to put her on the table and feast on *her* for dinner.

The desire stoked the flame inside her that had kindled the second she saw him. She leaned forward, checking his left hand. No ring. No tan lines, either. "What brings you to West Island?"

"It's paradise, isn't it? Who wouldn't want to come here to get away from it all?"

That wasn't quite an answer, but she was distracted by the intoxicating way his mouth moved when he spoke. *Get ahold of yourself, Allie. You're in danger of panting for him.* She took a quick drink of water that did nothing to quell the heat rising with each minute she sat next to him.

Luckily, a waiter appeared to save her from saying something truly embarrassing. He outlined the menu for the night and took their drink orders, then disappeared as quickly as he'd come.

They were in the middle of one of the most beautiful places Allie had ever seen, and she couldn't manage to tear her gaze away from this stranger. She licked her lips, every muscle in her body tensing when he followed the movement. She opened her mouth, but before she could speak, he took her hand, running his thumb over her knuckles.

The touch was innocent enough, but she felt that light movement in places that were most definitely *not* innocent. She didn't have to look down to know her nipples now pressed against the thin fabric of her sundress.

His smile was slow and sinful and promised things she never would have had the gall to ask for. "This is going to sound unforgivably forward, but what do you say we get out of here and go back to my villa?"

It was crazy. More than crazy. She didn't even know his name, and she sure as hell didn't know anything more pertinent about him.

But there on the softly lit patio with the tropical scent of some flower she didn't recognize and the soft shushing sound of the tide coming in, she didn't feel like Allie, gym owner and mother hen, the responsible one who could never afford to do anything out of line or make a misstep because too many lives depended on her.

Here, she was just Allie, a woman. A woman who desperately wanted the man staring at her mouth as if he was doing everything in his power to keep from kissing her right then and there. She licked her lips again, secretly delighting in the way a muscle in his jaw jumped. "Yes."

"Yes?"

"Yes, let's get out of here."

CHAPTER THREE

ROMAN TOOK THE woman's hand as they left the candlelit restaurant and made their way to the golf cart he'd driven there. He'd considered walking, but he was so goddamn glad now that he hadn't.

She looked even better up close than she'd been on the beach. Her white floral dress displayed her large breasts to perfection, hugging her ribs and then flaring out to swish around her thighs as she walked next to him. Her long blond hair was a mass of waves tumbling just past her shoulders, and he could picture it all too easily tangling between his fingers as he thrust into her.

Slow down.

He took a careful breath, and then another, focusing on keeping his stride unhurried and his hand loose on hers. Roman was hardly a saint, but he'd never had a reaction to a woman on such an intrinsic level like he was having now. He wanted to kiss her pouty lips and run his hands over her body and...

Slow. Down.

Not happening.

Not when she looked at him from under thick lashes, her blue eyes devouring the sight of him. She wanted this.

But he had to be sure.

He pulled her into his arms when they stopped next to the golf cart. She stepped against him easily—eagerly—and he let himself off the leash enough to run his hands down her back and to cup her ass, bringing her flush against him. Her breasts pressed against his chest, and he had to bite back a groan at how good she felt. "I'm going to kiss you now."

She didn't give him the chance to follow through. She tilted her face up and captured his mouth. It was chaste as such things went, her lips soft against his, but it didn't stay that way. Roman slid one hand up to cup the back of her head and deepened the kiss, tracing the seam of her lips with his tongue and delving inside when she opened for him. Her hands fisted the front of his shirt, pulling him closer even as her hips rolled against his.

Roman tore his mouth from hers. "Golf cart. Now." Or he was in danger of forgetting where they were and fucking her right here. Even ignoring the glaring lack of a condom, he wasn't a beast incapable of anything resembling control, and this beautiful wanting woman deserved better than to be bent over a goddamn golf cart.

At least for the first time.

First time? You're out of your damn mind.

He picked her up and set her on the golf cart, enjoying the way her lips parted in a surprised O. He was showing off and he didn't give two fucks about it, especially not when he slid behind the wheel, fired up the cart and started down the path leading toward his villa. He almost asked about hers, but just because she was alone didn't mean she was *alone*.

The thought brought him up short. He glanced at her. "Are you here with someone?"

"Just my friend." She correctly interpreted his expression. "I'm single. No boyfriend. No husband."

Thank fuck. "Same." He pressed the accelerator again. There were little eco-friendly lights scattered along the edge of the path to keep them from driving into a tree, and he made it back to his villa in record time.

Roman shut off the engine and turned to face her. "I—"

"Wait." She pressed a finger to his lips, and he instinctively nipped her lightly. Her eyes went wide. "Let's just…enjoy this. It's not like it's real life. It's the fantasy of this place." She motioned with her free hand.

He couldn't argue that, not with the low sound of some bird in the distance and the sky and sea fading from magnificent colors to true dark even as they sat there. He'd left on a scattering of lights in the villa, and he took her hand and led her inside. "Hot tub?"

"Maybe later."

There was no mistaking the intent in the way she watched him, so he didn't waste time. This was, after all, the fantasy. Roman embraced that and ignored the part of him that was curious about who this woman was and why she'd come to this place. About what her life was like wherever she spent her normal time. About a lot of things. He set it aside, because he craved another taste of her, and if he started talking about shit that didn't matter, he would ruin this perfect feeling of breathless need between them.

He led her into the main bedroom. It played up the island fantasy just as much as the rest of this place did: big windows overlooking the water, a massive mattress framed by a driftwood headboard. The white comforter was ridiculously fluffy, but he wanted to see her stretched out on top of it while he drove into her.

Slow, damn it.

Roman turned and framed her face with his hands. He kissed her, exploring her mouth as he took them deeper. She made a little helpless noise in the back of her throat that had his cock hardening even further. He licked along her neck and nudged off the strap of her dress before working his way across her upper chest to do the same to the other side.

As much as he wanted to rip the goddamn thing off her, he dragged his mouth over the swell of one breast and then the other, shifting the fabric lower with each pass. Her fingers tangled in his hair, and she arched to meet his mouth, her breath coming as quickly as his.

He captured one nipple, sucking hard until her back bowed and she let loose a little cry. "I'm taking this off."

"Good." She shimmied out of the dress in a move that made his mouth water, her breasts bouncing a little.

And then she stood before him in only a pair of pink lace panties.

"Fucking perfection," he breathed.

It was hard to tell in the low light, but a flush might have appeared on her cheeks and chest. "Don't make a girl stand here while you stare."

He shook his head, trying to clear it. "Give a man a few seconds to enjoy the view. I didn't get a chance to on the beach earlier today." He kneeled before her and ran his hands up her legs, enjoying the feel of her muscles flexing beneath his touch. He stopped at the generous curve of her hips and hooked his fingers into the edges of the panties. "It drove me fucking crazy that I didn't know the color of your nipples." The answer was a dusky rose, the contrast between her nipples and her tanned skin drawing him farther up onto his knees so he could see her better, could lick her there again.

She shook, just a little. "You could have come to find out."

"Mmm." He kissed her soft stomach as he drew her panties down her legs. "If I had, you would have run screaming up the beach and barricaded the door."

"Maybe." Her breath hitched as he ran his tongue around her belly button. "Or maybe I would have waded out into the water to meet you."

The image hit him with the force of a train. Of the waves cresting up to tease her breasts as she stood there waiting for him. Of him pulling her into his arms the same way he had here in the villa. Of her wrapping her legs around his waist and him tugging her bikini bottom to the side and— "Fuck, maybe I'll make another circuit around the island tomorrow and we can do it right."

She laughed softly. "Or maybe you can put that wicked mouth to good use and we can focus on the here and now."

That sounded even better. Roman moved, hitching one of her legs over his shoulder, and buried his face in her pussy.

Allie had half convinced herself that she was dreaming, but the feeling of his mouth latching on to the most secret part of her was all too real. She closed her eyes and gave herself over to his licks, long and slow as if relishing her taste and feel. It was the single hottest thing she'd ever experienced.

Right up until he turned them and toppled her onto the massive bed. She gasped, the sound morphing into a moan when he pushed a single finger into her, as slow and exploring as his mouth had been.

His eyes drank in the sight of her in a move she swore she could feel. He lingered on her thighs and pussy, hips and stomach, taking extra care over her breasts, before finally settling on her face. "Perfection," he said again.

"You're not too shabby yourself." She reached over her head to grip the comforter, knowing full well that it offered her breasts up for him.

He made a sound perilously close to a growl. "Thanks." A second finger joined the first, and he barely gave her time to adjust to that before he pushed a third into her. Stretching her. Readying her. "Fuck, woman, you feel good."

"You…too." She fought to keep her eyes open, to not miss a single second of the experience. This golden god looked at her as if he wanted to imprint himself over every inch of her, and she was more than happy to play sacrifice for the night. If he could bring such pleasure with his hands and mouth, there was no telling what he'd do with the rest of his body.

He twisted his wrist so that his thumb slid over her clit with each stroke of his fingers, the combined sensation leaving her feeling warm and melty. She let go of the comforter to reach up and cup his chiseled jaw. "I'm going to call you Adonis."

He barked out a laugh. "I'm hardly that pretty."

"You're even prettier." She never would have said

it in real life, without the island and pleasure making her drunk on him. Allie traced her thumb over his bottom lip, slightly fuller than the top. "You call me perfect, but you're flawless."

Another laugh, this one strained. "Trust me, I have more than my fair share of flaws." He turned his head and kissed her palm. "But we'll pretend that's not the truth tonight."

"Works for me." She didn't ask about his flaws. That wasn't what this was. She didn't even know his name, which somehow made the whole situation hotter—because Allie never did this. Ever.

Tonight she was going to.

With that thought buoying her, she reached for his pants. "I need you."

"You have me." He pushed his fingers deeper as if to demonstrate.

"No, I *need* you." She managed to get his belt off and shoved his shorts down his narrow hips. His cock was just as perfect as the rest of him, long and thick, and she swallowed hard. "I'm tired of waiting."

"That's too damn bad, because I'm just getting started." He slid his fingers out of her and looped an arm beneath her waist, sliding her farther onto the bed until he could place her hands on the bottom of the headboard. "I'm not going to tie you down."

Her heart tried to beat itself out of her chest at the thought. "I don't know how I'd feel about that." *Liar.* She wanted it. Allie didn't think she was particularly kinky before tonight, but the thought of being at the mercy of this man…

Slow your roll. He's a stranger. Getting tied up by a stranger is a bad idea, even in paradise.

He stopped, kneeling above her on all fours, his cock dipping down until it almost touched her stomach. Those hazel eyes were completely serious for the first time since she'd met him. *An hour ago. You met him an hour ago.*

He didn't touch her, though he was close enough that she could feel the warmth coming off his body. "If you've changed your mind, we can stop. I'll give you a ride back to your villa or, if you aren't comfortable with that, you can take the cart and the staff will return it to me tomorrow." No judgment in his tone. No trying to guilt her or pull some shady business. Just ensuring that this was exactly where she wanted to be.

She gripped the headboard. "I want to stay. I want you."

His grin had her breath fluttering in her chest like a trapped thing. "You won't regret it."

Before she could think too hard about what tomorrow would bring, he kissed her, long and slow. Reacquainting himself with her as if it had been days since they'd last touched instead of moments. Her Adonis worked his way down her body one torturous inch at a time, turning parts of her erogenous that she never would have considered before that night. The inside of her elbow. The bottom of her ribs. Her knees.

He stroked and kissed her body as if memorizing every inch, until she was a quivering mess. Her world narrowed down to where he would touch her next, to the only parts of her he *hadn't* touched—her breasts and the spot between her thighs where she ached for him. "Please. Adonis, please."

He chuckled against her inner thigh, and she felt it like a bolt to her pussy. "I like it when you call me that."

"I'll call you anything you want if you just *touch* me."

"I *have* been touching you." He shifted to lay next to her, his big palm coasting over her body, an inch off her skin. She shook with the need to arch up and feel him, but the slant of his brows told her that if she tried, he'd just move his hand farther from her. "Unless you mean something specific. Like here." His fingers drifted just above her nipples and then down until she could feel the air displacement above her clit. "Or here."

"Please."

The touch was so light, she thought she might have imagined it. But she didn't imagine the look in his hazel eyes. He leaned down until his lips brushed hers with each word. "I want to feel you coming on my cock."

CHAPTER FOUR

ROMAN HAD LAUGHED when he'd found the stash of condoms on his initial exploration of the villa, but he'd never been so glad for them as he was in the moment when he ripped through a foil packet and rolled the condom over his cock.

He looked at her sprawled on his bed, her long limbs askew, her pussy so wet he could see it glistening from where he stood, her breasts reddened from his mouth, her hair a tangle over the white comforter... Passion personified. "Aphrodite."

She tore her gaze away from his cock. "What?"

"If I'm Adonis, then you're my Aphrodite." He wanted to know her real name, but Roman wasn't a fool—if he pressed her now about it, it would ruin the fantasy they played at. He ran his hands up her thighs as he climbed back onto the bed. "You look like her statue."

Her lips curved in a sinful smile. "You already have me in your bed. You don't have to go overboard with the compliments." She leaned up on her elbows and kissed his throat. "If you don't slide your cock into me right this second, I'm liable to expire on the spot."

Fuck, she kept surprising him. Roman laughed; the sound was harsh with need. "Can't have that."

"No, we can't." She nipped the spot where his neck met his shoulder and then her hand was around the base of him, guiding his cock inside her.

He fought to keep the stroke steady and not drive into her like a goddamn beast. She clenched around him, one leg looping around his waist to take him deeper yet. *Heaven.* There was no other word to describe her little whimpers and shakes that he could feel all the way to the base of his cock. Or for her hands sliding down his back to grab his ass and drive him the rest of the way into her. He tangled his fingers in her hair and kissed her hard. "You know what you want."

"I want you."

He pulled almost all the way out of her and she rose to meet his thrust, her body moving in perfect time with his. As if they'd done this a thousand times before.

It was good. Too damn good.

He pulled back enough to create a little distance between their bodies. "Touch yourself. I said I want to feel you come on my cock, and I meant it."

She didn't hesitate, one hand snaking between her thighs, her middle finger circling her clit. The sight of her seeking her own pleasure while they were still joined threatened to toss him headfirst over the edge. He thrust again, hard enough to make her breasts bounce with each stroke.

Once. Twice. A third time.

She came with a cry, her mouth opening in a perfect O and her pussy milking him. He had no choice but to follow her under. Roman grabbed her hips and fucked her, pursuing his own pleasure even as her orgasm went on and on. Pressure built in the small of his spine and his balls drew up as he came hard enough to see stars.

He managed to collapse next to her instead of on top of her, but only barely. They lay there several long minutes as their gasping breath settled into something resembling normal. Roman pulled her closer, driven by some desire he didn't have a name for, and kissed her again.

She shifted toward him and hooked her other leg around his waist. "God, I just came harder than I've come in living memory and I already want you again. Do you have some kind of aphrodisiac in your sweat?" She licked his throat. "I think you might."

He rolled onto his back, taking her with him so she sprawled on his chest. "If I do, then you do, too." Sure enough, his cock was already stirring.

She squirmed against him, her smile conveying that she knew exactly how hot the move was. "Is it still a one-night stand if we keep having sex until we're both walking funny tomorrow?"

He opened his mouth, reconsidered and shut it. Telling her to stay as long as they were both on the island was premature in the extreme—and would interfere with his business here. He couldn't forget his purpose, not even for this beautiful creature staring at his mouth as if she wanted it all over her body again.

Business would wait until tomorrow.

Roman coasted a hand down her spine, bringing her more firmly against him. "It's still night, so the possibilities are endless."

"I like the way you think."

"Trust me, I'll give you reason to like a whole lot more than that."

Allie woke up to his mouth on her pussy. Again. In the few hours since they'd passed out after having sex again, he'd woken her up three—*three*—times like that, and proceeded to ravish her until her promise that they'd both be walking funny today was definitely a reality rather than a possibility.

His big shoulders spread her legs wide and he fucked her with his tongue, his low growls just as hot as his actions. She slid her fingers through his hair without opening her eyes. "Yes. Right there. Keep doing that." He zeroed in on her clit, mimicking the movements she'd made when she touched herself and pushing her to the edge yet again.

She didn't stand a chance of holding out.

She came with a cry, back bowing and her hands clenching him to her to prolong the pleasure as if she was totally and completely wanton. Maybe she was. She certainly had played the part that night, with no thought to what he'd think of her words or actions because this was only temporary. They were strangers, which was freeing in a way she'd never anticipated. It didn't mean she'd ever do anything like this again, but she was going to enjoy every single second of her time with her Adonis before dawn came.

He left her for several precious moments, but then he was back on the bed, flipping her onto her stomach and drawing her hips up. The position left her exposed, but she loved every second of it, especially when he stroked her between her thighs and then his cock replaced his fingers.

He pushed into her with a smooth move, sheathing himself to the hilt. And then he began to move, thrusting roughly into her and then withdrawing, only to begin again. Allie gripped the comforter and shoved back to meet him, until the only sound in the villas was the smack of flesh against flesh and their ragged breathing. She tried to hold out, tried to keep from being overwhelmed with the pleasure, but he did something with his hips that hit a spot deep inside her, and her orgasm crested in a devastating wave. She cried out, distantly aware of him fucking her harder until he, too, came with a curse.

He dropped to the side and guided her down with him so that they lay spooning with him still inside her. He kissed the back of her neck and palmed her breasts. "Morning."

"Mmm. And a good one at that." She still hadn't opened her eyes, but as one of his hands trailed down to her clit, she laughed hoarsely. "You're insatiable."

"Only with you." He kept up those slow kisses to the nape of her neck. "You make me crazy. I just came and I want you again already." He cupped her pussy, the possessive move making her moan.

But then she opened her eyes and realized how light it was outside. Allie froze. "What time is it?" If Becka woke up and realized she'd never come back last night, she'd be worried. Allie was reliable and dependable, and she most certainly didn't stay out all night while having amazing sex with a stranger. As beyond amazing as it'd been, she hadn't stopped to consider that her friend might think she was hurt or that something bad had happened.

He picked up on her tension and removed his hand. "What's wrong?"

"I have to go." She rolled out of his arms, her body crying out at the loss of warmth, but if Becka wasn't already awake, Allie had to make sure she got back to the villa before that happened. If she *was*, then Allie had some explaining to do.

Either way, she couldn't stay there.

He sat up and watched her scramble for her dress,

a frown marring his handsome face. "I know we joked about it being a one-night stand, but that doesn't mean you have to bolt the second the sun comes up. I thought we could have breakfast before you left."

It sounded just as wonderful and perfect as things had been since she'd taken his hand and embarked on this wild adventure.

Unfortunately, reality was calling—or as close to reality as a person got on West Island.

But she didn't like the look on his face—as if she'd somehow hurt him—so she paused. "I would love that, but my friend is back at our villa, and if she wakes up and finds me gone, she's going to think that I walked off the path and broke my leg or something and sound the alarm. I don't have an easy way to get ahold of her, so I have to go make sure she's not forming a search party."

His frown cleared. "I understand." He got out of bed and pulled on his shorts. "I'll give you a ride back."

She started to tell him she didn't need that, but the truth was she did. It was one thing to take his cart because she'd changed her mind about being with him and didn't want to walk the paths alone at night. It was another to want to skip a potentially awkward morning-after conversation. She was an adult. She could handle it.

She hoped. "Thanks. That would be helpful."

He threw on his shirt but didn't bother buttoning it. It gave him the look of a... She didn't even know, but she liked it. A lot. *Down, girl.* She found her shoes and followed him out to the golf cart.

Allie was so tense as she sat next to him, she was surprised she didn't jostle right out of the seat when he put the cart into gear, but he reached over and took her hand, interlacing their fingers as if they held hands all the time. She relaxed, muscle by muscle, but her nerves didn't calm. "I don't do that normally—any of it."

"You don't have to explain yourself to me." He squeezed her hand. "I had a good time last night."

"Me...too." She studied his profile. Adonis, indeed. "A really good time."

He shot her a look as he took a turn onto a path marked with her villa number. "I'm in danger of being pushy, but I'd like to have a repeat—or several. I'm here on business, but my nights are yours if you're interested."

Her breath caught in her throat, though she couldn't say why. To spend her days with Becka doing all the activities they had planned and her nights with her Adonis... That truly would be paradise. She licked her lips. "I... I'd like that."

He grinned and pulled to a stop where the cart path ended and the walking path began. "In that case, would you gift a poor man with your name? You'll always be Aphrodite to me, but I'd like to know the true identity of the woman I plan to have coming countless times in the next few days."

She blushed and then called herself an idiot for blushing. "I'm Allie."

He went so still, he might as well have turned into a statue. Those hazel eyes focused on her with unsettling intensity. "Allie? Allie *Landers*?"

She jerked her hand back, her heart beating for a reason that had nothing to do with desire. "How do you know my last name?"

He laughed, but not like anything was funny. "This is so fucked."

"What are you talking about?"

Gone was the devilishly charming Adonis who'd seduced her with little effort last night, replaced by a cold man she didn't recognize. "Roman Bassani."

She knew that name. She *knew* that name. Allie scrambled out of the cart and took several steps back, though he made no move to touch her again. "The guy who keeps hounding me? What the hell are you doing *here*?"

His smile was as cold as any she'd seen. "I'm here to convince you to sell your business."

CHAPTER FIVE

ROMAN WATCHED THE metaphorical shit hit the fan in slow motion. He looked at his Aphrodite—at *Allie Landers*—in disbelief. The horror in her expression, the way she took a step back and her body language closed down. Gone was the flirty siren he'd just had in his bed, replaced by a woman who didn't trust him as far as she could throw him.

Still, he tried to salvage it. "I can explain."

"Explain how you hunted me down to West Island and seduced me." She shook her head, blond hair flying. "Nope. Absolutely not. You pulled one over on me. Good job. Way to go. Points for being totally and completely unexpected. You don't get to stand there and tell me you can explain, because this is beyond explanation."

"I didn't know you were…you." He scrubbed his hands over his face. "I'm fucking this up."

"You think?" She took another step back. "Your reputation might be shady, but I never expected *this*."

He started to explain why he thought she couldn't

possibly be Allie Landers, but cut the words off before they reached the air between them. Telling her that her glorious curves didn't fit in a specialized gym was both shitty and wrong, and he'd have realized that he shouldn't assume a single goddamn thing if he'd stopped thinking with his cock long enough to function. *There has to be a way to salvage this.* "I don't see why this has to change anything."

Her blue eyes went wide. "You don't think this needs to change anything." She drew herself up to her full height, somewhere close to six feet. "You're out of your goddamn mind. Get out of here. I never want to see you again."

"Like hell I will." He hadn't wanted to do it like this. In fact, he'd crafted several well-thought-out arguments about how she needed to listen to his investment proposal. All of that flew right out the window in the face of his frustration. "You're going to lose it all if you don't stop being so fucking stubborn and let my investor help you."

She looked at him like she'd never seen him before. "Wanting to preserve what I worked so hard to create isn't stubbornness—and not wanting to sell it out to someone like *you* doesn't make me an idiot." She motioned at him.

"Someone like me." She'd made it sound like an insult, and maybe it was. Roman played dirty. He'd never had any qualms about that truth. He still wouldn't have tried to seduce Allie into seeing things his way—but he would have done everything else under the sun. He still would.

But her obvious disdain stung. He laughed harshly. "Someone like me," he repeated. "Honey, look in the mirror. There's only one reason Transcend is going under, and it's not me. I'm just trying to save it."

Her lips twisted. "How noble of you. Well, you can take your apparent white-knight complex and shove it up your ass." She spun around and marched down the path toward her villa, her middle finger in the air.

Stubborn, frustrating woman.

Admittedly, he could have played that better. Roman pinched the bridge of his nose for a long moment and then turned the cart around and headed back for his place. If he could just tell her *who* his investor was...

Impossible. He'd signed a nondisclosure, which his investor had insisted on. Even if he wanted to tell Allie the details of what his client had planned for her gym and shelter, he couldn't. Judging by her reaction, it wouldn't have mattered anyway. She would have called him a liar and told him he was full of shit.

He'd miscalculated. It wouldn't have changed the reaction he'd had to seeing Allie in person—he didn't think anything could have altered that—but he'd have kept control enough not to try to seduce her.

Fool. He could almost hear his old man's voice

as if the bastard sat next to him. *Took the easy way and look what happened—exactly what always happens. Failure.*

Roman shut that shit down. He didn't have time to wallow in shame for fucking up. He had to figure out a way around it. As tempting as it was to follow her back to her villa and continue the argument until she saw things his way, it wouldn't do anything but make her dig in her heels further. Allie had proved herself to be as stubborn as the day was long. For some reason, she was resistant to investors.

He needed to figure out why. It was the only way to get around her issues.

He took a shower and headed into the main lodge. It was the only place to get a call out on the island or to use anything resembling the internet. It took some convincing to get the woman on staff to give him access to the tiny business center, but he managed.

Roman sat down while the computer hissed and spit in the old-school dial-up sounds. He shook his head. Apparently paradise didn't like modern technology. Go figure. He considered his best options and dialed Aaron Livingston. It was late enough in the morning that the man should be at the office.

Sure enough, he answered on the fourth ring. "Aaron Livingston."

"Aaron, Roman here."

"Hey, Roman, it's been a while. What can I do for you?"

Roman hadn't spent much time out and about since the fiasco with Gideon and Lucy, and as a result, his social life had suffered a bit. He hadn't cared—it was a nice change of pace—but he hoped it wouldn't work against him now that he needed a favor. "I was hoping you could do a bit of a background check on a company I'm considering investing in. I've done the run-of-the-mill one, but the owner is being difficult and I need to know why."

"You mean they weren't down on their knees in awe at your greatness?" Aaron's amusement filtered through the line. "Color me shocked."

"You don't have to rub it in. I missed a step, and I need to figure out where."

Aaron laughed. "You'll have to give me a few minutes to get over my surprise that the vaunted Roman Bassani isn't perfect."

"Asshole."

"Without a doubt." Another laugh. "Give me the business name and I'll see what I can do. It might take me a few days, but I'll find the information you need."

"Thanks, man. I appreciate it."

"Yeah, well, I *am* charging you."

He grinned. "I wouldn't expect anything different." He hung up after Aaron told him to expect the information via email. It wasn't ideal, but he could wait through the long dial-up time to get it if that meant he had a leg to stand on with Allie.

Allie.

Roman sat back and scrubbed his hands over his face. It was time to deal with the fact that he'd fucked up. He might have fucked up badly enough that this account was lost...

No.

Damn it, *no*.

She was doing good work, but that good work could be increased exponentially if she allowed his client to invest and do the equivalent of franchising Transcend. It was a brilliant business model—or it would be if she moved a few things around.

Except she hadn't taken his meetings or returned his calls, and now she was doubly determined to stay the hell away from him. *Fuck me*. He had to fix this, to do something to get her to stop long enough to listen to what he had to say.

She was stubborn. She'd more than proved that. Well, it was too damn bad, because he could be a stubborn bastard, too.

Roman checked his email, verified that the sky wasn't falling back in New York and logged off. It was time to figure out a game plan to get moving again. They were trapped on this damn island together for the next six days, and he'd be damned before he let this opportunity pass because of one mistake.

Though he'd be lying if he considered last night a mistake. He should have gotten her name immediately, but if he had, the night wouldn't have happened. Having Allie in his bed… He stomped down on his body's reaction to the memories that rolled through him, one after another. Her taste on his tongue. The feel of her generous hips in his hands. Her pussy clenching around his cock. The little smirk she gave him when she knew her saucy attitude was flat-out doing it for Roman.

He'd give his left hand for a repeat. *Get your priorities in order, asshole. She might be hotter than sin and amazing in bed and funny as fuck, but she's still business.*

Roman couldn't afford to forget that—or let the lines blur.

"Roman Bassani followed you *here*?"

Allie adjusted her balance on the paddleboard and dipped her paddle into the water. "I already said that." She glared at the gorgeous water. Stupid paradise, making *her* stupid. She knew better than to go home with a man whose name she didn't even know. *You didn't go home with him, because neither of you are home right now.*

Not helping.

"I just… That's ballsy. Even for Roman."

She twisted so fast, she almost fell off the damn board. "You say his name like you know him." Something resembling jealousy curled thorny vines through her stomach. She had no right to the feeling, and it made no rational sense, so she ignored it.

"Well… I kind of do." Becka shrugged. She wore a bikini so tiny, it must have taken an act of God to keep it in place. It was a bright neon green that managed to complement her equally bright blue hair. "Or we have one degree of separation, but I've met him once, I think. He was a friend of my sister—*is* a friend of my sister." She shook her head. "You know the story, but yeah, he's really good friends with her boyfriend and so they all hang out sometimes now. But I know him by reputation, at least, and he's the best at what he does."

That was part of the problem—Allie wasn't one hundred percent sure what he *did* do. He'd contacted her about investing in Transcend, but it quickly became clear he was a middleman for someone else and… She didn't know. Trusting an investor was difficult enough without them hiding behind a third party. That extra distance didn't bode well for her being able to maintain control of the gym and shelter if she signed on the dotted line. She'd come to West Island to escape real life for a little bit, and it'd followed her here despite her best efforts.

And then she'd slept with it.

She frowned. *Way to make the metaphor weird, Allie.* "It doesn't matter. It was a mistake and I'm going to enjoy the rest of my damn vacation without worrying about him." She was lying through her teeth, but she sent a look at her best friend, daring Becka to call her on it.

Becka dipped her paddle into the water, moving farther away from the beach. "I don't know, Allie. He's one sexy golden god of a man. What would it hurt to bang him like a conga drum while you're down here and go back to hating him when you get home?"

"He's *Roman Bassani*. He's the enemy. I can't just separate things like he apparently can." Though he'd been just as shocked at her identity as she was at his. Allie knew that for a fact. The man might be a good actor, but no one was *that* good. She didn't believe for a second that he'd tried to manipulate her through sex, but that didn't mean she was about to roll over and offer herself and everything she'd worked so hard for to him just because he was beautiful and had an amazing cock and—

Not helping.

"What would a little hot and smoking sex hurt?"

She splashed water at Becka. "It wouldn't *hurt*, but the man already doesn't take me seriously. If he thinks he can seduce me into seeing things his way, who's to say he won't do exactly that?"

Becka sighed. "You're right. I know you're right. It's just so… This place. It makes everything sexier and less complicated, and even though vodka and I broke up, vodka would most definitely agree that it's a good idea."

"Then it's a good thing you and vodka broke up." They reached the mouth of their little bay and paused, letting the paddleboards shift with the water. She lay back on the board and closed her eyes, willing the sun to soak in and chase away her tension. "It's not fair. I am so damn furious that he pulled this shit, but my body hasn't got the memo. He's just so hot. It makes me crazy." She was pretty sure she had the self-control to keep her hands off him going forward, but Allie wasn't all that eager to put it to the test.

"Yes...yes, he is."

There was something in her friend's tone that made her open her eyes. Allie shot up to a sitting position. "Tell me that the sun has gone to my head and I'm hallucinating."

"If you are, we're sharing the view." Becka adjusted her kneeling position like she was going to war. "I can distract him if you want to make a break for it."

That ugly jealousy rose again, even though there'd been nothing resembling insinuation in her friend's tone. Anyway, Allie had *just* said that she wanted nothing to do with him. She couldn't have it both ways. And Becka was... Becka was a force of nature. *Stop that right this second. She's your friend, and he's not anything to you.*

The "he" in question rowed his kayak toward them in smooth movements that made the muscles in his shoulders and chest flex—kind of like they had when he was hovering over her and thrusting…

Her face flamed, and she shook out her hair, doing her best to pretend it was just the external heat and not his effect on her. When Roman got close enough for her to see his face clearly, she went still. He wasn't looking at Becka at all. His attention had focused on Allie like a laser beam, and he cut through the water, effortlessly back paddling to coast to a stop next to her paddleboard. "Allie."

"I'm not sure of the exact laws in this place, but I'm pretty sure they frown on stalking."

His lips quirked. "It's a small island. We're bound to run into each other."

How could he sit there so calm and collected while she fought between the desire to tip his damn kayak and to jump him where he sat? She steadied her grip on her paddle and fought for control. It was easier— so much easier—to be angry than it was to deal with the conflicting emotions inside her. "Is that what you call your kayaking past our villa—again?"

His grin was quick and unrepentant. "The view isn't as good this time." She sputtered, but he didn't give her a chance to reply, turning instead to look at Becka. "I know you."

"Not really. But you know my sister—Lucy Baudin."

He flinched—actually *flinched*—though he covered it up quickly enough that Allie wouldn't have noticed it if she wasn't watching him so closely. Becka had said her sister and Roman were friends, but it appeared to be more complicated than that. Allie filed that away, and irritation rose all over again. "We're trying to have a relaxing time, and you're ruining it."

Roman turned the force of his attention onto her again. His wearing sunglasses should have diluted the effect, but she swore she could feel his gaze dragging over her, taking in her high-waisted vintage swimsuit. It was a flirty black with pink polka dots, and she knew she looked damn good in it. From the way his grip tightened on his paddle, he agreed.

A strange sense of power rolled through her. He wanted her just as much as she wanted him. She'd known that, of course, but the shock of his true identity had twisted everything up in her head. Roman might be considering trying to seduce her into submission, but… What if she turned the tables on him?

Or maybe you want any excuse to get into bed with him again.

She ignored the internal voice and leaned forward, giving him a good view of the excellent cleavage the underwire top created. A muscle ticked in his jaw, and she reveled in the power for a breath before reason kicked back in. "Get lost, Roman. You don't have anything to say to me that I want to hear."

"We both know that's not true." His wicked grin widened, leaving no illusions to what he meant.

Her irritation flickered hotter. He was sitting there, the smug bastard, and thinking he had her number just because he'd made her come more times last night than she'd thought physically possible. Thinking he could railroad her into doing what he wanted.

Well, fuck that.

Allie lifted her chin. "I don't know anything of the sort. It was a forgettable experience across the board." She jerked her chin at Becka, who watched them with jaw dropped. "Let's go. Something stinks out here."

CHAPTER SIX

ROMAN SPENT THE rest of the day considering his game plan. Cornering Allie was all well and good, but from the look she'd given him before she paddled away early, if she thought he was trying to talk business, she'd cut him off at the knees. *Misplayed the hell out of this.*

There was no use bitching about it. The ideal situation was long gone, so he had to work with what he had.

What he had was smoking-hot chemistry with Allie Landers. Seeing her in that cocktease of a swimsuit with her hair in beach waves around her shoulders hadn't done a damn thing to help remind him why he couldn't have her.

He decided to give her until tomorrow—or, rather, to give *himself* until tomorrow—to figure it out. Rushing this wasn't going to accomplish the end he wanted.

He checked his email, more to distract himself than because he thought there'd be any information yet. There wasn't even a single fire for him to put out. Roman ran his hand through his hair. Paradise was all well and good in theory, but it was fucking boring here by himself.

On a whim, he made his way to the patio where sunset yoga would be held—and stopped short at the sight of Allie in a pair of yoga pants and a tank top that seemed to have too many straps but showed off her body to perfection. As he watched, she pulled her hair back into a ponytail and unrolled a mat.

The instructor—a tiny woman with dark eyes, curly hair and a wide smile—caught sight of him. "The mats are against the wall. Pick a place that feels best for you, but we do prefer to have classes in a single line when there's a small number of people."

Allie turned and her eyebrows shot up, then lowered just as fast. "What are you doing here?"

"Yoga." There was no backing out now, even if he wasn't going to get the relaxation he'd craved. He'd wanted to get time with Allie to talk, but this wasn't what Roman had in mind. He grabbed one of the mats and flung it out with a snap a decent distance from hers. On her other side, Becka looked between them as if she wasn't sure how she was supposed to react.

The instructor was all smiles and gentle hands as she picked up his mat and scooted it until it was only a few inches from Allie's. "Yoga is meant to be experienced as a group. We like to keep it intimate here—which we can't do if someone is creating distance." Once she was satisfied he'd obey, she moved to the front of their line and started her intro.

Roman tried to do yoga a few times a week. He spent too much time sitting behind a desk, and he preferred boxing as his outlet—both activities wreaked havoc on his joints. Yoga helped, and it settled his racing mind like little else, he found.

Today, there was no settling to be had.

He had too much awareness of Allie next to him, her body flowing through the positions effortlessly, her breathing deep and even. *She* didn't seem the least bit bothered to have him so close. It aggravated him in a way it shouldn't have, but he wanted to force her to acknowledge that he was *right there*.

"Roman, you seem distracted." The instructor— he couldn't remember her name, but it was something like Tiffany or Tracy—stopped next to him, using a light touch to adjust his Warrior I stance. "Focus on your breathing. Inhale deeply." She demonstrated, exhaling slowly through her nose in an audible sound. He followed suit, and she nodded. "Exhale your thoughts. Let your breath center you. You gave yourself this time today. Don't waste it."

He tried. Fuck, he tried. But each inhale brought a faint strain of Allie's lavender scent, and when she turned to face the side of the patio, he found himself captivated by the faint sheen of sweat on her golden skin.

It was too much.

With his being so goddamn in tune with his body, there was no fighting the threatening cockstand. Roman turned on his heel and stalked away, into the main building. He needed distance from that woman, but fuck if it helped. Her scent was in his system, her body a siren call he had no business hearing. She didn't want him—not now that she knew who he was.

He shouldn't want her, either.

But he did.

Roman considered heading straight back to his villa, but the thought of being alone right now only increased his agitation. *This was a mistake.* Which part was the biggest mistake was up for grabs, but he was considering chalking the entire situation up as a loss.

With nothing left to do, he walked into the bar. It was a small space—no more than a serving counter with a handful of lounge chairs facing the ocean— as everything on the island was. He motioned to the bartender. "I need two shots of whiskey, and a double seven and seven."

The man's eyebrows rose. "Sure thing. You've got the run of the place, so post up wherever you like." He turned back to select two bottles from the wall behind him.

Roman didn't want to sit, but standing there and hovering while the guy made his drinks wasn't going to win him any goodwill. He had enough people pissed at him currently, so he strode to the middle lounger and dropped into it.

Lazy streaks of color teased the darkening blue of the sky, the first sign of day giving way to night. Roman welcomed the change even as he dreaded what it meant. Another day down. Another night closer to failure.

It might not be the end of the world if he didn't secure Allie's cooperation in franchising her gym model, but her gym *would* go under. He'd seen the financials. She couldn't keep it afloat much longer, and it'd be a goddamn tragedy to see it fail. He knew she didn't look at it that way, but if she'd stop fucking *reacting* and listen to what he had to say, she might see things differently.

Right. Because I've been the very essence of calm and collected.

Her rejection stung. He wasn't about to lie and say it didn't. It sure as hell did. She hadn't just rejected the professional persona he displayed for work—she'd rejected *him*. The sex changed things, for better or worse. *Looking like for the worst at the moment.*

The bartender brought his shots over and lined them up, quickly followed by his drink. Alcohol wasn't the best choice—not when he needed to be sharp and fully present—but he wasn't going to be around Allie tonight, and the rest of the island could sink into the sea for all he cared. Roman downed one shot and then the second. The fiery burn of whiskey did nothing to chase away his... He didn't even know what the fuck to call what he was feeling. It wasn't pleasant—that was all that mattered.

Women's voices carried over the beach, and he tensed. Before she walked around the corner, Roman already recognized Allie's voice. She stopped short when she saw him, but Becka rolled her eyes and gave her friend a small shove. "Enough, already. I get it—he's a jerk. I won't even argue with you." She winked at Roman, not looking the least bit repentant. "But I want a drink, and this is the quickest way to get what I want." She gave a brilliant smile to someone behind Roman. "Hey, gorgeous. Can we get something fruity and alcoholic?"

"Sure thing, ma'am."

Becka launched into how horrified she was to be called "ma'am" while she walked to the bar, but Allie stopped at the foot of Roman's lounger. "You ran off pretty unexpectedly."

He gave her body a slow caress with his gaze, from her bright pink painted toes to her yoga pants to the tank top that offered her breasts up to perfection. "I was preoccupied."

She inhaled sharply, and he didn't miss the way her nipples pebbled against the fabric of her shirt. "Don't play games with me. It happened. We're done. End of story. Stop bringing it up."

"I didn't bring it up." He climbed to his feet

slowly and then closed the distance between them. "A word."

"Excuse me?"

"We need to have a goddamn conversation, so get your panties out of a twist long enough to unstopper your ears and hear what I have to say." He grabbed her hand and towed her into the growing shadows beneath the palm trees framing the walkway to the beach. Roman didn't stop until they were out of sight of the bar and far enough away that Becka's flirting with the bartender was barely audible. Only then did he release Allie and turn to face her. "Now, where were we?"

Allie was so furious, she could barely put two words together. "You don't get to just decide that we're having a conversation and haul me out here to do it."

"If I was going to *haul* you anywhere, it'd be over my shoulder."

Her body clenched at the thought of him doing exactly that, but she fought her reaction back. "You are insufferable. Do you know when the last time I had a vacation was? Ten goddamn years ago when I was still in freaking high school and on spring break. Ten. *Years.* Becka had to twist my arm to get me here, but I was enjoying myself—"

"I know *exactly* how thoroughly you were enjoying yourself."

She ignored that because if she tried to deny it,

she'd be a red-faced liar. "That changes nothing. The point is that I'm *not* enjoying myself now, and the only one to blame for that is *you*." She went to push him back a step, but her hands had a will of their own. They stayed on his chest, and she sucked in a breath at how warm his skin was. The man might be a corporate suit, but he looked perfectly at home in his shorts without a shirt on here in the growing darkness near the beach. It was almost enough to forget all the reasons she never wanted to see him again.

Allie stepped closer and lowered her voice. "Nothing you say can make me believe you're anything but a goddamn shark."

"Who said I'm trying to convince you of anything?" The words brushed her mouth as he leaned down, just a little. "I *am* a shark, Allie. I've never pretended to be anything else."

She started to call him a liar, but he was telling the truth. He hadn't tried to seduce her with sweet words to get her into his bed—he'd offered her exactly what she wanted in as many words. Black-and-white. Simple.

It wasn't simple at all.

"I despise you."

"You want me." His hands rested lightly on her hips. "It tears you up inside that you crave my cock, but you can't fight it no matter how hard you try." He backed her up, step by slow step, until she bumped a tree. Roman kept coming, the side of his face brushing hers. "Did you think about how good it'd feel to have my fingers sliding into these yoga pants?"

"No."

"Who's the liar now, Allie?" His lips caressed her earlobe. "I'd love a private yoga session. Just us. No friends, no instructors, no clothes. How long do you think we'd last before I was on my back and you were riding my cock?"

She couldn't breathe. Her skin felt too tight, as if it were several sizes too small, and her core pulsed in time with her racing heart. "I would never—"

"No, Allie. No more lies between us. You're pissed that I'm here—I get that—and you're even more pissed that you want me. Trust me, I know the feeling. I was never supposed to fuck you, and if I'd known who you were…"

She leaned back enough to look at his face—or what she could see of it in the darkness. "If you'd known who I was, you wouldn't have gone there with me."

Roman cursed. "Even if I'd known your name, that wouldn't have stopped me from wanting you. Needing you."

She stroked her hands down his chest to the waistband of his shorts. "Do you need me now?"

"I never stopped."

This was the worst idea. She needed her head clear, and it was nothing but muddled around Roman. He was too big, too beautiful, too overpowering.

Even now, she leaned forward, the few inches between them too much distance. He let her, his hands on her hips branding her—but not trying to guide her. Allie inhaled deeply. "Do you drug your cologne? Because, seriously, how am I supposed to think straight when you smell so good?"

He chuckled. "I'm not wearing any."

He was gorgeous and a god in the bedroom, and he had to smell good naturally. Because of course. "I don't like you."

"You don't know me."

She could argue that, but it didn't feel completely accurate. Allie traced the waistband of his shorts with her fingers. She shouldn't…but she was going to. She unbuttoned his shorts and slipped her hand in to grip his cock. "I don't have to know you—I know this."

"You're playing with fire."

"Maybe." Definitely. If she was smart, she'd release him, walk away and spend the rest of her vacation in as close to bliss as she could get, throwing herself into relaxation before she had to go back to reality. She stroked him again, liking the way his body went tense but his hands stayed still on her hips.

As if he was waiting for permission.

The realization sent a thrill through her. She kept stroking his cock, teasing him. "Did you really think it would be that easy?"

"What would?" He spoke through gritted teeth, and her body gave another thrill of pleasure.

"Getting your way." She squeezed him around the base and nudged his pants down a little farther so she could cup his balls with her free hand. "You thought you'd show up here, interrupt my vacation and what? I'd fall all over myself to give you exactly what you wanted?"

Roman released one of her hips and braced his hand on the tree behind her. The move brought him closer to her, but not so close that he impeded her movements. She stroked him harder as he slid his cheek against hers, his breathing hitching with every downstroke. He nipped her earlobe. "Isn't that exactly what happened last night?"

She glared and gave his balls a squeeze that was just shy of vicious. "You're awfully cocky for someone who's got their nether bits in my hands."

"They're very capable hands." He shifted to press butterfly kisses along her jaw and down her neck even as his hand on her hip squeezed her. "Don't stop."

"I should." She didn't. "I should stop right now and leave you with a wicked case of blue balls." Why was her breath coming as harshly as his? He'd barely touched her, but having his cock in her hands and him so close… Intoxicating. There was no other word for it.

Roman gave her collarbone an openmouthed kiss

and dragged his hand up her side to palm her breast. "I'll just go back to my villa and jack myself off thinking of your sweet pussy. Not as good as the real thing—nothing is—but you gave me more than enough inspiration to get the job done." He tugged the strap of her tank top off her shoulder. It was one of those things with a built-in bra, so the motion freed her breast. He repeated the move with the other side, and she shivered as the breeze coming in off the water teased her nipples. "Beautiful," Roman murmured.

"You go overboard with the compliments." She kept up her leisurely stroking. It was like the rest of the world ceased to exist outside their little sphere. It was just her and Roman, driving each other crazy.

"I give credit where credit is due." He bent and sucked one nipple into his mouth. The position meant she had to let go of his cock, which she did with reluctance. He cupped her through her yoga pants, the coolness of the tree against her back only highlighting how warm his body was. "If I slipped my hand in here, would I find you wet and wanting? I think so." He traced a single finger up the seam of the pants— right over her clit. "I think having my cock in your hands turned you on as much as the fact that we're ten yards away from the bar and anyone coming up from the beach will get the show of their life."

She pushed back against him even as her hips rolled into his touch. "That's not true."

"Liar." She felt more than heard the word as his breath caressed her neck. "You get off on this as much as I do." Another stroke through the fabric. "Would you take my cock right here, right now?"

She started to say yes, but common sense reared its ugly head. "I'm not fucking you without a condom."

"Mmm." He kissed her neck. "I know." Roman pulled her pants down in a swift movement. She started to protest, but he went to his knees in front of her and yanked her foot free. *Oh*. He looped one leg over his shoulder and she caught the glimpse of white teeth when he grinned. "Have a little faith, Allie. I'm not a complete monster." And then his mouth was on her pussy and she didn't have the breath to argue.

CHAPTER SEVEN

ALLIE FORGOT ALL the reasons she wanted nothing to do with Roman under the slow slide of his tongue. He tasted her pussy as if he'd been years without it and wanted to imprint every last detail on his memory. She bit back a cry and covered her mouth with one hand even as her other laced through his hair and pressed his face closer to her.

His dark chuckle vibrated over her clit, nearly sending her to outer space. What was he *doing* to her? She didn't act like this. She didn't screw strangers, and she definitely didn't let a man she was pretty sure she didn't like give her oral while in clear view of anyone who happened by.

He pushed two fingers into her and zeroed in on her clit, sucking and then flicking it with his tongue in a rhythm she couldn't have fought even if she wanted to. His fingers deep inside her circled that sensitive spot and he mirrored the movement with his tongue, driving her ruthlessly over the edge. Her hand muffled her cry, but only barely. Allie slumped against the tree and watched him press his forehead to her stomach as if trying to get control of himself.

As if fighting not to rise and drive that glorious cock into her right then.

Finally, he helped her get her foot back into her yoga pants and stepped back while she righted her clothing. Roman didn't speak, didn't look at her, and she couldn't help the dip of disappointment deep in her stomach.

Allie took a fortifying breath and turned for the bar. She needed a drink and to get the hell out of there. She could smell him on her skin, and between that and the orgasm, she was having a hard time remembering why Roman was off-limits.

So off-limits that I just had his mouth all over me.

She managed one step before a hand closed around her arm. Allie looked back, waiting to see what he'd do. Roman finally cursed and released her. "We need to talk, Allie. Actually talk."

Disappointment warred with righteous anger. "Wrong. As I've said half a dozen times already—I am on vacation." Her orgasm-induced high brought more words. "On the other hand, if you want this." She motioned to herself. "Then that's something we can negotiate." At the look on Roman's face, Allie almost took the offer back.

He stepped closer. "You want to separate business and pleasure."

"Business and pleasure should always be separate." She lifted her chin, half-amazed at how brazen she was being, but it wasn't as if she had anything to lose. Roman wasn't going to give up—the limited interactions she'd had with him up to this point reinforced that belief—and she also wasn't going to back down. They could either blow off some steam here on the island before they got back to her dodging his calls and his trying to buy her business out from under her, or they could go their separate ways now.

There was no happy medium. Not for them.

His gaze dropped to her mouth. "I can't promise that. The timeline is too tight and—"

"I don't want to hear it," she cut in. "If you can't promise you won't talk about business, then don't talk at all."

That delicious muscle in his jaw ticked. "You make it sound so simple."

"It is. It's exactly that simple."

Roman stared at her long enough that she had to fight not to squirm. He smiled, the expression doing nothing to quell the urge. She crossed her arms over her chest. "What?"

"I don't have to make any deals with you, Allie."

Again, disappointment tried to take over. She fought it back down, but she was less successful this time. She had to make a conscious effort not to let her shoulders dip or her spine bend. "And why's that?"

"Because you want me as much as I want you." He traced a single finger down her throat and over her sternum. "You want me so badly, if I crooked my finger, you'd be back at my villa, naked and coming on my cock. You say you'll draw the line in the sand, and that's fine, but you'll be fighting yourself more than you'll be fighting me to keep from crossing it."

Her growing anger was almost a welcome relief. Allie knew how to be angry. She didn't let it control her, but most of her successes in life could be chalked up to doing things out of spite. A trailer trash girl from upstate New York couldn't go to college? Like hell she couldn't—and she'd get the majority of it paid for while she was in the process with volleyball scholarships. Having a forward-thinking women's-only gym that paired with a women's shelter was unconventional? Sure, it was. But that wasn't going to stop her from going for it full throttle.

Roman thought he could sit back, kick up his heels and let the lure of his cock draw her in after she'd laid out her terms?

Not fucking likely.

She pushed his hand away from her. "You're wrong."

"Am I?"

She wanted to smack that smug look off his face, but that wasn't how she operated. She stepped back and then stepped back again. "The terms are what they are. If you can't respect that, stay the hell away from me."

He blinked, as if he hadn't expected her response. "Allie—"

"No, you will not 'Allie' me as if I'm being irrational. I want you. We both know it. What *you* don't seem to be able to wrap your brain around is that while you might be ruled by your cock, *I* am more than capable of making decisions that aren't based in sex." She forced herself to turn around and walk away from him. "If you change your mind, you know where to find me."

She didn't give him a chance to respond before she picked up her pace and made her way back into the lantern light now illuminating the bar area. Becka turned away from the handsome bartender and raised her eyebrows. "You look like you've been up to no good."

"I have no idea what you're talking about." She took the bar stool next to her friend and downed the tequila shot waiting for her without hesitation.

"That was mine," Becka said mildly.

"I'll get you the next one." She shook her head. "What am I saying? They're included." She'd lost her damn mind. There was no other explanation for how she was acting—like a horny teenager who didn't care what was at stake as long as she got hers. Allie was better than that. She had to be.

The bartender poured them each another shot and set a fresh margarita in front of Allie. "Ring the bell if you need me."

"Sure thing, sweetie." Becka barely waited for him to walk out of eyesight before she swung around to face Allie. "Explain yourself. I didn't think you needed assistance, but I can't tell if you've been in a fistfight or fucking against a tree."

Allie's face flamed. "We didn't have sex."

"But you did *something* against a tree." She shook her head. "For a woman who says you despise that man, you are having a hell of a time keeping your hands off him."

She started to protest, but what was the point? Allie could chalk up the night before to her not knowing who he was, but she didn't have that excuse this time. She knew who Roman was and why he was here, and she'd still stuck her hand down his pants. "I get around him and my rational brain shuts off. It's like I have a lady Neanderthal in there, and she's decided she really likes the look of Roman and wants to bang his brains out and to hell with the consequences."

"This is a new thing for you." Becka downed her shot and set the glass on the bar with a faint clink. "It's disconcerting, huh? To have rational Allie who follows all the rules overrun by the hindbrain."

That was exactly it. She kept saying she didn't do things like this, but only because it was the truth. Back in New York, Allie never would have laid down the offer she'd just given Roman. She wouldn't have gone home with him in the first place. She glared at her tequila shot. "I think they pump something into the air on this island to make people act irrational."

"Or maybe...just maybe—" Becka nudged the

shot into her hand "—it might *possibly* be that you've been wound so tightly for a seriously long time that the first situation that arose where no one was depending on you, you let yourself live a little. You don't have to play whipping girl about this, Allie. It's okay to want him."

But it *wasn't* okay.

She didn't know how to reconcile the person she was back home and the woman she was acting like here. "I'm not supposed to want him. Anyone but him."

"Ah." Becka nodded and took a long drink of the pink thing in front of her. "I don't have an easy answer for that. You going to his place tonight?"

"No." She might want him more than she had a right to, but that didn't change the fact that she *didn't* want to talk business with him—or, rather, fight about business. If he couldn't agree to that bare minimum, then the pleasure wasn't worth the pain.

She just had to keep reminding herself of that.

Roman didn't sleep well. Every noise brought him fully awake, sure that Allie had changed her mind. He knew she wouldn't. She had drawn that line in the sand and she was stubborn enough not to cross it. He might have bullshit her yesterday, but he knew the truth.

The ball was in his court.

He woke early and attended the sunrise yoga

class. There were a few people there he didn't recognize, but neither Allie nor Becka showed up. It was a relief to turn off his mind for a bit, but the feeling lasted until he walked into the tiny business center and went through the irritating process of checking his email.

Aaron had come through for him.

Roman stared at the document for a long time before he printed it. Even if he decided to take Allie up on her offer, he still had his eye on the prize for when they got back to New York. That meant he needed the deeper research so he could figure out how to play this. They were down to the wire.

It wasn't completely his fault, but that didn't change the bottom line.

He gathered the papers, double-checked to make sure the document hadn't downloaded on the computer and logged off. There was plenty of time to get his reading done and then figure out how he'd plan the rest of the day. Accidentally running into Allie might be entertaining as fuck, but it wasn't accomplishing anything. He had to figure out a better way to go about this.

I could take her up on the offer.

Roman hesitated in front of his cart. It seemed simple enough—leave business out of things. It meant passing up valuable opportunities to talk to her, but...it wasn't like Allie was talking to him at this point. She wasn't going to, either. She'd made that more than clear.

There was no goddamn reason not to say yes.

He turned around and headed back into the main building. The hostess smiled when she saw him coming. "Mr. Bassani, are you enjoying your stay?"

"Very much so." He was about to enjoy it a whole hell of a lot more. He stopped next to the desk she stood behind. "I was hoping you could help me with something."

"Of course." She smiled brightly, her brown eyes lighting up with the rest of her face. "Let me know what you need and I'll take care of it."

"I'd like to send a message to one of the other villas—villa six."

Her face fell. "Oh, I'm sorry. We do our best to create an isolated and relaxing atmosphere here. If guests choose to come into the lodge, that's one thing, but we don't seek them out unless they need something." And she clearly thought that whatever he wanted to send wouldn't be relaxing.

Roman put on his most charming smile. "It's just a little note. If they order dinner tonight, there would already be someone going out there. You can just include the message with the food."

Still she hesitated. "I'm not sure."

"If it makes you feel better, you can read the note. Just to ensure it's all on the up-and-up."

Another hesitation, shorter this time. "I sup-

pose…" She passed over a thick piece of island stationery. Roman accepted the pen and scrawled a quick
note. The hostess frowned. "That's it?"

"She'll know what I mean."

She smiled, obviously put at ease by the fact he
hadn't written anything inappropriate. Roman could
have corrected her assumption, but he needed Allie
to get that note. *Passing notes. That's what I've been
reduced to.*

It would be hours yet before he knew what *her*
answer was—possibly longer if she decided to make
him wait. The entire thing was beyond his control,
and it irritated the fuck out of him. What was he
supposed to do with this? Roman was used to seeing
what he wanted and going for it—and heaven help
anyone who thought they could stand in the way.

He wanted his client happy, and the only way that
would happen was acquiring the gym.

He wanted Allie, too.

Therein lay the issue—he couldn't have both.
There might not be any sort of future with Allie,
but there sure as fuck wasn't one if he kept pushing
her. She'd made that more than clear.

If he stopped pushing her, they could relax into
the insanely hot sex, but he'd have to let his plan for
Transcend go. It might not be the end of the world, but
Roman's career was built on the faith that he could
provide exactly what he promised. He'd never met
an obstacle he couldn't account for and overcome.

Until now.

He turned and strode out of the main building and to his cart, gripping the stack of papers. All the information he could come up with for Allie and her gym—something Roman should have done a long time ago. Oh, he'd done the basic background check and pulled the available financial statements he could get ahold of, but he hadn't dug deeper than that, even when she'd refused to meet him.

Stupid of him.

He didn't need to navel gaze for the rest of his goddamn life to know why he hadn't pushed as hard as he normally did. *The shelter.* He admired the hell out of what she was doing there, and he knew it was pretty damn likely that she had some kind of history that drove her to create a safe space like she had. Having a man try to bulldoze her might trigger shit that he'd have to be a monster to pull up.

He'd played softball with her.

Now that he'd met Allie, he was forced to re-evaluate. She wasn't anything like he'd expected. She wasn't a wilting flower that would crumble at a sharp word. The woman had thorns, and she had no problem using them. Roman gripped the papers. The gloves were coming off. Now.

CHAPTER EIGHT

ALLIE BARELY WAITED for the man to leave their covered food before she yanked the lids off. "I'm starving." If she'd spent any time wondering if she'd be active enough while on vacation, she needn't have worried. Swimming and paddleboarding had left a pleasant soreness in her muscles and an equally pleasant tiredness.

Also, she'd been ready to wade into the ocean and try to catch her own fish if dinner hadn't shown up when it did.

Becka laughed and bumped Allie with her hip. "They also brought vodka. Your priorities are suspect."

"Food always trumps vodka." She speared a glazed shrimp with her fork and then grabbed a chair. "I'm glad to see that you and vodka are back on speaking terms."

"We're taking it slow." Becka pulled up a second chair and sank into it. "My shoulders are killing me. I obviously need to add more push-ups to my routine."

Allie laughed. "The girls will love that." Her friend had a reputation for being a brutal fitness instructor—a reputation she'd more than earned—and this would only cement it. One of the biggest draws Transcend offered was high-energy spin classes with combined exercises that worked the entire body. She reached for the pitcher of cucumber water in the middle of the table and froze. "What is that?"

Becka reacted first and snatched up the little folded note. She read it and frowned. "What the hell *is* it?" She turned it around, and Allie's heart skipped a beat.

Yes.

The word had been scrawled with a careless masculine hand, and even though it wasn't signed, she had no doubt who had written it. *He accepted my terms.* A flush spread over her skin, and even though she tried to fight it, Becka saw.

Because of course she did. She dropped the note and pointed a finger at Allie. "It's from Roman. You sly fox, I thought you were calling the whole thing off."

Allie pushed her food around the plate with her fork. "I told him if he could keep from badgering me about business—or even talking about it—then we could spend more time together."

"That was the tamest euphemism for banging your brains out that I've ever heard." Her friend slouched back into her chair and laughed. "Vacation has done wonders for your stress level. I told you so."

"The guy trying to convince me to sell the gym that I worked my entire adult life to get started and keep running followed me to another country to pitch his sale, and you call this trip a success."

Becka shrugged, completely unrepentant. "You took care of that by removing business from the equation. Now there's only the hot monkey sex to worry about, and I think you two have proved that you're more than capable of keeping your eye on the prize." She made an obscene gesture.

Allie spit out the sip of water she'd just taken. "Oh. My. God."

"Just calling it like I see it." Becka winked. "But seriously—if he's willing to shelve that big black mark against him, are you going for it?"

There was no reason to think he was telling the truth. He could be trying to pull a bait and switch to get her alone. But that didn't make sense. He could have found a different way. Roman had more than proved how capable he was in tracking her down. He had no reason to agree if he wasn't interested in exactly the same thing she was—sex.

Her body clenched at the thought. Allie set her fork down. "I think so."

"Woot!" Becka gave a little wiggle. "That's my girl. In that case, I'm bringing that delightful bartender, Luke, back here for some of said hot monkey sex."

She shot her friend a look. "You wouldn't, by chance, be throwing me at Roman so you can hook up with Luke?"

"Oh, please. We both know that I'm more than capable of finding a suitable place to get under that uniform if I have to." Becka sobered. "But I don't want to get him into trouble, so the villa is a better option." She held her straight face for all of two seconds. "What are you waiting for? Go! Get your…" Becka stopped short, her expression turning wicked. "He's stacked, isn't he? You can just tell by how he carries himself that the man is packing serious heat."

"Becka." Allie laughed, which broke the tension that had been building from the moment she realized Roman had changed his mind. She sat back in her chair. "You did that on purpose."

"You're stressing, which is the opposite of what you're supposed to do here." Becka popped a strawberry into her mouth. "I helped."

"Yes, you did." She looked at the food, but her stomach was tied in too many knots to think about eating right now. Allie pushed back her chair and stood. "I guess I should…change?"

Becka picked through the food and added more to her plate. "You want my advice?"

"As if saying no would stop you from giving it to

me." She snagged one of the bright red strawberries and took a bite.

"Wear that." Becka waved a fork at her.

Allie looked down at her muscle tank top and sleep shorts. "This is not sexy."

"Lose the bra and whatever you're wearing under the shorts." She grinned. "If he doesn't take you right there on the floor, I'll give you twenty bucks."

Allie walked across the warm sand to Roman's brightly lit villa. Soft music emerged, and though she couldn't quite place the lyrics, the lilting melody drew her in. She made her way up the porch stairs and stopped just outside the ring of light from the foremost lamp.

"You're teasing me."

She jumped and then silently cursed herself for jumping. Allie searched the spot where his voice had come from, only making him out of the shadows when he moved closer. "How long were you lurking there, waiting to make your grand entrance?"

"Would you believe me if I said I went for a swim to burn off some energy and just got back?"

She started to call his bluff, but he walked into the light and, sure enough, he wore wet swim trunks and his hair dripped tiny rivers down his shoulders and chest. It took more effort than it should have to drag her gaze to his face. "Swimming in the ocean at night is stupid."

"I survived." He held out his hand, as imperious as a king. "Come here."

Allie had never been one to make an entrance, but she found herself wanting to prove Becka right. She threw her shoulders back and put a little extra hip into her walk, knowing it would make her breasts sway more than normal.

Sure enough, as soon as she breached the circle of light, her chest was exactly what held Roman's attention. His hazel eyes went wide and then hooded. "AC/DC."

"I'm a fan." She looked down and pulled at the hem of her shirt, which drew the fabric forward and revealed a bit more side cleavage. "They're classic."

"How attached are you to that shirt?"

The question brought her head up. She found him closer than before and stopped. "I've had this shirt since I was thirteen."

"Mmm." He circled her, and she didn't bother to try to keep him in sight. Allie already knew what he'd see. The tiny sleep shorts that her ass filled out, the slits in the side teasing even more skin. The carefully ripped sides of the shirt that showed her breasts and part of her side. She normally wore the shirt for sleeping or working out—*with* a bra. It was practically indecent without one.

Which was the point.

Roman stopped in front of her, closer than before. He reached out and ran his hands slowly down her arms, his thumbs caressing the sides of her breasts. "I'll show the required restraint not to rip it off you right this fucking second."

Allie shivered. "If you did, we'd have a problem."

"Noted." His hands moved back up her arms, thumbs again making the movement a tease. "Were you wearing this when you got the note?"

"I might have made a few alterations." *Thanks for the tip, Becka.*

"Mmm." The sound was somewhere between a purr and a growl. Roman released her arms and hooked his fingers into her shorts. A swift yank and they hit the deck. "No panties. Allie, I think you're going to fucking kill me."

She started to pull her shirt off, but he stopped her. "Keep it on. It's just as much a tease as you are."

"If anyone is a tease, it's you."

"Is that so?" Roman undid the ties at the front of his suit and slid it off without taking his eyes from her. "You came earlier, Allie. I suffered."

She smacked his hands away when he reached for her again. "Don't pull that shit with me. You said you'd jerk yourself. If you didn't, that's your problem, not mine." She tried to make herself believe the words. She wasn't some idiot teenager who thought blue balls meant she owed a guy something, but the thought of Roman suffering didn't sit well with her, even if he was the enemy outside of this island.

"If you think my hand can compare to your pussy,

you're sadly mistaken." He went to his knees right there in front of her and lifted her shirt to bare her completely from the waist down. "It's been hours, Allie. Fucking *hours* that I've wanted you and haven't been able to do a goddamn thing about it." Roman dragged his mouth from one hip to the other, just below her belly button. He inhaled deeply. "I crave you. What are you doing to me?"

"Me?" She didn't get more than that out before he nudged her legs wider and gave her pussy a long lick. The position didn't leave her open nearly enough, and she tried to spread her legs farther without toppling over.

Roman hooked the backs of her thighs and lifted her to straddle his face. She blinked down at him, but he was too busy taking advantage of the access. He delved his tongue into her, and pleasure made her stop worrying about if he was going to drop her. She clung to his head and gave herself over to what he did to her, trusting him.

He fucked her with his tongue the same way he fucked her with his fingers and cock. Thoroughly. She could barely shift against him in her current position, though, and frustration warred with desire. "Not enough. I need more."

His growl vibrated through her and seemed to center on her clit. He shifted and she let loose a cry as he stood and walked them to one of the lounge chairs arranged to look out over the beach. With the light of the villa, the contrasting darkness felt absolute, but Allie didn't have a chance to think too hard on that before he laid her on the lounge chair and lifted his head. "Not enough."

"That's what I said."

He pushed two fingers into her. One stroke. A second. A third finger joined them. Roman used his other hand to tug her shirt to reveal one breast. He flicked her nipple with his tongue as he plunged his fingers into her again and again. "Is this enough, Allie?"

Yes. No.

She thrashed, shaking her head. "I need *you*."

He nipped the underside of her breast. "You missed my cock. You've been empty and aching for me since you left. That orgasm earlier only made it worse, didn't it?"

"Yes," she sobbed out. It was the truth. Instead of taking the edge off, she'd been acutely aware of what she was missing, rather than what she'd gotten.

"You need me, Allie." He kept up the punishing rhythm with his fingers. "You need what I can give you."

"Yes! I need you." She grabbed his shoulders. "Tell me you have a condom nearby."

She felt his grin against her skin. "I stashed some earlier." He reached under the lounge chair and she heard the familiar crinkle of foil. Roman ripped it open and stopped touching her long enough to roll it on. "Up."

Allie scrambled to obey, already anticipating what came next. He took her place on the lounge chair and guided her to straddle him. "That shirt won't last much longer." He cupped her exposed breast and went still as she positioned his cock at her entrance. "That's it, Allie. Take what you need."

I need you.

She didn't say it again. It felt too big, too vulnerable, to give voice to, when she was going out of her mind with what he was doing to her. She sank onto his length, enjoying teasing them both by taking it slow. Only when he was sheathed completely inside her did she breathe out. "Yes. This."

He pulled her shirt up. "I want to see all of you while you ride me."

There were no shadows to hide in out here on the patio. Anyone who walked up could see them, but that was the point of paradise—there was no one but them. She liked the thought of being interrupted, though—more than she wanted to admit.

Allie took her shirt off, braced her hands on his chest and began to move. A long slide up, and another down while she rolled her hips. It felt so fucking good, she had a hard time keeping up the rhythm. Roman's grip on her hips urged her on, her pleasure cresting all too soon. She dug her nails into his perfect chest. "I'm close."

"I know."

So damn cocky. It would have been unbearable if not for the way he watched her, as if she was something he wanted. Needed. Allie couldn't close her eyes, couldn't look away, couldn't do anything but ride him with one slow stroke after another, pushing them both toward oblivion.

"I love your body." He skimmed his hands over her stomach and up to her breasts. A few breathtaking seconds spent plucking her nipples and then he coasted his hands back down to her ass. "Fucking phenomenal."

"Stop talking." She had decent self-confidence, but that didn't mean his showering her with compliments made her comfortable. Allie knew Roman wanted her—he wouldn't have acted the way he had since meeting her if he didn't. He sure as hell wouldn't have compromised his business plans to give them a reprieve. She might not know him well, but she knew that much. But the way he spoke to her—about her—was as worshipful as if he really thought she was Aphrodite.

But she was only a woman, and not one that he'd like all that much outside of paradise.

Allie might not be sure of a lot of things, but she was sure of *that*.

CHAPTER NINE

ROMAN HELD ALLIE'S BODY, but her mind was a million miles away—just like it'd been since they'd finished having sex. He had no right to push her. He knew that. The agreement that had brought her here in the first place was the same one that kept him from asking anything that might link back to New York.

Except…

"What are you thinking about?"

"Hmm?" She blinked those impossibly blue eyes at him and gave herself a shake. "Sorry. I was mentally wandering."

It was tempting to let it go. Hell, it was the right move to make. But when Roman opened his mouth, that wasn't what came out. "Tell me."

"It's just boring stuff." She shifted off him and climbed to her feet. A small petty part of him was pleased to see her legs shake a little. The sex had been…beyond words. Desperation—that was what he felt for her. He'd hoped she'd respond favorably to the note, but Roman hadn't been sure she'd actually come to him.

He wasn't sure of a lot of things when it came to Allie.

She scooped up her clothes but made no move to pull them on. He liked that. She was so comfortable in her body, and that confidence was just as attractive as her looks were. But all that was surface-level shit. He wanted to know *her*.

Roman stopped short. Knowing her wasn't part of the bargain. It was supposed to be just sex—strictly physical with nothing else involved.

She didn't say no emotion. She said no business. Apples and oranges.

He steadied himself and followed her into the villa. She meandered to the kitchen and pulled a bottled water from the little fridge. Allie watched him as she took a long drink. "What?"

"What?"

She frowned. "Now you're the one mentally wandering. What's going on in that devious brain of yours?"

He grabbed his own water and contemplated it. "I was thinking about the terms of our agreement."

She went still. "And?"

This was the moment he could back off, change course and keep them in a safe spot. But Roman had never met a woman that both turned him on and called him on his shit the same way Allie did.

He might never again. Letting her slip through his fingers without at least poking at the potential for more was a stupid move.

Roman didn't make a habit of making stupid moves.

"And I want to know more about you." He watched her closely, noting the tension that crept into her shoulders.

Allie set her water bottle down on the counter. "Why?"

"I haven't connected with a woman the way I've connected with you. Ever. I want to know if it's just lust that will run itself out or if it has the potential to be more."

"Normally…" She shook her head. "There is no normal in this situation. In another world, I'd think that sounded downright nice. But this isn't another world, this is ours—and no matter how great the sex is or how compelling the connection, there remains the fact that you want to buy my business out from underneath me."

"Ah-ah." Roman held up a finger. "No business talk. That was part of the agreement."

She glared. "That was before—" Allie cut herself off and looked at the ceiling. "Damn it, you're right."

"Taking business out of it—"

"Roman, that's crazy."

"You keep throwing around that word. Maybe you're even right." He set his water bottle next to hers and placed his hands on either side of her hips on the counter. "But what if you're not, Allie? Do you run into this kind of thing so often that you're willing to pass it up?"

She frowned harder. "Your argument is compelling. Irritating, but compelling."

He'd given her a lot to think about, but he wasn't planning on giving her recovery time to think *too* much. Roman traced her collarbone. "Any siblings?"

"Only child." Her expression closed off, as clear as if she'd lit a neon sign warning him away.

Family is off-limits. Got it. It was almost enough to confirm that Allie's pushing so hard for the women's shelter had something to do with her past. He set the thought aside—for now. He wanted her to tell him when she was ready. He might have the file on her history, but he decided right then that he wouldn't read it. Better to hear from Allie whatever she wanted to share with him.

What happens when we get back to the mainland? We'll figure it out.

She pulled her hair off her shoulder to give him a clear path to stroke to her arm and back again. "You have siblings?"

"No. I always wanted one or two, but my parents had other priorities."

"Like what?"

He glanced at her face, but there was only curiosity there. Roman stroked her knuckles. "They're both from old money, and while I was growing up, their only priority was making the family even richer. My old man was a stockbroker, and my mother was a consultant like I am."

"Was?"

He shrugged. "They retired a couple years back. I haven't seen them since, but they bought a boat and have been traveling the world. It's large enough to house a small army, because my parents never do anything halfway. They'll come around again when they get tired of the travel, but I don't expect them to stay. They're nothing if not restless. Always have been." He loved his parents, in a way, but it was a distant sort of feeling that meant talking to them once every few months and the occasional Christmas card if they stayed in one place long enough to receive it. He had friends who'd grown up with loud families filled to the brim with messy love that manifested in jokes and hugs and the occasional heated fight. There was no room for that in the deep stillness of the Bassani household. "Even when I was little, they traveled regularly. They'd be gone for weeks at a time."

"That must have been hard to deal with as a kid." She looped her arms around his neck, bringing them chest to chest. "I don't know anyone with perfect parents—mine included—but at least most of them were *there*. The absent figures must have sucked."

"I thought it was a grand old time when I was in high school. Parties every weekend and girls staying over most days of the week." He tried to give the comment lightly, but it came out bittersweet.

Allie saw it. She smiled and ran her finger along the shell of his ear. "You turned out all right—except for the whole business thing that we aren't talking about."

He laughed. "Except for that—which is my life."

"Seriously? You don't have anything else going on but work?"

He squeezed her hips. "Do you?"

She opened her mouth but seemed to reconsider. "That's a fair point. I could argue that my business is more honorable, but… I'm not in the mood to argue."

Roman liked this side of her, playful and almost coy. He turned them so he could lean against the counter with her in his arms. "What, pray tell, are you in the mood for?"

"I'm so very glad you asked." She kissed his throat, his shoulder, his pectoral muscle, sliding to her knees in front of him.

The wood floor would be hell on her knees, but she gave him a look from beneath her lashes that stilled the words in his chest. Allie knew exactly what she was doing, and she wasn't about to let him drive the show this time. The sight of her stroking his cock with an exploratory hand had him in danger of swaying. It was only the promise of her wetting her lips that kept him pinned in place.

"Your cock is ridiculous." She gave him another stroke. "There isn't another word. Just *ridiculous*."

He tried to laugh, but the sound came out strangled. "Thanks?"

"You're welcome, but seriously, with you packing this around, it's no wonder you're an arrogant ass." She flicked her tongue along the underside. "You've gone down on me like a dozen times in the last few days and I haven't had you in my mouth even *once*."

"Show me."

She gave him a saucy smile and then his cock was between her lips. Allie sucked him down, down, down, until he bumped the back of her throat. Roman gripped the counter, using every ounce of self-control he had to keep from moving other than to brace his legs a little wider.

She took the move as an invitation and cradled his balls with one hand while she kept sucking him. Just when he thought he couldn't take another second of it, she released him. But Allie wasn't done. She gripped him around the base of his cock with her free hand and licked him like he was her favorite flavor of lollipop. That evil, wonderful tongue of hers damn near made his eyes roll back in his head. "Fuck, Allie."

"We're about to."

Allie barely got the words out before Roman was on her. He paused long enough to pull a condom out of a candy bowl she hadn't noticed before and then he was between her thighs, his cock sliding home. He cradled her head with one of his big hands, saving her from knocking herself silly against the hardwood floor with the strength of his thrusts.

It was...brutal. There was no other word to describe the way he moved over her—in her.

She loved every single second of it.

She was the reason he'd lost control.

Allie clung to him, rising in time with his strokes. "I should give you head more often."

"Every single goddamn day." He kissed her, which was just as well because she didn't have a response to that. *Every day* sounded a whole lot like time after they left West Island. Allie couldn't promise him that. He *knew* she couldn't promise him that.

She kissed him back with everything she had. Their limited time only made the whole thing hotter—or that was what Allie told herself as Roman rolled them. She slammed down onto him without missing a beat, leaning back to brace herself on his big thighs. The man was a monster in the best way possible. The wood floor bit into her knees, but the faint pain only spiked her pleasure higher. She bent down and kissed him without throwing off their rhythm. *Yesyesyesyesyes.*

"After this. Bed."

"Yes."

Roman palmed the back of her head and pressed a hand to the small of her back, effectively caging her. He thrust up, fucking her from below while she was helpless to do anything but take it. Allie took his mouth even as he took her pussy, the pleasure so intense there was no holding out. She came with a cry that he ate down, her legs shaking from the strength of her orgasm. He followed her over the edge with a curse, his rough grip at odds with the sheer pleasure written across his face.

They lay there for several long moments before he shifted her to the side. She gave a small cry of surprise as he climbed to his feet, lifting her into his arms in the process. "What are you doing?"

"We might not be too old to fuck on wood floors, but it's hell on the back." He shifted her and pressed a soft kiss to each of her knees. "And on you."

"Totally worth it."

"Without a doubt." He chuckled. "We'll call the bed a nice change of pace."

But he wasn't going to the bed. He turned left inside the bedroom and walked through the doorway leading into the bathroom. It was similar to the two in her villa, but the coloring was all soft grays and a bright blue that reminded her of the ocean surrounding the island. The tiled walk-in shower was large enough to fit ten people, with two sunflower showerheads and a bench that made her think filthy thoughts despite the exhaustion that broke over her in a wave.

Allie lay her head against his shoulder. "I should get back."

"I don't think so." He set her on the bench. "It's late, and it's dark, and I promise to let you get some sleep tonight if you stay."

She raised her eyebrows. "*Some* sleep?"

Roman turned on the water and shot her a look. "You can't honestly expect me to have you in my bed and keep my hands to myself."

"God forbid." She stood and ducked under the closest showerhead. The water was the perfect temperature, and Allie let herself just *be* for a few seconds. She could hear Roman washing himself, and as tempting as it was to watch, her thoughts kept her feet rooted in place. *He wants to know me.*

The thought shouldn't scare the shit out of her. Roman was gorgeous and successful and… It would never work. Irreconcilable differences about summed them up. Those differences might not matter while they were on West Island, but they would be glaringly obvious when they got back to New York. He was a rich…whatever the hell he was…and she was having to rob Peter to pay Paul and make ends meet. They lived in two different worlds.

They always had.

He'd grown up rich with distant parents. Her heart ached a little for the boy he must have been. So alone. In that, at least, there was a thread of similar experiences. The main difference was that Allie would have given anything for her parents to be gone and leave her alone. Well, her father at least. She shuddered.

"It's okay." His arms slid around her from behind. She tensed, waiting for him to ask what was wrong, but Roman just turned her to face him and held her closer. Comforting her without prying.

Even though she knew better, Allie clung to him. She wasn't weak for wanting to lean on someone for just a few seconds. *It's so hard being strong all the time. I don't know if I can take it. I'm about to fail, and when I do, I'm going to take so many women down with me.* Words pressed against the inside of her lips, all her worries and fears that she never gave voice to bubbling up inside her. She clamped her mouth shut and buried her face against his shoulder.

No matter how good the sex, or how wonderful he seemed to be, she couldn't afford to forget what Roman's ultimate goal was—the gym and shelter. He might have shelved his ambition temporarily, but that was all it was. Temporary. Spilling her fears would just give him ammunition later.

What if he could actually help?

He can't. No one can.

Worse, his version of help might be to sell the damn thing out from underneath her. It wasn't as easy as that, but once she started missing bills, it opened a door she couldn't close. If she didn't figure something out, and fast, she wouldn't have any choice at all in the matter. *I need a plan...a better plan than just pushing forward and hoping for the best.*

"It will be okay," he murmured and stroked a hand down her back. "Whatever it is, it'll be okay, Allie."

She wished she could believe him.

Allie took a breath, and then another. Self-pity wasn't her MO. She was the fighter, the one who took people under her wing. She stepped back, and Roman let her go. To hide her embarrassment, she ducked under the spray again. By the time she cleared the water from her eyes, Roman had turned off his showerhead and was drying himself off with an oversize fluffy white towel. He returned with a second one, and she stepped into it after turning off the water.

Roman kissed her forehead. "Come to bed with me, Allie."

Despite the turmoil in her head, there was only one answer. "Yes."

CHAPTER TEN

ROMAN WOKE TO find Allie gone. He sighed and rolled onto his back. It shouldn't have surprised him that she'd bolted, but disappointment was sour on his tongue. He stared at the vaulted ceiling for a few long moments before he forced himself out of bed. Lying around all morning wasn't going to do anything but give him more time to debate what the fuck he was going to do.

Accepting her terms was probably a mistake. But the thought held no strength against the memories from last night. He wouldn't take that choice back, no matter how thoroughly it might bite him in the ass later.

He pulled on a pair of shorts and headed out into the main living space of the villa. It was a sprawling room containing a kitchen and furniture artfully arranged around the wall that opened to the beach. Roman stopped short at the sight of Allie walking up the steps, sand on her feet and her blond hair windblown.

She grinned. "The sunrise is seriously beautiful today."

She didn't leave. He tried to get his reaction under control and to smile in return. "It *is* paradise."

"That's true." Allie dropped a kiss on his lips as she walked past. "I got coffee started. How do you take yours?"

Roman had never lived with a woman before. Even when he'd dated—occasionally seriously— his schedule prevented this kind of casual morning interaction. It had never felt like a loss until that moment. He followed Allie into the kitchen. "Black."

"I should have known." She'd reclaimed her shirt and shorts, and they looked even better in the daylight than they had the night before. She brought two mugs from the open-faced cupboards and poured coffee into them. After setting his in front of him, she doused hers with enough cream and sugar to make his teeth hurt. She shot him a look from beneath her lashes. "What can I say? I like sweet."

"I see that." Even this early in the morning, he was smart enough not to comment on it. He took a cautious sip. "You stayed."

She stirred her coffee. "I almost left, but it didn't seem right to sneak out like a thief." Allie made a face. "Plus, Becka was otherwise occupied last night, so I don't expect her up and around until a little later. I do *not* need to walk in on some kind of morning-after shenanigans."

He almost asked, but Roman was… He didn't know how to term his relationship with Becka's sister anymore. They were friends once, albeit not close ones. They might be friends again if Gideon ever forgave him for meddling in their relationship. At this point, he'd be lucky if he was invited to the wedding.

Either way, it was none of his damn business who Becka Baudin went to bed with. He wasn't her brother, and he wasn't her friend. Her sister might have an opinion on that, but Lucy wasn't here and Roman wouldn't win any points by running back to her and telling tales. No, Becka was a grown-ass woman and he was going to stay the hell out of it.

Roman leaned against the counter. "Big plans today?"

"We were going to go snorkeling off the reef on the other side of the island. They have a boat that takes you out and they provide lunch, too." She hesitated. "Do you want to come?"

Yes.

He tempered his reaction almost as fast as it arose. Jumping at her and yanking her into his arms was only going to spook her and make him look like a fool in the process. Instead, he saluted her with his mug. "Only if I'm not intruding."

Allie raised her eyebrows. "As if you'd let that stop you."

He laughed. "Fair point. Yes, I'd like to come snorkeling with you." Saying it felt like he was agreeing to something more serious than a daytime outing, but Roman didn't let himself think about that too hard. He liked Allie. He liked spending time with her. She wasn't going to let him get any ground on talking business while they were down there, and even if he went back to New York, he couldn't make any forward progress without her. All that aside, he *wanted* to be on West Island. With her.

"When's the last time you had a vacation?"

He shrugged. "I visited my parents in Morocco a couple years ago."

Those blue eyes saw too much. She gave a soft smile. "When's the last time you had a real—*relaxing*—vacation?"

"Ah, that's something else altogether." He thought hard and came up blank. "I don't know. Maybe spring break in college, but that's hardly the idea of relaxing you're talking about." He'd had his eye on the prize even back then, so Roman had used the time to network. Nothing brought people together as much as getting drunk and doing stupid shit, and those relationships had panned out nicely in the years since.

But an actual vacation? Just to relax?

He cleared his throat, not quite able to meet her gaze. "Never."

"That's what I thought." Allie set down her mug and slid into his arms as if she'd made the move a thousand times before. "We have four days left on

West Island. Why don't we treat it like a real vacation and just enjoy ourselves?"

It sounded a whole hell of a lot like she'd just smacked an expiration date on them. Roman wasn't surprised at that. What *did* surprise him was how her words made him feel—like he wanted to bend her over the counter and fuck her until she admitted that there might actually be something *there*.

Instead, he palmed her ass and gave her a light squeeze. "You'll stay here at night."

"Yes." No argument for once. Her gaze dropped to his lips. "I have to talk to Becka, but judging by how excited she was by my leaving last night, I don't think she'll have a problem with the change of plans. Especially if it leaves the villa open for her to have her own vacation fling."

I'm not a fucking fling.

Once again, he smothered the response. Roman didn't know what he wanted from this yet, other than more time with Allie, but he'd be damned before he did or said something to spook her. There would be plenty of time to hash it out later. Right now, they were just talking about the next four days.

He smoothed her hair back. "Why don't you bring your things here for the duration—it'd save you the multiple trips."

"Trips I'll still have to make to arrange things with Becka for our daily plans." Allie shook her head. "No, this is better with clear boundaries. I'll bring enough stuff for overnight—toothbrush and that kind of thing—but the rest stays."

Stubborn woman.

"You're being difficult."

She grinned. "What I'm being, Roman, is non-compliant. I get the feeling that you don't get told no a lot, but you should get used to it. You might have a magical cock, but that doesn't mean you get a permanent free pass to run my life."

"You think I have a magical cock?" He pulled her closer, lining up their hips so she could feel exactly what she'd just described.

Allie's eyes went wide. "I might have said that." She palmed him through his shorts. "Then again, my memory is a bit faulty. It's been ages since I've had you inside me."

"Woman, it's been a few hours at most." He laughed and scooped her into his arms, liking the little yip sound she made. "But never let it be said that I don't take care of your needs."

"Heaven forbid." She arched up to murmur in his ear. "I'm desperate for you, Roman."

His cock went rock solid and he tightened his hold on her. "In that case, I think your friend can wait another hour or two." He strode for the bedroom.

Allie sat as rigid as she was able to while the boat wobbled its way through the waves away from the island. When she'd invited Roman along to go snorkeling, she hadn't really thought it through. Becka hadn't seemed to mind, so it didn't really sink in until they'd left the island that this was…a date.

No, not a *real* date.

But it was as close as she'd come to a date in *years*. *Not loving what that says about my social life.*

What social life?

It was different when it was just her and Roman in his villa. She didn't have to think too hard about the implications, because it was clearly just sex. Or maybe the sex just fuzzed her mind and *that* was why spending all that time with him didn't bother her.

Either way, it was different now.

They were out in what passed for public on the island. The little boat was maxed out with her, Roman, Becka and a trio of giggling women who kept shooting Roman significant looks. All three had wedding rings, but that didn't look like it'd stop them from taking him somewhere to be alone if he so much as crooked a finger.

Allie clenched her fists and stared pointedly at the ocean. Roman wasn't hers. If he wanted to run off with someone else, she didn't have a right to be pissed. She certainly didn't have the right to punch him over it. *Get it together.*

"You look like you're about to shove someone into the ocean." Roman's murmur was barely loud enough to be heard over the waves they cut through. "What's wrong?"

"Nothing's wrong." She'd answered too quickly. *Might as well have put a sign over my head claiming the opposite.*

"Allie."

She glared at the horizon. If she was smart, she'd fake a smile and play this off. Admitting to feeling something as damning as jealousy would give Roman even more ammunition than he already had. Then again, if she'd wanted to prevent him from having ammunition, she shouldn't have slept with him a second and third time…and she shouldn't be planning on doing it again at the earliest available opportunity. There was no taking back those actions, and she had no intention of stopping until she really had to.

"Allie." He pressed his hand to the small of her back. "You've been checking out on me ever since last night."

"Maybe it's just what I do. You don't actually know me, so you don't know that it's not something I don't do." It sounded just as jumbled as her head felt. She battled the truly ridiculous urge to cry. Allie shook her head. "I'm sorry. I think it all just became real to me and I'm trying to come to terms with the fact that I'm not really protected against you and it's my own damn fault."

Roman moved closer, his body blocking her from the rest of the people on the boat. "You think you need protection from me?"

She couldn't read his tone, but the words didn't sound any happier than she felt. "Not like *that*. I know you'd never hurt me, but…" But once they left West Island, all bets were off. She also knew that. She'd known that going into this thing with him.

So why did it bother her so much now?

I like him.

It was as simple as that. It might have started with just sex, but it wasn't *just* sex. She'd never been all that good at compartmentalizing, and even if she had been, Roman's sheer presence would overwhelm whatever barriers she put up between them. It was easier when she could pretend she loathed everything about him except for his body.

That fallacy hadn't held up against their interaction that morning. He wasn't just an unfeeling suit. He was a man, with a past and a present and a future, and they had at least a few superficial things in common. She understood his loneliness, because she held the twin feeling inside her. He spoke to her as if he cared what she thought, even if most of the time they'd been too busy to talk about much of anything. It didn't matter. That focus was *there* and he'd have her confessing her deepest desires if given half a chance.

She turned to face him, putting her back against the boat railing. His expression wasn't a happy one. He hadn't had a vacation, and she'd invited him out here to continue their feel-good time together…and now she was ruining it. She hated that, hated that she'd been the one to damper his enjoyment of the boat ride. *Of the sight of those women.*

Stop it.

She bit her lip, but there was no holding back the torrent of words. "I hate the way they look at you."

He blinked and then blinked again as comprehension dawned. "You're jealous."

"I wouldn't say *that*." That was exactly what she'd say.

Roman moved closer and skated his hand up her side until his thumb brushed the side of her breast through her swimsuit top. "Do you honestly think I have the slightest interest in anyone else?"

She didn't really know. That was the problem. It was entirely possible that the only reason he'd come onto her the first night was because they were literally the only two people in the restaurant. *Oh, for God's sake,* stop. Allie gave herself a shake. She didn't do this. Crippling self-doubt was exactly that—crippling. She hadn't had time for that nonsense up until this point, and she'd be damned if she would let it prevent her from enjoying her remaining time with Roman.

She took a long, slow breath, and then another. "Okay, yes, I'm jealous. You might not be mine, but you're mine right now, and I don't like them looking at you like you're a piece of meat they'd like to share over dinner."

Roman burst out laughing, the sound taking up residence in her chest...and lower. His thumb dipped beneath her swimsuit, wandering dangerously close to her nipple. "You know damn well that you're the only one who gets to have me for dinner."

She couldn't find the air to laugh. Not when he pressed his hips into her, letting her know *exactly* how much he wanted her to have him for dinner. Allie ran her hands up his chest. "There isn't anywhere private on this boat."

"If there was, we'd already be there, and I'd be inside you." Roman's thumb found her nipple. "I wouldn't even tell you to be quiet, Allie. I'd fuck you hard enough to make you scream as you came around my cock, so everyone within hearing range would know exactly who it belongs to."

Belongs to.

She didn't know what to say to that, so she went onto her tiptoes and kissed him. Allie looped her arms around his neck and pressed her body against his and tried to tell him without words how hot he made her—how much she appreciated the distraction.

Distantly, she was aware of the boat turning and stopping. The guy driving it cleared his throat. "We'll gear up here and you can explore the reef." He went on, but she was too focused on the heat rising to her cheeks to pay attention.

Roman backed off just enough to fix her top and

then slid behind her and wrapped his arms around her waist. His cock pressed against her backside, the hard length preventing her from focusing fully on the instructions. He knew it, damn him. His lips brushed her ear. "Pay attention."

"Stop distracting me." She rolled her hips a little, rubbing her ass against him.

The instructor finally finished up and started handing out snorkels and life vests. Allie slipped out of Roman's grasp and headed for Becka. Her friend gave her a significant look. "I thought you two were going to go at it right there."

Her face flamed, but she tried to laugh it off. "Don't be ridiculous."

"It's not ridiculous if it's true." Becka grinned. "Get it, girl." Her gaze went over Allie's shoulder and her eyebrows inched up. "Would you look at that?"

She turned around in time to see one of the other women saunter up to Roman. Her bikini was tiny enough to border on indecent, and she wore it with utter confidence. Normally, that would have been enough for Allie to want to give her a high five, but with the way the brunette was eye-fucking Roman, the only thing Allie wanted to high-five was her face—with a chair. She sidled up to him, all flirtatious moves and sweet smiles, and placed her hand on his arm, leaning in so her barely covered breasts pressed against his biceps.

He took off his sunglasses and looked down at the

spots where she touched him with such coldness that she actually jumped back a step. Roman gave her one last long look that wasn't in the least bit friendly and then turned to take his snorkel gear from their guide. He donned it quickly, dropped his sunglasses on top of his towel and slipped into the water.

All without saying a word.

Becka whistled under her breath. "He gets a nine for takedown, with a plus-two bonus for dramatic exit."

Allie snorted and then tried to cover the sound with a cough. "You're horrible."

"No, what's horrible was that attempt to poach your man." She spoke just loud enough that there was no way the other woman didn't hear her. "Who the hell does that? He was two seconds from dragging you into the ocean to bang you against the side of the boat and *she* thinks she has a chance?" Becka tsked. "Girl's got issues."

Allie smacked her friend lightly even though she agreed with everything Becka had said. All her worries seemed silly in the face of what had just happened. Hell, they were silly even before Roman rebuffed the woman. *A fling in paradise. Don't complicate things for no damn reason.*

Easier said than done.

CHAPTER ELEVEN

ROMAN ENJOYED THE hell out of the day. The weird tension riding Allie disappeared once they got into the water, and they spent several hours exploring the reef and then floating in the waves. By the time the boat dropped them back to the island, she was tucked comfortably under his arm and chatting animatedly with Becka. Roman kept expecting her friend to say…something…about their arrangement, but Becka seemed content to hang out as if this was the most normal thing in the world.

He drove them both back to their villa and left the women there. Though he wanted to take Allie back to his place, he recognized that she needed a little space.

Frankly, he could use a little space himself.

Roman had never been more conflicted in his life. He liked Allie. He wanted to see her succeed. Fuck, he just flat-out wanted her. But she was right this morning. There was a lot more to take into account than what they'd experienced together on West Island.

With that in mind, he strode into his villa and sat down with the papers he'd stashed there the day before. As much as Roman wanted Allie to give him the information voluntarily, the truth of the matter was that she was blocking him. She had her reasons for not wanting to open up, and he respected that, but this wasn't about his growing feelings for her—it was business.

He had to separate the two.

He couldn't afford not to.

She needed his help. She just didn't know it yet. If he let her wait until she was comfortable talking about this stuff with him—*if* that ever happened—the opportunity would pass and she could lose everything.

He needed to know what he'd missed about that damn gym, and he needed to know now. Stomping down on the guilt that tried to dissuade him, Roman sat down and fanned out the papers. He started at the beginning—with Allie and her family.

A story that he'd seen played out before. Alcoholic father. A mother who fled with her child when the abuse transferred to her daughter. A hard life lived, but which didn't stop Allie from graduating from college with honors and very little student debt. She'd worked her ass off to get Transcend up and running with money her mother had left her when the woman passed away three years ago. The shelter was set up under a nonprofit bearing Allie's mother's name.

But a successful nonprofit took a lot of work and shmoozing, and Allie obviously didn't have a taste for it. It didn't bring in enough to cover the costs, so she'd been draining the income generated by the gym—and her own personal savings.

Roman shook his head. It was an easy fix. Pass off the nonprofit to someone else, franchise Transcend and things would even out—and transfer from red back into the black.

So why was she so resistant to the idea?

Once he knew the answer to that, he'd know how to play things. He sighed. *Except it isn't that simple.* This wasn't a prospective client he could manipulate into doing what he wanted without remorse. This was Allie. He didn't want to hurt her, even if it was ultimately for her own good. He wanted her to trust him—to let him help her.

He kept reading. Her abusive father was horrible, but it didn't explain why she was so determined to do this alone. The woman Roman had started to get to know over the last couple days was strong and smart, but not a control freak like he'd expected. That was the only thing that would explain her insistence on not allowing the investor he represented to buy into the company.

Frustrated, Roman flipped through the papers again. Nothing, and he'd essentially breached her trust by doing this search to begin with. *Fuck*. He'd done the basic background on her when he first found the business, but Allie Landers kept her nose clean and, aside from the business's financial records and her school history, he hadn't dug deeper before.

He wished he hadn't now, either.

Roman threw the papers back into the folder and tucked it into a drawer under the kitchen counter. There was no easy answer here. He'd promised that they would leave business in New York, but the only way he could figure out what was stopping her was to *talk* to her… Some fucking businessman he was. He'd painted himself into one hell of a corner with this.

Enjoying their time together was the only option. If he tried to push her, she'd call an end to the whole thing. Allie didn't care about the pending deadline, since she had no interest in selling her business.

Which was a problem, because the whole damn ship was sinking. She'd be underwater inside of six months and then she'd lose everything. If she would just trust him, he could take care of everything. That was the problem, though. Roman knew he wanted what was best for the gym and Allie, but *Allie* didn't know that. It didn't matter how many different ways he tried to tell her, the truth was that he hadn't done anything to earn her trust, and it was doubtful he'd manage that feat sometime in the next four days.

Roman sat there and contemplated it for nearly an

hour, no closer to finding a solution by that point than he had been when he'd first started thinking about it.

What the fuck am I going to do?

Come to dinner with me. Dress to the nines.

Allie looked at the masculine scrawl on the note that had been delivered to their villa with the snack Becka had ordered. She felt a stupid grin pulling at the edges of her lips and tried to fight it. A single note from Roman shouldn't be a highlight of her day—especially after the glory that was snorkeling off the coast of the island—but her heartbeat kicked up a notch knowing that he was thinking about her... and planning something for tonight.

"He sent you another note, didn't he?" Becka stepped out of her room, wearing a wrap dress that showed off her legs and lean frame. She'd pinned her blue hair up into a style that could only be described as shabby chic. And she was grinning like the cat who'd eaten the canary. "I don't know if that's adorable beyond measure or cheesy as hell."

"Both." She tried to sound unimpressed, but the stupid smile wouldn't go away. "It's lame."

"It is not lame. He's smitten." Becka eyed her. "You're both smitten."

"I can't be smitten with Roman Bassani. We only have a few days left and then it's back to being enemies again." The thought dimmed her smile like nothing else had been able to. It was strange to think a time would come when she and Roman would be adversaries, but there was no real alternative. He wanted her gym. She would never give it up. End of story—end of them. Nothing that happened while they were on the island would change that.

Becka poked at the snacks that had been delivered and chose a selection of fruit. "You know he has a client who wants to invest in Transcend. Do you know why?"

"For the same reason all the other investors came around when they realized I wasn't making ends meet as well as I would have liked. They think they can jump on the trendy fitness-nutrition combo and franchise it. They don't care about the shelter—and they'd probably cut it out completely if they had control. It's a money pit, after all, and it's not like they're invested in any of those women's futures." Allie shook her head sharply. "No. I can't risk it. Business isn't so bad that we have to give in to the kind of offer Roman and people like him are bringing us. We're doing just fine." *Not really fine at all.* She should have organized a fund-raiser or something for the shelter, but she was so busy running the gym that the thought of adding anything else to her plate was too much to deal with. So she'd put it off.

She was regretting it now.

Too little, too late.

"How do you know?"

She pulled herself back into the present. "What?"

"How do you know what Roman has planned for Transcend?" Becka popped a piece of pineapple into her mouth. "Have you talked about it?"

"No. And we're not going to." At her friend's incredulous look, she glared. "You wanted me to have hot vacation sex, and hot vacation sex includes not talking about work. That's the only condition Roman and I put on this thing, so hell if I'm going to break the rules. It's just going to end in another fight, and this one we might not be able to screw our way out of." She ran her hand over her face. "What am I doing? This whole thing was a mistake."

Becka jumped to her feet. "Oh, no, you don't! I'm sorry I pushed buttons. I thought I was just asking a question." She hurried to Allie and guided her toward her own room. "Go get ready. Then get your ass back in here and have a shot with me for sure mutual courage. Then we'll never speak of this again—at least for the next few days."

"You don't have to be sorry. I'm the one acting batty." She paused just inside her doorway. "I like him."

"I know you do, honey."

She didn't know if that was comforting or worrisome, so she didn't comment on it. She just gently shut the door between them and dug through her suitcase for something that would be qualified as dressing to the nines. She'd packed a couple nice dresses, just in case, and she laid them both out on her mostly unused bed. One was a simple little black dress that was flowy and showed her cleavage to perfection. The other was a two-piece with a stretchy nude pencil skirt and a cropped bustier top that showed a sliver of skin between them. Normally for something resembling a first date, she'd play it safe with the LBD and leave the trendier choice for once she'd figured out if the guy was a douche or not.

But she already knew what Roman was—and what he thought of her.

Allie's grin reappeared. The cropped top and skirt it was.

She took extra time getting ready, styling her hair in perfect beach waves and keeping her makeup light enough that it wouldn't melt off her face the second she left the villa—or once she and Roman got to whatever he had planned for dessert. She finished off the look with her strappy wedge sandals. With their three-inch heel, she'd be almost as tall as him, and the idea pleased her more than it probably should have. Roman's masculinity wasn't so fragile that he needed her to cut herself down to make him feel better. It was one of the things she liked about him.

I like a lot of things about him.

Stop it.

Becka grinned when Allie walked back into the main area of the villa. "Ooooh, someone has their seductive panties on tonight."

"I'm not wearing any."

Her friend laughed. "Which just serves to support my point. After that little show on the boat earlier, if he doesn't fall on you like a starving man the second he sees you, I'll eat my shoe."

Allie wasn't prepared to take Roman's response to seeing her—whatever it would be—for granted, so she just shook her head and started for the exit. "See you in the morning?"

"As long as by morning you mean after eleven." Becka set her fork and plate in the sink. "Luke is meeting me here after his shift, and I plan to rock him all night long."

"You like this guy?"

Becka shrugged. "I like parts of him. He doesn't have the most stimulating of personalities, but he's got a monster cock and magic hands, so he's perfect for the time and place." Her smile was sunny but didn't quite reach her eyes. "You know me—I don't do that messy emotional bullshit. I like my life how it is. I don't have time for some needy dude expecting me to bend over backward to rearrange it for him."

There was a story there, but in all the years Allie had known Becka, she'd never got to the heart of it. Despite her friend's carefree spirit, Becka had a hard line when it came to anything resembling a relationship. She liked to laugh away the serious stuff whenever they got close to talking about it, and Allie respected the unspoken request to not bring it up.

Then again, Allie hadn't done more than casually date in that time, either, so she wasn't one to talk.

"Shots!" Becka poured vodka into two glasses and passed one over. "To a night of wall-banging sex and living our vacation to the fullest."

They clinked glasses. "Tomorrow, why don't we do something with just us?" Allie suggested.

"Sure…as long as you aren't using me as a shield against Roman." Becka downed her shot without a grimace. "If you want to spend the rest of this trip with him, then you should. I'm more than capable of keeping myself occupied, and it's not like we don't spend more time with each other in New York than we do with anyone else in our lives."

There was no arguing that, but… She took her shot, closing her eyes as the alcohol burned its way down her throat and created a comforting warmth in her stomach. "I don't want to abandon you." She wasn't sure she wanted to be that close with Roman, either. It was already hard to keep the boundaries in her head between them—between the island and New York, between the present and the inevitable future. Getting to know him better would make it worse.

Except…

"I'll think about it."

"Do that." Becka plucked the shot glass from her hand. "Now get out of here. Five bucks says he bangs you right there on the patio."

"You really need to stop making bets about how quickly Roman and I get to banging." But she laughed all the same. She could shelve all her worries about what the future held—at least for a few more days.

Allie would figure out the rest when she got back to New York.

CHAPTER TWELVE

ROMAN HAD EVERYTHING prepared for Allie. A table set up on the patio overlooking the sunset. The food prepped and ready in its various warming plates. Candlelight. The best of intentions.

And then she walked out of the jungle and the blood rushed out of his head and took up residence in his cock. She wore a skintight beige skirt that his hands were itching to slide over, and her little crop top bustier thing offered her breasts up as if begging for his mouth. The sandals had a little heel on them, which only served to highlight the muscles in her legs and...

He rubbed the back of his hand over his mouth. "Fuck, Aphrodite."

Her sweet smile was reward enough, but he wasn't going to be the gentleman he'd planned to be originally. Not with her looking at him with those come-fuck-me eyes and strolling right up to slide her arms around his neck. Her smile widened as she pressed her hips against his. "Hey."

"Hey." He cupped her ass with one hand and her hip with the other, dragging his thumb along the exposed few inches of her upper stomach between the skirt and top. "You look amazing."

"Thanks." She looked him over. "You, too."

It was too hot for pants, but he'd chosen a pair of khaki shorts and a linen button-down that passed as dressed to the nines for island fashion. "Are you hungry?"

"Starving." She hooked her fingers into his belt loops. "But not for food. I've been thinking about you since we were on the boat." She gave a delicate little shiver that had his cock hardening further. "Dinner will hold. I need you now." Allie had his belt undone in the space of a heartbeat and shoved his pants down his legs.

Shock stole his reasoning when he recognized the look on her face. "You're still jealous."

"No, I'm not." She knelt in front of him and wrapped her fingers around his cock. "I was. It wasn't anything you did, and it wasn't anything I have a right to feel, but it was there all the same."

He laced his fingers through her hair. "You're entitled to feeling anything you damn well please."

"Yes, I'm aware."

He watched her lick her lips, his heartbeat kicking up a notch. She was jealous of the woman on the boat. Roman hadn't bothered to remember her name, but she had been beautiful and confident and someone he might have looked at twice if he wasn't totally and completely wrapped up in Allie. "Do you really think another woman can compare when you're in the room?"

"We were on a boat." She gave him another stroke but seemed content to talk for the time being.

"The point stands."

Allie pinned him with a look. "I'm not interested in competing with another woman for a single damn thing. Life isn't a zero-sum game, and too often we're pitted against each other when it's not beneficial for anyone but the men around us." When he just looked at her, she relented. "*Fine*. I hated seeing her touch you. I wanted to march up and toss her over the railing. I'm not proud of that."

He wished he'd seen the obvious fury in her gaze when it all went down, though it was probably for the best that he hadn't. Roman had no business being pleased with the fact she was jealous, but he was all the same. He slid his fingers deeper into her hair and lightly massaged her scalp. "I'm not interested in anyone but you."

"For the next few days."

For always. He couldn't say it. Even with all the extenuating circumstances, it was too soon. Roman had never shied away from what he wanted, though—and what he wanted was Allie Landers.

He just had to give her a reason to give him a shot. *Focus.*

"Suck me, Aphrodite. Show me how disinclined you are to share."

She arched a perfectly shaped eyebrow. "I find myself very disinclined to share." Allie licked the underside of his cock like a lollipop and then sucked him down.

Roman had to fight to keep his eyes open, to watch her pretty pink lips move over him. She licked and sucked, her gaze never leaving his face. She worked him like she was laying claim to his cock in a way that had lightning sparking at the small of his back and pressure building in his balls. He wasn't going out like that, though. Not without touching her. "Come here." He guided her off him and lifted her onto a chair.

Roman hit his knees and slid his hands beneath her skirt, pushing the soft fabric up. She wore nothing beneath it, and his breath caught in his throat when he found her wet and ready for him. *Not yet.* But a taste couldn't hurt. He hooked her legs on the outside of her chair arms and dipped his head to drag his tongue over her. As long as he lived, he'd never get enough of the taste of Allie on his tongue.

She moaned and arched her back, offering herself further. "Stroke your cock, Roman. For me."

He froze, nearly coming on the spot at her words. *Fuck, woman, I'm keeping you.*

Keeping one hand bracketing her thigh, he made a fist around his cock and stroked hard. He was already close from her sucking him off, but he wasn't about to let himself come before she did. He flicked her clit with his tongue, alternating between circles and those vertical motions that he knew she liked. A frenzy took hold and he devoured her, driven on by her moans and writhing. She was close. So fucking close. His balls drew up, and he fucked her with his tongue, growling against her pussy. Needing more.

Needing *her*.

Allie laced her fingers through his hair, riding his mouth and crying his name as she orgasmed. He gripped his cock harder, roughening his strokes as he followed her over the edge, coming hard enough that he saw stars. He drew back enough to kiss first one of her thighs and then the other, then he pulled her skirt back down over her hips. "Now it's time for dinner."

Allie slouched in her chair, feeling completely boneless. "That's one way to start a meal."

"Mmm. Yes." Roman kissed her stomach and then adjusted her clothing to its correct place. He did up his pants just as efficiently, and she mourned the loss of the sight of him. The man was built magnificently and as good as he looked in clothes, he looked even better out of them.

He set about doling out food onto two plates with an easy, almost professional quickness. When he nudged a crooked fork back into place, she knew it had to be true. "How long were you a waiter?"

"Six years. My parents paid for my college, but they are big believers in working for anything worth having, so the rest was up to me. I handled room and board and books and all the other bullshit expenses that show up when you're in college by working at a local restaurant." He shook his head. "I will never do it again. Lifetime food service workers are either saints or insane, because nothing brings out the asshole in people as much as the little power they think they have when they're out to dinner."

From the comments he'd made, she'd assumed he'd grown up with money, but knowing he'd had to work for at least part of it made her like him better. "Bet you tip really well."

"I can afford to." He shrugged as if that made a damn bit of difference.

Allie examined her food, giving him a brief break from a subject that obviously made him uncomfortable. *Interesting.* He hadn't minded talking about working the job, but anything resembling evidence that he might be a good guy and he was suddenly closemouthed. She took a sip of wine. "I was a bartender my college years. O'Leary's." She saw from his look that he knew it. "Rich guys are the worst tippers out there—unless they think they have a shot at getting into your pants. Trust me, it's not something that your waitstaff take for granted."

"You don't have to do that."

"Do what?" She set her glass down and gave him her full attention.

Roman studied her. "Convince me that I'm not a total piece of shit. I already know I'm not. I might not be the best guy out there, but I'm a far cry from the worst. I'm solidly average."

Allie snorted before she could stop herself. "Roman, you are many things, but average is not one of them." And she wasn't just talking about the size of his cock. He was obviously driven and smart and clever, and he'd done well for himself.

Even though she knew better, she still asked, "Why are you in this brand of investments? Why not stockbroking or something that—" Allie cut herself off before she could finish that thought aloud. *Why not something that doesn't involve taking from other people?*

From the look he gave her, he knew exactly where her mind had gone. "I know it doesn't seem like it, but I'm not the enemy—not yours and not any of the others whose businesses I help pair up with investors. Most of them thank me in the end."

She had no doubt about that. Roman was hardly a snake oil salesman, but the force of his personality was often in danger of eclipsing all else—like common sense and reason. If he focused the entirety of it on a person, eventually he'd have them convinced that the sky was green and up was down. Even now, *she* was trying to find a way for it to make sense that he was the good guy and not the boogeyman under the bed that she'd assumed for months.

In truth, he was neither the bad guy nor the dream vacation fling—at least not in full. Reality was a lot more complicated.

Allie took a long drink of her wine and poked at the food on her plate. "You understand where I'm coming from with this."

He didn't answer for several beats. "You want to talk about business?"

Did she? The longer they were together, the clearer it became that they'd have to talk eventually—probably before they actually left the island… but she didn't want it to be tonight. She shook her head. "No. I'm sorry I brought it up."

Another of those searching looks. "We can talk, Allie. We're both adults, and as much as I enjoy the hell out of fucking you, I want to get to know you better."

That sounded like… She didn't know what that sounded like. It didn't fit in with her preconceptions of their boundaries. It didn't fit with *anything*. Allie swallowed against the panic welling inside her. It was just a conversation. She wasn't agreeing to anything just because she was talking with him. She'd *been* talking with him this entire trip. It just felt different this time.

Meaningful.

She took a breath, and then another. "Do you have...hobbies?"

Roman smiled gently, as if he knew what the question had cost her. "I work a shit ton, so I don't have much in the way of time. But I box a couple times a week at my gym—nothing crazy or competitive. Just sparring."

She could see it. He certainly had the upper body of a boxer, though his legs were just as solid as the rest of him. "Boxing and yoga. That's quite the combination." He was experienced with yoga. She'd been doing it for years, and she still had trouble with some of the poses he'd pulled off the other morning.

"They both help with my stress level, albeit in different ways."

"I bet they do." She cocked her head to the side. "Doesn't leave much time for social stuff." Like recognized like—between running the gym and teaching classes, she had nothing in the way of free time.

"How did you get into the gym business?" He held up his hand before she could speak. "I'm not talking about your business right now—I want to know why you chose that route."

She started to consider how she wanted to answer that, but exhaustion rolled over her. Allie was so damn tired of having to watch what she said around him. If she trusted Roman enough to give him full control of her body, she should trust him enough to have a conversation without worrying that he'd twist it around to use it against her.

Maybe it was time for a tiny leap of faith.

Allie took a bite and chewed slowly, finally swallowing the food, though she couldn't have begun to guess what it was she'd eaten. Her entire focus was on Roman and their conversation. He had no way of knowing that the seemingly innocent question would open a whole Pandora's box of history for her. She finally set her fork aside. "When I was growing up, I didn't have the healthiest of childhoods. It could have been a lot worse than it was, but the only high points during those years were when my mom would let me tag along to the gym. When she was there, she was…" She had to search for the word. "Free. In control in a way that she never was while married to my dad. When that relationship ended for good, it was a new city, a new gym, a new sense of purpose. It was in that place that I saw her find herself again, make friends, start the long road to what healthy looked like."

She tried a nonchalant shrug, but every muscle in her body was tense. "I initially started going so we would have something in common, but I really liked it. I never got super into the nutrition aspect of it, but I eat healthy enough." She motioned at her body. "I like food. I like working out. I like giving women like my mom a safe place. It all came together in Transcend."

Roman was so still, he might not have breathed the entire time she spoke. "I'm sorry your father was such a piece of shit."

"Me, too." Once upon a time, she'd wondered if her being born was the thing that ruined her parents' relationship, but Allie had seen too much—heard too many stories out of the same playbook—for that guilt to hold any water. Her father would have been the same if it was a different woman, whether there was a child or not, regardless of the external stressors he liked to blame for his flying off the handle.

She looked at Roman and tried to picture him drinking so much he actually hurt a woman—anyone, really—and couldn't wrap her mind around it. Maybe she was being naive, because he had a ruthless streak a mile wide, but nothing about him rang that warning bell. *Why am I even thinking about this?*

Because you can't afford not to.

Except this ends when we go back to New York, so it won't matter what he's like when he's not on vacation because you won't be around to see it.

The thought had her sagging in her seat. She poked at her food again. Wanting more with Roman was out of the question. The whole condition of their being together was *not* to talk about the most important thing in their respective lives—her gym and his work. It wasn't sustainable.

But part of her wanted it to be.

CHAPTER THIRTEEN

ROMAN SAW THE exact moment Allie started to shut him out. He'd been pushing it with that question and he'd known it, but there was too much he didn't know about her. He *should* be prodding her with questions to help spin things to his advantage, but the only reason Roman had asked was because he genuinely wanted to know.

He cleared his throat. "I envy you, in a way."

"Why's that?" The distance in her blue eyes retreated, leaving her present and accounted for.

In for a penny, in for a pound. She'd bared part of herself with that little window into her past—he couldn't do anything less than the same. "I mentioned before that my parents weren't around much when I was a kid." He snorted. "I might have understated it. They were gone more often than they were there. There was nothing traumatic about my upbringing, other than a bit of benign neglect, but when I was younger, I would have given my left arm to have designated time with either of them like you had with your mom."

Allie leaned forward, now fully engaged. "Why didn't they have more kids, if only to give you someone who wouldn't leave?"

"My mother didn't like being pregnant all that much, and she wasn't a fan of what came after, either." He made a face. "Hearing that at the tender age of five was eye-opening, to say the least."

"Oh, Roman."

"No, none of that." He casually slashed his hand through the air. "I don't need pity any more than you do. All my needs were met and my parents loved me in their own way. They just loved each other and travel a bit more. I had a whole staff of people who ensured I didn't turn out a monster, though I wager my nanny, Elaine, would feel differently if she'd lived to see me as a business acquisitions consultant." At her raised eyebrows, he continued, "She found money to be a necessary evil but always told me that she hoped I'd pick a good honest job that didn't revolve around it."

He hadn't thought about that conversation in over a decade. Elaine had passed when he was in his first year of college, and by that time he was firmly in his rebellious stage. Too much drinking, too many girls, too many attempts to do something crazy enough to force his parents to acknowledge him. Elaine's death had snapped him out of it like being thrown into a freezing ocean. He'd taken a good hard look at his life and realized that the only person he was hurting was himself. His parents would never change who they were, and trying to push them to be different was a lesson in futility.

Roman shook his head. "This got heavy. Sorry."

She tucked a lock of hair behind her ear. "I appreciate your sharing. It's kind of strange that we don't know much about each other, but…" Allie motioned between them.

"We fuck like we were made for each other." He wished he could recall the coarse words the second they were out of his mouth. He and Allie had bypassed mere fucking days ago. This was something on another level and cheapening it was a shitty thing to do.

She smiled. "Exactly that."

It stung that she agreed with him so quickly, but had he really expected anything else? In an effort to distract them both, he said, "So how did you meet Becka?"

As she launched into a tale of two broke college students desperate enough to take second jobs at the scary campus gym, he sat back and indulged in watching the animated way she spoke. Allie really was beautiful. He'd known that, of course—he had two eyes in his head, after all—but she was beautiful right down to the core. A genuinely good person.

Let me help you.

He couldn't say it. Even talking about the gym in more abstract forms had caused her to shut him out. Trying to talk more explicitly was a recipe for disaster. He had to play the game within the terms they'd set out. It was the only way.

"You're not even listening." She didn't say it like she was mad—just stating a fact.

"I am." Roman managed a smile. "That boss you had at the campus gym sounds like a real piece of work—though he should have been reported for forcing you to be in those conditions."

She raised her eyebrows. "Okay, that's a neat trick. You were a million miles away, but you still retained everything I said. That's nuts."

"Necessary evil." Though he'd never once been called on it before now. "I learned early in my career that it's best to have several options for plans by the end of a meeting with a new client—that means listening to what they're saying while still thinking strategically to create a game plan. They fill out preliminary information, of course, but until I meet them face-to-face, I rarely know exactly what they're looking for." He shrugged. "Some things sound better on paper than they are in reality."

Allie bit her bottom lip, and he could see the conflict clear on her face. "Okay, I'll bite—tell me about your job. Broad strokes, please."

Easy enough, though he couldn't help feeling it was a test. "I am a glorified numbers monkey. I research various businesses that look like good investments and then line up investors that will fit well with them. The ultimate outcome varies. Sometimes they take it to the ground level and build it up again. Sometimes they expand. Sometimes they franchise. Usually it's successful for both business and investor and I get a nice fat bonus."

"Depends on your definition of *successful*, doesn't it?"

He knew where she was going with this, and as much as he didn't want to fight, maybe it was better to get it out there now and expose the elephant in the room. "I won't pretend that every business owner is thrilled with the process, but most of the time the alternative is rock bottom and losing everything they worked their ass off to accomplish. Sometimes compromise is necessary."

She looked directly at him with those big blue eyes. "And do you ever compromise, Roman?"

Allie should have…well, she should have done a lot of things. She regretted the question as soon as she put it to voice—like she regretted much of what she'd said around Roman since they'd met. She pushed to her feet. "Never mind. We just got through saying we shouldn't talk about this—should keep it light—and we keep doing the exact opposite of that."

There was one thing they were good at—better than good at.

She slid her thumbs into the band of her skirt and pushed it down in a smooth move. The top took a little more effort, but she managed to unhook it and drop it without looking like a total fool. Roman hadn't moved once, but his knuckles were white where he held on to the table. He managed to tear his gaze from her breasts to her face. "What are you doing?"

"We're going to ruin this by talking too much. I don't want to ruin it."

Still, he didn't move. "It's okay for us to disagree on things. It's unrealistic to think that we'd match up on every subject the way we match up physically."

She knew that. Of course she knew that. Only a child or an idiot thought there was such a thing as a perfect relationship. Everyone had problems, though most of the time they weren't as catastrophic as her parents' had been.

But this wasn't a relationship. She had to keep reminding herself of that, and *that* was as much a problem as anything.

She shook her head. "That's the thing—this is fantasy. There is no room for disagreements in fantasy. I want you. You want me. Let's just leave it at that."

"Allie—"

She turned and strode into the darkness. He'd follow. He'd be unable to help himself. And then they'd get their hands on each other and all her conflicting feelings would disappear for a while. *That* was what she wanted. She already had a complicated life. She didn't have room for *more* complications—even if they arrived in a package that made her body ache and her heart beat too hard.

Sex was easier. Sex was safe.

Even if it didn't feel particularly safe as she hit the sand and kept going. The wildness of the island was closer to the surface here, with the villa lights seeming at a distance and the stars a blanket overhead. The soft shushing sound of the water sliding over the sand let her draw her first full breath since she and Roman had started talking about things better left unsaid.

She tilted her head back and inhaled deeply, taking the salty air into her lungs and letting it chase away her worries. She was still on vacation, no matter how stubbornly real life kept trying to intrude. Relaxation was the name of the game and Allie would be damned if she was drawn back into all the crap before she was good and ready.

Footsteps padded behind her, and she didn't turn to watch Roman approach. She wouldn't be able to see more than the outline of him, and it was better to soak up what little peace she could as she waited to see if he'd let the conversation go.

He stopped next to her, close enough that his

shoulder brushed against hers. "You can't run from this forever."

"I'm not running from anything." *Liar.* "I'm holding to the arrangement we made. Everything can wait until we leave West Island." What happened then… No, she wasn't going to talk about it. She wasn't even going to *think* about it.

"Allie…" His exhale was lost in the sound of the small waves hitting their feet. "This is what you really want? For me to fuck you until neither of us is capable of words and we just ignore everything unspoken between us?"

This was the moment of truth. If she said she'd changed her mind about their bargain, she had a feeling Roman wouldn't judge her for it. He seemed to want to talk—actually talk. Maybe he was starting to feel the same thing she was—that this thing between them wasn't just about mutual orgasms.

That maybe it could be more.

All she had to do was tell him that she was willing to talk.

But when she opened her mouth, it was cowardice that won. "We can talk when we're in New York."

He turned to face her, his expression lost in the darkness. "Promise me that we will."

"What?"

"Promise me that you won't run when we get back. You'll have dinner with me and we'll talk."

It'll never happen. It sounded good in theory right

now, beneath the stars and with their bodies gravitating toward one another, but once they got back to the city and were grounded in their real lives, it wouldn't hold up. He'd get busy. She'd have to cancel a few times. They'd both lose interest and move on with their lives.

The thought made her chest ache, but she set it aside just like everything else she'd set aside since she came here. "I promise."

Roman shifted closer, sliding his hands over her hips and up her back, fitting her body against his. He'd stripped before following her out here, and all his skin against all of hers sent a delicious thrill through her. He kept calling her beautiful, but he was a work of art. "Adonis."

"Aphrodite." He lifted her easily so she could wrap her legs around his waist. "Let's go swimming."

She didn't protest as he walked them into the ocean. Roman didn't go far, stopping as the water lapped the bottom of her breasts. It felt absolutely wicked to be out here in the dark with him. Even if it'd been broad daylight, no one would have seen them, but the thrill of the risk still heightened every sensation.

The water teasing her breasts. The slick slide of his skin against hers. The feel of his breath ghosting across her lips.

She arched against him, trying to take his mouth,

but Roman dodged her kiss. "Do you know the legend of Aphrodite?"

She blinked. "Yes, of course. She came from the sea." The words were barely past her lips when Roman launched her away from him. She was airborne for a single breathless second and then she hit the water and went under.

Allie surfaced with a curse that turned into a laugh. "You're crazy."

"Come on. You can't skinny-dip in the Caribbean without horsing around a bit." He splashed her and then disappeared beneath the surface.

Allie skittered back, searching the inky water for a sign of him, but the only warning she got was a hand around her ankle and then he pulled her under. They twisted beneath the surface and tangled together. She used his shoulders to shove him farther down and push herself up for a breath.

And then his arms were around her waist and he was hauling them closer to shore. His cock pressed against the small of her back and her breath hitched in her throat. "Playtime's over."

She laughed at the cheesy line, but the sound came out strained. "You just wanted to get me all wet."

"Mmm." He cupped her breasts and rolled her nipples between his thumbs and forefingers. "Come on. As much as I need you right here, right now, the condoms are back in the villa."

She almost threw caution to the wind and said it

didn't matter. Allie clamped her mouth shut to keep the words inside and nodded sharply. Unprotected sex with Roman, no matter how much she wanted him in that moment, was the worst possible idea. "Yes. Villa. Now."

Before she did something they'd both regret.

CHAPTER FOURTEEN

ROMAN CARRIED ALLIE across the sand. He ignored the tension bleeding into her body the farther they got from the waves. *Too much time to think.* They were being so damn careful not to edge too close to subjects that would put them at odds with each other, but he craved that part of her as much as he wanted the rest. Allie wasn't just the beautiful siren who looked so at home in the sun and sand, with the turquoise water creating the perfect backdrop.

She was a strong woman who hadn't let circumstances beyond her control beat her. She'd fought tooth and nail to accomplish so much in such a short time, and it was a fucking tragedy that it hadn't gone according to plan. He didn't want her to lose Transcend any more than she wanted to lose it, if only because he now recognized the pain it would cause.

Roman would go to extraordinary lengths to save Allie from whatever pain he could.

He padded up the porch steps and headed straight for the bedroom. She wouldn't thank him for ruining their good mood with serious talking, and she might go so far as to leave if he tried to broach the forbidden topic. There wasn't a damn thing Roman could do to change that, and he wasn't used to being so effectively painted into a corner.

He couldn't use words to reassure Allie.

But he could use his body.

"Roman?" The hesitance in her tone killed him.

He set her on her feet but didn't release her. Naked and wet from the ocean, she really did look like a siren who'd been sent to tempt him. Allie blinked those big blue eyes. "Are we okay?"

"Yeah." *Not as okay as I want us to be.* He *liked* Allie. He admired her strength. He wanted to bolster it, to be the immovable object she could lean on when she needed it. If there was one thing he was sure about when it came to the woman in his arms, it was that she didn't allow herself to rest, to pass the burden on to another.

He wanted to bear all her burdens, at least for a little while.

Roman framed her face with his hands and stroked his thumbs over her cheekbones. "I want it to be just us while we're here. No past, no worrying about the future. Just you, Allie, and me, Roman. Two people enjoying their time together."

"That sounds good." She bit her bottom lip. "But I don't know if it's possible to just put all that aside and pretend it's not there."

"Aphrodite." He kissed the spot on her lip where there was still an indent from her teeth. "Nothing exists but us. The goddess of love and her Adonis."

She laughed a little. "You know that myth didn't end happily, right?"

"It's Greek mythology. There are no happy endings." He shifted to kiss her stubborn chin. "Fuck them. This is our story."

Her hesitation was so brief, it might not have existed. "Yes. Tonight. The next three days. You and me. I'm in."

As much as Roman didn't want any kind of limit, he knew when not to push his luck. Allie had given him more than he'd hoped, and he'd have to be happy with it. "I'm taking you to bed now."

"Finally." She gave a dramatic sigh. "I thought we'd never get to the good part."

"All of it is the good part." He walked her back to the bed and laid her down, leaning over her. "Tell me what you want. Your wish is my command tonight."

"Just tonight?" There it was again, the slightest hint of vulnerability.

Not just tonight. Always. Promises he had no business making rose, pressing against the inside of his lips like live things. He'd known he wanted Allie, but the realization that he had only three days left with her pulsed up inside him, desperation building with each heartbeat. He looked down at her, her open expression of need cleaving into his chest as if she'd actually struck him. *I don't want to lose you.* He swallowed hard. "We'll start with tonight and see how it goes."

Her grin brought out an answering one from him. "Kiss me, Adonis." She arched up, pressing all of her body against all of his. "Touch me. Hold me. Fuck me."

There was no room in this night for fucking. They'd passed that point days ago, though he couldn't pinpoint the exact moment when Allie went from a gorgeous woman who drove him out of his mind to a woman whose inside was just as compelling as how she felt when she rode his cock. It wasn't just sex between them, no matter what lies she told herself.

Maybe it never had been that uncomplicated.

Roman joined her on the bed and kissed the long line of her neck. "Here." He shifted to the side so he had full access to her body, and moved to the curve of her shoulder. "Perhaps here."

She shivered. "I could think of a few places I'd like."

"I bet you could." He urged her onto her side so he could fit himself against her back. The position gave him free reign, and he wasted no time cupping her full breasts, weighing them in his hands. "Open your eyes."

She obeyed and froze when she met his gaze in the reflection of the windows across from the bed.

The deep darkness outside and the single lamp he'd left on inside created a mirror of the glass.

Roman pressed an openmouthed kiss to the back of her neck and retreated just enough for his breath to ghost over the damp skin. She shivered and arched her back against him, pressing her breasts more firmly into his hands. "That feels good."

"I'm just getting started." He lightly pinched her nipples, rolling the tight buds between his fingers. "I love how rosy your skin gets when you like what I'm doing to you."

She lifted her head and frowned. "The reflection isn't that damn good."

"No. It's not." He skated a hand down her stomach and hooked her thigh, lifting her leg up and setting her foot behind his legs. It left her open for him and he delighted in her shiver. "Cold?"

Allie reached back to run her fingers through his hair. "I'm burning up. Touch me, Adonis."

He loved it when she called him that. It was something they alone shared. Something special and meaningful. Roman dragged a single fingertip over the inside of her thigh, teasing her. "Where do you want me to touch you?"

"You know where."

"Mmm. I might." He palmed her pussy, and cursed when he found her warm and wet and wanting. "This is where you want me." He traced her opening. "Where you're aching with need."

"Yes." She shifted her hips to guide him, but he nipped her shoulder. Allie hissed out a breath. "Bossy."

"Always." He spread her wetness up and over her clit and circled the little bud of nerves with the pad of his finger. "You love it."

"Maybe."

"Definitely." Roman pushed two fingers into her, stroking her leisurely while he watched her face. Her sinful lips parted and her blue eyes went hazy. "My Aphrodite." He released her long enough to reach over and snag a condom.

"Let me." Allie turned in his arms and plucked it out of his hand. She ripped it open and then gripped his cock. A stroke. Two. The desire in her eyes a match to the furnace inside him. "You shouldn't be this perfect, you know? It's got to be a mathematical improbability."

He barked out a laugh. "Not perfect. Never that." He had more than his share of faults. He always had. Too selfish. Too driven, often at the expense of his relationships. Too stubborn by half.

"Well, obviously." She rolled the condom over him, taking her time. "I was talking about your cock, Adonis."

That surprised another laugh out of him despite the fact she started stroking him again. "Quite the backhanded compliment."

"Only if you want to look at it that way." She

nudged his shoulder, pushing him onto his back. Allie climbed on top of him and ran her hands up his chest. "Seriously, though. You don't have a single physical imperfection. I've never had a man take my breath away just by looking at him, and you do."

He looked at her, this woman that he'd never planned on. She was trying so fucking hard to keep as many barriers up between them as she could. Easier to focus on the physical than to admit that he might not be as evil as she'd assumed. To admit that she liked him for more than his ability to make her come hard enough to see stars.

Allie positioned his cock at her entrance and sank onto him in a slow movement. Her eyes fluttered closed and her pink lips parted. "Oh, God." She rolled her hips a little, adjusting. "I always think I can anticipate how good it will feel, and I'm always wrong."

"Because it's me."

Her eyes flew open and she frowned down at him. "What?"

"You lose your fucking mind every time I touch you because it's me. Just like I can't keep my goddamn hands to myself when I'm in the same room as you. We make each other crazy, and yeah, some of that has to do with how smoking hot you are. But it's more and you know it." He reached between them to circle her clit with his thumb. "I'm not a glorified dildo or a blow-up doll. I'm *me*."

* * *

Allie stared down at Roman. All she wanted was to lose herself in the perfection of the moment, of how good it felt to have him inside her, his big body between her thighs. She didn't want to turn this into something it wasn't supposed to be. *Too little, too late.*

"I know it's you." As if she could detach the man from his body. She couldn't. She'd tried. Roman's personality was just as overwhelming as his good looks. "Damn it, I see you."

Driven by the pounding pleasure in her blood, she shifted, swirling her hips a little in a move that made them both gasp. "I see you," Allie repeated. "You're not a bad man, no matter how much you pretend to be." He might not be a *good* man, but that wasn't something she could determine inside of a week. *Liar.*

She leaned down to kiss him, answering the temptation of his mouth as much as she wanted to silence the little voice inside her. *You won't be able to take this back. It's already complicated and it's only going to get more so.* She didn't care. She'd worry about complications when she came to them. All that mattered in that moment was removing the flicker of hurt she'd seen in Roman's hazel eyes.

She tasted the ocean on his lips, felt the warmth of the sun in his skin. Roman was like this island personified, beautiful and more than a little bit wild beneath the carefully cultured exterior.

"It stopped being just sex with you. You know it. I know it. We're still not talking about it."

He hesitated but finally nodded. "I can play the patient hunter, Aphrodite. We won't talk about it tonight. Maybe not for the next three days. But we *will* talk about it."

That was what she was afraid of. "Guess you really *are* Adonis," she murmured against his lips.

"Only when it comes to my Aphrodite."

She didn't want to talk anymore. Every time he'd spoken tonight, he'd chipped away at the fragile balance she'd worked to keep in place. Boundaries were there for a reason and, damn it, Roman seemed determined to trample all over them. He'd stopped playing by the rules, but he hadn't pushed so hard that she could call him on it.

Do I even want to call him on it? What's the harm in enjoying this?

It won't last.

What if it does?

She kissed Roman again, pressing her body into his. She rode him slowly, not worried about the destination. They'd get there eventually. They did every time. No, right now what Allie wanted was to be fully present in the moment. Right there. With him. The rest of the world could wait.

He dug a hand into her hair and grabbed her ass

with the other, guiding the long slide of her strokes. Sweat slicked their skin, and the drag of her nipples across his chest made her moan. *So good. Everything* about them was *so good*. Nothing else mattered but how his tongue moved expertly against hers, the feeling of him inside her, big and full and almost too much, and where he would touch her next. "I need more."

He rolled them, and the second her back hit the soft mattress, Roman began to move. He rolled his body like the waves they'd just been playing in. Smooth and steady and hitting all the right places. He ground his pelvic bone against her clit, the friction drawing a moan from her lips. His big body kept her pinned even as he wrapped himself around her. All she could feel was Roman. All she knew was Roman. The feel of his strong hands gripping her hips, the pounding of his cock between her thighs, the little curses he uttered with each exhale.

Glorious. So incredibly glorious.

"Yes. *There*. Don't stop."

"Come for me, Aphrodite," he growled against her neck. "Come for your man."

She was too lost to the pleasure of what he was doing to her to think too hard on his words. Or that was what she told herself as she buried her face in the curve of his neck and orgasmed hard enough to shake the earth on its axis. Roman pounded into her, wild with a need she felt to her very soul.

This isn't going away. I don't know if it's real or not...but I want it to be.

Roman tucked her against him and held her tightly, as if he expected her to leap out of bed and flee into the night. Considering how hard her heart pounded in a way that had nothing to do with the outstanding sex, she wasn't sure his fears were unfounded. "I don't know how to do this."

"Do what?"

She kept her face pressed against his chest. It was easier to be honest when she wasn't looking directly into those hazel eyes. "This. You. Us." *Us.* One little word, but it somehow changed everything. The realization that this wasn't simple vacation sex had been growing inside her every time Roman touched her. Every time she came with his name on her lips.

He smoothed a strand of her hair back from her face, tilting her head up so she could see him. "Why do you have to do anything at all?" There was something in his expression, something tight and guarded despite his warm smile.

"What's wrong?"

He hesitated and sighed. "Look, Allie, I like you. A lot. But I can tell that this whole thing freaks you out, so I'm trying to not put any pressure on you while we're here."

While we're here.

They wouldn't be on West Island forever. Hell, they wouldn't be here this time next week. This thing they had was temporary. She knew it and he knew it. Allie took a careful breath as the knowledge settled in her chest like a stone. They had an expiration date. There would be a time in the very near future when she'd no longer have the right to spend her nights tangled up with Roman.

I have to shore up enough memories during these last few days to last me a lifetime.

The thought made her want to cry, but she shoved the feeling down deep. There would be plenty of time for tears later. Right now, the only thing that mattered was gorging herself on everything Roman. On the little touches. On his kisses. On the feeling that rose inside her as she came apart around him.

"Aphrodite?"

She tangled her fingers in his hair and pulled him close for a desperate kiss. She put all her frustration and fear into the slide of her tongue against his. Three days. She had so much living to pack into three tiny twenty-four-hour periods.

Roman pulled her closer yet, his big hands cupping her ass and grinding her against him. He broke the kiss to nip at her jaw. "This is what you need, isn't it? Not to think anymore."

"Yes." He always seemed to know what she needed, even when she couldn't put it into words. "I just want to feel you. To be here and present and not worried about what happens when we get back to New York."

"Consider it done." He captured one of her nipples in his mouth, sucking hard. "Trust me, Aphrodite. I'll take care of you."

For the next three days, she finished silently, even as he rolled her onto her back and began kissing his way down her body. She couldn't bear to think about what happened after.

So she didn't.

CHAPTER FIFTEEN

ROMAN SMOOTHED ALLIE's hair back from her face. "You'll have to get moving if you're going to make your flight."

She swatted at his hand without opening her eyes. "Screw it. I'm not going back to New York. I'll just stay here until they kick me out."

He felt the same way, though it wasn't the island that had Roman wishing he could make this moment last forever. He wasn't ready to let this thing with her go. It was a truth he'd been working toward for some time, but this morning, knowing that they were going to board their respective flights back to New York and go back to their normal lives… The stakes were suddenly sky-high. "Come out with me tonight."

"What?" She finally opened a single eye. "What are you talking about?"

"Tonight. After we're both settled. I want to take you on a date." He didn't exactly form it as a question, but Roman knew all too well how fragile the limb he stood on was. They'd spoken about changing the rules, but he'd just thrown every single one of them out. Roman stroked his hand down her arm and laced his fingers with hers. "I'm not ready for this to be over."

"Roman, we talked about this. Our lives don't match up outside of this island. Our worlds are too different—our world*views* are too different. We wouldn't last the week before something happened that ruined us for good." She shifted to look down at their joined hands. "And that's not even getting into the whole 'your investor's trying to buy my gym out from underneath me' thing."

She was determined to see the worst in that situation, and he hadn't had the chance to convince her otherwise because every time it came up, suddenly they were having sex. Roman knew damn well that Allie was trying to keep them both distracted, and he couldn't exactly be pissed at the side effect, but he wanted to *talk* to the infuriating woman. "Have dinner with me. We'll talk about all the shit we've been avoiding up until now. If at that point you're sure you don't want me to facilitate someone investing in the gym, then I won't."

"Just like that?"

"Just like that." It wouldn't be just like anything. His client was interested in the gym and she had a clear vision over what she wanted for its future—a vision Roman shared. It wouldn't be easy to find a replacement, but he'd make it work. *If* Allie actually talked to him. "What do you say?"

Still, she hesitated. He could practically see her weighing her desire not to go to that dinner against the chance to get him to back off once and for all. Finally, Allie nodded. "I can't do tonight, but tomorrow I'm free."

"Tomorrow it is." He pressed his lips to her forehead. "As much as I want to seal this with a kiss, if I start kissing you, we won't stop until lunch and you have a plane to catch." He bit back the impulse to tell her to stay—that they really could just live on the island indefinitely and leave their lives behind. That peace wouldn't last. No matter how effectively they'd checked out of reality for the week, given enough time, real life would come creeping into their time here. Hell, it already had. Allie had done her best to avoid it, but Roman was a realist—they needed to get their shit out in the open so they could deal with it.

They had no chance of a future without that.

Before he could reconsider kissing Allie, she was out of the bed and pulling her clothes on. "I'd better go. If left to her own devices, Becka will pack my stuff and her version of packing is to shove everything in and wrestle with the bags until the zipper is in danger of breaking. Better for both me and my luggage if I do it myself."

"Give me your number."

Again, the slightest of hesitations. She grabbed a piece of stationery from the nightstand and scrawled her number on it. "See you tomorrow."

Tomorrow. In New York.

No matter how much he wanted to pretend otherwise, it was a big fucking deal to bring their budding relationship home. Roman managed a smile. "Have a safe flight."

"You, too." And then she was gone.

He listened to her footsteps leading out of the villa, and only after they'd faded did he climb out of bed and throw on a pair of shorts. His flight was in a couple hours—the early one off the island—so he wouldn't have a chance to see Allie again beforehand.

It took fifteen minutes to pack everything he'd brought and comb every room twice to ensure he didn't miss anything. He took extra time to shred up the information he'd gotten about Allie. He didn't need it. She'd given him everything when she spoke about why she'd started the gym. He knew what pressure points to push to incite the reaction he wanted... but he couldn't do it.

She wasn't just a stubborn business owner who needed a little pressure to do things his way. This was *Allie*. For her, he'd bypass the manipulations and shady dealings for plain old honesty.

Roman grabbed his bags and made his way to the lodge. It was time to get this show on the road, and he had a shit ton of work to do on the trip. All the pieces had to be in place before he saw Allie again.

The stakes were too high for it to be any other way.

Allie couldn't wrap her mind around being back in New York. It was more than the weather, more than the sheer amount of people. It was almost like her life didn't quite fit the same way it used to, as if it was a sweater with a tag she'd never noticed before but that itched every time she moved. To distract herself, she taught an early-morning spin class and spent the rest of the day holed up in her office going over bills and the budget for next month.

It was a shitty distraction. Nothing lined up. They'd taken their usual summer months hit in attendance to the classes, which meant less income. She was already in the red, but both the gym and the shelter were rapidly reaching the point of no return. Allie would have to start laying off her girls soon— like next week—and the thought made her sick to her stomach. The only other option was to turn away some of the women in the shelter, which wasn't an option at all. It was like having to choose between two of her children and she didn't even know where to begin.

She set it aside to work on later. She couldn't call Becka, because Becka would quit on the spot. She wouldn't worry too much about finding another job—Becka was the type of woman to jump out of a plane and figure out how a parachute worked on the way down. It was part of her charm, but Allie couldn't ask her to make that decision.

No, who she really wanted to call was Roman. They'd spoken briefly last night—mostly to arrange a time and place for their date today—but it was nowhere near enough after having him within arm's reach for a full week. She wanted to be wrapped up in him and have him tell her that it'd all be okay and that they'd figure it out together.

Weak. I shouldn't have to lean on a man for strength. I should be strong enough to stand on my own.

Especially since Roman's solution would undoubtedly be to try to convince her to sell the business and let it become someone else's problem.

For the first time, she was actually tempted. She'd been shouldering the burden alone for so long. It was no one's fault but her own that both the shelter and gym were in danger of going under. Running either of them was a full-time job and Allie was trying to do both by herself. If she'd just been willing to find a business partner she could trust...

At twenty-two, she'd been sure that the only person she could trust was herself. She'd needed some way to work through her grief over her mother passing, and this seemed like the best option. She *was* doing good; it just wasn't working like the well-oiled machine she'd anticipated. *There has to be a better way.* She just didn't know what it was.

Frustrated, she headed out. The evening classes were already covered, so there was nothing holding her there except a strange sort of guilt. There had to be something *more* she could be doing, but hell if she knew what it was. Maybe if she scrambled, she could throw together a fund-raiser or two this month, before it was too late. It would mean relying on her girls to run the gym while she devoted herself to event planning, which had never been her strong suit. Making cold calls to the few donors who'd helped her get the shelter off the ground was the next step, but it had always made her feel awkward and shameful—like she was begging for charity. As it was, her presence at the gym was totally and completely unnecessary at that moment, and all she'd accomplish by staying was working herself further into a spiral of worry.

Allie went upstairs to her apartment. She took her time showering and getting ready, battling nerves that told her this date was a giant waste of time and would only end in heartbreak for her. Roman had his eye on the prize—and the prize wasn't her. It was her gym and the investor interested in it.

Knowing that didn't douse the slow excitement building in her stomach at the thought of seeing him again. It hadn't even been forty-eight hours and she already longed for his touch. *Dangerous.*

She checked the time and decided that being a little early wasn't a bad thing. Nerves were in danger of getting the best of her as she made her way to the restaurant, but she knew Roman well enough at this point to know that he'd find a way to get ahold of her if she no-showed him. What was more, he wouldn't make the same offer twice. This was her chance to get what she wanted—freedom.

Too bad the thought of that didn't fill her with the expected relief. Free meant she wouldn't be seeing Roman again. How could she when he represented such a different set of priorities than she had? Even if she was willing to give it a shot, their respective schedules would mean dates were few and far in between. If things didn't fall apart because of their differences, they'd fall apart because neither one of them could come up with the time to make it work.

Wow. Talk about being fatalistic.

No, I'm being realistic.

She walked into the restaurant Roman had chosen. It wasn't one she was familiar with, and she stopped just inside the door to take it all in. Everything was very modern and minimalist, which was a far cry from the shabby beach chic clutter of West Island. Nothing about the choice screamed Roman to her, but that could very well be because she didn't know him nearly as well as she would have liked to pretend. *You're seesawing all over the place. Get ahold of yourself.*

She told the waitress she was meeting Roman

Bassani and was led back to a little booth tucked into the side wall facing the street. The windows weren't big, but they offered plenty of fodder for people watching. Or they would if she could look anywhere but at Roman's perfect face. He rose to meet her, and she couldn't help comparing this man with the one she'd felt so connected to on the island. *Her* Roman was there, beneath the expensive suit and the perfectly styled hair. She could see a hint of him in those hazel eyes, but even the way he held his shoulders was different here. Harsher.

"Hey." She wrapped her arms around herself, wishing she'd worn something fancier. But that wasn't Allie any more than the relaxed guy in the cargo shorts was Roman. Her wrap dress was nice, but if she didn't miss her guess, he could pay her rent for several months with that suit.

"Hey." He took her hand and pulled her gently closer. The quick kiss he dropped on her lips made her heart ache because it was different, too. Cursory. Distracted. Lacking the heat she'd grown used to that was present in even the smallest of touches between them before.

She disengaged her hand, forced a smile and slid into her seat. "You look nice."

"You're stealing my line." His lips quirked up as he sat across from her. "How was your day?"

Horrible. I can't pay my bills. I'm realizing I care about you a whole lot more than I expected, and the writing is on the wall that both this budding relationship and my ownership of my gym will end awfully. I'm in a funk I don't know that I'll ever get out of. She tried to smile. "It was okay."

Roman's brows slanted down. "What's the truth, Aphrodite? Because that's not it."

She tensed. "Let it go. Please." The last thing Allie wanted to do was rip herself open for him. She didn't do that for *anyone*. She was the strong one. The one who got through things that would break other people and came out the other side swinging with everything she had. It couldn't be clearer that this dinner was the end. Roman wanted things she couldn't give him—and she wasn't talking about her gym and the shelter. He wanted parts of *her*.

No way.

She gritted her teeth and resolved to get to the end of this date so she could secure Roman's promise to leave her business the hell alone. Then she'd walk. Better to end things here and now instead of letting them drag on and enact any one of the horrible scenarios she'd tortured herself with earlier.

The waitress appeared to take their drink order, and Allie was pathetically grateful for the distraction. She ordered a white wine and Roman had whiskey. Then the woman was gone and there was nothing to stand between them. She took a steadying breath. "I'm ready for your pitch."

CHAPTER SIXTEEN

ROMAN STARED AT Allie across the table from him, feeling like he was on a boat headed for a storm, watching the receding shore of paradise and knowing he'd never see it again. Regardless of what she'd told him when she'd agreed to this date, it was clear she'd already made up her mind about both his proposal and him. It made him want to shake her, to force her to see that good things were within reach if she'd just lower the barriers the slightest bit.

If she'd let him in.

He sat back. Might as well get this over with, because he could already see that she wouldn't let him get anywhere near anything personal until they'd both fulfilled their part of the bargain connected to her beloved gym. "I don't have to tell you about the stats of women who feel harassed in their gyms, let alone their daily lives. With Transcend you've created a unique hook that my investor thinks will go over well as a small franchise. Something exclusive to a handful of big cities at first—LA, San Antonio, Seattle, Atlanta, Chicago. Boutique gyms are in right now, but this has the potential to last longer than the fad does, especially if there's some kind of health plan and smoothie bar that goes hand in hand with it."

"That's not what Transcend is about."

"That's exactly what Transcend is about. You are a bastion of safety for women. They flock to that gym because it's one of the few places they can let their guard down a little. *You* are the reason they feel safe, and the little community you've created." He leaned forward and braced his forearms on the table. "Don't women outside this city deserve that feeling, too?"

She met his gaze directly. "There are other women-only gyms out there. Mine is far from unique."

"But yours is the only one connected with a shelter for battered women." This was it. He'd lose her or have her based on this last part. "My investor is interested in continuing and expanding the work you do with the shelter." The hope in her eyes killed him, so he spoke quickly. "With the caveat that you sign over the nonprofit entirely."

"What?"

No use pussyfooting around it. "It's not your passion. The brainchild was all yours, but the delivery has been lackluster at best. You help those women, and *that* is your passion, combined with the gym. But a successful nonprofit requires shmoozing and networking, and that's a full-time job—a job it couldn't be clearer you are not interested in. You haven't done much with it up to this point."

"That's not fair. I—"

He held up a hand. "That wasn't a criticism. You're running two full-time businesses by yourself. It's natural that things have fallen through the cracks as a result. My point—my investor's point—is that if you delegate and hand off a few things, the whole operation could expand and run smoother as a result."

Allie sat back, the golden tone of her skin going pale with worry. "Even if I was interested in signing away everything I've worked for, what guarantee would I have that this investor of yours wouldn't turn around and do exactly the opposite of what they're proposing now?"

"It's something that could be stipulated in the contract." He found himself holding his breath while she seemed to think it over.

But she shook her head. "No. I can't risk it. Those women depend on me to keep them safe, and I don't know a single damn thing about this investor of yours. I've seen how flimsy paperwork can be when it comes to protection—might often makes right, and your investor has all of it."

She was technically right—even with the protections written into the contract, there were limits to what Allie could demand—but Roman knew this investor and he knew that the offer was legit. He wouldn't have fielded it otherwise. "Trust me. I wouldn't have brought this to you, especially after the last week, if I didn't think it would honor what's important to you."

"You keep saying that—to trust you. You haven't done a single thing to earn this level of trust."

And fuck, that stung. He'd shared things with her last week that he didn't talk about with anyone. Even though Allie was still guarded, he'd thought she'd shared shit with him, too. He wasn't a sappy romantic, but that *meant* something.

Or at least, he'd thought it had.

Roman forced the tension from his shoulders. "I have only your best—"

"No."

He waited for some kind of explanation, something he could work with, some sign that she wasn't just shutting him out without explanation. None came. With a slow sinking in his stomach, he sat back. "And if I ask you on another date—if I want this to go somewhere—am I going to get the same answer?"

Allie fiddled with her fork and then set it aside. "I'm sorry, Roman, but I just don't see how this could possibly work out. We're too different."

A nice pat explanation—and it was bullshit. "How are we supposed to give this a shot if you won't talk to me? If you *never* talk to me. You came to dinner tonight with your responses already planned out. It didn't matter what I said, because you were always going to tell me no to investing in the gym, and no to us dating."

She flinched. "I'm saying no to your investor because I don't trust their intentions. And there is no *us*. I had a wonderful time with you on West Island, but that wasn't reality. This?" She motioned between them. "This is reality. You in your expensive suit and me in my secondhand dress. I do whatever I can to help people, and you hurt them *for your job*. We're just too different."

"That's bullshit and you know it." Frustration grabbed him by the throat. She was determined to see the worst in his choice of career, no matter what evidence he provided to the contrary. It didn't matter if he laid out a list of all the happy business owners who had benefited from him doing his job—Allie would pick out the one from the bunch who was pissed and then use it as proof that he was a monster. "You're being a chickenshit. Newsflash, Allie—I'm not your father. I'm as far from that bastard as a man can get, but if you can't see that, then maybe you're right—we don't stand a chance."

Roman wasn't saying anything Allie hadn't said to herself, but somehow hearing those words—that condemnation—come out of his mouth sucked all the air out of the room. "That's not fair."

"Neither is sacrificing a potential future with me because you're scared." He spoke low and fiercely, and part of her wanted to give in and just let him take the wheel. Roman was more than capable of taking care of both of them and guiding the relationship toward...

What am I thinking?

She knew what came from having to depend on a man. Even if Roman would never hurt her—and he wouldn't—he was too overpowering and overwhelming. He would swallow her whole and all that would be left of her identity would be connected to him. Roman's woman.

Not Allie, strong and mostly confident business owner who didn't need to lean on anyone. That person would be gone, and she'd never be able to get her back.

If Allie didn't have her gym, she didn't have anything. She'd be starting over from scratch, selling her soul in the process. It was easy for Roman to tell her to trust him, to talk to him, when *she* was the one making all the sacrifices and he was making none.

"Is that what you really think?"

She hadn't realized she'd spoken all those thoughts aloud, but she'd put it out there and she wasn't about to take it back now. "Isn't that the truth?" Roman had all the chips in this scenario—he had since they'd met. *No, not since we met. That first night, we were on equal footing.* There was no going back now, though. They were who they were, and neither of them could really change that.

He clenched his jaw hard enough that she feared for his teeth. "Talk. To. Me."

"That's exactly what I've been doing this whole time. Just because I'm not saying what you like doesn't mean I'm wrong." She slid out of the booth and stood. "This was a mistake."

"Allie, if you walk out that door, that's it. I'm not going to chase your ass down just so I can keep bashing my head against the same damn wall." He said it with such finality, her throat burned and her eyes prickled.

Because this was it. They'd been hurtling toward this moment since the first time they'd realized each other's identities. Part of her had thought they'd find a way around, but he was too uncompromising, too sure that he knew what was best for her.

And he was right—he was nothing like her father or the abusive men who drove the women to her shelter in flocks. Roman would never hurt someone like that, no matter how angry. She'd stake her life on it.

No, the damage he dealt wasn't physical. It wasn't even intentional. That didn't stop her from feeling like he'd reached into her chest and ripped out her heart. "Goodbye, Roman."

"Allie, wait."

Her feet stopped, even as her brain demanded she

keep moving. Almost against her will, she turned and looked at him.

Roman stood and glanced around them. She'd been vaguely aware that they had an audience before then, but the reality of the situation came crashing down on her. She was having a very public breakup with a man who wasn't even her boyfriend. *This is what my life has come to.* "If you have anything left to say, now's the time." She waited, holding her breath, wondering if maybe he'd say something that would override her fears and put them back on something resembling solid ground.

He stepped closer and lowered his voice. The warmth was gone from his eyes, leaving the cold businessman in his place. "If you don't take this investor's offer, you'll be sentencing both your gym and the shelter to death."

Allie flinched. She knew that she was in trouble better than anyone, but that didn't mean she'd put the women who depended on her at risk. Not until she'd exhausted all other options. "I'll find another way."

"Good fucking luck." He shook his head and walked around her. "I do mean that, Allie. It'll take a goddamn miracle to save you at this point, and you just turned down the helping hand I offered. That's on you—not me."

She watched him walk away, a pit opening up inside her with no end. Allie had hit so many snags since she'd set herself on the goal of opening her own business and nonprofit, and every single one of them she'd fought her way through. By all rights she should be furious at Roman, and that should drive her to figure out a solution to this problem.

But all she wanted to do was go home and cry herself to sleep.

She turned to pay for their drinks but caught sight of a fifty that Roman had left on the table. Even pissed as hell, he had ensured that he held up his end of the bargain, at least when it came to this. *Stop thinking about that.* She'd given him the only answer she could. Ultimately, his investor could paint whatever pretty picture they wanted, because when push came to shove, money talked. Once the papers were signed and Allie was no longer in control, the investor could do as they pleased and she'd have no power to stop them.

She'd made the right call. She was sure of it.

She just didn't know why it felt so freaking awful to have pulled the proverbial trigger and put an end to both the investor talk and her time with Roman. She should be relieved. It was over. She'd held up her end of the bargain, and she was free. Not to mention a vacation for the record books, the kind she'd remember fondly for as long as she lived...

Even if all she felt right at that moment was overwhelming sadness.

Allie left the restaurant, thought about grabbing a cab and ultimately decided to walk. She needed to expend some energy, to work her way through the crap circling in her head. Roman's words kept ringing through her mind, telling her that she'd never figure out how to save her gym and the shelter on her own. That she was destined for failure.

Fuck that.

It was easier to focus on business than to deal with the yawning chasm of loss taking up residence in her chest. It didn't matter how much she told herself that she and Roman would never work—she'd secretly hoped that he'd have a solution that would take care of her fears. *Depending on Roman to shoulder all of that was totally fair.* It wasn't that... Allie shook her head and picked up her pace. Maybe it was partly that. She didn't want to depend on him for everything—for anything—but she had still kind of been on the verge of doing exactly that. *Weak.*

She couldn't afford to be weak. Not in business, and not in her yearning for Roman.

Allie still had to fight not to call him as she strode down the block toward her apartment. She wanted to talk to him, to yell, or cry, or...something. Connect. She'd been adrift for so long, and she hadn't realized it until his grounding presence had slammed into her life. The fact they'd spent only a week together should have been a bucket of cold water on her, but it didn't seem to make any difference. They had a connection, and it scared her. It didn't seem to scare him as much, but what did he have to lose? The scales of their risk were not equal.

Roman would move on with his life after this. She had no illusions that he'd be happy to leave her behind, but he was a driven individual who wouldn't let a little heartache stop him from reaching his goals. He'd find a better-fitting investment for this client. And the next, and the next.

Eventually he'd start dating. Even as chaotic as his schedule had to be, he was too much of the full package *not* to find a woman willing to put up with it. They'd date the appropriate amount of time and then he'd propose on an island a whole lot like West Island. Hell, maybe he'd actually propose *there*.

The thought made her sick to her stomach.

Just get home. You can break down when you get home.

She flagged down a cab and rattled off her address. Through the entire drive, Allie focused on breathing, putting every bit of concentration she had on that single task. It got her as far as her front door and then she slumped to the floor. "Oh, God, what am I going to do?"

CHAPTER SEVENTEEN

"You're in a pissy-ass mood."

Roman stared at his drink. It was his second, and he forced himself to sip it instead of shooting it like he wanted to. No matter how good of a friend the man next to him was, he still couldn't afford to lose control. *Mostly because I'll end up drunk texting Allie and making a damn fool of myself.* "I'm fine."

Aaron Livingston snorted. "You're about as far from fine as a man gets. I've never seen you this out of sorts about a deal falling through."

The deal and Allie were all twisted up in his head, and he couldn't untangle them. That investor would have *helped* her. He couldn't divulge details until the contracts were set, but his client, Clare Belford, was the perfect fit for that company. She had one of the biggest nonprofits for abused women in the country, and she'd loved the idea of Allie's gym being linked up with several of them.

Because of a nondisclosure agreement he had with Clare, he hadn't been able to tell Allie that, but if she'd just trusted him, she would have found out shortly.

Except she hadn't trusted him.

He was good enough to fuck, but anything beyond that was strictly off-limits. The thought had him downing the rest of his drink despite his best intentions. He motioned to the bartender to refill the glass, doing his best to ignore the curious look he could feel Aaron giving him. "I don't want to talk about it."

"Holy fuck." Aaron leaned against the bar, blue eyes narrowed. "It's not business at all—it's woman trouble."

"What part of 'I don't want to talk about it' don't you get?"

"You do want to talk about it. You wouldn't be here otherwise." Aaron waited for the bartender to slide the newly filled glass over before continuing. "You weren't seeing anyone before you left for the island, and that place has a limited population of guests, so there was only one woman there who'd be twisting you up like this." He whistled softly. "You and Allie Landers? I thought you didn't mix business with pleasure."

"I don't—didn't." He eyed his glass but didn't pick it up.

"You might as well get it off your chest. I can't say I've ever had that look on my face, but I have three sisters, so I know a thing or two about women."

Roman almost commented on the fact that if he

had to recall his sisters for advice instead of his own dating history, he wasn't much help. But the truth was that Roman had a varied dating history and he'd never been this fucked up over a woman. Even his worst breakups and the respective aftermaths had been filled with a sense of peace because it was the right call.

There was no peace in this.

He nudged his glass farther away. "I had all the answers. The solution to everything she needed. All I got for my trouble was a kick in the ass as she showed me the door." When Aaron made a noncommittal noise, he kept going. "I never planned on her. Fuck, man, she's strong and gorgeous and smart as hell. I'm talking full package. I thought we were on the same wavelength, but she didn't even try to see that I might actually be right. She's so determined to do things her way, she won't even give us a shot."

"You want the bro-supportive view or real talk?"

He finally looked at Aaron. Roman could have called Gideon to come drink with him, but his other friend was so deep in his romantic bliss with Lucy Baudin that he wouldn't be able to commiserate. Aaron, at least, was single. All Roman had really wanted was someone to drink with who wouldn't press too hard, but he'd underestimated Aaron. It was tempting to say he wanted the supportive viewpoint, but Roman had never shied away from the shitty side of things, so he went with the hard truth option. "The latter."

"You fucked up."

He blinked. "How do you figure?"

"Look at this from her perspective—you crashed her vacation and, yeah, maybe your intense chemistry made everything else take a back seat for the week, but nothing really changed. You were still the conquering enemy force once you two got back to New York. You have the standard contract with the prospective investor?"

"Yeah. Always."

Aaron nodded. "So even if it's the best fit, you aren't telling her shit about this person and you're expecting her to just take your word for it. From all accounts, Allie Landers is a woman who's been holding the world on her shoulders and dealing with every issue that's arisen on her own. You can't seriously have expected her to just flip on a dime and put everything she's worked years for on the line on your word alone."

"I expected her to trust me," Roman snapped. The fact she hadn't still stung like a bitch.

"Why?"

He growled. "Because I would never hurt her or what she cares about."

"Maybe you know that. Maybe she even knows that on some level." Aaron shrugged. "If your delivery was anything similar to the one you've given tonight, you can't blame her for telling you to fuck off. Maybe the sex changed things for you both, but if you didn't tell her that, how's she supposed to know? She's not a damn mind reader."

He wanted to rail at his friend—at Allie—that she should have trusted him anyway, but... What had he really done to earn that trust? A multitude of orgasms was great, but it didn't translate—a fact he damn well knew. He'd opened up about his past a bit, but he hadn't exactly made himself overly vulnerable to her. He'd held back. They might have established a connection, but it certainly didn't earn him the amount of trust he could expect her to stake her business on. He drank some of his whiskey, forcing himself to go slow. "I care about her."

"And it's making you stupid. Don't worry—you're not the only one who's done it. She made mistakes in this, too, but we're not talking about her. We're talking about you." Aaron took a pull of his beer. "The question remains—what the hell are you going to do about it?"

Allie cared about him. Roman would bet everything he owned on that fact. His pride might be demanding he let the whole thing go and move on with his life...but he couldn't wrap his mind around moving on from this. Allie was special. More than what he felt for her, he wanted her to succeed in the vision she'd put into play. He wanted to be by her side when she saw it realized. If he walked now, he wouldn't do any of that.

What was his pride when compared with his happiness—and hers?

He checked his watch and stood. "I'm going to go get my girl."

"There you go." Aaron toasted him with his beer. "Though I'd recommend waiting for morning, since it's after ten."

Roman was already turning for the door. "I have a few calls to make. I'll catch up with you later." He had several things to line up before he could talk to Allie. If he wanted a chance to succeed in winning her back, he had to be able to present new information—to change the narrative.

A pounding on the door brought Allie out of her light doze. She shot to her feet before she realized that she wasn't in her bed, and nearly tripped over the coffee table. She scrubbed a hand over her face and headed for the door as whoever was on the other side kept knocking. For one crazy moment she was sure it was Roman, coming to find her after last night to say... She didn't know what. Something.

But when she opened the door, it was Becka on the other side. Her friend took one look at her and shook her head. "Oh, God. It's worse than I thought."

"What?"

Becka nudged her back into the apartment and

shut the door. "You. You are worse than I thought. Look at you—you're wearing holey sweats, you have powdered sugar on your shirt and there are ink stains all over your hands. Something is going on with you, and I want to know what it is. Did Roman do something? Do I need to kick his ass to Brooklyn and back?"

"What? No." *Yes. Sort of.* She smoothed her hair back, belatedly realizing that she hadn't showered today and her messy bun was more mess than bun. "Roman and I had a vacation fling and it's over now."

Becka narrowed her eyes. "Bullshit."

"Excuse me?"

"You heard me. You were well on your way to head over heels for that guy, and from the way he looked at you, he was right there with you. So what gives? Because you were fine when we flew back to the city, and now you're on the verge of a breakdown."

She opened her mouth to make some excuse and change the subject just like she always did when Becka put her on the spot, but despair got the better of her. "I'm in trouble, Becka. Big trouble."

Instantly, her friend's half-joking demeanor disappeared. "Tell me so we can fix it."

"I don't know if there's any fixing this." She walked back to the couch and sat down, waiting for Becka to join her before she started in. Allie detailed how far behind they were on bills, how she'd been borrowing from her own income to supplement both the gym and the shelter, how she was almost drained dry.

How she'd told Roman no even though he'd offered her a potential way out.

"Well, yeah." Becka nodded. "He didn't give you much in the way of assurances, and I get why you said no." Before Allie could relax, she continued. "What I don't get is why this is the first time I'm hearing about all this."

"I thought I could handle it." Even when she'd realized she couldn't, putting that burden on someone else went against everything Allie was. She was the problem solver, and she knew she could depend on herself. *Other people* depended on her—she didn't depend on other people. She didn't know how to reach out when she was in trouble.

Becka gave her a look. "You know, it's not the worst thing in the world to ask for help. You're allowed to not be perfect."

"I know I'm not perfect."

She snorted. "But you don't know how to lean on other people. As your best friend, I'm all about blindly hating anyone you hate, but I have a question and I want you to answer it honestly."

Even knowing where this was going, she couldn't help nodding. "Okay."

"Did you even stop to consider for a second that maybe Roman was on the up-and-up? That maybe he cared about you and was telling the truth about his investor and he only wanted to help?" She held up a hand. "I mean, the man is not a saint. He went after this account because he knew it would make his investor happy, and he didn't really care about what you wanted before he met you—but that doesn't mean that the investor is an evil mastermind who wants to destroy everything you've worked toward. Did you ask Roman if you were going to be able to stay on in any capacity?"

"No." Heat climbed her chest and throat to settle in her face. Embarrassment. "He wanted me to compromise on everything and just have faith that he wasn't screwing me. I just…reacted."

Becka nodded. "I mean, I'm not saying you were 100 percent in the wrong. He played that poorly from beginning to end. But I also think that maybe, just maybe, you reacted instead of thinking it through. I know you want to be able to do this all yourself, but there's no shame in letting someone else share your vision—and help you realize it."

She took a slow breath. "All those women are depending on me to help them."

"Whoa. Slow down there, Wonder Woman. Those women are grateful for a safe space, yes, but they're not helpless. They're not children who need you to see to their every need. You can't put all that on your shoulders." She leaned forward. "Let's be honest here for a second, okay?"

Allie managed a half smile. "We weren't being honest before now?"

"You know what I mean. I love the shit out of you, but you can be bullheaded to a clinical degree. Roman scared you. He made you feel things and he offered you something you want desperately but are afraid to take because it might blow up in your face. I get that. I do. But I also think you latched on to any reason why it wouldn't work and just ran with it, ignoring any indication that you might be—just maybe—dead wrong."

She didn't want to admit that. Roman was as bullheaded as she was—if not more so. She couldn't afford to show weakness because he'd steamroll her.

Except by not showing weakness, she'd put them in a position where it was all or nothing. There was no compromise because *she* hadn't tried to compromise. She'd just turned him down and cut things off because it was easier than putting herself out there and trying. Becka's words wouldn't smart so much if they didn't have more than a grain of truth in them. "Damn it, you're right."

"I often am." Becka slouched back onto the couch and pulled her legs up to her chest. "So, to simplify— you like Roman a whole hell of a lot, and you're in trouble with the gym—the kind of trouble an investor would solve, but only the right investor."

"That about sums it up." She twisted a lock of hair around her finger. "I guess if I had the right investor, it wouldn't be hard to sign over control—at least partial control. Someone who has the same vision I do, and who wants the same things."

"That makes sense." Becka grinned. "Good thing we know someone with a whole list of people wanting to invest in start-up companies that have promise. I imagine if you went to Roman with a counteroffer, he'd fall all over himself to give you whatever you want."

Since Allie couldn't imagine a scenario where Roman fell all over himself, she just nodded. She could go to a different person to make this connection, but that seemed the height of stupidity—and cowardice. Facing Roman and admitting that she was wrong shouldn't be the end of the world. It wouldn't be comfortable, but what if he really had been serious about giving them a real shot? She'd spend the rest of her life wondering if she'd missed the love of her life because she was too stubborn to ask for help. "I should call him, huh?"

"If you think so."

She considered it for a full thirty seconds. "I'm going to shower and *then* I'm going to go find him."

"That's my girl!"

CHAPTER EIGHTEEN

ALLIE'S INTENTIONS WERE all well and good, but she couldn't find Roman. He wasn't in his office, and no one seemed to know what his schedule was—and he hadn't answered any of her calls. By the time the afternoon rolled around, she was on the verge of despair. *Maybe I misread the entire situation and he really wasn't interested beyond the gym and now he wants nothing to do with me.*

Not sure what else to do, she sent him a quick text. I'm sorry. I'd like to talk. Can we meet somewhere?

Her phone buzzed before she had a chance to set it down. Where are you?

He wouldn't respond to any of her calls, but he responded to a text—because of course. Down was up and up was down, just like it had been since she'd met Roman. The gym.

Stay there. On my way.

Her heart leaped into her throat and she had to

swallow several times before she was able to force
her thumbs to type out a reply. Okay.

She tried to busy herself with paperwork, but she
kept watching the clock and wondering what was
going on. Allie wanted to talk, for sure, but Roman's
abrupt texts made her wonder all over again if this
was a mistake.

*No. Stop it. You care about him, and you're going
to fight for him, damn it.*

She clung to that thought for the next twenty-five
minutes. When someone knocked on her office door,
she nearly bolted out of her chair. "Come in!"

Roman walked through, and the sight of him was
like coming home. He wore a pair of dark slacks and
a button-down shirt that did wonders for his shoulders, and the look he gave her when he breached the
door was one of a returning hero. As if he had craved
the sight of her as much as she'd wanted him.

She opened her mouth to say all the things she'd
had running through her head for the last day, but
stopped when she registered that he wasn't alone. A
petite silver-haired woman stepped into the room.
Her face was ageless enough that Allie couldn't tell
if her silver hair was trendy or all natural, but she
could only be termed a handsome woman. Her bone
structure was a little too strong to be merely pretty,
and she carried herself with a confidence that filled
the room.

Roman shut the door and turned to Allie. "I'd

like to introduce you to Clare Belford—the investor who hired me."

She froze. "I know that name… You're the woman
who runs Safe Places."

"I am." Clare's voice was low and melodious. "I'm
really impressed with the operation you're running."

"I— Thank you. I love your work. You make such
a difference in so many women's lives."

Clare moved closer to her desk. "Roman here
told me about your concerns—which are perfectly
valid—and I wanted to meet you to reassure you
that I have every intention of staying true to your
vision. I would like to incorporate your shelter into
Safe Places and expand Transcend to pair new gyms
with the current shelters in the cities Roman suggested. And I would also like to hire you to stay
on as general manager of both the local shelter and
the original gym. I know it's not the same thing as
owner, but I'm prepared to allow you full autonomy
provided you operate within the parameters you've
already established."

Allie couldn't breathe. She couldn't think. It was
everything she could do not to cry. In all her imag-
inings of how things would go down with her shelter
and gym, *this* wasn't even on the list of possibilities.
She cleared her throat. "That sounds wonderful."

"Don't give me an answer now. Think it over and
let me know by the end of the week." Clare reached
out and shook Allie's hand. Her grip was just as con-

fident as her personality. "I'm glad we were able to meet."

"Me, too."

Roman waited for the door to close behind Clare to speak. "I'm sorry."

She still couldn't quite process the turn of events. "I thought you couldn't talk about who your investor was."

"I signed a nondisclosure agreement. It's standard because the job can get a little sticky when it comes to negotiations and some investors would rather not be identified beforehand for their own reasons."

The dots connected with a snap she could almost hear. "You asked her to talk to me."

He hesitated. "While it would have been great if you'd trusted me on this, I understand why you didn't now. You have more than just your life at stake, and going into the situation with only my word isn't sufficient. I knew if you met with Clare, you would understand that this will only mean good things for both the shelter and the gym—and more women than you can reach on your own."

Allie took a breath, and then another. "Roman, I don't know what to say."

"Then just... I have to apologize—actually apologize. I was pissed that you wouldn't trust me, but I was asking you to do all the bending and I wasn't putting anything on the line to keep us on equal footing. So here it is—I love you, Aphrodite. I know it's too soon and you have reservations, but I'm willing to do whatever it takes to be with you. If that means you need time, then I'll give you as much time as you need." The tense look on his face conveyed how much he liked that idea, but he charged on. "We can go as fast or as slow as you want, but *I* want *you*. So unless you don't want me back, this is happening."

God, she was more than a little in love with him, too.

Allie stood and rounded the desk to stand in front of him. "If we're going to restart this on the right foot, I have to apologize, too. I went with my knee-jerk reaction to take care of things myself and didn't stop to think that maybe it's okay to lean on someone or to ask for help." She shifted closer to him, not quite willing to touch him yet, but wanting to. "I was actually calling you today to ask if you'd help set me up with an investor." She smiled. "I guess we were on the same page, after all."

Roman took her hands, his expression serious. "If you aren't comfortable with what Clare is offering, we can find someone else. I'm not going to push you on this. I promise."

"I'm going to take her offer." She'd known it the second Clare had made it. As much as it had initially been her dream to own her own business, being the GM wasn't much of a step down. If she was able to keep control and be assured that all the women who came through her shelter were cared for... It was worth it. It was more than worth it. "Thank you. I'm sorry I didn't trust you."

"You have nothing to apologize for."

She slipped into his arms. "I do have one other thing to say."

"Just one?" A smile flirted with the edges of his lips.

"I love you, too." She kissed him, showing him she meant the words, putting everything she felt into the contact. "This might be too soon, and it might be a little crazy, but I wouldn't have it any other way."

* * * * *

WILD THING

NICOLA MARSH

MILLS & BOON

For Nic's Super Novas, the best support team a girl could wish for.
Your input on covers, characters and buffed guys is invaluable!

CHAPTER ONE

MAKAYLA TARRANT HAD done some embarrassing things in her twenty-four years on the planet.

Falling off the stage as an awestruck seven-year-old at her first ballet recital? Check.

Flashing a nipple courtesy of a wardrobe malfunction during her stage debut at sixteen? Check.

Stripping in front of sleazy strangers at a dive bar in Kings Cross to ensure her mum had the funeral she deserved? Check.

But nothing came close to the mortification making her muscles spasm as she strutted into the most important audition of her life to date and discovered the casting director was Hudson Watt.

Her best friend growing up.

Her confidant.

Her go-to guy.

The only guy she'd ever really trusted.

Until that night five years ago when he'd seen her naked on stage and her world had imploded.

She hadn't seen him since. Not after the hateful

accusations exchanged. He'd misjudged her without giving her a chance to explain. She'd cut him from her life without a second's remorse.

Okay, so that was a lie. At a time when she'd been reeling from her mum's unexpected death, a time when she'd needed her friend the most, a time when she'd done the unthinkable to make sure she could afford a decent funeral, Hudson had morphed into a judgemental monster and she'd lost the best friend she'd ever had.

Back then, she'd pretended she didn't care when in fact she'd grieved for her lost friendship almost as much as for her mum.

'Next,' Hudson said, impatience lacing his tone as he flipped pages on a clipboard.

Makayla didn't move. She couldn't, her feet heavier than her heart as she hovered left stage, wishing she had the guts to turn around and make a run for it before he saw her.

But she needed this job, desperately. Her roommate, Charlotte, was on the verge of leaving and Makayla's pay cheque from working part-time at Le Miel, the hippest patisserie in Sydney, wouldn't cover rent let alone anything else.

She'd auditioned eighteen times for various dance roles over the last few weeks. Nada.

Embue was the coolest nightclub in a city brimming with trendy hotspots and the moment she'd heard they were trialling live shows she'd applied, determined to nail her first dancing role in months. A determination that was rapidly fading when faced with the prospect of dancing for Hudson.

Crap.

What the hell was she going to do?

At that moment, he raised his head and her chance to flee unobserved vanished.

Shock widened his eyes, his lips parting in surprise before compressing into a thin line. A frown slashed his brows. No great surprise he wasn't pleased to see her, considering what she'd called him the last time they'd met.

'Hi, Hudson,' she said, injecting enough fake enthusiasm into her voice to convey nonchalance, but her hand shook as she raised it in a wave. 'Long time no see.'

She inwardly cringed at her blasé, clichéd greeting as she forced her legs to move, heading for centre stage. Where she'd be under the spotlight. Exposed. Vulnerable.

Hell.

After what seemed like an eternity of him pinning her with a laser-like glare, he nodded. 'Mak. So you're auditioning for the lead dancer?'

Mak…only Hudson uttered that one short syllable in a way that touched her deep, like a warm hand strumming her spine in a long languorous caress. His voice seemed lower, huskier, than the last time she'd seen him…when he'd hurled vile assumptions at her and their friendship had crumbled.

'Mak?'

Damn, he'd caught her daydreaming. Now that the option to flee had gone—she wouldn't give him the satisfaction of seeing how rattled she was—she squared her shoulders.

'Yes. I'd love to be lead dancer in Embue's new production. Thanks for the opportunity.'

She didn't give him a chance to respond, shooting the music co-ordinator a quick nod to start her track.

She'd be okay once the song started. The dread making her gut churn would fade. The nerves making her muscles seize would ease. It had to. Because she couldn't fail this audition. Not with so much at stake.

As the first booming bass beat of a Lady Gaga hit blasted from the sound system, an instant wave of calm washed over Makayla.

She could do this.

Music and dance and moving to a rhythm, she understood.

Men who abandoned her when she needed them most, not so much.

As the tempo increased, she began her routine. Steps and twirls and kicks, a high-energy routine designed to dazzle. She let the music take her, her feet pounding to the beat, her arms slicing through the air in perfect synchronisation.

It had always been like this, from the moment she'd seen her mum dance on stage in a nightly Kings Cross revue, a wide-eyed three-year-old mesmerised by the glittery costumes, the make-up and the applause.

She'd adored her mum, had wanted to be exactly like her. Emulating her grace and elegance and vibrancy on stage. But Makayla also wanted more. More kudos. More recognition. More.

Broadway. The pinnacle. Her dream.

But unless she scored a leading role soon, her dream would be in tatters, like her bank account.

The song drew to a close and Makayla threw herself into the finale, a run across the stage complete with high scissor split, before landing nimbly on her feet, arms flung high in victory.

The music cut off, the silence deafening.

At some auditions, she'd seen directors clap for outstanding performances.

Hudson didn't move a muscle.

Swallowing the burgeoning lump in her throat, she stepped to the edge of the stage, out of the spotlight.

He scribbled something down before glancing up at her, his face unreadable.

Her heart sank but she forced a smile. A smile that wavered the longer he stared at her through narrowed eyes.

'We'll be in touch,' he said, and, with a curt nod, dismissed her.

Disappointment made her knees wobble, but she'd be damned if she gave him an insight into her devastation.

Mustering what little courage she had left, she strode offstage.

And flipped him the bird behind the plush gold curtain.

CHAPTER TWO

HUDSON BIT BACK a guffaw.

Mak had flipped him the bird when she thought he couldn't see. But Embue was renowned for its many mirrors and he'd seen her, clear as day, as she'd exited the stage.

Feisty. Bold. Confident. Still the same old Mak. Yet she wasn't the same, not by a long shot.

It had been five years since he'd seen her in that Kings Cross strip club, naked in front of a room of slobbering Neanderthals. Five years since he'd fucked up. Big time.

She'd matured since then, her curves more womanly, her legs a tad longer, her eyes a deeper blue, her hair a rich glorious auburn. She'd always been a stunner growing up but now Mak could knock a guy to his knees and make him grovel to get back up.

When he'd seen her name on the audition sheet, he could've sworn his heart had skipped a beat; she had that kind of impact on him. Always had.

He'd clamped down on his initial reaction to

score a line through her name. It wasn't her fault he couldn't erase that night he'd seen her strip and the resultant fallout.

How many times had he picked up the phone afterwards to apologise? To see if she was okay? To talk her out of heading down a nefarious path that he'd seen first-hand resulted in tragedy?

Countless times, when he'd tried to formulate the right words yet had been lacking. He'd wanted to lecture her against the dangers of scoring easy cash via stripping. He'd wanted to warn her of the potential to spiral out of control. He'd wanted to tell her the truth behind his funk in the hope she'd understand why he'd freaked out.

Instead, he'd hung up the phone each and every time, knowing nothing he could say could erase the damage he'd done that night.

He'd said awful things, hateful things, in his shock-induced rage. Sadly, there'd been no coming back from it.

A week later he'd left Kings Cross, moving into a small Manly apartment and into the manager's job at Embue. He'd deliberately avoided going to clubs in the Cross for fear of seeing Mak performing. He couldn't face it, couldn't face seeing her innate innocence tainted in that sleazy world.

Not that he hadn't thought about her over the years. Some women were unforgettable and Mak was one of them.

Seeing her name on his audition sheet had given him a jolt. Could he really face seeing her dance again, when the last time he'd seen her gyrate and shimmy she'd been naked? He feared it would bring back all the old feelings: anger, disgust, with a healthy dose of jealousy. Crazy, out-of-control emotions, when he had no right to feel any of them.

He'd dithered for two days before the agency had called and demanded a list of potential dancers he'd like to trial. Before he could second-guess his decision, he'd added Mak's name to the list.

After seeing what she could do a few minutes ago, he was glad.

Mak could dance. Really dance. Exhibiting the kind of talent that would establish Embue as *the* venue for live shows.

He'd been worried that when she moved on stage, he'd be catapulted back to that horrible night five years earlier and his impartiality as a producer would be shot.

Thankfully, it hadn't happened. He'd been mesmerised by her lithe movement, her ability to command a small space, her stage presence.

Quite simply, as a dancer, Mak was a knockout.

It made him regret all the more that he'd missed out on seeing her come of age the last five years. In a world where he didn't trust easily, Mak had been a good friend. One of the best, next to Tanner.

'Auditions done?' Tanner slumped into the seat

next to him and braced his hands behind his head. 'Because Abby is getting angsty with the end-less trail of long-legged babes strutting their stuff through here.'

Hudson snorted and placed a thumb in the middle of Tanner's forehead. 'Your girlfriend is well aware you idolise her and that you're right under this.'

'She's the best.' Tanner swatted away his hand, his friend's goofy grin making Hudson want to puke.

Not that he begrudged his best mate and boss a little happiness. If anyone deserved it, he did, after the shit Tanner had tolerated growing up. But ever since Abby had come on the scene a month ago Tan-ner had been a shadow of his former self. Staring into space at the oddest of times. Leaving the nightclub early to watch chick-flicks with Abby. Refusing to go out on the town like they used to.

Relationships were for suckers.

Tanner steepled his fingers and rested them in his lap. 'So? Am I wasting my time, giving you a shot at making this live gig fly?'

Hudson sure as hell hoped not. He needed his idea to work. He owed Tanner and he always paid his dues.

'Once I finalise the lead, rehearsals can start.'

Tanner nodded, thoughtful. 'How did Makayla go?'

Hudson startled, immediately followed by a sink-ing feeling deep in his gut. The kind of feeling that made him want to punch something, preferably Tanner, if he'd slept with Mak.

Women fell at Tanner's feet, always had. Not that Hudson was jealous. He did okay. But the thought of his Mak with anyone…not that she was his. Not any more. Not that she ever had been, really. His outburst that night five years ago had seen to that.

'Mak did well.' Keeping his voice steady with effort, Hudson pretended to study the call-back sheet. 'How do you two know each other?'

Tanner laughed so loud it echoed around the club. 'Man, you should see your face. You look like you've sucked a lemon.'

'Fuck off,' Hudson growled, that urge to thump Tanner growing by the minute.

'I think a more pertinent question is how you know *Mak*?' Tanner's laughter petered to chuckles. 'By your thunderous expression, I'm assuming you know her a hell of a lot better than me.'

'You still haven't answered my question, dickhead.'

Infuriatingly calm and determined to make him sweat, Tanner linked his fingers and stretched forward. 'Makayla works at Le Miel with Abby. So when I filled in there while Remy was in hospital, I got to know her a bit then.'

'Oh.' Hudson deflated in relief, feeling like an idiot for allowing jealousy to cloud his judgement.

He had no right to be jealous of Mak. She could've

slept with the entire north shore of Sydney and it still shouldn't bother him. But it did. Deep down in that place where a part of him still missed her dreadfully, he cared. A whole damn lot.

'If you call her Mak, you've known her longer than me?' Tanner's smirk didn't hide his blatant curiosity.

Hudson could lie. But he didn't bullshit Tanner. They'd been through too much together, from the time they were at Kings Cross High, two misfits without mothers, trying to do the best they could with asshole fathers.

'Mak and I go way back,' he said, rubbing the tension cramping his neck muscles. 'When I was working the clubs at the Cross, our paths crossed constantly because her mum danced and waitressed there. We became friends.'

Tanner must've sensed the seriousness behind his declaration, because he stared straight ahead rather than grinning like an idiot. 'How come you never mentioned her back then?'

Because Mak had been all his. The one bright spot in his lousy world. Someone he could confide in, someone who understood the daily battles of growing up in the Cross, because she faced them too.

But he didn't say any of this to Tanner. Instead, Hudson shrugged. 'I didn't want you giving me shit. She's younger than me and I wanted to protect her.'

'A regular Sir Galahad,' Tanner scoffed, the lame-ass grin returning. 'What happened?'

'We had a falling out.' Massive understatement considering the blowout they'd had the night he'd stumbled upon her stripping. 'Haven't seen her in years.'

A speculative gleam made Tanner lean closer. 'So you two haven't…you know?'

'No.'

Not that he hadn't wanted to. But Mak had been off-limits due to her age—and her naivety, if he were completely honest. She'd radiated an innocence that shone bright in an otherwise grimy world. A world of pimps, prostitutes, drugs and strippers. A world he'd worked in out of necessity but had done his damnedest not to let taint him.

It was one of the many reasons he'd flipped out that night he'd seen her gyrating naked on stage.

That, and because of his mum.

'Well, I don't know what's wrong with you, man. Makayla's a bombshell and if I were single I'd take a shot at—'

'Shut the fuck up.'

'Whoa, easy, big fella.' Tanner held up his hands. 'Just giving my opinion. And if you overreact like that to a simple suggestion, I advise you to get laid, pronto.'

Hudson wouldn't give his doofus friend the satisfaction of knowing he wasn't far off the mark. What with getting this show off the ground, he hadn't had time to date lately. In fact, it had to be at least three months since he'd had sex. Maybe that was the reason he'd wanted to bound onto the stage and drag Mak into the nearest dressing room when he'd first seen her up there ten minutes ago?

Yeah, like that was the only reason.

'I need to organise call-backs so if you'll excuse me I've got work to do.' He brandished the clipboard at Tanner, who grinned as if he could see right through his feeble excuse.

'Get laid, buddy. It takes the edge off.' Tanner stood and clapped him on the back. 'According to Abby, Mak hasn't dated anyone in ages, so you two should get *reacquainted*.'

His glare was lost on Tanner as his friend sauntered away, lifting his hand in farewell. Damned if Tanner's advice didn't resonate.

He'd love to put the past behind and move forward with Mak. But how could he approach her as a friend, when she'd just nailed the lead dancer role in his show?

He might have found his leading lady but once he told her, it ensured they could never be anything but professional.

Mak's talent had floored him. She deserved this role.

So where the hell did that leave him?

CHAPTER THREE

By THE TIME Makayla made it back to Le Miel to start her shift she'd managed to come up with forty-three different ways she could make Hudson hurt.

Decapitation, evisceration, circumcision...not that she knew if he needed the latter or not, considering they'd never got that far, but she'd be willing to do it without anaesthetic.

His laconic, trite 'we'll be in touch' mocked her, echoing through her head until she'd thumped the steering wheel of her car several times. It hadn't helped. Hopefully, venting to Abby would.

Because if Makayla knew one thing, Hudson wouldn't call her. After the way they'd parted five years earlier, he had no freaking intention of calling her. Ever.

Even if he did, would she accept the job? Could she work with the guy who'd judged her and found her lacking, effectively ending their friendship?

She'd heard the rumours on the entertainment grapevine. That landing the lead gig at Embue could be a good segue into the latest dance extravaganza staging at the Opera House in a few months. And from there…well, dancing at the Sydney icon would look mighty fine on her CV if she ever made it to Broadway.

Broadway…her dream since she'd donned her first tutu and slipped on her first tap shoes.

Growing up, she'd spent countless hours poring over the Internet, watching video clips of shows at the many theatres in midtown Manhattan, wishing she could be a part of it.

Her mum had never scoffed at her dreams. Instead, Julia Tarrant had fostered her love of all things dance, spending every cent she earned on Makayla's dance lessons. It wasn't until her mum had died that Makayla realised the extent of her mum's sacrifice: Julia had no savings, but a detailed record of where her money had gone over the years. A budget that indicated Julia's love for her daughter.

Makayla had adored her mum and discovering she couldn't afford a decent send-off…it had driven her to take drastic action and accept that stripping job for one evening only.

The night Hudson had lost the plot and their friendship had imploded.

'Ugh,' she muttered, knowing she wouldn't be able to stomach her usual *beignet* and cappuccino before she started her shift.

Of all people to audition for, it had to be Hudson.

What the hell was he doing anyway, producing a dance show at Embue? Back then he'd been a gofer for the clubs at the Cross. Doing whatever jobs that came his way. He'd always talked about getting out when he was older, doing something in the club scene, so how did that equate to producing a stage show?

Entering the kitchen, she slammed the back door harder than intended, causing Abby to jump, the pastry brush in her hand clattering to the work bench.

'Sheesh, what's got your knickers in a knot?' Abby waggled a finger. 'Don't you know it takes precision and genius to create the perfect lemon tartlet?'

Makayla rolled her eyes. 'You could make pastries in your sleep and they'd still turn out delish, so quit your moaning.'

'Ouch. Someone's in a mood.' Abby frowned as Makayla slumped onto the nearest stool and scowled. 'Hey, what's wrong?'

'I had an audition this morning. It didn't go well.' Makayla folded her arms, belatedly realising that not even the delicious aromas of cinnamon and sugar wafting from the ovens could lighten her mood today. 'It was a biggie. And I danced my ass off.'

Concern creased Abby's brow. 'And they said no on the spot?'

'Hudson said "we'll be in touch".' She made inverted comma signs with her fingers. 'But I know that's BS.'

'Hudson? I know a guy called—'

'Yeah, he's Tanner's bestie. I didn't know he worked at Embue when I signed up otherwise I wouldn't have auditioned.'

Abby had just answered Makayla's unasked question but she had to be sure. 'You and Tanner didn't have anything to do with me scoring a chance at auditioning for the lead, did you?'

Confused, Abby shook her head. 'I had no idea and I doubt Tanner would, either. He gives his staff free rein while he manages the financial side of things.'

'Thought so.' Makayla slumped further on the stool. She should be happy she'd scored an audition of that calibre on her own. Instead, all she could think about was how she would've landed the role if anyone else had been casting.

'I don't know Hudson well but he seems like a nice guy.'

'He's a prick.'

Not entirely true, and she felt guilty immediately for saying it. Hudson was one of the good guys. At least, he had been until he'd gone berserk, lecturing her and admonishing her when he hadn't had a clue about her motivation for taking off her clothes.

She'd been stunned by the ferocity of his anger. He hadn't given her a chance to explain. He hadn't done much of anything that night he'd watched her strip but lose it backstage, ranting like a madman.

She'd been mortified enough at taking off her clothes in front of a roomful of slobbering idiots, but she'd got through it by blocking out the club and everyone in it, and focussing on her mum.

Then Hudson had to dump another shit storm over her at a time she needed his support the most. She'd never forgiven him and had told him so.

Abby wiped her hands and came to sit beside Makayla. 'What happened?'

'Nothing.' She closed her eyes, took a deep breath and opened them. 'Okay, that's not entirely true. Hudson and I were good friends once. Then we weren't any more. And I rocked up today, he was the guy I auditioned for, so it makes sense that's the end of that.'

Abby raised an eyebrow. 'I don't know what happened between you but do you think he's that petty?'

'Who knows?' She snagged her hair and pulled it back into a ponytail. It did little to cool her down. She'd been hot and bothered since she'd strutted out onto that stage at Embue and locked eyes with the devil. 'We didn't exactly part on amicable terms.' She held up her hand. 'And before you ask, shit happens. That's all I'm going to say.'

'Okay.' Abby shot her a sideways glance. 'So what you're saying is you think Hudson won't judge you on your dance ability? That he'll let what happened in your past affect his judgement?' Abby shook her head. 'Doesn't strike me as professional.'

Before Makayla could respond, her cell rang. When she slipped it out of her pocket and glanced at the screen, she didn't know the number.

'I'm waiting on another audition so I need to get this,' she said as Abby nodded, and she hit the answer button. 'Makayla Tarrant speaking.'

'Hey, Mak, it's me.'

Crap. She knew that 'me'.

And he was the last person she'd expected to hear from.

She managed a curt 'hi' before he continued.

'I wanted to let you know that your audition impressed and I'd like you to come in so we can talk.'

She should thank him. Sound enthusiastic. But in that moment, with shock making her gape, all she could think was, *I have the opportunity to score a great job working with a not-so-great guy.*

'Mak?'

She cleared her throat. 'Sure, I'll come in, thanks. When do you want me?'

Damn, that didn't sound good. But he seemed to think so, as he chuckled. 'Can you meet me back at the Embue studio around seven tonight?'

'Fine,' she said, still surprised by his offer but managing to sound as if she weren't. 'See you then.'

She hit the call end button before he could say anything else to further discombobulate her and stared at the phone as if she couldn't quite believe it.

'Good news?' Abby tapped her on the arm, and Makayla nodded.

'I got a call-back from Hudson.'

'That's great, sweetie.' Abby leaned over and hugged her. 'See? Told you he was a good guy.'

'Yeah…' She sounded less than convinced.

Something in Hudson's tone bugged her. A touch of condescension? Like he was doing her some giant favour. Probably all in her overactive imagination but for a moment she considered calling him back and citing a prior engagement.

Foolishness, considering how badly she needed this job and how it could lead to something much bigger. But she didn't need anyone's pity and she'd be damned if she backed out of this before she'd given it a real shot.

'At the risk of getting my head bitten off, I'm going to offer some advice.' Abby eyeballed her with surprising seriousness. 'Your heart is in dance, not working part-time at a patisserie to pay bills. So whatever happened between you two, forget about it and concentrate on making the most of this opportunity, okay?'

Makayla grunted in acknowledgement. 'Who made you so wise?'

Abby grinned and tapped her temple. 'Considering the mess I made of my own life until recently, guess I learned a thing or two about putting the past behind me.'

'Thanks, Abs.' She leaned over and hugged her friend. 'I've wanted a dance role like this for a long time. So I'll nail this call-back if it kills me.'

The part where she had to meet a guy who'd once been her best friend after hours at a hip club? Not a problem at all.

Not really.

CHAPTER FOUR

HUDSON DIDN'T MAKE it back to the Cross much these days. Not that he shunned his past so much as he'd moved on. But Bluey McNeil had called and when the man who'd given him his first job telephoned, Hudson made an effort.

Bluey hadn't sounded good. In fact, he'd coughed three times during their brief conversation. Hacking coughs that invoked an image of Bluey's packet-a-day habit and how haggard he'd looked the last time Hudson saw him about three months ago.

Foreboding lengthened Hudson's strides as he rounded the iconic El Alamein Fountain, skirted the bar he'd found his father passed out in too many times to count, and into the tiny jazz club aptly named Bluey's after its owner.

While the sun blazed outside, inside the club channelled the darkest midnight, with blackout drapes ensuring the wall sconces glowed and the faux candles created an atmosphere of intimacy. A few patrons dotted tables around the small stage, where a solo saxophonist did his thing. No older than twenty, the kid wasn't bad. And obviously another of Bluey's charity cases, as he'd once been.

'Hey, Squirt, thanks for coming.' A hand clapped him on the back, and Hudson grinned. He'd been a late bloomer, so Bluey had always called him Squirt and the nickname had stuck, even after he shot past six foot at seventeen.

However, when he turned around and caught sight of his friend, Hudson's grin faded. Bluey looked terrible. A walking skeleton. Parchment-thin skin stretched across cheekbones. Furrows bracketing his mouth. And a pallor that indicated just how ill his friend was.

'Any time, you old reprobate.' Hudson enveloped Bluey in a man hug, not surprised that his arms met at the back when they once couldn't. Bluey had lost a shitload of weight and his earlier foreboding blossomed into full-blown panic.

They disengaged, and Bluey gestured at the bar. 'Let's have a seat. What can I get you?'

'The usual,' Hudson said, knowing it got a rise out of his old friend every time.

Bluey's nose wrinkled. 'Orange juice with a spritz of soda is a girl's drink.'

'So you've told me a million times before.' Hudson leaned his forearms on the bar, taking comfort in watching Bluey fill a glass with orange juice and adding a shot of vodka rather than soda, something he'd seen countless times before. 'What's up, old man? Woman troubles?'

Bluey grunted and slid the glass along the bar towards him. 'You've got a big mouth for a whipper-snapper. You know my heart belonged to Julia and no woman has come close since.'

'Who's talking about your heart?' Hudson raised his glass in a silent toast, wondering if Mak's mum ever knew about Bluey's crush on her.

This place wasn't just special because of his first boss. Bluey's was the place he'd met Mak, doing homework on a makeshift bench set up in a nook off the main hallway leading to the kitchen, while her mum worked tables. She'd been a beaming fifteen-year-old high on life; he'd been a jaded twenty desperate to get out of the Cross. But there'd been something about her, something refreshing, and once they'd started chatting their friendship had been born.

Back then he'd watched Bluey make puppy dog eyes at Julia, who'd taken it in her stride, as pleasant to Bluey as she'd been to his customers. Everyone had loved Julia and he could've been well on his way to feeling the same for her daughter if he hadn't screwed up so monumentally.

'Listen, Squirt, I've got something to tell you.' Bluey braced himself on the counter behind the bar and Hudson knew the news was bad from the way his eyes darted away. 'I'm heading to the big jazz bar in the sky. Lung cancer. Terminal. Few months left, tops.'

Hudson's stomach fell away, and he downed the orange and vodka in two gulps as Bluey continued. 'I wanted you to hear it from me, not by a second-hand phone call after one of the geezers here rang to invite you to my funeral.'

Hudson wanted to say something, anything, to make this better. He remained silent, anger and regret roiling in his gut alongside the vodka.

'And before you go getting all sentimental on me, stop.' Bluey thumped his fist against the bar. 'I've been around for sixty-one years and been lucky enough to run this place for most of it. So don't feel sorry for me. I've had a good inning. And enjoyed sucking back on each and every one of those bloody cancer sticks that gave me this bugger of an illness.' He thumped his chest. 'So now you know. What's happening with you?'

The ache of impending loss blossomed in Hudson's chest. He'd experienced the same feeling before, the night he'd strode into Le Chat and seen Mak stripping on stage. In that moment he'd laid eyes on her, wearing a thong and little else, he'd known they were over.

And when she'd removed that thong…there'd been no coming back from that, and he grieved the loss of their friendship almost as much as he'd grieved the mother he'd never known.

This time he waited until the ache eased. Took his time formulating a response. If he'd done the same thing with Mak back then, maybe they would've had a chance.

When the lump in his throat finally subsided, Hudson said, 'Thanks for telling me but damn, it's fucked up.'

'Yeah, Squirt, it is, but what's a man to do?' Bluey shrugged and blinked rapidly. 'Tell me something to take my mind off it.'

'Mak auditioned for me today.' The words tripped out in haste and he instantly regretted them because if he'd cottoned on to Bluey's crush on Julia the old guy definitely noticed his on Mak and had teased him endlessly about it.

'How's she doing?'

'Good.' Hudson ignored the knowing glint in Bluey's astute gaze. 'She's got talent. I'm casting her as the lead dancer in the revue I'm producing at Embue.'

'Well, well, well.' Bluey folded his arms, his grin smug. 'This should be interesting.'

'We'll be working together in a professional capacity,' he said, sounding like a pompous ass and hoping he could keep it that way.

He needed to delineate clear boundaries from the start: he would be Mak's boss, she'd need to follow his orders. He couldn't afford to blur lines. Not when he had no frigging idea how he'd go seeing her dance for him every single day. Just because he'd coped at her audition didn't mean he had a grip on his memories.

Seeing her dance for those few minutes already had him thinking about her way too much and imagining how their future interactions would go, professional or otherwise.

Bluey sniggered. 'I have no idea why you two fell out and I haven't seen that darling girl in years but you tell her I said hi. And if you've got half a brain in that big head of yours, you'll treat her right this time.'

'What do you mean, this time?'

Bluey rolled his eyes. 'Because, numbskull, it's always the man's fault, and if you haven't figured that out by now, you're thicker than I thought.'

Hudson managed a wry grin. 'I'm going to miss you.'

'Right back at you, kid.' Bluey's eyes glistened before he turned away to cough, the harsh sound raising the hairs on the back of Hudson's neck.

Life wasn't fair. He'd figured that out pretty damn early when his mum did a runner and he was left in the custody of a mean drunk. But losing Bluey would hit hard and he knew it.

When Bluey's cough petered out, he turned back around. 'Now get the hell out so I can do some work.'

'Propping up the bar, you mean?' Hudson stood, moved around the bar, and enveloped him in another hug. 'You call me, okay? Any time, day or night, if you need anything.'

'Thanks, kid.' Bluey shoved him away with half-hearted force. 'You always were a soft touch.'

Not always. Hudson had taken a hard stand with Mak and look how that had turned out.

'I'll pop in next week,' he said, and Bluey saluted in response, his mouth downturned and worry clouding his eyes.

Bluey had said he had months to live but with a death sentence hanging over him, Hudson understood the old guy would be living each day as his last.

The injustice of it all swamped him anew and he headed for the door, desperate for air before he bawled. He stumbled outside, and it took a while until his eyes adjusted to the sudden glare and he made for the nearby fountain, slumping onto a bench next to it.

Tourists streamed by, snapping pics with their phones or giggling excitedly about being in Australia's most notorious suburb.

To him, Kings Cross would always be home in a way no one could understand unless they'd lived here. Unless they'd braved the back streets. Unless they'd used every ounce of savviness to survive.

Mak understood. And catching up with Bluey had clarified his situation with her in a way he could never have anticipated.

Life was too short to hold on to the past. Ironic, he'd strived so hard to become successful and put the past behind him yet here he was, back where it all started, feeling as lost and lonely as he had back then.

He'd come a long way. Mak probably had, too. He had no right to judge her. Not any more.

When she came in tonight, he'd keep an open mind. Be friendly. Try to forget the past and focus on the future.

They both deserved that.

CHAPTER FIVE

MAK STRODE INTO Embue as if she owned the place, confident that she'd achieved the impression she'd aimed for and then some.

Smoky eyes. Siren-red lips. Sleek blow-dried hair. Killer heels. And a strapless, knee-length, figure-hugging emerald sheath that had got her more second dates than she could count.

Earlier today, auditioning for Hudson had rattled her. Tonight, she wanted to assert her dominance and show him who was boss.

A tad overdramatic, maybe, and in reality she'd have to be deferential and respectful because she really needed this job. But dressing like this ensured she felt good and the way her insides quivered with nerves she needed all the help she could get.

Her mum had taught her many life lessons, and dress to impress had been one of them. It didn't matter whether she was doing a yoga class early on a Saturday morning or picking up groceries on her way home, she always wore lipstick and mascara.

She felt naked without them. And while her budget might be verging on dire, she managed to find outfits at second-hand shops that garnered compliments.

As she caught sight of herself in one of the many mirrors lining the club, she squared her shoulders and stood tall. She could do this. Meet with Hudson. Convince him to hire her. Dance her ass off for however long this show ran. Definitely doable.

Until she caught sight of him striding towards her, and her tummy went into free fall, her confidence following suit.

This was Hudson.

The guy she'd secretly crushed on for years.

The guy she'd idolised.

The guy who'd been the best friend a girl could wish for.

The guy who'd seen her stark naked, at her most vulnerable, and turned his back on her.

Crap.

'Hey, Mak, glad you could make it.' He held out his hand, like it was the most natural thing in the world they shake in greeting, when it had once been customary for them to exchange a kiss on the cheek. 'Let's head into the studio to talk.'

Mak managed a mute nod, surreptitiously swiping her palm against the side of her dress when he released it. Yeah, like that would stop the tingles creeping up her arm.

It had been years since she'd seen him, so why

the same irrational reaction, as if her body recognised on some visceral level what her brain refused to acknowledge?

She should hate him for how he'd treated her, how he'd dismissed their friendship without a second thought. But she couldn't afford to let her residual bitterness towards him flare now. This job had to come first.

'How was your day?' He cast her a sidelong glance, as if he couldn't gauge her mood. Join the club. She didn't have a clue how to act around him now that her faux confidence had dwindled on sight.

'Same old,' she said with a shrug. 'I work part-time at a patisserie. Le Miel. You may have heard of it?'

Of course he had, considering his boss Tanner had worked there temporarily while his brother Remy had been laid up in hospital following a fall. And Abby knew him, which meant he'd know she worked there, too. But she wanted to see how honest he'd be, how their new working relationship would pan out from the start.

He was staring at her as if he knew she'd been trying to trip him up somehow. 'Tanner's my best bud, so yeah, I know it. And I've met Abby, she's lovely.'

Relieved he'd been honest, she nodded. 'They're both good people.'

He cast her a quizzical look. 'Are you okay?'

No, she wasn't. She couldn't do this. Couldn't pre-

tend they didn't have a past. Like the argument that
had ruined their friendship never happened. Like
she wasn't still hurting that he'd thought so little
of her; that he hadn't known her as well as she'd
thought he did.

'Honestly? I'm having a hard time accepting you
as my potential boss considering we share a past.'

He didn't react. In fact, she couldn't see a flicker
of acknowledgement on his stoic face bar a slight
clenching of his jaw. How did he do that? Hold his
emotions so closely in check when she was having a
hard time not blurting every single thing she wanted
to say to him?

'Let's talk in here.' He pushed the double doors to
the studio open and waited until she'd passed through
before closing them.

Makayla should've relaxed stepping into the studio with its familiar set-up of stage, mirrors, steel
rails lining the walls and spotlights. The space was
new, or rarely used, because it didn't have the familiar smell of stale sweat and greasepaint. Maybe that
explained her nerves.

A crock and she knew it. Her nerves had everything to do with the man staring at her with trepida-
tion, as if he knew she was about to unleash years'
worth of home truths.

Before she could speak, he held up his hand, an-
noyingly imperious. 'I know we need to talk about
what happened back then. But before we do, I want

you to know you've got the job of lead dancer. Your audition blew me away and I'm not saying that out of some warped case of guilt because of how things ended between us, I'm saying it because you're incredibly talented and I need this show to succeed, so I want you in it.'

He blew out a long breath after his ramble and in that moment she realised he was nervous, too. Hudson didn't do long-winded speeches. Less was more for him when it came to words. So the fact he'd blurted all that indicated he was just as nervous as she was.

'Thanks, I'm thrilled to get the job.' She sounded formal, stilted, and cleared her throat, wondering how long she'd have the job for once she said what needed to be said. 'But the last time we saw each other you basically called me a whore and it's difficult getting past that.'

He flinched as if she'd struck him. 'I didn't—'

'You didn't use the word but it was pretty damn clear from everything else you said what you thought of me.'

That night was imprinted on her brain. The night she'd been so desperate to give her mum the funeral she deserved that she'd shelved her principles and done whatever it took to get the money she needed.

Hudson hadn't given her a chance to explain. He'd taken one look at her stripping on stage and flipped out. She'd expected better from her best friend. She'd expected so much more than what she'd got.

While time should've eased her resentment it hadn't, and seeing him again seemed to bring it all back in a mortifying rush.

She remembered every single moment of that humiliating night in excruciating detail. Pretending not to care when the club owner leered at her, demanding she strip down to bra and panties so he could see the goods before he gave her the gig. Throwing up before she went on stage. The stench of cheap aftershave and beer when she'd been taking her clothes off.

And in the midst of her degradation, she'd spotted Hudson, staring at her as if she were the worst person in the world.

His opinion mattered to her. *He* mattered to her and having him witness her shameful, demeaning show had crushed her. She'd been desperate to explain. He hadn't let her. His appalling lecture had rung in her ears long after he'd stormed out.

Now she had to dredge all that up so they could move forward as professionals. Ugh.

'I'm sorry.' He leaned against the nearest wall, looking like a cool, impervious model, not a guy hell-bent on repentance. 'That was the night I landed the job at Embue and I came looking for you to share my good news. Bluey told me he'd seen you entering Le Chat so I headed there.' He shook his head, remorse twisting his mouth. It was an improvement on the loathing she'd seen all those years ago. 'I freaked out. Said some things I shouldn't have—'

'You were my best friend! You should've trusted me.' She swallowed down the lump of emotion lodged in her throat, making her voice embarrassingly squeaky. 'I didn't owe you any explanations then and I sure as hell don't owe you any now, but that was the worst night of my life and having you witness my mortification, then berate me for it, sucked big time. Then you turned your back on me...'

Damn, if she didn't wind this up soon she'd end up crying and that wasn't the professional impression she wanted to present.

'Maybe it was for the best, us moving on with our lives separately, leaving the Cross behind, but there isn't a day that goes by that I don't miss the friendship we once had.' There, she'd said it, though she ended on an embarrassing half hiccup that had her wishing the ground would open up.

Hudson didn't say a word. He just stared at her, sadness down-turning his mouth, before he crossed the short space between them and enveloped her in a hug that squeezed the air from her lungs.

She resisted for a moment, not wanting the physical contact, not wanting anything from him bar this job. But this was Hudson, the guy she'd depended on almost as much as her mum, and if her brain resisted her body had other ideas. His arms were strong around her, crushing her like a steel band, his warmth staving off the chill that had invaded her bones around the time they'd started this conversation.

Breathless, she finally relaxed into him, and as if sensing her capitulation, he hugged her tighter if that were possible. It should've ended there. An apologetic embrace between two old friends who'd been torn apart in the past but now had to work together.

Instead, she felt the shift between them, the exact moment the hug became something else. His woodsy aftershave, something expensive, probably designer, made her nose tingle. His warmth turned to heat where it pressed against her. His hand splayed in her lower back, grazed the top of her ass. Something semi-hard nudged her hip.

He pulled away but didn't release her, as she tilted her head up. 'I'm not proud of the way I treated you that night and I've regretted losing our friendship over it. But I care about you, Mak, I always have, so if you'd let me I'd like to be friends again.'

He sounded sincere and his eyes blazed with untold emotion, but she couldn't forget how badly he'd once hurt her. If young Hudson had had the power to do that, the older, sexier version would be a lot more dangerous if she let him get close again.

'We can try,' she said, sounding flippant, but still caught up in the weird unspoken tension shimmering between them. 'I'm a professional and I intend on making the most of the opportunity you've given me.'

'I wasn't talking about work and you know it,' he said, his low voice rippling over her like a caress, making her all too aware she hadn't pulled out of his arms yet.

She should. She should establish a clear boundary between them from the outset, but when his burning gaze dropped to her mouth and her nipples hardened in response she knew it would take more than putting space between them to reinforce all they shared was a working relationship.

She'd always been like this around him, hyper-aware, like her body was somehow invisibly, intrinsically attuned to his. He hadn't known back then; she'd been too good at hiding it. It should've dissipated over the years, disappeared completely, but the longer he stared at her with blatant hunger, the harder she found it to remember why she had to maintain distance from him.

'We can try the friendship thing,' she said, finally willing her legs to move and breaking free of his embrace by backing away a few steps. 'But I'll give you a heads-up. I'm not the same naive girl I once was.'

'And I'm not the same narrow-minded jerk I once was.' His lopsided grin catapulted her back in time to the many times that same smile had made her young, impressionable heart beat faster. 'Now we've established we've both grown up, shall we talk business?'

'Absolutely.' Her emphatic nod sent her hair tumbling over her shoulders and she pushed it back, a simple, innocuous action with complicated results when Hudson's gaze locked on her hair as if he wanted to bury his face in it.

Hell. She could do friendship in a pinch but anything more between them would be disastrous. He might not know it but he'd given her a big break professionally in hiring her for this lead dancer role. She couldn't screw it up. She wouldn't. No matter how much intrigue spurred her on to see exactly how hot Hudson was beneath that cool facade.

'Tell me about the show,' she said, sounding fake and upbeat and perky, while she couldn't ignore the way heat flared inside at the way he stared at her like he'd been given the keys to his favourite ice-cream store.

He eyeballed her and in that moment she saw he faced the same inner battle she did. Lust versus logic. Curiosity warring with common sense. Desire battling deprivation.

Crap. She might have just landed a dream job but she had a feeling she'd landed neck-deep in a load of trouble, too.

'Tell me about you first.' He gestured at a bar stool, indicating she sit. She didn't want to. She wanted to stand so she could make a run for it if she needed to.

Because being in Hudson's arms had resurrected

a whole host of feelings she'd long suppressed. She should hate him for how he'd treated her and their friendship. Instead, she'd accepted his apology, even though he hadn't explained why he'd behaved so appallingly towards her, and agreed to try the friendship thing now.

Was she insane?

'Not much to tell.' She perched on the edge of the stool, ready to flee at the slightest sign of awkwardness. 'I attended uni for a while, doing a bachelor of applied dance in the hope I could teach as well as perform. But I hated the rigidity of classes so lasted less than six months.'

His eyebrows rose, as if he couldn't believe she'd even consider a career in teaching. 'I can't imagine you being an instructor.'

She instantly bristled. 'Why not?'

'Because you've always had talent and haven't you heard the old cliché, those who can do, those who can't teach?'

Assuaged by his compliment, she continued. 'Guess I'm a cliché then, because once I focussed on dancing, I never looked back.'

'The agency sent across the CVs of all applicants auditioning.' He hesitated. 'You've had tons of experience but no starring roles?'

Damn him for homing in on her weakness.

'What's with the twenty questions?' She sounded snappish and didn't care.

He was her boss, she was his employee, that was where it ended. She didn't need him treating her like a friend catching up for old times' sake. It blurred lines and she preferred perfectly delineated boundaries. She couldn't deal with anything else, not now, when seeing him again had resurrected so many feelings, many of them bad.

'Because I want to know what makes you tick these days.' He reached out and touched her above her heart. 'In here.'

It had been nothing more than a fleeting brush of his fingertips against her skin; a barely there touch that shouldn't have mattered. But it did, because heat flooded her body, most of it ending up in her cheeks.

'I said I'd try the friendship thing. Don't push it,' she said, easing him away with her index finger.

He laughed, the same rich, deep sound she remembered and damned if she didn't prickle with awareness. Everywhere.

'Friends ask about each other's interests. They chat. They tease—'

'No teasing.'

It was one of the things she'd loved most about him back then, his ability to make her laugh.

'You used to love it when I taunted you.' He leaned forward as if to prove it, invading her personal space, his mouth mere inches from her ear. 'Just because we haven't seen each other in years doesn't mean I've forgotten anything.'

Damn.

Did he know how she'd felt back then? Was that why he was torturing her now?

Though it was more than two friends getting re-acquainted and she knew it. There was a sexual tension between them, simmering beneath the surface, deliberately ignored but there all the same.

Not good.

'Then you'll remember how much I hated you bugging me when I was doing homework and not much has changed.' She elbowed him away, and he clutched at his side in mock outrage. 'I'm your employee. I need to focus, not be distracted by...by... you,' she finished lamely, not wanting to articulate exactly how badly the ever-present attraction between them was making her lose focus and her cool.

'You find me distracting?' His low voice made it sound like she'd found him naked.

'I find you painful.'

Her dry response made him laugh again. 'Tell me you don't feel more comfortable now than when you first came in?'

So that was what he'd been doing. Trying to put her at ease. She should've been relieved. Instead, a familiar mortification in his presence swamped her; had she imagined the attraction between them?

His boner during their hug could've meant nothing, a simple physiological reaction guys got when in close proximity with a woman. And his banter could've been exactly as he'd said, a way to put her at ease.

To her chagrin, he squeezed her hand, like a friend would do.

'Look, Mak, we have to work together. I think it's great we've confronted the past and reached a point where we can talk like this. It'll make the next few weeks a hell of a lot easier.'

He was right, of course. While they couldn't resume their old friendship, they had to be civil.

But he hadn't released her hand, and as she stared at it, his strong tanned fingers wrapped around hers, she couldn't help but think that for a guy who professed friendship, he'd been teetering on the brink of overstepping the mark.

As if to reinforce it, his thumb brushed across the back of her hand in a slow, languorous sweep that made her tingle and bite back a moan.

Hell.

She could do friendship with Hudson.

Anything else could only end in disaster.

CHAPTER SIX

HUDSON COULDN'T HAVE been more relieved to see the entire dance cast troop into the studio five minutes later, after he'd given Mak a brief rundown of her duties in the show.

The longest frigging five minutes of his life.

He'd always been attracted to her but now…fuck, he got hard again just thinking about that moment when she'd been in his arms, her lithe body pressed against him, her familiar exotic fragrance befuddling his senses.

She'd worn that perfume for as long as he could remember. One of the dancers in the club her mum had worked at had brought it back from Hong Kong for her and damned if he wanted to know how she still managed to get her hands on more.

Had she travelled? Worked overseas? Had a boyfriend obtained more from there? So many questions he had no answers to and it irked that he knew so little about her when he'd once known everything.

Or so he'd thought.

He was glad they'd cleared the air. As much as could be expected, that was. He hadn't told her why he'd freaked out that night he'd caught her stripping and she hadn't told him why it had been the most mortifying night of her life.

He'd wanted to ask. Hell, he wanted to know what drove her to it when she'd been ingenuous and sheltered despite growing up in the sin capital of Australia.

But prying wouldn't have served any good, not when they had to work together. He'd tried to put her at ease, to ask innocuous questions, but she'd been defensive and wary. He didn't blame her, considering how their friendship had ended. But he wanted some semblance of their old camaraderie now so they could at least work together and not have to deal with old wounds.

He'd invited her over earlier than the other cast members to smooth things over between them. He'd succeeded to a point but having Mak look at him with anything other than loathing only served to remind him how much he wanted her and, unfortunately, his dick had no problem keeping up with the programme.

He'd touched her, several times. More to prove to himself that his reaction to having her in his arms had been an aberration, his body's way of telling him to get laid sooner rather than later.

It hadn't been, because even with a simple handhold, he'd felt *it*, that insistent tug of attraction that grabbed him by the balls and wouldn't let go.

A major problem, considering Mak was his lead dancer and he was her boss, not to mention they both carried enough baggage to fill an airport carousel.

'See you at rehearsals Monday, boss.' The lead male, a short guy named Shane, clapped him on the back with an overfamiliarity that set his teeth on edge.

But Hudson forced a smile and nodded. 'Have a good weekend.'

The rest of the eight-person crew filtered out. Everyone except Mak, who had vanished. Surely she wouldn't have snuck out without saying goodbye?

The thought saddened him and just as he'd poured his first bourbon from the makeshift bar in the corner, she slipped back into the room, her eyes widening in surprise as she noted it had emptied.

'Where is everyone?'

'Gone home to start their weekends early.'

She glanced at her watch. 'It's eight-thirty.'

'Early by clubbing standards.'

'I know that.' She rolled her eyes as she padded towards him, having discarded her stilettos ages ago. 'I'll have you know I'm the dance queen of Sydney.'

He liked her haughty playfulness, remembered her often throwing out challenges to best him. 'There's a difference between dancing for a living and burning up the floor for fun.'

'I'm the best at both.' Her chin tilted as she stared him down. 'Single in Sydney means let the good times roll.'

Grinning, he said, 'We're still talking about dancing, yeah?'

She snickered, a cute sound that catapulted him back in time. 'You're such a guy.'

'Glad you noticed.' He flexed his biceps, garnering a dry chuckle. 'Because I'm single in Sydney and I can guarantee that whenever I get anywhere near a dance floor my right foot morphs into my left, so I have two of them.'

She muttered something that sounded like 'bullshit' under her breath, before flashing him a teasing smile he hadn't seen in forever. 'As I recall, whenever you were working the Kings Cross clubs you'd manage to squeeze in a boogie and trust me, your moves were far from a guy with two left feet.'

'You kept an eye on me? I'm touched.' He clutched his chest, thrilled that they'd reverted to swapping banter as they used to. It was what he'd been aiming for earlier but she hadn't responded, too guarded as she'd tried to get a read on him.

Now that she'd loosened up, he hoped they could continue in the same vein. It had been so natural back then, teasing each other like this, sharing laughs. He'd missed this light-hearted fun the most.

'You know all the girls had a crush on you back then.'

'Even you?' He leaned on the bar, trying to appear casual when he wanted her answer to be affirmative too much.

'I had more sense,' she said with a nonchalant shrug, but not before he glimpsed the cheeky spark in her eyes.

Yeah, the old Mak was back and he couldn't be happier. 'Would you like a drink?'

She hesitated, her gaze drifting to the door a second before she surprised him and nodded. 'Vodka and lemon, please.'

'Coming right up.' He didn't need to measure out the quantities. He'd helped out behind bars since he could practically walk and he found the familiar action soothing. Or maybe that had more to do with Mak watching his every move.

He should've found her scrutiny off-putting. He didn't. Instead, her presence had a calming effect, the way it always had.

Back then she'd steadied him in a topsy-turvy world he'd rallied against with every fibre of his being. He'd done whatever it took to survive, saving every cent he'd earned from odd jobs to formulate a plan to escape the life that had threatened to drag him down.

These days, he spent way too much money on caring for the man who'd done his best to make his life hell, but the way he saw it, paying for his father's care facility kept the old bastard away from him. When he saw him, it was on his terms. Just the way he liked it.

'What's wrong?' She perched on a bar stool and rested her chin in her hands, studying him. 'You look sad. Are my lame jokes at your expense that bad?'

He shook his head, impressed she could still read him so well. 'Just thinking about Dad.'

Wariness clouded her eyes. Like most people who lived at the Cross back then, she'd known Wiley Watt was a deadhead drunk and a mean prick. 'How is he?'

'Dementia claimed him a few years ago. Drifts in and out. He's in a private facility.'

Before she could say anything else he changed the subject, not wanting to taint their reawakening friendship by discussing the one subject he'd rather avoid at all costs. 'I saw Bluey today.'

Her eyes lit up and for a ridiculous second jealousy stabbed him as he wished she'd look at him like that. 'Haven't seen him in years. How is he?'

Damn, when he'd wanted to change the subject, he'd grabbed at the first thought that popped into his head. Not the smartest move, considering that brightness in her eyes would fade the moment he divulged the truth.

'He has lung cancer. Terminal. Few months tops.' He slid her drink towards her, and when she slumped he felt like he'd revealed there was no Santa. 'But he's happy. Brash as ever. Wanted me to hear it from him and not get a call for his funeral.'

'That's Bluey,' she said, blinking rapidly, as he quelled his first instinct to bundle her in his arms. 'He was so cute, the way he mooned over Mum.'

'Did she know?'

'Of course.' A soft smile of remembrance played about her mouth. 'But Mum was too smart to mix business with pleasure.'

She eyeballed him as she said it, a clear warning he should heed. But damned if keeping his hands off her wouldn't be the hardest thing he'd done in a long time.

'Smart woman, your mum,' he said, taking a slug of his bourbon. 'You must miss her.'

'Every single day.' She downed two thirds of her vodka in one gulp. 'That's what I hated most after you weren't around any more because I'd just lost Mum. And not having my best friend there to bounce ideas and feelings off, the kind of friend who moved in the same circles, the friend who knew me almost better than I knew myself…'

She trailed off and for a horrifying moment he thought she might burst into tears.

Before he could say anything remotely comforting, she tossed back another gulp of vodka. 'Don't mind me. It's the alcohol loosening my tongue and making me maudlin.'

'I missed us too,' he blurted, wishing he hadn't

said anything when she stared at him in hope as she used to.

Back then he'd known he couldn't be Mak's hero, no matter how much he wanted to. He wasn't built that way. He'd learned from a young age to take care of number one and that was him.

He hadn't fostered anything beyond friendship between them because of it, even after Mak had turned eighteen. It would've been so easy to slip into a relationship with her, especially considering how much he'd wanted her.

But he'd known he wasn't the kind of guy Mak deserved, not the kind of guy she wanted. Not really. Mak craved stability and he could never give that to her. Not after what he'd been through. Pushing her away that night he'd seen her strip had almost been a relief in some ways.

Now she was back. Tugging at his heartstrings all over again. Making him want to slay a goddamn arena full of dragons in order to protect her from bad stuff.

Not good.

He was a different man now. He'd moved on from that guy who'd felt unworthy. But he still couldn't be her guy. He had too many demons, most of them linked to that night he'd seen her strip, a night he might never get past no matter how close they became.

'Here's to us,' she said, raising her almost empty glass. 'To friendship.'

Friendship he could do. Contemplating anything else would be beyond madness.

'To friendship.' He clinked his glass against hers but when he took a slug of bourbon it burned all the way down his throat, testament to the lie he'd just uttered.

He didn't just want friendship with Mak. He wanted *her*. He always had.

In his arms. In his bed. Wrapped around him.

It was going to be one hell of a tough time ahead.

CHAPTER SEVEN

MAKAYLA DIDN'T BELIEVE in magic. Not since she'd watched a show backstage as a ten-year-old and discovered the magician was merely good at fooling people into believing what they wanted to believe.

But someone had sure sprinkled a handful of fairy dust over her today because she'd never danced so well. Rehearsal had started at five p.m. Monday and she'd been at it for two hours. Feet flying, legs kicking, arms spinning. Nailing every single move. The dancers around her were good—it looked as if Hudson only hired the best—but today, she was better.

She didn't get it. Usually when she landed a new role it took her a day or two to pick up the rhythms, to trial the steps, until it clicked. Today, from the moment she'd stepped onto the studio stage at Embue and the choreographer had outlined the major moves, she'd been on fire.

Now, with sweat pouring off her and her damp leotard clinging to her skin, she slumped onto the nearest bench and reached for her drink bottle. Maybe it was something in the water. Or maybe it was dancing for the man heading towards her, admiration making his eyes glow indigo.

'Wow, that was impressive.' Hudson sat beside her, his thigh almost brushing hers, and she forced herself to relax. 'You're good.'

'Tell me something I don't know,' she said, raising her water bottle to him in a mock toast before downing half of it.

He chuckled. 'What do you think of the show?'

She was paid to dance, not give an opinion, but she liked the fact he'd asked. 'It's great. High energy, good tempos, catchy songs.'

'I've been working part-time in local theatre, behind the scenes mostly, for a while. It's something of a hobby.' Concern pinched his mouth, at odds with his usual confidence. Even as a guy in his early twenties doing whatever it took to survive he'd had a cockiness about him, a self-assurance that she'd wished she could emulate. 'Tanner's never done anything like this at Embue before. He took a chance on my idea. I need it to rock.'

'It will,' she said, instinctively patting his thigh in reassurance before belatedly realising she'd made a dumb move.

Being attracted to her boss was one thing. Touching him entered a whole other stratosphere of stupidity.

His muscle flexed beneath her palm and she

snatched it away before insanity prevailed and she slid her hand higher.

'With your talent, why haven't you had any long-term roles?'

She appreciated his switch back to business-like. That impulsive gaff with her hand had been beyond embarrassing. 'Not for lack of trying.'

She picked up a towel, draped it across the back of her neck and dabbed at her face with it. 'I bust my butt attending auditions. I get countless call-backs. But the big roles seem to elude me.'

'But you're phenomenal.' He sounded a tad awe-struck, confusion creasing his brow, and she smiled.

'Thanks.' She bumped him with her shoulder, wishing she could hug him for his rousing endorsement. 'I'm hoping being the primary dancer in this show will lead to bigger things.'

'Like?'

She hadn't articulated her dream out loud to many people for fear of being laughed at. But Hudson had connections. She'd done some online research after she'd landed the lead dancer role and discovered he did a lot of theatre stuff in addition to his management job here at the club that ensured he'd meet a lot of influential people. If he had contacts in the industry, he might be able to help.

But before she could say anything, he snapped his fingers. 'How could I forget? You always wanted to be on Broadway. Is that still your goal?'

Heat flushed her cheeks that he'd remembered something so trivial and she nodded. 'Sounds far-fetched, huh? But it's been my end goal since I started dancing as a kid. I want the bright lights. The big stage. In the most happening city in the world...'

She trailed off, lost in her musings as she usually was whenever she thought of New York City and how utterly fabulous it would be to visit, let alone live and perform there.

'From what I've seen today, you're good enough to get there and then some,' he said, staring at her in frank admiration. 'You've got the moves, kid, the kind that could take you all the way.'

She resisted the urge to preen under his praise; that and fling herself at him in gratitude. Usually, she didn't need other people inflating her ego; she was a realist and knew she had talent that could flourish given time, effort and the right environment. She'd been lucky enough to have two of the best dance teachers in the biz growing up and they'd never minced words. Giving praise when it was due. Kicking her in the butt when she needed it.

But having Hudson praise her meant something and she knew why. She'd always valued his opinion. Had sought it out, from his views on her latest lip-gloss colour to upcoming pop bands. Despite their five-year age difference, he'd never made her feel stupid or inept. He'd listened to her; truly listened, then offered sage advice. Yet another thing she'd missed when their friendship ended, not having a sounding board she trusted.

'Hey, did I say something wrong?' He touched her arm, a brief impersonal touch that sent a jolt all the way down to her toes.

'No, just thinking how much I appreciate having your input again.' She grabbed the end of her towel and swatted him with it. 'But careful, I might get a big head with all that flattery.'

'You're too grounded for that, always have been,' he said, batting away the towel. 'I think that's one of the things that drew me to you back then. Low tolerance for BS, you saw the world how it was yet it didn't get you down.' Something akin to darkness, a fleeting shadow, clouded his eyes. 'Growing up in the Cross was tough but you took it in your stride and didn't let it taint you.'

'Yeah, I did,' she said, remembering the one night when she'd succumbed to the seedier side of Kings Cross and why.

She could've let the memory of that degrading night drag her down but she hadn't. She'd taken the money and walked away without looking back.

She could've taken the easy option and done more strip shows. That one night, she'd earned more than dancing two months' worth of gigs. The owner had offered her a sizeable pay, enough to set her up. But she'd knocked it back for the reason Hudson had articulated: she hadn't wanted to be tainted by the kind of life she didn't want.

She'd never regretted it but she couldn't help but wonder at times how much easier her life could've been if she'd had that kind of money as a nineteen-year-old.

Hudson stared at her, a host of unasked questions hovering between them, before he blinked and glanced away. 'I don't do anyone favours unless they deserve them but if what I saw today is any indication of what you can do on stage, I'll keep my ear to the ground. Let you know if I hear of any big opportunities here in Sydney, maybe even overseas, okay?'

'Thanks, that would be great.' This time, she didn't hesitate in wrapping her arms around him in a grateful hug. It felt right, comfortable, and nothing like the tension-fraught comforting hug last week. 'Anyone ever tell you you're the best boss ever?'

'Only every single day,' he said, his smile bashful when she released him. 'Speaking of work, I better get back out there otherwise Tanner will fire my ass for slacking off on my management duties.'

'And I've got an appointment for a one-off show.' She glanced at her watch and leapt to her feet. 'Crap. I didn't know rehearsal ran overtime. I'm going to be late.'

She glanced at her drenched workout gear and grimaced. 'No time to head home for a shower. You don't have one around here that staff can use, by any chance?'

Hudson hesitated, a flash of something indefinable in his stare, before he huffed out a breath, as if he'd come to some momentous decision. 'I live in the apartment over the club. You're welcome to shower there if it makes things easier for you.'

A ripple of awareness made her skin prickle. She couldn't turn up for a dress fitting for another show sweaty and flustered; or worse, late. But taking advantage of Hudson's generous offer meant getting flustered in another way entirely.

Standing in his shower stall, imagining him in there, soapy and slick and naked...

'Uh, thanks, that would make life easier,' she said, clearing her throat when her voice sounded a tad high. 'I appreciate the offer.'

'No worries,' he said, waiting until she gathered her stuff before heading for the door.

Easy for him to say, she thought as she followed him. Because getting a glimpse into Hudson's home life, getting naked in his bathroom, getting ideas into her head that she shouldn't, had her very worried indeed.

CHAPTER EIGHT

GROWING UP AS a jack of all trades in Kings Cross, doing odd jobs for whoever would pay, had garnered Hudson a reputation for having sound business sense and good ideas.

Offering his shower to Mak hadn't been one of them.

What was it about this woman that brought out his latent knight-in-shining-armour complex in a big way?

It had been bad enough sitting through two hours of rehearsal. One hundred and twenty excruciating minutes of watching Mak gyrate and contort and flaunt her hot body encased in skin-tight cotton and Lycra.

Pure torture.

And this was only the first day. How the hell would he keep a grip on his lust and pretend having her back in his life as a friend was all he wanted?

His only saving grace was the tight turnaround on this project. Two weeks of rehearsals. Two weeks of nightly shows. Then Mak would move on to the next show, and he could breathe again. Because right now, with the thought of her naked behind his bathroom door, he couldn't. His lungs felt as if they'd been clogged with concrete. His cock, too.

'Idiot,' he muttered, kicking a heavy wooden leg of the coffee table. It didn't do much to relieve the frustration.

The bathroom door creaked open, and Hudson swore his heart stopped. If Mak came out here dressed in only a towel he'd have to make a run for it before he followed through on every single filthy fantasy running on repeat through his head.

'Uh, I hate to be a pain, but there's a problem with the flick mixer and I can't get the water temperature right.'

He risked a glance towards the bathroom and saw her poking her head around the barely opened door. Caught a glimpse of creamy bare shoulder. The hint of a towel lower.

Fuck. He'd forgotten to call the plumber this morning to fix the dodgy shower mixer. He'd had the same problem, unable to adjust the perfect temperature, and it had taken a lot of jiggling and fiddling to get it right earlier that day.

'Have you tried moving it around?'

She wrinkled her nose. 'I've tried everything. Do you think you could fix it for me? I really can't afford to be late to this costume fitting.'

'Sure,' he said, when he should've said 'hell no' and headed down to the club where the music would be so loud it could drown out his licentious thoughts. As if. 'But only if you're decent.'

He'd meant it as a joke but he caught the flare of awareness in her eyes as he broached the distance between them. It didn't help.

Neither did the sight of her wrapped in one of his navy towels. It ended mid-thigh, exposing her long dancer legs, toned and tanned. Stunning. He couldn't help it: he looked his fill before letting his gaze drift upward to where she clutched a loose knot over her chest.

That was when he saw the telltale poke of nipples through the cotton. It wasn't cold in here, which meant Mak was as turned on as he was.

His cock gave a throb, as if to remind him he had a beautiful, half-naked woman in his bathroom and what the hell was he going to do about it.

The smart answer would be nothing.

But he'd given up being smart around the time he'd been dumb enough to drive this woman away first time around.

He took a step towards her. 'Mak, I—'

'Fix the shower, Hudson, please.' She held up one of her hands, letting the towel slip a little. Revealing a swell of breast that left him salivating.

'I'll fix it for you on one condition.'

Her eyes widened imperceptibly, her irises expanding. 'What?'

'You let me watch you.'

The dare tumbled from his lips and he didn't regret it. If he was to have any chance of convincing her he wanted her beyond friendship, he needed to see if he could get past that night five years ago that changed everything. Seeing her stripping on stage had brought up a host of awful memories he'd rather forget and he'd reacted accordingly. This time, he had to get past his hang-ups before he told her how much he wanted her and to do that, he had to see her naked.

Testing himself might be the stupidest thing he'd ever done but better to know now before he fucked up their tentatively re-established friendship because his libido couldn't be quelled.

Her lips parted on a shocked O. It wouldn't surprise him if she slapped him. He half expected it. Braced for it. Tension made his muscles bunch beneath his shirt.

He needed a workout after this; should hit the gym tonight, no matter what the time. He had a feeling he'd have a lot of tension to work off.

'The last time you saw me naked, it didn't work out so well,' she said, aiming for flippant, but he caught the worried undertone to her comment. Like she was testing him.

This time, he wouldn't be so foolish as to fail.

'Don't do that, try to trivialise something I did

that screwed up our friendship,' he said, taking another step towards her. 'We've moved on from the past and this thing between us now? So frigging potent I can't see straight. You feel it too?'

He held his breath for an eternity, her indecision clear in the conflicted emotions flickering in her eyes, before her barely perceptible nod encouraged him to continue. 'I want you, Mak. No complications. No expectations. But I know you have to be somewhere so, for now, let me watch.'

It sounded so dirty when he said it out loud, but she hadn't turfed him out yet. In fact, the longer she stared at him with a mix of fascination and wariness, he got the impression she wasn't so averse to his suggestion.

'Fix the mixer, fast,' she finally said, so soft and breathy he wasn't sure he'd heard right.

'So that's a yes?'

'Just fix the thing,' she said, releasing her grip on the towel.

It slithered to the floor. Along with his jaw.

She was breathtakingly beautiful, the kind of exquisite that made his chest ache.

The first time he'd seen her naked he'd been angry and resentful and out of his mind with worry. He hadn't wanted that life for her. He'd seen what it had done to his mum and it killed him deep inside every time he thought of what she'd done to make ends meet. For him.

Since that fateful night he'd deliberately blotted out the memory of Mak naked, hadn't wanted to taint his image of her.

Now, with her standing in front of him, uncertain yet unabashed, he looked his fill. Imprinting every single detail on his memory. Her perky C cups. Pale pink nipples. Mole above her belly button. Trimmed golden-red bush.

Perfection.

She snapped her fingers, breaking him out of his trance. 'The shower, remember?'

He managed a rueful grin and pointed to his head. 'Sorry. My little brain was caught up admiring the splendour of your beauty while my big brain,' he said, pointing lower, 'is telling me to strip naked too.'

'Don't you dare. I don't have time.' She waggled her finger at him, which would've held more sway as an admonishment if her breasts hadn't jiggled with the action too. 'Shower. Now.'

How he managed to fix the damn shower mixer he'd never know, considering his hands were as fumbling and clumsy as his efforts to not stare at her. Damn near impossible.

After four botched attempts, he had the water at a reasonable temperature and stepped back, allowing her to enter the double stall.

'Room for two in there,' he pointed out, clenching his hands into fists to stop from reaching for her as she stepped past him, smelling of sweat and arousal.

'Maybe some other time.' And with a jaunty flick of her hip, she closed the door in his face.

But didn't turn her back on him. Instead, she pumped body wash into her hand from his dispenser and slowly, leisurely ran it down the front of her body from neck to navel.

Damned if it wasn't the most erotic thing he'd ever seen.

The shower stall started steaming up and no way in hell would he tolerate his view being obliterated, so he flicked the exhaust switch and perched on the edge of the bath tub to enjoy the show.

He couldn't believe his luck. When he'd thrown out his challenge he'd expected Mak to verbally flay him, calling him anything from pervert to sicko.

Never in his wildest dreams had he expected to be privy to this.

Eyes closed. Water sluicing down her body. Her hands rubbing her breasts, over and under in hypnotic circles, lathering up so that bubbles covered her. Drifting lower to her stomach. Lower yet…

His breath caught as her fingers skirted her mound, before momentarily delving between the folds.

Lust pounded through his body in time with his heart. Every muscle tensed in his desperation to hold back. Every ounce of common sense swamped by how badly he wanted to touch her. Fuck, he was in blue ball hell watching her. Wanting her. Craving her with every horny cell in his body.

When she let out a low moan, Hudson couldn't take it any longer. He sprang up from the bathtub, wrenched open the shower door and knelt.

Her eyes flew open. 'What are you doing?'

'This.' He leaned forward and grasped her ass with his hands, edging her towards him.

'This wasn't part of the deal…ooh…'

He tongued her, a long, slow sweep between her slick folds that had her bracing against the shower walls and arching into his mouth ever so slightly.

It was all the encouragement he needed to devour her. Alternating between sucking and nibbling. Teasing her clit with repeated little flicks before returning to laving her deeper.

She went a little crazy. Hips undulating. Thrusting at him. Urging him on. Her incoherent pleadings escalated along with every lap of his tongue. So responsive. So fucking hot.

The moment before she came he slipped a finger inside her, another, pumping into her as he licked her. She fell apart, her knees buckling as she yelled, 'oh, yeah,' so loud his ears rang.

Smug that he'd satisfied her the way he wanted but calling on every ounce of restraint not to push her up against the shower stall and bury himself deep, he stood, water dripping down his face. That was nothing compared to his soaked clothes.

When he started to back away, her hand snaked out to capture his.

'Where do you think you're going?'

'To change.'

Confusion clouded her eyes and she gnawed on her bottom lip. 'But… I mean…what about you?'

Suddenly shy, she glanced away. 'Why don't you join me in here?'

It was the best invitation he'd heard all day—all frigging decade—but the first time they had sex he intended to make it count. All night long.

'I'd like nothing better but you've got an appointment, remember?'

Her muttered 'Fuck the appointment' made him smile as he closed the shower door.

'Trust me, babe, if I joined you, we wouldn't get out of there for a week, so how about you take that as a prelude and I'll do the right thing and wait for you out there?' He jerked a thumb towards the hallway.

She didn't respond, staring at him in wide-eyed wonder, as if she couldn't believe what had just happened.

Join the club.

Eventually, she nodded and turned away, but not before he saw something that made his heart soar.

The coy smile of a well-satisfied woman who wanted more.

CHAPTER NINE

'HEY, HONEY, I'M HOME,' Charlotte called out her standard greeting as she entered the lounge room of their tiny Bondi apartment, dumped her satchel and fell into the nearest seat. 'I hope you had a better day than I did.'

Makayla's day had been average. What had happened after rehearsal in Hudson's bathroom had more than made up for it.

Even now, three hours later, she couldn't believe it.

He'd gone down on her.

Giving her an orgasm to end all orgasms.

What that man could do with his tongue...

'Why was your day so bad?' Makayla managed a sensible question while inside she still screamed, *Oh, my God, Hudson and his tongue!*

'New boss from hell.' Charlotte took off her heels and stretched her legs out, scrunching her toes. 'Haven't even met him in person yet but taking orders from him remotely is bad enough.'

'I thought all accountants were perfectly polite

types who treated each other with dignity and respect?'

Charlotte flipped her the bird. 'That's how much I respect your opinion. As for my boss being an accountant, I think he's one of those business drones who only see the bottom line and couldn't give a flying fig about personnel.'

'Sounds like a rough day,' she said, busting to get Charlotte's opinion on what had gone down with Hudson—literally—but not sure she wanted to talk about it.

'Looks like yours wasn't.' Charlotte tucked her legs under her, eyeing her with curiosity. 'You've got this weird smug smirk thing happening.'

'Rehearsal went well,' she said, her lips twitching, unable to stop a grin spreading over her face, the kind of grin that made her cheeks ache. 'Really well.'

'What the...?' Charlotte's eyes narrowed before she squealed. 'No way. You slept with someone on your first day?'

'Of course not.' But she'd wanted to drag Hudson into the shower with her. She'd admired his self-control while cursing him for it.

When he'd first asked to watch, she'd been shocked at his cheekiness. He'd asked her to do the very thing that had ensured he'd ended their friendship five years earlier.

Yet her surprise at his audacity had quickly given way to intrigue and she'd been turned on by the suggestion. But she'd wanted to make him sweat. In trying to prove a point—that he was duplicitous for wanting to watch her naked when he'd freaked that one time she'd done it with good reason—her plan had backfired.

Having him watch her shower had been the most erotic thing she'd ever experienced. She'd tried to stick with the programme of deliberate torture as revenge for how badly he'd treated her the last time he'd seen her naked, intent on purposely driving him crazy. Unfortunately she'd driven herself nuts in the process.

She'd never been so turned on, had been shocked yet relieved when he'd opened that shower door. Not that she was a complete fool. She'd known what might happen when she'd agreed to let him watch her. Had counted on it, so she could call him out for being a hypocrite and release all the pent-up regret that she'd harboured despite their newly awakened friendship now. She'd planned on stopping him with a few terse words. She hadn't expected to admire him because he'd been man enough to acknowledge the attraction simmering between them.

Even as her resistance had crumbled and her residual anger had faded, she'd had reservations. Getting physical with Hudson would change everything. He'd already seen her naked and found her lacking once. What was to say his freak-out that night years ago wouldn't happen again because of his baggage she didn't know about?

She'd been an idiot. She should've known that in agreeing to his challenge out of anger, it would backfire on her. She'd been curious to see how far she could push him. She hadn't expected him to push back...and how. But she couldn't get past one question that kept bugging her: was he genuinely so damn hot for her that he couldn't resist or had he been trying to prove a point—to himself—as she'd been doing?

Whatever his rationale, when her anger had dwindled and she'd released the bitterness of the past, she'd realised Hudson was staring at her with admiration, not disgust, and she'd never felt so empowered as she'd showered in front of him. Knowing he was finally looking at her the way she wanted him to look. Knowing he wanted her.

'You so did sleep with someone. Look at your cheeks!' Charlotte yelled. 'You're crimson.'

Makayla pressed her palms to her scorching cheeks. 'I didn't sleep with anyone but there may have been other stuff going on.'

'Ooh, do tell.' Charlotte rubbed her hands together, but before Makayla could reveal the partial truth, the doorbell rang.

'That'll be Abby,' she said, glancing at her watch. 'She's bringing leftovers from the patisserie.'

'Good, I'm starved.' Charlotte leapt nimbly to her

feet, her petite frame always making Makayla feel like an ogre. 'Dealing with an asshole boss gives me an appetite.'

Dealing with Makayla's boss gave her an appetite too, but not for food.

'Hi, lovelies.' Abby breezed into the room brandishing the distinct pink and gold cardboard bags from Le Miel. 'I come bearing gifts.'

'Whatever you're offering, I'll have three of each,' Charlotte said, padding into the kitchen to get plates. 'Chardonnay okay for you two?'

'Please,' Abby said, shooting Makayla a 'what's up?' look when she hadn't said anything.

'Tell you in a minute,' Makayla said, waiting until Charlotte had poured them each a glass of wine and their plates were covered with lemon tartlets, petite croissants and *beignets*.

'Makayla's been up to no good with someone at work,' Charlotte said, popping a tartlet into her mouth whole. 'And she's about to spare this poor, pathetic spinster no details.'

'Someone at work?' Predictably, Abby's ears all but twitched. 'Tell me it's Hudson. He's gorgeous.' She swivelled towards Charlotte and wiggled her eyebrows. 'You know the actor Tom Hiddleston?'

Charlotte's forehead crinkled before she snapped her fingers. 'English, right? Tall, blond, blue eyes, incredibly hot?'

Abby nodded. 'Hudson could be his twin.'

Charlotte wolf whistled. 'But isn't he your boss?'

Makayla sighed, knowing she should've remembered that salient point around the time he'd opened that shower door. 'Technically, yes, but we're old friends.'

'Friends or *friends*?' Charlotte made smoochy sounds. 'I do love a good juicy friends-to-lovers saga.'

Makayla snorted and pointed to a towering stack of novels on a side table. 'Stick to your romance novels because there's not much to tell.'

Abby's grin channelled pure evil. 'Maybe I should ask Tanner—'

'Don't you dare.' Makayla glared at Abby, who feigned innocence before taking a bite out of one of her signature croissants.

Makayla loved Abby's pastries but if she ate half of what Abby did she wouldn't be able to fit into her leotards, let alone dance.

'You'll have to give us something, my friend, otherwise I'm getting Tanner to do some digging.' Abby dusted off her hands and reached for her wine glass. 'And trust me, he's more of a gossip than I am.'

'Okay, okay, sheesh.' Makayla blew out a breath, keen to get her friends' take on what had gone down with Hudson—literally—but nervous they'd reiterate what she already knew. She was stupid for complicating a working relationship with her boss. 'But you promise not to breathe a word of this to Tanner, okay?'

Abby hesitated before nodding. 'We tell each other everything, but considering you're my best friend and Hudson's his, we'll stay out of it.'

Makayla glanced at Charlotte, who held up her hands. 'Hey, who would I tell? You two are the only friends I have.'

Makayla searched for the right words, something to tell her friends that didn't involve revealing everything. Before realising if she left out the juicy stuff there wouldn't be much to tell.

'The short version? I had a dress fitting tonight for another show I'm doing, a one-off. Rehearsals ran late so I wouldn't have had time to get back here to shower. Hudson lives in an apartment over Embue so he offered me his shower to save time.' Makayla felt heat flush her cheeks as Abby's eyes widened to saucer proportion.

'You didn't! He showered with you?'

Charlotte blew a raspberry. 'I'm so freaking jealous. You lead the most exciting life ever.'

Not usually. Exciting things didn't happen to Makayla often. Today had been an aberration...that she'd remember for a very long time. 'Do you want to hear the rest or not?'

'Yes!' both girls yelled in unison, so she continued. 'The shower mixer thingy wasn't working and I couldn't get the water temp right. So I called out to him to fix it.'

'And?' Charlotte prompted, her elbows resting on

her knees, chin in her hands, leaning forward and hanging on her every word.

'He said he'd fix it.' Makayla paused for dramatic effect. 'If I let him watch me shower.'

Charlotte squealed and Abby's mouth dropped open. 'No way. That's so hot.'

'I know, right?' Makayla's skin pebbled at the remembrance of having Hudson watch her with that intense gaze of his. Like he couldn't look away. Like he was really seeing her for the first time. 'I should never have agreed but we've got this attraction going on, always have, so I thought why not?'

'Why not indeed?' Charlotte sighed and slumped back on the sofa, wistfulness clouding her eyes. 'You are so lucky.'

Since they'd been flatmates, Makayla had never seen Charlotte date, let alone have a boyfriend. She'd tried to encourage her to go clubbing or go out for drinks at their local bar on a Friday night, but Charlotte preferred reading to socialising. She hoped she could drag her to Embue to watch her perform. If Makayla was in a man slump, Charlotte was in severe drought.

'So what happened after that?' Abby prompted.

'I was angry at first, really mad.' For reasons she wouldn't go into with her friends. She'd left the past behind and had no intention of rehashing it. 'I wanted to tell him to stick his ludicrous challenge.' Her grin turned sly. 'But then I wanted to make him sweat for being so audacious, so while he watched I may have played up to him a tad and…he, uh…ended up in the shower…' Hell, there was no easy way to say this, so she blurted, 'He went down on me.'

'Hells bells.' Charlotte almost fell off her chair she leaned forward so far, while Abby tut-tutted. 'Bad girl.'

'Or good, very, very good, depending how you look at it.' Makayla couldn't keep the smug grin off her face now she'd come to terms with her fall from grace. And she'd fallen far. From indignant woman scorned to moaning, wanton goddess, she'd given in to Hudson when she should've rallied against his injustice. But the moment he'd lapped at her with his tongue her outrage at his double standards had been obliterated and, considering the ferocity of her orgasm, she couldn't be sorry for that. 'Let's just say if I hadn't had to rush off I'd probably still be there, returning the favour.'

'You two are so going to end up together,' Charlotte said, sounding pensive. 'I can sense it.'

Abby, the more practical of her friends, seemed less caught up in the romanticism. 'What does he think about this fling?'

Something in Makayla's chest tightened at Abby's casual labelling of what she'd shared with Hudson as a fling. She shouldn't care, because if things proceeded with them that was exactly what it would be.

But having Abby articulate it meant her friend either thought she wasn't up for anything more or she knew more about Hudson via Tanner and he wasn't.

'We didn't really get to talk,' Makayla said, some of her earlier enthusiasm at getting the girls' opinions dwindling. 'But I like him. He likes me. The shower thing could be a prelude to more.'

'Do you want that?'

'Of course she does,' Charlotte answered for her. 'If this guy is as hot as you say, why wouldn't she?'

Abby's furtive glance away made Makayla's heart sink. 'What aren't you telling me, Abs?'

Abby hesitated before giving a brief nod. 'Tanner and Hudson have been mates since high school. According to Tanner, Hudson hasn't been in a relationship ever. He dates a few times max, moves on. Are you okay with that, considering you share a past?'

Makayla's heart foolishly lifted at the thought of Hudson never being involved with a woman long term. Not that she was interested in changing his track record—far from it—but it meant that if they did have a fling it wouldn't change the status quo for either of them.

She didn't have time for mess. Not when this job could be the first step to achieving her dream.

'We both grew up in Kings Cross. Our paths crossed regularly and we ended up friends. Then we had a falling out and we weren't any more. But all that's in the past, and whatever happens now we'll both know where we stand.'

Sounded nice in theory but Makayla knew it had the potential to be way more complicated than that.

Working with Hudson could provide her with contacts she needed to climb the industry ladder. It could lead to her big break. So what happened if they had a fling but it soured? Their friendship had gone south once before and she still didn't know the real reason behind his outburst that had effectively ended them. This time, it could have far more severe consequences.

The concern creasing Abby's brow faded. 'As long as you both know the score before you start something up, you'll be fine.'

'I think they've already started something up,' Charlotte said with a cheeky wink. 'You should go for it, sweetie. Have some fun. You deserve it.'

'Here's to both of you getting clean in many showers together.' Abby raised her glass in a toast. 'Or should that be getting dirty?'

Makayla chuckled and clinked glasses with the girls. While she didn't need their approval to take things further with Hudson, it had been helpful to use them as sounding boards.

Not that she had a hope in hell of backing out. She'd made her decision the second she'd let the towel drop and allowed Hudson to see her naked several hours ago.

A bold move or a moment of madness?

Guess she'd soon find out.

CHAPTER TEN

WORK HAD KICKED Hudson's ass tonight.

Patrons flocked to Embue for a good time on a daily basis but some nights were crazy busy. Being the manager for Sydney's hottest nightclub had its advantages. He counted the coolest celebrities and sports stars as friends, knew every up-and-comer in the city and had his pick of gorgeous women.

He should've been rapt that Australia's biggest beauty pageant contingent had chosen Embue as their venue for an after-party tonight. Instead, as he watched countless stunning women swan by him wearing next to nothing, sporting bodies that could make a guy grovel, all he could think about was Makayla.

Was she regretting their earlier encounter?

Was she looking forward to the next?

Was she thinking about him at all?

He sure as hell couldn't stop thinking about her.

He'd never expected to take things so far. He'd wanted to test himself, to see if he'd moved on from the past, to ensure that seeing her naked again wouldn't resurrect the old feelings of repugnance; not against her, but for what seeing her naked the first time represented to him.

Thankfully, nothing but desire had filled him, pounding through his blood to a relentless beat he couldn't ignore. He'd never been prone to impulsiveness but watching her soap and stroke herself had lit something within he couldn't deny.

He had to prove—to both of them—that he saw her as a beautiful, desirable woman. That he'd left his reservations from the past behind. That he'd moved on, for both their sakes.

When he'd opened the shower stall, he'd had no idea what to do. Kiss her maybe. Touch her. But the look in her eyes had slayed him: as if she half expected his rejection all over again.

That realisation had gutted him and he'd known he had to give her pleasure and keep a tight rein on his.

Tasting her, hearing her tiny mewls of satisfaction, had been amazing. But he couldn't forget that damn look in her eyes and the fact he'd put it there with his appalling treatment of her five years earlier.

Scowling, he made his umpteenth round of the club, doing impromptu spot checks on everything from the cleanliness of the cocktail glasses to dance-floor spills. Staff must've sensed his mood because they steered clear, ensuring their workstations were spotless, not giving him the usual grief.

His cell buzzed in his pocket and he fished it out, his heart giving a traitorous leap when Mak's name flashed up on the screen.

She'd sent him a text. Short and sweet.

I've got 2 tix for show @ Opera House 2moro nite. U free?

He worked nights, but if Mak wanted to spend any time with him after what had happened earlier, it meant she didn't want to castrate him for his boldness and was open to more.

Nothing could keep him away.

Spying Tanner near the sound booth, he crossed the club with determined strides, eager to give her an answer before she changed her mind or asked someone else to accompany her.

'Hey, bozo, what are you putting in the drinks?' Tanner gestured around. 'This place is packed tonight.'

'Word travels. That, and you've got the best manager in the business.'

'Modest, much?' Tanner leaned against the console, his white T-shirt fluorescent in the club lights. 'What's up?'

'Speaking of being the best manager in the business, can I have tomorrow night off?'

Tanner's eyebrows rose. 'You never ask for time off. What gives?'

'A show at the Opera House I want to check out.'

'Uh-huh.' Tanner tapped his temple, pretending to think. 'Is this technically work? You checking out a show to get ideas for the show here?'

Hudson didn't lie to his best friend. But he knew if he told the truth, he'd never hear the end of it.

'Something like that,' he said, the half-truth lodging in his throat.

'Sure, go ahead. Knock yourself out.' Tanner shrugged. 'Say hi to Mak for me.'

'What?'

Tanner guffawed and slapped him on the back. 'Listen, dickhead, when a workaholic like you asks for a night off for the first time in five years it must involve a woman. And seeing as Mak had you in a spin after the audition, it has to be her. Correct?'

'You're full of shit,' Hudson said, glad his friend knew him so well. 'She has a spare ticket, she asked me to go, that's it.'

'Keep telling yourself that,' Tanner said, grinning like a doofus. 'Though you've heard the saying, right? Don't screw the crew?'

'Like you did with Abby?'

'*Touché*, my smitten friend.' Tanner shrugged. 'Don't say I didn't warn you.'

Hudson flipped him the bird and stalked off, already tapping a response to Mak.

He didn't need any warnings. He already knew that getting involved with Mak could lead to disaster.

But with relentless desire pounding through his body, making him want her with a mindless intensity he couldn't shake no matter how hard he tried, he knew that some things were worth the risk.

CHAPTER ELEVEN

HUDSON HAD OFFERED to pick Makayla up but she'd cited a late shift at the patisserie and arranged to meet him on the steps of the Opera House instead.

Pathetic, considering she'd invited him. No use chickening out now. But that was exactly what she'd done, ever since Charlotte had presented her with the tickets last night after their gossip session.

At the time, she'd justified her decision to invite him as a way to thank him for the job opportunity. Now, twenty-four hours later, with the prospect of sitting next to him in the dark, trying to keep her mind on the recital and not on the delectable guy making her think naughty thoughts, her decision didn't seem so smart.

In reality, she could dress up her invitation any way she liked but the truth was she wanted to spend more time with him.

He'd been out of her life for years and in less than a week, he'd insinuated his way back into it without trying.

She couldn't stop thinking about him.

Probably her hormones wanting a repeat of what went down in his shower too, but she owed it to herself to explore this thing they had between them.

She'd been dating regularly for years. Not without any thought for the future, but for the simple pleasure of having fun. She hadn't slept with a lot of guys—she was too picky for that—but she liked dating, enjoyed sex, and hadn't had enough of either over the last year.

Time to rectify that with a guy she actually respected and admired.

Hudson had always been larger than life for her. The kind of guy who strode into a room and everyone took notice. Back then, he'd been amenable and pleasant and a hard worker, friendly to everyone. His *laissez faire* attitude had got him regular work around the Cross, because no one doubted if they hired Hudson their work would get done.

Despite his busy schedule, he'd always had time for her. Had listened to her wax lyrical about everything, from her favourite boy band to her crappiest teacher. She'd never mentioned any crushes, because he'd been it for her.

Here they were, five years later, with her crush stalking towards her, looking incredible in black trousers, black shirt and dark grey sports jacket. Perfectly tailored designer clothes that accentuated

the lean hardness of his body. A body she'd be seeing naked by the end of tonight if she had her way.

'Glad you could make it,' she said when he
reached her and leaned down to brush a kiss on her
cheek.

'Wouldn't miss it.' He straightened, but his aftershave lingered, a heady mix of crisp citrus and
deeper exotic undertones. Mysterious. Alluring.
Scrumptious.

'I didn't know you're that into opera?'

'I'm not.' His enigmatic stare left her in little
doubt what he was really into. 'But I'd be a fool to
pass up the opportunity to spend an evening with
you.'

'Smooth talker.' She smiled and gave him a gentle
nudge with her elbow. 'Shall we go in?'

'Sure.'

She forced her body to relax when he placed a
hand in the small of her back, an innocuous gesture
to guide her. But she couldn't stop her nerve endings from going haywire, firing and zapping and
making her want to ditch the opera in favour of the
nearest hotel room.

'I love this place,' he said as they stepped inside
the iconic Opera House, the soaring ceilings inside
as beautiful as the white sails outside.

'Have you been to many shows here?'

He nodded, glancing around with an interest bor-
dering on reverence. 'The theatre company I'm in-

volved with attends shows regularly here so I tag along whenever I can.'

'I'd never have picked you to have an interest in theatre,' she said, wondering how many other things she didn't know about him.

It had been five long years since they'd last spoken and it struck her anew. What did she really know about Hudson Watt?

Back then, she'd known he favoured orange juice over pineapple, preferred Aussie Rules football over rugby and liked jazz over pop. Now, she knew next to nothing about him and it saddened her.

What would their relationship be like now if they'd stayed in touch?

'I guess working around the Cross clubs all those years, seeing the dance shows, rubbed off on me.' His tone was curt, clipped, and she knew why.

He didn't want to talk about some of the club shows at the Cross. Not when some of them involved stripping, the reason they'd fallen out in the first place. But if she wanted to know more about him, she couldn't back down, even when the going got tough.

'So you're interested in the production side of things?'

He nodded, his shoulders still rigid with tension. 'I've done a lot of behind-the-scenes stuff in the theatre company. Got me thinking what it would be like to combine the show side of things with clubbing.'

He shrugged. 'I put together a proposal, Tanner gave me a chance.'

'So that means I need to dance my ass off so you can impress your boss to do more shows?'

'Something like that,' he said, his mouth curving into a slow smile. 'But please look after that ass. I happen to like it.'

Her pulse leapt, but she managed a demure, 'I'll bear that in mind.'

'You do that.' They'd reached their seats, and he waited until they'd sat before leaning across to murmur in her ear, 'Because if you need any assistance looking after it, I'm your man.'

She turned towards him and their eyes met. Even in the dim lighting she could see the spark, the lust, the heat. It gave her courage to reach across and rest her hand on his thigh. Low enough to be decent. High enough to be suggestive.

'You'll kill my concentration if you do that.'

In response, she slid a little higher and squeezed.

'I never did like opera all that much anyway,' he said, covering her hand with his, waiting until the lights went out before guiding it higher.

Yowza. He was big. Hard. Her fingers curled around him a little and she heard a muffled groan.

Makayla had no idea how they lasted through the first act: forty-five long excruciating minutes of exquisite costumes and pitch-perfect singing. Usually, she would've been enthralled. Instead, all she could focus on was how Hudson felt beneath her hand. How he could hold himself perfectly still, not moving a muscle, yet his rigidity conveying a restraint that left her awestruck.

As the falsetto strains of the lead vocalist faded and the lights flickered on, Hudson released her hand and she straightened, blinking at him as her eyes adjusted.

'What do you fancy for intermission?'

She couldn't imagine sipping champagne, making small talk and sitting through a torturous second act, wanting him more with every passing minute.

So she looked him in the eye and said, 'You.'

CHAPTER TWELVE

HUDSON DIDN'T CARE about speeding fines at this time of night. He happily broke the land speed record between Circular Quay and his apartment. Besides, he couldn't have driven slowly if he'd tried. Not with Mak sitting next to him, radiating a barely restrained energy that had the air between them almost crackling.

He'd felt it the moment he'd greeted her on the Opera House steps. As if something had shifted between them. Something minute and indescribable but there all the same, pulling them together, as if it were inevitable.

He'd been determined to fight it because he viewed her invitation to attend the opera with her as a huge step between them. An unspoken acknowledgement on her behalf that she'd forgiven him and they might have something more than friendship between them.

So he'd made small talk. Planned on sitting through

the entire performance before suggesting they head back to his place for a drink.

Never in his wildest dreams had he anticipated Mak wanting to leave halfway through the opera because she couldn't keep her hands off him.

When she'd touched him…did she have any idea what she did to him? He'd been rock-hard for forty-five goddamn minutes and he could've shouted for joy when she'd wanted to leave.

As he pulled into his car spot in the underground car park and killed the engine, he knew they were on the cusp of a massive shift in their relationship.

The point of no return.

So being an idiotic gentleman to the end, he gave her a last chance to back out.

'You sure about this?' He stared out of the windshield, unable to look at her. If he did, he knew he wouldn't be able to resist hauling her into his arms and that would take the decision out of her hands completely.

'Never been surer.'

She didn't touch him. She didn't need to. The conviction in her tone brooked no argument.

She wanted this as much as he did.

Which meant he couldn't get her upstairs fast enough.

She'd stepped out of the car before he had a chance to open her door, so he offered her his hand.

She took it and didn't let go until they were inside

his apartment, the door barely closing before she was on him. Pushing him against the nearest wall. Slamming her body against his. Reaching for his zipper.

The thing with quick gratification, it could be incredibly hot but was over too fast. For his first time with the woman who'd featured in his fantasies for years he wanted to take things slow. Real slow.

'Hey, I want you,' he said, holding her arms and easing her back a fraction. 'I've wanted you for ever. So let me savour every single moment of this.'

The corners of her lush mouth kicked up in a devilish smile. 'So you want to torture me?'

'Call it building anticipation rather than torture.' He relaxed his grip on her arms and started sliding his palms up and down her bare skin, feeling it pebble beneath his touch. 'Quite frankly, you drive me crazy and I want to be buried inside you in two seconds flat.'

'Way too fast,' she said, her glance coy from beneath lowered lashes. 'But considering you sat through that entire first act rock-hard, how slow exactly do you want to take this?'

She pressed her pelvis against him. 'Because, honey, there's a difference between building anticipation and killing me slowly.'

He laughed, loving her honesty, loving that they could talk like this. They'd always been open with each other, had trusted each other. Until it had all imploded.

But he couldn't think about that night. Couldn't think about the secrets she probably harboured. Secrets that could drive him to distraction and wreck this before they'd even begun, if he was stupid enough to let them.

He had Mak in his arms.

Wanting him.

Mak.

No way in hell would he let the past or any doubts derail what promised to be the best night of his life.

'Dance with me,' he said, smiling when her eyebrows rose in surprise. 'Ever since I saw you audition for me, I imagined what it would be like having your incredible body moving close to mine.'

'Vertical sex, huh?' She pretended to ponder a moment, before nodding. 'I like it.'

He would too, as he led her by the hand to his stereo system, did a quick scroll through a smooth playlist, and chose one of his favourite classic songs.

'Prince? Seriously?' She slapped him playfully on the arm. 'Exactly how old are you?'

'Old enough to know better, old enough to not give a damn and do the bad stuff regardless.'

As the first sultry beats filled the air, he took her other hand, his body pulsing with barely controlled desire for her. Then she started moving in time to the music and all he could do for a moment was stare.

She had an inherent elegance that transformed into unadulterated heat as she danced. Her body took on a life of its own, as if the bass were a part of her. Sinuous writhing combined with sensuous hip rolls. Languid shoulder shimmies alternating with some seriously hot ass wiggling.

He was a goner.

He tugged on her hands, hard, intent on devouring her. But she resisted, her sexy smile ratcheting up the sizzle between them.

'I thought you wanted to prolong this?'

'I lied,' he muttered, his plans to take things slow shot to hell the second she wiggled her ass at him. 'Sitting through that opera was foreplay enough and my self-control is shot to shit with you putting the moves on me.'

She quirked an eyebrow, her faux innocence not fooling him for a second. 'I'm merely dancing, just like you wanted to.'

'Don't listen to me. I'm an idiot.'

She chuckled and took a step closer. Close enough he could smell her, sweat mingling with her sultry fragrance, a heady combination that drove him wild.

'But you didn't dance?'

'You danced enough for the both of us,' he said, palming her ass and pulling her close. 'God, you drive me wild.'

Her slow, seductive smile made his heart pound. 'Show me.'

He didn't have to be asked twice. 'You look sensational in this dress but I've been wanting to get you out of it since the moment I saw you tonight.'

The simple black halter that ended below her knees screamed understated class, but the silky fabric that clung to her body in all the right places ensured it transformed the dress from demure to sexy as hell.

'Be my guest.' She turned around, giving him an unimpeded view of smooth skin. No tan lines. Interesting.

Thankfully, she'd tied a simple knot at her neck and he had it undone with a flick of his wrist. The material slithered down her front, and he bit back a groan as his fingertips skated down her spine to her waist.

He toyed with the zipper for a moment, his throbbing cock urging him to rip the damn thing and be done with it. But there had to be something to delayed gratification so he slid it down slowly.

Revealing a black satin thong.

Hot damn.

The dress fell to the floor in a whisper of silk, leaving her standing before him in stilettos and that thong.

Her ass was as sweet as he'd imagined, rounded yet taut. A good handful. He palmed it. Kneading it. Her low groan better than any aphrodisiac.

'Turn around,' he said, his order a growl.

He stepped back as she did so, allowing himself to look his fill.

Exquisite.

The first time he'd seen her naked, he'd allowed himself one illicit glance before looking away, incensed. In his shower, he'd been too gobsmacked to stare too long.

This time, he intended to take his time.

Her breasts were perfect. Perky, full. With pretty pale pink nipples that stood to attention, begging to be sucked.

He glanced lower, zeroing in on where he wanted to be. Saw her hook her thumbs under the elastic of the thong. Push it down. Revealing heaven. Golden red, a deeper shade than her hair cascading around her shoulders.

In his shower, he'd devoured her too quickly. Had been hell-bent on giving her pleasure and giving in to the fantasy of tasting her. Tonight, he'd make sure he took his time.

Later.

She kicked away the thong and kinked a hip in a purely provocative pose. 'Shoes on or off?'

'You won't have time to take them off,' he said, launching himself at her.

But she stepped back and held him off with a hand on his chest. 'Uh-uh. One of us is way overdressed.'

'I don't need to undress.' He unzipped his fly,

where his cock strained against the briefs beneath. 'There. Done.'

'You're not the only one who gets off by looking.' She gave him a little shove. 'I want to see you naked. Now.'

'Bossy,' he muttered, grinning as he shrugged out of his jacket and flung it away.

'Faster,' she said, sounding breathless.

So he obliged by popping buttons quickly and letting his shirt fall to the floor.

She made an appreciative sound deep in her throat as he unsnapped his trousers and stepped out of them. With her gaze riveted to his groin, he pushed down his jocks and almost crowed with pride as her jaw dropped.

'You felt big but…wow,' she said, sounding awed. 'This is going to be one hell of a night.'

He bit back his first response, 'Just one night?'

Because if that was all Mak was willing to give, he'd take it. No questions asked. He'd waited too long, wanted her too much, to spoil tonight with awkward conversations.

'Don't move,' she said, and stepped forward before kneeling at his feet.

'Mak, I want—fuck…' he groaned as she wrapped her mouth around him. Taking the tip of his cock between her lips. Flicking her tongue out to tease him. Licking him like she couldn't get enough. Driving him frigging nuts.

He watched her take him in deeper, the moist heat of her mouth making him grit his teeth. What she couldn't take into her mouth she wrapped her hand around and that was when the fun really began.

She started moving her hand and mouth in sync, sucking and licking as if he were all her favourite ice cream flavours rolled into one.

The hottest fucking thing he'd ever experienced.

But the pressure in his balls built too quickly so he had to stop. The first time he came he wanted to be inside her.

'Baby…' He laid a hand on her head and eased her away. She glanced up at him, questioning, and he knelt, bringing him to eye level. 'As much as I'm in blow-job heaven, I need to be inside you.'

'Okay,' she said, her lips curving in a saucy smile. 'Heaven, huh?'

'You have no idea.'

Then finally, after waiting forever to do this, he kissed her. Slow grazes of his lips against hers. Increasing the pressure each time. Lingering longer. Until her tongue darted out to touch his and he was lost.

Their tongues tangled as he hauled her against him, her breasts crushing against his chest, her skin soft beneath his touch but incredibly hot, as if she were burning up from the inside out.

He knew the feeling.

Breaking the kiss long enough to fish a condom

out of his trouser pocket, he sheathed himself and returned to where he wanted to be. In Mak's arms.

'Lean back,' she said, pushing him slightly, until his back rested against the couch.

She straddled him, arms braced either side of his head. He held his breath as she lowered herself, her entrance nudging his cock.

Without breaking eye contact, she slid lower. Inch by exquisite inch. Her mouth open, eyes glazed, until she'd taken all of him inside her slick heat.

'You make me feel…wanton,' she said, raising her arms to lift the hair off her shoulders, tilting her head back, thrusting her breasts at him in a pose of sheer abandonment.

He thrust upward, garnering a smug smile from her, so he did it again. Holding her hips. Pushing upward. Savouring her moans, her pants.

She undulated on him, rising and falling in perfect synchronicity with the pounding in his head reverberating all the way down his spine to his balls.

He wanted to suck her nipples but he couldn't take his eyes off her, the way she rode him with wicked intent.

It was too much, too soon, but he had as much chance of not coming as he did of forgetting this incredible night. So he reached between them, circled her clit with his thumb. Felt the first ripples of her orgasm deep within.

She picked up the pace, sliding up and down

with abandon, the sheen of sweat making her body glow. Unable to hold back a second longer, his body tensed and he gave one last flick against her clit, savouring the moment she fell apart. Her body stiff, breasts thrust upward, expression cataclysmic as she screamed his name and he came so hard he saw spots.

She slumped against him, clung to him and he held her tight.

There were no words.

Superfluous, considering what had just happened. Mak had blown apart his world as he knew it.

CHAPTER THIRTEEN

MAKAYLA KNEW SHE should've left the moment her heart rate had returned to normal the first time they'd had sex in Hudson's living room.

But she'd been too sated, too languid to move, so she hadn't protested when he'd swept her up in his arms like some goddamn hero out of those romance novels Charlotte devoured and taken her to his bedroom.

Where she'd stayed all night.

Makayla never slept over with any of the guys she dated. She enjoyed the foreplay, tried to enjoy the sex, then left.

That was another thing. The sex. Usually, she got off more on the foreplay. The teasing. The flirting. The touches. The glances. The act itself, not so much. In her experience, most men didn't pay enough attention to her body beyond sticking it in and giving her orgasm a passing thought.

Not Hudson. Hudson had strummed her body like a maestro. Caressing every inch. Exploring every crevice with his mouth, his hands. Licking every erogenous zone. Coming back for more. Four times.

She'd never had sex five times in one night. Incredible. Memorable.

Diabolical.

Because as the first fingers of dawn stole through the blinds, highlighting the slumbering sex god by her side, all she could think was where the hell did they go from here?

'I can hear you thinking.' A low rumble came from beneath the covers as he rolled over to face her. 'Stop overanalysing.'

She tugged the sheet higher, feeling oddly vulnerable despite the many ways he'd already seen her body last night. 'Hey, I just woke up. I'm not overanalysing anything.'

'Sure you are,' he said, trailing a fingertip down her cheek in a tender gesture that brought an unexpected lump to her throat. 'To be expected after the way you ravaged me last night.'

She feigned mock outrage and swatted his hand away. 'As I recall, you did most of the ravaging, mister.'

'I remember.' His eyes darkened to indigo, the spark of lust unmistakeable. 'And I plan to do it all over again, starting now.'

Makayla would like nothing better than to lose herself under his skilful ministrations but she knew walking away without clarifying what had happened between them would be wrong considering she'd be seeing him at rehearsals this afternoon.

'Wait,' she said, placing a palm against his chest. His heart pounded beneath it. Strong. Steady. Dependable.

Just like Hudson. He'd been her rock growing up. Her friend. Until he'd misjudged her and ended up leaving her alone like everyone else in her life.

She'd learned a hard lesson then: never depend on anyone but herself. A mantra she'd stuck to. It had served her well. Independence above all else.

But there was a fine line between independence and foolishness. And that was a line she'd be treading if she didn't acknowledge that thanks to Hudson she now had a shot at a serious career boost, but she might have screwed it up by sleeping with her boss.

'What's wrong?' A frown marred his brow and she itched to reach out and smooth it away.

'Don't get me wrong, last night was amazing, but…' She floundered, searching for the right words to convey her confusion and concern.

'But you don't want a repeat, is that it?' His frown deepened, his mouth twisting with regret.

'I… I don't know what I want,' she admitted, rubbing her neck to ease the tension making her muscles bunch. 'The sex we had was phenomenal and so damn rare I want to do it over and over again. But I've worked my ass off as a dancer for years and your show is the first big break I've had in ages, so I don't want to mess with that. Plus you're my boss and I don't want rumours circulating that I score roles by sleeping with the boss. So even if we do keep this thing between us going, it'll have to be a secret, but that sounds so dirty, and that's not us—'

'Whoa, slow down, take a breath.' He rested his hand on her waist, the heat comforting through the cotton. 'So the sex was phenomenal, huh?'

She huffed out an angry breath. 'Typical guy, homing in on the sex and ignoring the rest.'

'I'm kidding, sweetheart.' He leaned forward to brush a soft kiss against her lips. 'Are you saying you want us to continue this?'

She wanted to lie. She wanted to run, far from his persuasive mouth and soul-searching eyes. But this was Hudson, the guy who'd once looked out for her, and she wouldn't mess with their friendship again. Not when having him back in her life now was like a precious gift she'd unwrapped and savoured.

'At the risk of sounding like a complete idiot, I had a crush on you way back when, so last night was pretty damn incredible,' she said, relieved when his frown cleared. 'And yeah, call me greedy, I want more.'

A slow grin eased across his face. 'I'm all for more—'

'But I don't want it at the expense of my career.' She sounded callous, calculating, but it had to be this way. Self-preservation was the only thing that had kept her going all these years when she'd scrimped to get by. 'Call me heartless, whatever, but I've never let a relationship come between me and my goals and I'm not about to start now, even for you.'

'Wow,' he said, wariness creeping into his eyes. 'You're a straight shooter.'

'I have a low tolerance for BS.' She shrugged. 'So I guess we play this my way or not at all.'

'I have a low tolerance for ultimatums,' he said, his frown returning. 'But I get where you're coming from.'

An ache filled her chest and spread outward, numbing her arms. In telling him the truth, had she lost him before this had really begun?

'Where do we go from here?'

He took an eternity to answer, conflicting emotions scudding across his steady gaze. Hope. Concern. Excitement. Recalcitrance.

When he opened his mouth to respond, she braced for an answer she wouldn't like.

'Mak, I've fantasised about you for years and now that I've had one stupendous night with you, do you honestly think I'm stupid enough to let you go?' His hand resting on her waist drifted upward in a slow caress that ended at her face, where he cupped her cheek. 'We'll play this your way. Whatever you want. Whenever you want. No one needs to know but us.'

Relief made her tremble, and she launched herself at him, burying her face against his chest. 'Thank you.'

His arms slid around her, warm, comforting. She snuggled deeper, feeling like she'd just won the lottery, a great job and a sensational guy as a bonus. It had been a long time since luck had been on her side. She didn't want anything to mess this up.

'Mak?'

'Hmm?'

'If this is our secret, can we get to the dirty part now?'

She chuckled against his chest before easing away, feeling more light-hearted than she had in ages. 'I need to get to work.'

'This won't take long.'

His wolfish grin made her tingle with anticipation as he slid a condom on and scooted down the bed, taking the cover sheet with him. Leaving her bare and exposed, the faint red marks on her skin evidence of their wonderful night of debauchery.

He slid a finger between her folds, a long sweep that had her arching towards him. 'So wet,' he said, lifting the finger to his mouth before licking it. 'So sweet.'

Makayla stared at the most erotic thing she'd ever seen, him tasting her unashamedly. She loved how uninhibited he was, as if the sex was merely an extension of their friendship.

'What are you going to do—? *Ooh...*' He nudged her knees apart, positioned himself and drove into her in one smooth thrust.

'No time for foreplay, you said.' He lifted her ass with his hands and slid a pillow under it, lifting her hips, giving him better access to hit her sweet spot when he thrust again. 'So I better make this quickie count.'

In response, Makayla wrapped her legs around him and interlocked her ankles, while bracing her hands behind her head. 'Go right ahead.'

He laughed at her devil-may-care posture and reached down to rub her clit. 'You look like you're floating on a daybed in a pool.'

'Except for this, of course.' She gave his butt a little kick with her feet. 'This posture would not be suitable poolside.'

'True.' He withdrew slowly and drove into her with renewed purpose to prove it. Over and over. Hard thrusts. Long thrusts. Making her body wind tight with every exquisite movement.

His thumb circled her clit, light flicks alternating with deeper pressure, keeping time as he pumped into her. She watched him touching her, watched him driving into her, more turned on than she'd ever been.

The pleasure built as he picked up speed, pounding into her so hard that her elbows knocked the headboard repeatedly.

'Hudson…' Her body stiffened, spasmed, as she came on a low moan, echoed by him a second later.

Boneless, she unlocked her legs, and he collapsed

on top of her, generous to a fault even now as he rolled his weight to one side so as not to crush her.

'Have I made you late for work?' he mumbled against her neck, nipping the tender skin below her ear.

'All good,' she said, too sated to move but knowing that Remy would kill her if she rocked up late for the second morning in a row. 'In fact, I have time for a shower, if you'd like to join me?'

'You'll be late.' He nuzzled her, making her skin pebble as his hand drifted up her thigh, his fingertips skating across her stomach, before coming to rest a fraction away from her mound. 'Better ring ahead and let them know now.'

Makayla did exactly that.

CHAPTER FOURTEEN

THE END OF the week couldn't come quick enough for Hudson.

Usually, he dreaded weekends for the simple fact he worked long hours at the theatre followed by busy nights at the club.

This weekend would be different.

He had a date lined up with Mak, a step back in time, that he hoped would solidify what he already knew.

They were frigging great together.

Being a couple hadn't interfered with their work. If anything, her dancing had moved to a new level, filled with a passion and grace found lacking in many on stage these days. Or maybe he was just biased and saw sensuousness in her every move considering they'd spent every night this week wrapped in each other's arms.

He couldn't get enough and, thankfully, the feeling was entirely mutual.

'Hey, Hudson, how's it hanging?' The booming

voice of Reg Grober, Sydney's leading backer of every single show to hit Australian shores, rang out across the stage as the tall, grey-haired power broker strode towards him. 'Unearthed any stars lately?'

Hudson had gained something of a reputation over the last few years for taking unknown talent and casting them in well-known stage musicals, only to find their star taking off. He prided himself on his eye for talent and was proud to call Reg a friend.

He might have a great job managing Embue and knew he could always count on his bestie Tanner, but he'd learned from a young age that jobs weren't always rock solid and people weren't always dependable. He viewed Reg as a security blanket, a contact that could come in handy one day if the bottom of his world ever fell out, as it had before.

'I've got a new show starting next week at the nightclub I manage. Some great performers there. You should come see.' He shook Reg's hand when he stuck it out. 'Let me know which night and I'll leave your name on the door.'

'I might just do that.' Reg gestured around the empty theatre. 'Can't believe we've had a sell-out here for the duration. Who knew people liked musicals about Aussie icons at the beach?'

'Whatever you touch turns to gold, mate.'

Reg acknowledged the compliment with a broad grin. 'Speaking of gold, know any outstanding dancers? I'm involved in a start-up on Broadway and one of the chorus busted her leg. We need someone good to start over there in a month.'

Hudson's heart pounded in his chest, making him oddly breathless. He knew a dancer, one of the best, whose dream was to star on Broadway.

However, when he'd told her he might have contacts to help her get there he'd never anticipated it would be so soon.

If he put Mak's name forward, she could leave him in a month.

Four short weeks.

And they'd be over before they'd really begun.

For a long moment, he considered lying. But this was *Mak* and he couldn't do it to her, no matter how selfish he was and wanted to keep her to himself for a little longer.

'I do know someone. She'd be perfect.'

Reg beamed. 'Great. We'll be auditioning in a week so I'll send you the details.' He tapped the side of his nose. 'And I'll make sure to be completely unbiased, even though I know that anyone you send me will have an automatic walk-up role.'

'Thanks, Reg.' Hudson shook his hand again and waved the clipboard in his free one. 'Got to get back to work.'

'Sure thing, I'll leave you to it.'

As Reg walked away, Hudson knew he should call Mak and share the good news. He delved into his pocket, pulled out his cell and brought up her name.

However, his thumb hovered on the call button as a host of unwelcome thoughts flooded him.

Once she found out, would she end this thing between them now to focus on her big break?

Would she stay with him for the next few weeks out of obligation, as a thank-you for getting her the job?

Or the biggie, if he laid it all on the line, would she still leave him regardless?

Hudson hated secrets. He'd grown up with them. Keeping his father's alcoholism from the schoolteachers and welfare workers. Watching men cheat on their wives in the strip clubs. Seeing women whoring. A world of secrets that festered and left him feeling tainted because of it.

He couldn't keep this secret from Mak to suit his own ends.

He glared at her name on the screen, clutching the cell so tight he wouldn't have been surprised if it cracked.

He would tell her.

He had to tell her.

Later.

Hating himself, he slipped the phone back in his pocket and focussed on ensuring this production went off without a hitch, unable to shake the feeling that in making all Mak's dreams come true he was ruining his.

CHAPTER FIFTEEN

'I THINK I liked you better before you were getting laid regularly,' Charlotte said, perched on her favourite stool in the window at Le Miel. 'You're way too smug.'

Makayla grinned at her flatmate and placed a steaming hot chocolate in front of her. 'Can't blame a girl for being satisfied.'

Charlotte held up her hand. 'Please. Spare me the details.'

'Lucky for you, I'm not one to shag and tell.' Makayla winked. 'Anything else I can get you?'

'One of those decadent *beignets*.' Charlotte pointed at the display cabinet where Abby's amazing creations made every customer's mouth water. 'And throw in a *pain au chocolat* too.'

Makayla's eyebrows rose. 'Hungry?'

'Drowning my sorrows in pastry.' Charlotte sighed and slumped a little. 'That new boss I mentioned? The one working remotely so I can't even tell him what I really think of him to his face? He's making my life hell.'

'So quit. You're diligent and there must be stacks of jobs for good accountants.'

A flicker of fear flashed across Charlotte's face. 'Nerdy introverts don't do well making grand gestures like quitting before we have a new job to go to.'

'Then start hunting. Or better yet, sign up with one of those agencies that'll find you a dream job just like that.' She snapped her fingers. Yeah, like it was that easy. She'd registered with every talent agency on the eastern seaboard for years and she knew first-hand that dream jobs were few and far between. But Charlotte looked so morose she had to pump her up somehow. 'No boss should make you this unhappy.'

Charlotte's eyes narrowed but not before Makayla glimpsed a wicked gleam. 'Unlike your boss, who's making you exceedingly happy.'

'Hudson's a great guy,' she said, her dismissive shrug belying just how great he was.

Work-wise, he knew his stuff and he treated her with nothing but professionalism. He demanded perfection from his crew and ran to a rigid schedule. She liked working with a boss who respected his dancers and knew what he was doing.

But away from rehearsals, Hudson was simply… amazing.

He made her feel cherished in a way she'd never

had with a guy. His main goal seemed to be giving her pleasure, and she returned the favour and then some.

But she'd learned the hard way that if something was too good to be true it usually was and she knew this fledgling relationship wouldn't end well.

And it would end. There was no doubt. She'd never lost sight of her goal, making it on Broadway, all these years. Every audition she attended, every dress rehearsal, every dance show no matter how small the crowd, had been part of her grand plan.

She could never give it all up for a guy, no matter how special. Especially one who had let her down badly once before.

They might have lain the past to rest but a small part of her deep down still resented him for not giving her an explanation for his behaviour that night.

She'd deliberately pushed the memory of his unwarranted freak-out to the back of her mind since they'd got together, not wanting to spoil the amazing fun—both in and out of the bedroom—they were having.

But having that residual doubt, no matter how deep she'd buried it, still niggled. Would she be foolishly setting herself up for a fall if she threw herself wholeheartedly into a relationship with Hudson?

Her heart encouraged trust, her head screamed logic that couldn't be denied.

He'd left her once without an explanation.

He could do it again.

'You're so lucky to have found a guy like Hudson.' Charlotte rested her chin in her hand, whimsical as usual, her eyes dreamy as she envisioned a hero out of one of those novels she couldn't put down.

'Someone talking about my right-hand man?'

Makayla stiffened as Tanner appeared behind her and draped an arm across her shoulders. 'Hud is a great guy and I've never seen him so happy, so I'm guessing that has something to do with you? He won't give me any details, which is a pain in the ass because I want to hang shit on him but can't. Maybe you'll give me the low-down?'

Heat suffused her cheeks as she shrugged off his arm and elbowed him in the ribs. 'I'm not saying a word.' She made a zipping motion over her lips. 'And leave him alone.'

'Protective too, I respect that.' Tanner winked at Charlotte, who always appeared shell-shocked that a guy as hot as Tanner was talking to her. 'Ain't love grand?'

'You should know, bozo, considering you're gaga over Abby,' Makayla said, chalking a point up in the air.

She didn't need to see Tanner's goofy grin to know the guy was head over heels for her best friend.

'Hey, here's an idea.' Tanner's gaze turned positively evil. 'We should double date some time. You and Hud, me and Abby. That way, I'll get the low-down first-hand.'

'Not going to happen.' Makayla hesitated, not wanting to make a big deal over the fact her relationship with Hudson was a secret, but having to tell her friends so they wouldn't accidentally hassle her in front of the wrong people, like the show's cast. 'Hudson and I are keeping this thing between us secret.'

Tanner and Charlotte wore matching comical WTF expressions so she continued. 'He cast me as the lead in his show so I don't want rumours starting that I slept with the boss to score the role.'

Understanding sparked in Tanner's eyes. 'Good point. I won't say a word.'

'And I've got no one to tell,' Charlotte added, sounding morose.

'I'll leave you ladies to it.' Tanner backed away, hands up, as if he didn't want to be on the receiving end of a lecture. 'But for what it's worth, I approve of you and Hud getting together. I've never seen him like this, relaxed and approachable. You're good for him.'

Before she could respond, Tanner swivelled and strode away, leaving Makayla more worried than ever.

They hadn't actually spelled out the boundaries of their relationship, beyond keeping it secret. Did Hudson understand they had an expiration date? That she would ultimately head overseas to pursue her dream?

'What's wrong?' Charlotte touched her arm, concern creasing her brow. 'You look like you've choked on a croissant.'

'This love stuff is tough,' Makayla said, propping on a stool, wishing her shift could end now so she could head home and hide away in the apartment to mull this latest development.

Charlotte's eyebrows shot heavenward. 'You love him?'

Startled, she shook her head. 'No. Just a figure of speech.'

She couldn't afford to fall in love with anyone right now, least of all Hudson. He'd broken her heart once by walking away from her, had seriously hurt her. She didn't want to return the favour but that was exactly what she would do when she ended this.

If love entered the equation for either of them, it would be disastrous.

'Have you ever had a serious relationship?'

Charlotte snorted and gestured at her sedate outfit of grey trousers, white blouse and flat pumps. 'Do I look like the type of woman to inspire grand passions in any man?'

'Don't sell yourself short,' she said. 'Any guy would be lucky to have you.'

'Yeah, tell that to the hundreds of hotties batting down my door.'

Makayla grinned at her friend's dry response. 'So that's a no, then? No serious relationships?'

'No relationships, period.' Charlotte sighed and

shifted on her stool, uncomfortable. 'I dated occasionally in uni. Fellow accountancy students. No muss, no fuss kind of guys that were boring as hell.' She shook her head. 'At the risk of sounding like a cliché from one of those fabulous romances I read, I need a bad boy. Some big, bold, annoying, arrogant guy to rattle my cage.'

Makayla bit back her first retort, that the kind of guy Charlotte described would break her heart faster than she could say number-cruncher. 'Trust me, sweetie, you'll meet some great guy when you least expect it.'

Charlotte rolled her eyes. 'Yeah, and I'll morph into a sexy siren too.'

Makayla chose her next words carefully, not wanting to offend. 'We could do a makeover if you like? Play around with some different looks? Change it up a little with hair and make-up?'

Charlotte wrinkled her nose as if the milk in her hot chocolate had curdled. 'All that stuff just isn't me. Besides, when I meet a guy I want him to like me for me, not because of a few fake eyelashes and hair extensions.'

Makayla could relate. Hudson knew about her past, knew her faults, but liked her regardless. He'd even moved past his freak out of seeing her strip and that kind of acceptance was rare.

Hudson was a keeper. Pity she wouldn't be the one doing the keeping.

Makayla glanced at her watch and pulled a face. 'I have to get back to work.'

'Sure.' Charlotte pointed at the cabinet. 'Starting with serving me those pastries I ordered.'

Makayla smiled. 'Whichever guy is lucky enough to have you, I hope he has a French pastry addiction like you do.'

'If he doesn't, I'll convert him.' Charlotte hid a smile behind the mug as she lifted the hot chocolate to her lips, but Makayla recognised bittersweet when she saw it.

Charlotte was a homebody. The kind of woman who coveted the girly dream of a husband, kids, dog and a mortgage. From the way she kept their apartment spotless and whipped up comfort meals, she'd make a good wife. Makayla hoped that in chasing her dream, she didn't get her heart trampled on by some jerk in the process.

'One *beignet* and *pain au chocolat* coming up.'

However, as Makayla served Charlotte her order, then headed back to the kitchen, her thoughts circled back to what Tanner had said earlier.

She made Hudson happy, and Tanner had never seen him like that.

How happy would Hudson be when she walked away?

CHAPTER SIXTEEN

'WHEN YOU SAID we'd be eating the best burgers in town, I had no idea you'd bring me here.' Makayla stared around the run-down diner in the heart of Kings Cross, her eyes alight with joy. 'It's been at least six years since I last had one of Jonnie's specials.'

'That's what I thought,' he said, leaning against the faded red vinyl seat in a booth in the far corner near the jukebox. 'You rarely ate burgers back then anyway, always watching your weight.'

She crinkled her nose in disgust. 'Yeah, it almost became an obsession, until Mum talked sense into me.'

'Dancers need to be fit, not stick insects.' He snagged her hand across the table and lifted it to his lips. 'Besides, I happen to think you've got a sensational bod and I wouldn't change a thing.'

'Sweet talker,' she muttered, grinning when he brushed a kiss across the back of her hand before releasing it. 'I'm way too curvy for a dancer but I bust my ass working out in the gym and jogging daily to ensure I can still score the roles I want.'

Guilt lodged in his chest, as heavy as a stone, and he resisted the urge to rub it away.

He still hadn't mentioned the Broadway role Reg had told him about. The audition was a few days away and he knew he had to tell her. But he'd been looking forward to this date, to a stroll down memory lane, too much to spoil it.

Because he knew what would happen the moment he told Mak about the audition. She'd become obsessed, wanting to research the show, rehearse and focus on the biggest break of her career.

He didn't blame her. He would do the same. But that small stubborn part of him deep inside resisted telling her, at least for another day.

He would lose her. Nothing surer. He'd spent a lifetime doing right by other people; he could be a selfish prick for a few more hours.

'Is everything okay?'

He stiffened. He should be glad she could read him so well but it didn't help the guilt eating away at him. 'Yeah, why?'

'You keep drifting off the last two days, like you've got something on your mind?'

'Only you.' This time, when he reached for her hand, he didn't let go. 'I've never had a real relationship before and it's kinda distracting.'

'I know the feeling,' she said, giving his hand a

squeeze. 'I need to focus on opening night next week and making sure my footwork in the final samba is perfect, but sometimes at rehearsal I find myself thinking of other things.'

A cute blush stained her cheeks, making him want to haul her across the table and do wicked things to her.

'Like?'

The blush deepened. 'Like the way you take me in the shower every morning. Like the way you're so eager we barely make it to your bedroom most nights.'

The tip of her tongue darted out to moisten her bottom lip, an innocuous action that shot straight to his already hard cock. 'Like the way you use your tongue to make me forget every goddamn thing.'

Hudson shifted in the booth, trying to ease the constriction in his jeans. Yeah, like moving around would do that. Buried deep in Mak or being sucked dry by her luscious mouth was the only way to ease his aching cock.

'Do you have any idea what you do to me?' He threaded his fingers between hers. 'I'm tempted to say screw the burgers and let's get out of here.'

'You're hard?' She quirked an eyebrow, feigning innocence, and he bit back a groan. 'Pity these old booths don't have tablecloths.' A wicked smile curved her lips. 'I could've taken care of that little problem for you.'

'There's nothing little about my problem and you know it.'

'Modest, much?'

They laughed and this time it wasn't guilt making his chest heavy but his heart, doing some weird flip-flop that made breathing difficult.

This was what he'd always imagined it would be like between them. Friends who became lovers and it only solidified their bond. The kind of connection born of years of shared confidences. The kind of relationship bred from trust.

But she hadn't always trusted him. Not enough to tell him the entire truth, like that night indelibly etched on his brain when she'd ripped the blinkers from his eyes.

Now he was doing the same, withholding information from her.

What did that say about their relationship?

'Why did you start stripping?'

Damn, the question popped out before he could censor it, or at least dress it up in better terms.

Predictably, she tugged her hand free of his, wariness descending over her expression as it blanked.

'Is that why you brought me here, to bring up the past?' Her upper lip curled in disgust. 'You thought plying me with burgers like old times would get me to spill my guts?'

Shit. He'd blurted the question at a vulnerable moment, desperate to discover something that had bugged him for years. But in doing so he'd driven a wedge between them. So much for a day of sweet reminiscing.

'Our date here has nothing to do with me trying to soften you up,' he said, showing his palms to her like he had nothing to hide. 'I guess the closer we get, the more I don't want anything tainting what we have. And while we've moved past that night, I hate that it happened in the first place. That it's this thing between us, like an elephant in the room that we keep ignoring.'

Her eyes blazed with anger as she leaned forward, resting her forearms on the table. 'Do you have any idea what you did to me, saying all that hurtful stuff that night you saw me stripping before walking out of my life?'

She shook her head, but not before he glimpsed the sheen of tears.

Fuck. He'd made her cry.

'That night I saw you at Le Chat, I freaked because I didn't want that kind of life for you—'

'It wasn't your call to make,' she said, her voice barely above a hiss. 'You didn't question my motivation. You didn't ask for an explanation. Instead, you jumped to conclusions and judged me for it.'

She dragged a hand through her hair, making his palms itch to do the same. 'God, Hudson, I missed you so much. You were my best friend back then, the only person who really got me and suddenly you weren't there any more.'

She tapped at her chest. 'It was like you stuck a knife right here and I never recovered.'

Hudson never cried but for the first time in a long time, he felt the burn of tears. 'I'm so, so sorry. A lot of what I said that night had nothing to do with you and more to do with my own shit.'

She lifted her head a fraction, studying him with curiosity. 'What do you mean?'

Hudson had never told anyone about his mother. About his early suspicions, later solidified into the horrible truth. As a young kid he'd watched her spiral downhill, from a respectable waitress, to a stripper, to something far worse he'd discovered later...

It had killed him inside, watching the woman he idolised walk away from him without looking back.

That was the real reason he'd fought with Mak that fateful night, unable to stick around to watch her follow the same downtrodden path.

Losing his mum had devastated him. Losing Mak the same way would've finished him off.

So he'd removed himself completely, had cut ties with her and hadn't looked back.

He could trust her with the truth but something held him back. Some long-seated, deeply buried, self-protective mechanism that screamed he couldn't trust anyone, least of all the woman he'd hurt and who had the potential to hurt him right back.

'I'd been working the clubs, doing odd jobs, since I was ten. You knew that.' He rubbed a hand over his face. It did little to ease the tension. 'I saw too many women fall into the temptation of easy money by stripping. Then it became harder and they couldn't walk away. Some turned to drugs, others took the next step…' He trailed off, horrified when her expression turned glacial, as if she'd never look at him the same way again.

'I hated seeing you up there. Hated that you hadn't turned to me if you needed money. Hated that you hadn't trusted me enough to confide in me before you did it—'

'You're a moron,' she said, her tone low and lethal. 'Do you think I wanted to take my clothes off for a roomful of slobbering sleaze-bags? I needed the money fast to pay for Mum's funeral. She deserved that at least, after all the sacrifices she made for me over the years. So I accepted that job for one night. That's it.'

Sick to his stomach, he stared at the woman he'd misjudged, searching for the right thing to say and coming up empty.

'I saw how hard you worked, how desperate you were to escape the Cross, so no way in hell I would've approached you for that kind of money.' She shook her head, her glorious red hair tumbling over her shoulders and semi-shielding her face. 'I was ashamed of how far I had to go to get that money and no way in hell would I have told you about it. Then you walked in that night and you were a prick to me.'

'Fuck, I really messed up.' He rested his hands on the table, palms down, needing some kind of anchor in a world suddenly tipped on its ass. 'I wish I could turn back time and do it differently that night but I can't. I'm an idiot. But know that I was trying to protect you from a life you didn't deserve.'

The fury twisting her mouth eased. 'You're right about one thing. You're an idiot.'

'Was.' He tried a tentative smile. 'I'd like to think I'm smarter these days.'

'Debatable.' When she placed her hands over his, the tight band of anxiety squeezing his chest dissolved. 'So now that we've confronted the elephant, can we shoo him away and concentrate on the here and now?'

Hudson would like nothing better, but guilt still gnawed at him. He'd misjudged her badly that fateful night, had let his own preconceptions colour his judgement and make him jump to conclusions.

He felt like an idiot. Pissed too, that she hadn't come to him because he'd made such a big deal out of escaping the Cross. He'd known how she felt about stripping, how she'd vowed to make it as a dancer without having to do it, yet he hadn't trusted her enough and had jumped to conclusions.

He should've known there had to be something big

behind her decision to strip that night; he should've given her the benefit of the doubt.

Unfortunately he couldn't change the past, but he could make up for it by giving her the future she'd always dreamed of.

'Speaking of here and now, I've got some news you may like.'

She quirked an eyebrow, and he continued. 'Don't get your hopes up because nothing may come of this, but remember I mentioned I have contacts in the theatre industry?'

Her fingers involuntarily dug into his hands as she leaned forward a fraction. 'Yeah?'

'You've heard of Reg Grober?'

Her eyes widened. 'He's huge. Backs all the major theatre productions here and many overseas.'

'I ran into him yesterday and he mentioned an opening for a dancer in his latest show on Broadway. Asked me if I knew anyone—'

'Oh, my God, you didn't?'

'I did.' He grinned as she released his hands to clap hers in excitement. 'The audition is next week but Reg trusts my judgement, so you should be in with a good chance. In fact, I think he said that anyone I recommend would be a walk-in.'

She flopped back against the booth seat, her expression incredulous, two spots of colour staining her cheeks.

'You're serious?'

'Would I kid about something as important as this?' He smiled as he glimpsed the shimmer of tears in her eyes. 'I know this is your dream.'

'I—I don't know what to say…' She stood and moved around to his side of the booth, shooing him over.

When he moved over, she slid in next to him and flung her arms around him, burrowing into the crook of his neck. 'Thank you.'

'You're welcome.' He slid his arms around her and held her close, inhaling the tempting vanilla fragrance of her hair, wishing they could stay this way forever.

But all too soon she pulled away, returned to her seat and their burgers arrived. They ate, traded banter and swapped trade talk as they usually did.

Yet beneath it all Hudson could feel an undercurrent, a powerful force pulling Mak away from him.

He knew he'd done the right thing in telling her about the Broadway audition, even if it had been out of guilt.

But at what cost?

CHAPTER SEVENTEEN

MAKAYLA KNEW SHE should be listening to Hudson as they strolled the familiar back streets of Kings Cross, but her mind kept drifting back to the news he'd given her, casual as you like, over dinner.

He'd put her forward for an audition with Reg Grober. *The* Reg Grober. For a dance role on Broadway.

Freaking *Broadway*!

She'd pinched herself several times when he hadn't been looking then proceeded to digest one of Jonnie's famous burgers without tasting a thing. She could've been ingesting arsenic sprinkled on a mud pie for all the attention she'd paid her food.

Broadway.

Her dream from the first moment she'd slipped on tap shoes at age three.

Her mum had never laughed at her. Instead, she'd fostered her love of dance, scrimping and saving from her own jobs, as a part-time waitress and dancer, to pay for lessons. Jazz, tap, ballet, Makayla had done them all. And she'd practised until her toes bled, repeating routines in front of the cracked second-hand mirror in their tiny lounge room in a one-bedroom flat on top of Bluey's bar in Darlinghurst Road.

Though they'd lived in the heart of Kings Cross and Makayla had grown up around dive bars, her mum had instilled values in her from a young age. She might have seen stuff a kid shouldn't but she could never do those things herself.

That was part of why Hudson's misjudgement of her that one and only night she'd stripped had stung so damn bad. Makayla wouldn't have done it unless she was desperate, and he should've known that.

But after their earlier discussion it looked as if they'd finally moved past that night. He'd freaked out because he was trying to protect her. Good intentions, bad execution.

They'd cleared the air before he'd dropped his little bombshell.

And she hadn't been able to focus on anything else since.

'Hey, are you listening to me?'

She laughed and squeezed his hand. 'Honestly? I have no idea how far we've walked and I haven't heard half of what you've said.' She did a little jig on the spot. 'I can't stop thinking about the audition.'

'I knew you'd be like this when I told you.' He

grinned and swung their arms between them as they resumed walking. 'You're nothing if not predictable.'

'Hey, I resent that,' she said, bumping him with her hip.

However, he missed the wall and stumbled into a small opening between two buildings, tugging her with him. It could've passed for an alley if it weren't so narrow, barely enough room for the two of them. A snug fit. Snugger when she pressed against him and his back hit the wall.

'Predictable, huh?' She ground against him a little, his cock rubbing her sweet spot and making her breath hitch. 'Want me to show you how non-predictable I can be?'

Makayla had done many things in her lifetime. Sex in public wasn't one of them. But they were in a back alley, secluded from prying eyes. No one ever strolled this way. In fact, the only reason why they'd taken this route was because they'd done it years earlier, when he'd walked her home many times, defiantly confident that nobody would lay a finger on them because he was so well known in the Cross.

'You're serious?' His eyes glittered with excitement in the wan light spilling through the alley opening.

'Well, I need to dispel this preconception you have of me,' she said, snaking her hand between their bodies to cup his burgeoning boner. 'And what better way than to ravish you in an alley?'

She rubbed the length of him, savoured his low groan. 'Hot, fast, alley sex. What could be less predictable than that?'

He claimed her mouth in response, their teeth clashing a little in his eagerness to devour her. His tongue swept into her mouth, commanding and demanding, teasing and taunting until she strained against him, needing more.

She'd never been so thankful for wearing a dress when he rucked up the skirt, a firm hand kneading her ass while the other delved beneath her panties to finger her hot spot.

'I love how responsive you are,' he murmured against her ear, nipping the soft skin beneath it as he slid one finger inside her, another, while his thumb worked magic on her clit. 'So tight. So wet...'

She moaned as his thumb increased pressure, driving her to the brink faster than she could've thought possible. She had no idea if it was the fear of being seen, the bite of chill against her naked butt, or her being so confident in Hudson's ability to pleasure her, but whatever it was, her orgasm built quickly, making her quiver and strain towards it.

She clung to him as his thumb changed the angle on her clit slightly and pushed harder, faster, and she was gone. She sank her teeth into his shoulder as she came, pleasure spiralling upward and outward, wave upon wave until she sagged limp against him.

She was barely aware of him rummaging in his

pocket, unzipping and sheathing. But she knew what was coming and her body tensed in anticipation.

When he pressed against her, she hooked a leg around his waist, giving him all the access he needed to drive into her in one hard thrust.

Maybe it was the narrowness of the alley and the angle of their bodies, maybe it was the wantonness of the situation, maybe it was the heightened awareness of outdoor sex, but she'd never felt so turned on in all her life.

With every thrust she came alight, ripples of awareness spreading through her and making her tingle, her skin hypersensitive to his every touch, her body finely attuned to his in a way it had never been.

Every inch of her craved, every nerve ending buzzed. She'd turned into one of those static electricity balls, sparking wherever he touched her.

'You wanted hard and fast, right?'

'Yeah…' she gasped as he drove into her harder, faster, the beginnings of another orgasm teasing at the edges of her consciousness.

'What the lady wants,' he murmured, grabbing her ass and picking her up, angling her just right so she came apart again, so swiftly and spontaneously that she let out a yell he quickly silenced by covering her mouth with his.

He stiffened a moment later, and she swallowed his groan, the power of his orgasm making her wish they could do this all over again.

But all too quickly he'd lowered her until her feet touched the ground. Withdrew. Smoothed down her skirt before turning away to take care of business. While all Makayla could do was prop against the wall until the wobble in her legs subsided.

When he turned back, his grin lit up the alley. 'That was…' he shook his head, momentarily lost for words '…the hottest damn thing ever.'

He reached for her, hugged her tight. 'You're incredible, you know that?'

'Tell me something I don't know.'

Her sassy retort earned a chuckle, his chest reverberating against hers, before he eased back.

'Have you worked up an appetite for dessert? Perhaps we can have a nightcap and apple pie at Bluey's?'

'I'd like that,' she said, searching his face for some sign that what had just happened between them meant as much to him as it did to her.

She'd just had the hottest sex of her life—in public—which made her realise something: she never would've trusted any other guy this much.

Hudson made her feel cherished and safe and, dare she say it, loved.

It frightened the hell out of her.

She couldn't lose sight of her goal, especially when it could be within her grasp. If all went according to plan and she nailed the audition for Reg Grober she could be moving to New York sooner rather than later, and falling for Hudson would only complicate matters.

She couldn't fall in love with him.

She wouldn't.

But what if it was too late?

CHAPTER EIGHTEEN

HUDSON HADN'T BEEN a monk over the years. Being a manager in Sydney's hippest club ensured he never had any shortage of beautiful women wanting a piece of him. It didn't make him conceited. It was a fact he accepted with eternal gratitude.

But never in the years since he'd lost his virginity at fifteen to a much older woman who ran a bar in the Cross had he indulged in the kind of risqué sex he'd just had with Mak.

She'd blown his mind. Literally.

He'd brought her to the Cross for a stroll down memory lane. Never in his wildest dreams had he anticipated raunchy alley sex.

He'd never felt like this. Totally discombobulated. Mak constantly surprised him, with a knack for throwing him off-guard regularly. It made him wonder; did she do it on purpose, to keep him at an emotional distance? His musing was soon replaced by a darker supposition.

Had the phenomenal sex been her way of repaying him for the Grober audition?

He hated the mere thought of it, as it cheapened what they'd shared ten minutes ago. He didn't want her to feel grateful. Or as if she owed him anything.

What would she think if she knew he'd only blurted the news about the audition out of guilt for being such a prick in the past?

She'd reacted the way he'd anticipated too, her mind drifting and her responses vague, already pulling away from him. If they hadn't stumbled into that alley, would she have wanted to spend the rest of the evening with him or would she already be home, researching the Broadway show and all it entailed?

He hated feeling like this. Confused and concerned. So he'd done the only thing he could think of to re-establish equilibrium; brought her to Bluey's and hoped that memories of their shared past would strengthen the bonds between them now.

'How long since you've been here?' He held the door open for her and waited until she entered before following.

'Too long,' she said, rapidly blinking as she glanced around the bar. 'I can't believe it looks the same.'

'You know Bluey. If it ain't broke, don't fix it.' He guided her through the throng of late-night jazz fans that crowded the bar.

Every table was full and the standing-room area near the stage had people ten deep. Hudson was glad.

A packed house would keep Bluey busy and hopefully not focussed on his impending trip to see the big guy upstairs.

'It even smells the same,' Mak said, inhaling deeply and closing her eyes. 'Fried onion rings and bourbon.'

Hudson knew what she meant. Every place he'd ever worked back then had its own smell, some more pleasant than others. Bluey's had always smelled good to him because he knew he'd find Mak here, holed up in a small room off the main bar. Doing homework. Flicking through magazines. Keeping busy while her mum worked a shift.

He touched her hand when he spotted Bluey. 'I spy someone who would love to see you.'

Her eyes opened and zeroed in on the hallway leading from the main bar to the back. 'Oh, my God, he looks awful.'

'You might need to keep that gem to yourself,' he said, guiding her towards Bluey, whose eyes lit up the moment he spied them. 'Bloody cancer. So unfair.'

'He looks skeletal,' she murmured, reaching for Hudson's hand and holding on tight. 'Poor Bluey.'

However, as they neared him, she pasted a smile on her face, released Hudson's hand and enveloped the older man in a hug. 'It's been too long.'

'You got that right, girlie.' Bluey's arms wrapped around her, and Hudson had to look away for fear the emotion clogging his throat would be too easily read on his face.

When they eventually disengaged, Hudson glanced back to find Bluey staring at Mak with tears in his eyes.

'You're the spitting image of your mother.' He reached out to touch her hair. 'Even the same striking colour.'

'Mum was beautiful so I guess I'm lucky.'

'She sure was.' Bluey cleared his throat and gestured at the bar. 'What'll you have to drink?'

'Chardonnay for me, please.' She glanced at Hudson. 'You?'

Hudson needed something stronger tonight, something that would chase away his funk and the insistent rumblings deep inside that he'd already lost Mak.

'Whisky, neat.'

Bluey's eyebrows raised in comical disbelief. 'First time you've ever had a man's drink in all these years.'

'I'm shaking things up tonight.' Hudson shot Mak a meaningful look, and she blushed.

Bluey snorted and poked Mak in the arm. 'Word of advice, girlie. Don't let this fool sweet talk you.'

'Might be too late for that,' she said, smiling as she slid an arm around his waist and rested her head against his shoulder. 'He's kinda charming when he wants to be.'

Bluey snorted again, unable to hide a grin. 'I'll be right back with those drinks. Make yourself comfortable in the nook.'

'So you think I'm charming, huh?' He backed her into the nook where they'd once spent countless hours chatting and nuzzled her neck. 'Because you ain't seen nothing yet.'

'Hmm…' She almost purred as he nibbled his way across her jaw, down her neck, to the tender spot above her shoulder. 'Want to hear something perverted?'

He lifted his head to stare at her. 'Always.'

'What you're doing now, here? I used to fantasise about it happening a lot back then.' An adorable blush stained her cheeks. 'And I filled an awful lot of notebooks with our initials intertwined in hearts when everyone thought I was doing homework.'

Nostalgia gripped him, squeezing his chest in a vice. 'Your crush was reciprocated one hundred per cent but the age thing…'

'Yeah, I know. Everybody would've flipped if we'd started dating back then.' A cheeky glint darkened her eyes. 'Especially if we were as naughty then as we are now.'

'Naughty doesn't begin to describe it,' he said, his cock instantly at half-mast at the mention of what they'd indulged in less than twenty minutes earlier.

'Then maybe we can think up other words. Later.'

She arched her pelvis into his, her smile positively wicked.

'You're insatiable,' he muttered, brushing a kiss across her lips. 'And I like it. A lot.'

'For Pete's sake, get a room,' Bluey said, entering the nook and placing a tray with drinks on the table in the corner. 'I always pegged you for a smart girl, Mak. Don't know what you see in this bozo.'

'He has his good points.' She laughed and slipped out of his arms, before taking a seat at the table. 'One of them being the fact he doesn't forget his friends.'

She winced and reached to cover Bluey's hand with hers where it rested on the table. 'I'm sorry I haven't been around.'

'Shit happens.' Bluey shrugged but Hudson saw how much Mak's admission meant in the set of his jaw. 'You moved on after your mum died. A natural progression.'

'Yeah, but I should've popped in to visit.' The corners of her mouth downturned. 'Hudson told me. About the cancer.'

'Like I said, shit happens.' Bluey blinked a few times before his jaw clenched. 'I'm dying. So let's not waste this visit overstating the obvious and talk about other stuff.'

Bluey's gaze turned shifty. 'Tell me what's going on between you two.'

Mak said, 'Nothing,' at the same time as Hudson and Bluey laughed.

'Hey, I won't tell anyone.' Bluey tapped the side of his nose. 'What happens at Bluey's stays at Bluey's.'

Hudson waited for Mak to say something, not wanting to overstep and say the wrong thing: like the fact he was in a relationship with Mak but it could end at any moment.

Mak flashed a cheeky smile at them both. 'Hudson's sort of my boss at the moment so I'm not supposed to say anything, but…' She crooked her finger at Bluey. 'I had a massive crush on him years ago so you can't blame a girl for losing her head and falling for him a little.'

Hudson grinned. She'd admitted to falling for him. That had to be a good thing moving forward. So why did he feel like her admission was some kind of consolation prize considering she'd be leaving soon?

Bluey rolled his eyes. 'At least he's a good guy.'

'Thanks for that rousing endorsement.' Hudson lifted his Scotch in a toast. 'To old times. And old timers.'

Bluey picked up his dark rum, his poison of choice for as long as Hudson could remember, and clinked glasses. 'To making the most of every minute.'

'To us,' Mak added, her simple toast meaning more than she could've imagined when she locked gazes with him, trying to convey a message he had no hope of interpreting.

Was she realising that his revelation earlier meant the end of them? That the odds were in her favour to pack up and head to New York without him? Did she care?

They'd never stipulated a time line for this relationship. Hell, they'd never spelled out much of anything. They'd given in to a long-held passion without articulating what this would mean if things got serious.

Because they'd both been stupid enough to believe it wouldn't.

After their first stupendous night together, Mak had said she wouldn't let a relationship stop her from achieving her career goals. He'd said he was happy to play this whatever way she wanted.

But what happened when Mak wanted to end this before it had really begun?

'Speaking of old times, want to hear something crazy?' Bluey slammed his glass down on the table a tad hard and winced. 'Because of the insane crush I had on your mum, I didn't touch your flat after she died and you moved out.'

'What?' Mak stilled, shock widening her eyes. 'You didn't rent it out to someone else?'

Bluey shook his head. 'Couldn't bear to change it.' He blushed and rubbed a hand over his face. 'At the risk of you thinking I'm a looney old man, I like going in there sometimes, reminiscing.'

'Wow.' Mak slumped back in her chair. 'Can I ask you something?'

'You can ask. I might not answer,' Bluey said, sounding embarrassed.

'Why didn't you ever tell Mum how you felt?'

'Are you kidding? She was way out of my league.' A deep frown slashed Bluey's brow. 'But there isn't a day that goes by now that I don't regret not having the balls to speak up and tell her.'

Something shifted in Hudson's chest, an uncomfortable flip-flop that left him wanting to rub away the odd ache. Did he have the balls to speak up? To tell Mak that, for him, this relationship was more than a transient thing?

He'd never been in a relationship that lasted beyond a few dates. Had never met a woman that captured his attention for longer than that. But Mak was the whole package. She entranced and captivated and totally bamboozled him on so many levels he wouldn't know where to start if he did try to articulate his feelings.

Initially, he'd thought the powerful pull between them had more to do with the past; that he'd finally got what he'd wanted and it was as good as he'd imagined.

But it was more than that and he knew it. Problem was, did she?

'For what it's worth, she never talked about guys but your name slipped into conversation often,' Mak said, patting Bluey's hand. 'In fact, I could've sworn you two might've had something going on in secret but were trying to shield me from it.'

Bluey's blush intensified and he swore under his breath. 'I wish. The closest I got to letting your mum know I was sweet on her was the requisite smooch on New Year's Eve.' A slow grin spread across his face. 'I always made sure she worked that shift.'

'Real smooth,' Hudson said, wishing Bluey had taken his chance when he'd had the opportunity.

Whatever happened with him and Mak, he'd never regret the time they'd spent together. But he still wanted more. He was greedy like that.

'You can go up and check out the flat if you like?' Bluey downed the rest of his rum. 'I need to get back out front.'

Mak's eyes lit up. 'I'd love to.'

Hudson hesitated, unsure whether to follow Bluey or stay with Mak. He didn't want to intrude on her stroll down memory lane but had the damnedest impulse to stay by her side. Like she was already slipping away if he let her out of his sight. Crazy.

Bluey waved as he headed into the main bar, leaving Hudson feeling like an extra wheel.

'Want to come with me?' Mak stood and held out her hand. 'Get a glimpse of my old bedroom, where I spent way too many hours lusting over you.'

He exhaled in relief and took her hand. 'You had exquisite taste.'

'Or way too much time on my hands and a woe-

ful social life where I didn't get to meet any boys
but you so—'

'Quit while you're ahead,' he said, tugging her
into the corridor to sneak a kiss.

A long, deep, open-mouthed kiss that quickly escalated into his cock being hard and yearning to be
inside her.

'We'll combust if we're not careful,' she whis-
pered against the side of his mouth, kissing her way
along his jaw towards his ear, where she nipped the
lobe. 'I like how hot we are together.'

'Me too.' He ground against her to prove it, enjoying her soft mewl of pleasure. 'But doing it in
the hallway of Bluey's seems almost sacrilegious.'

'Then let's get upstairs ASAP.' She tugged on
his hand, half bounding up the stairs, leaving him
no option but to follow, bemused and hopeful and
incredibly horny.

He liked the fact she wanted him as much as he
wanted her. That she'd instigated that frigging hot
alley sex. But it seemed that whenever they entered
emotional territory, like her admissions at the table
a few minutes ago, she immediately reverted to the
physical stuff. Whether as a distraction or a coping mechanism for feeling out of her depth, he had
no idea.

He should question it. Ask her. But he couldn't
formulate the words, with all his blood drained south.
He'd ask. Later. Much later.

'I've never been up here,' he said when she paused outside a door at the top of the landing.

'Bluey never let anyone up here but his tenants.' She leaned against the door, her hand still gripping his. 'I almost plucked up the courage to invite you up here one day when Mum was out, but Bluey must've got an inkling of what I was up to because he invented some lame-ass job to send you on when you arrived and that was the end of that.'

'Better late than never, I guess.' They smiled at each other, goofy grins reflecting their shared pasts and how far they'd come.

'Come on, before this trip down memory lane makes me blubber.' She turned towards the door and tested the handle.

The door swung open and the first thing that hit him as they stepped inside was how clean the place was.

'Looks like Bluey has someone come in here once a week.'

'Yeah,' she said, so softly he barely heard.

When she tugged her hand free he released her, closing the door behind them as she drifted into the tiny apartment.

The place appeared threadbare: a frayed cotton two-seater sofa, cracked vinyl armchair, dining table for two, kitchenette. Two doors led from the sole room: one into a bathroom, the other into a bedroom.

Amazing that Mak and her mum hadn't got on

each other's nerves in such a confined space. He'd
had much more room at home but it hadn't helped
his relationship with his father. It wouldn't have
mattered if they'd had the entire continent between
them—dear old dad would've found a way to make
his life hell.

'It seems so much smaller now,' she said, as if
reading his mind, slipping off her shoes to pad towards the bedroom. 'Mum always made me take my
shoes off at the door. Said it was better for my dancer
feet, to let them flex and extend naturally.'

'You've never felt the urge to come back here?'

It surprised him. For someone who loved her mum
as much as Mak had, to go as far as stripping to get
money for her funeral, that she hadn't been back to
the place she grew up.

She shrugged and leaned in the bedroom doorway, her expression downcast. 'This place held no
interest once Mum died. It wouldn't have mattered
where we lived because Mum was home to me, not
the apartment.'

'You're lucky you were so close.' He hesitated,
before adding, 'I envy you that.'

'You've never thought of trying to find your
mum?'

The familiar sick feeling deep in his gut that
thoughts of his mum elicited made him wish he'd
never come up here. He couldn't tell Mak the truth.
Couldn't ruin this night, the evening she might have

finally got her big break, and taint it with what he'd discovered when he'd gone in search of his mother. The truth had almost killed him. He didn't want Mak's pity. Not tonight. So after a lifetime of practice, he schooled his face into lack of interest. 'No point trying to find someone who doesn't want to be found.'

'Your dad never tried?'

'My dad's an asshole,' he snapped, instantly regretting his show of emotion for a subject that was off-limits.

He never discussed his shitty family life with anyone. Only Tanner had an idea of how bad things had been with his dad back then, but even his best friend didn't know the half of it.

Now, having Mak prod at a deep festering, well-hidden sore spot only served to reinforce what he already knew.

That his past had no right interfering with his future.

He worked his ass off so he could pay for his dad's special accommodation fees. He did his part. Even though the old bastard didn't deserve it.

He made the obligatory visits at Christmas and on his father's birthday—that was it, the extent of his familial obligations. Much easier to throw money at the problem and maintain his distance than be a sadist and inflict pain on himself that inevitably happened whenever he saw the old man.

Mak held up one hand and pretended to write on it with the other. 'Note to self. Avoid all talk of families.'

'Sorry.' He swiped a hand over his face. 'Sore point.'

'I gathered.' She crossed the tiny living room and held out her hands to him. 'Want the grand tour?'

He glanced around. 'Looks like I've seen most of it.'

'Not the bedroom.' She slipped her hands into his and stepped into his personal space, close enough that her nipples brushed his chest.

Just like that, he forgot his past and focussed on the here and now.

'Lead the way.' He backed her towards the bedroom, step by step, slow and steady, not breaking eye contact.

'What would you have done if I'd tried to lead you astray five years ago?' She batted her eyelashes, her smile coy.

'Being older and wiser, I would've been the ultimate gentleman, of course.' He paused in the doorway of the bedroom, quickly scanned the small interior. Two single beds. Uncomfortable but doable. Considering the alley hadn't posed any problems, a single bed wouldn't stop him.

'Lucky for me, you're not so wise any more.' She clutched at his shirt and tugged him close for a kiss. One of her signature 'I want to devour you as fast as humanly possible' kisses that never failed to leave him breathless and hard.

She had this way of using her tongue that drove him wild. Short thrusts, languid sweeps, keeping him guessing. Off-kilter and lusting.

'You sure this isn't too weird?' He backed her towards the nearest bed, hoping like hell she wouldn't renege now.

'Are you kidding? I fantasised about you being in here with me all the time back then.' She unzipped his fly and slid her hand inside, making him groan. 'I'd fall into bed at the end of a day, exhausted from homework and dance classes, too wired to sleep.'

She stroked the length of him, the gleam in her eyes beyond wicked. 'So I'd imagine you here. Lying with me.' She rolled her thumb over the head of his cock and he tensed. 'Touching me.'

Carefully withdrawing her hand, she proceeded to unsnap the top button of his jeans and push them down his legs, along with his jocks. 'Lucky for me, the reality of you far surpasses my imagination back then.'

'Did you touch yourself while thinking of me?'

'Yeah. Just like this.' She blushed and slid her hands slowly down her front in response. Skimming her breasts. Tweaking her nipples. Before rucking up her dress and sliding her fingers under the elastic of her panties.

'Fuck me,' he said, mesmerised by the sight of Mak pleasuring herself.

'All in good time, my friend,' she said, her smile coy as she pushed her panties down, then returned to playing with herself.

Pushing her middle finger between her folds. Circling. Rubbing. Until her breathing altered, coming in short pants.

Torn between pleasure and pain, he gripped his cock, sliding his fist up and down, wanting to be inside her but unwilling to stop the erotic show.

'Would you like to finish me off?' She lifted her finger, glistening with moisture, towards him, like some prized offering, and his cock twitched.

He didn't have to be asked twice.

Thankful he'd had the foresight to start packing several condoms in his wallet since they'd started dating, he rolled one on in record time before hoisting her slightly and sliding in to the hilt. Savoured the first slide into tight, wet heat, slightly wondrous as she clenched around him, making him feel like a goddamn king.

It was like this every single time. So good. So bad, because he couldn't help but acknowledge the fleeting thought that each time could be their last and where the fuck would that leave him?

'I need to come now,' she said, her demand throaty, as she lifted one leg to rest her foot on the bed.

Determined to eradicate his doubts and focus on

pleasure, he grabbed her ass, angled her forward so he dragged across her clit with every thrust.

'Oh, yeah, just like that.' Her head fell back as she arched her body against his in abandon, the sexiest damn thing he'd ever seen. Her skin sweat-slicked. Her lips parted. Her eyes glazed with passion. 'Now, Hudson. Now…'

He drove into her like a man possessed, oblivious to everything but the exquisiteness of being inside this woman. The mind-blowing ecstasy when his orgasm ripped through him like a freight train, shattering his barriers, exposing him like never before.

Mak yelled at the same time he did, her head snapping up so fast she almost knocked him out.

He didn't care. The only thing he cared about was keeping this woman in his life for longer than today, tomorrow and the day after that.

'I love—' Fuck, he'd almost slipped up and said he loved her. Too much too soon, if her startled expression was any indication. So he quickly added, '—doing this,' throwing in a bashful half-shrug for good measure.

'Me too,' she said, brushing an all-too-brief peck on his lips before disengaging.

Uh-oh. Was her abrupt withdrawal a result of his botched admission or a figment of his imagination?

A knock on the door sounded, and her eyes widened in surprise. 'I'll get that.' She jerked her thumb over her shoulder. 'There's another door through to the bathroom if you need to tidy up.'

Considering he was standing there with a condom to be disposed of and naked from the waist down, that might be a good idea.

'Thanks,' he said, his heart sinking as she all but bolted from the bedroom.

Yeah, there was definitely something up. Just frigging great.

He heard murmured voices from the living room so slipped into the bathroom, closed the door to the lounge room and tidied up. When he heard the door close, he opened the bathroom door and peered into the living room. To find a veritable feast laid out on the small dining table.

She waved him over. 'I don't know whether to be appalled or grateful that Bluey sent this up, thinking we may have worked up an appetite.'

'He said that?'

She shook her head. 'No, he sent one of his minions up with the message and the food.'

'Crazy old coot.' As Hudson neared the table and spied the food, his stomach rumbled. 'But remind me to thank him when we get downstairs.'

Bluey had sent up fried onion rings, buffalo wings, BBQ ribs and fries, with two gigantic pieces of apple pie and two bottles of lemonade.

'I'm starving,' Mak said, handing him a plate to dish up. 'Feels like I had that hamburger days ago.'

'I think we've worked off that meal twice,' he deadpanned, watching her reaction carefully, thankful when she laughed, the awkwardness of a few minutes ago gone.

'I've certainly worked up an appetite,' she said, piling her plate high before taking a seat at the table. 'Best workout ever.'

He held up his hand. 'I'm more than happy to assume the role of your personal trainer.' He winked. '*Very* personal trainer.'

'You're hired,' she said, raising a bottle of lemonade at him in a toast. 'To many sweaty workouts together.'

'I'll drink to that.' He clinked his lemonade bottle against hers and took a healthy swig. 'You really think Bluey sent us up here because he thought we'd fuck?'

'No idea, but considering the way you look at me it wouldn't take an Einstein to figure it out.' She picked up a wing and started gnawing on it with indelicate bites that made him laugh.

'And how do I look at you?'

'Like I'm this.' She brandished the wing. 'And you're particularly ravenous.'

He grinned and shrugged. 'A guy's gotta eat.'

'Yeah.' Her eyes darkened with passion, hopefully remembering the many ways he'd eaten her since they'd got together.

'You need to stop looking at me like that,' he

said, helping himself to some food. 'I need energy if you're about to pounce on me again.'

'Fair enough.' She made short work of the wing and consumed five ribs before he'd eaten a few onion rings.

'Wow, you really are hungry.'

'It's this food,' she said, gesturing at the diminishing feast. 'Bluey used to send up this stuff regularly for Mum and me if she'd pulled a double shift or danced at another club. He's so thoughtful.'

With that, a lone tear trickled down her cheek and she swiped it away with her free hand. 'Damn, being back here has me all sentimental.'

'I get it.'

And he did. He'd felt the same way when he'd come in to see Bluey last week yet he'd never lived here. How much worse must the nostalgia be for Mak?

'Being back here, in this flat, makes me realise perhaps I shouldn't have shunned my past so much.' She laid down a rib and wiped her hands on a napkin, her expression guarded. 'After Mum's funeral I got the hell out of the Cross and never looked back. But I shouldn't have done that.' She shook her head, her mouth downturned. 'I shouldn't have let that one night I stripped taint all the great memories of growing up here.'

'Is that why you left?'

She gnawed on her bottom lip, nodded. 'Yeah,

I felt so dirty. I couldn't walk down the street any more without thinking every guy was leering at me, that they'd taken a front-row seat to my humiliation.' She held up her hand. 'And before you can apologise again, my leaving had nothing to do with your freak out.' She patted her chest. 'It was all me. But I shouldn't have ignored my past. I loved growing up in the Cross. This was my home and I felt safe. I should've kept in touch with Bluey. He was always so good to me.'

'He knows you care, in here.' He pointed to his heart. 'People who mean the most to us know how we feel about them even if we haven't seen them in ages and Bluey's one of the good guys. He knows how you feel.'

'Stop, you'll make me bawl,' she murmured, swiping a hand across her eyes. 'Did you know he used to buy my favourite teen magazines and leave them lying in the nook for when I got home from school?'

The image of big, bad Bluey raiding the local newsagent for teen magazines made Hudson smile. 'That's going above and beyond.'

'And not just that,' she said, her eyes glazed, lost in memories. 'He'd make sure the dance floor was clear for an hour a day after school so I could practise. No band rehearsals, no roadies doing sound checks, just me and my music.'

'He's a thoughtful guy.' Hudson didn't add that maybe Bluey had lavished affection on Mak because he'd never had kids of his own and he'd had a massive crush on her mum.

'He even lent me money once, when I wanted to buy Mum a special perfume for her birthday.' She pressed the pads of her fingertips to her eyes and took a few breaths, blowing out slowly. 'Doesn't seem fair, that I've only just reconnected and he'll be gone soon.'

Sadly, life wasn't fair. He knew that better than anyone. But Mak didn't need his cynicism right now.

'Bluey's a realist. And I think you are too. Life's hectic, for everyone. He gets it. Just pop in when you can. He'll appreciate it.'

He made it sound so simple when in reality if Mak nailed the Grober audition she'd be heading overseas sooner rather than later. But he didn't want to think about that now and he certainly didn't want that putting a dampener on what was left of this evening.

'Who made you so wise?' She balled her serviette and threw it at him.

He caught it and waggled a finger at her. 'I've always been wise, babe. Took you long enough to wake up to it.'

She poked her tongue out at him, grabbed a few fries and swiped them through ketchup. 'Thank you,' she said, popping the fries into her mouth and chewing, eyeing him with gratitude.

'For what?'

'For bringing me here today.' She gestured around

the room. 'I needed to reconnect with my past. I just hadn't realised how much until tonight.'

'You're welcome.'

Damned if that uncomfortable ache in his chest wasn't back, as if he'd eaten too many barbecue ribs.

She glanced at him from beneath lowered lashes. 'Can I tell you something?'

'Anything.'

'Sharing this trip down memory lane has been extra special because you're here.'

That annoying ache intensified, making him want to blurt exactly how he felt. But she hadn't called him on his earlier slip-up. In fact, she couldn't have run out of the bedroom any faster if she'd tried, which told him exactly how this would go if he blabbed his true feelings.

'I've enjoyed being here.' He forced a warm smile, when in fact he wanted to haul her into his arms and bury his face in her hair.

'Okay, enough of the mushy stuff.' She snapped her fingers. 'Let's demolish this amazing food, then you can take me home.' Her eyes sparkled with enthusiasm. 'I have a very important audition to research.'

Any hope he'd harboured of spending the night withered and died right then. This was important to her. Her lifelong dream. He got it.

Didn't mean he had to like it.

CHAPTER NINETEEN

SINCE CHARLOTTE'S NEW boss had appeared on the scene, it wasn't unusual for her flatmate to stay late at work and get home around midnight. Makayla had never been gladder to have the place to herself than tonight.

Hudson had dropped her off thirty minutes ago. She'd showered, changed into her old cotton rugby jersey and sat on the sofa ever since, doing an online search for Reg Grober's upcoming shows.

The extent of Reg's backing in the theatre world blew her mind. As for the Broadway show she'd be auditioning for…if she got it, she'd be set. A major gold star on her CV. Leading to the type of roles she'd only ever dreamed about until now.

This was it.

Her big break.

So why the niggle of worry that wouldn't quit?

She knew the cause. Hudson. The guy who'd stolen her heart once before and had recaptured it a second time around.

But this time was worse, so much worse. This time, she'd become emotionally invested to the point of envisaging him in her life every single day and he had too.

She'd been sure he'd been on the verge of blurting his feelings in her old bedroom. He'd said the L word, before masking it with some lame sidestep. And she'd been glad. Relieved. It was too much, too soon. She couldn't handle landing her dream job and dream man in the same night.

Unfortunately, the two would be mutually exclusive.

Get the job, lose the guy.

It should be a no-brainer. She'd told him right from the start that she'd never let any man jeopardise her dream. He knew the score. But outlining a bunch of clear-cut rules to continue having the best sex of her life was a far cry from falling for him and realising she couldn't have it all, no matter how much she wanted it.

A key rattled in the door a second before it opened, and Charlotte padded into the room, holding her shoes in one hand, a briefcase in the other. She jumped when she caught sight of Makayla sitting in the semi-darkness.

'Hey, everything okay?'

'Grab the wine and I'll let you know.'

'Okay.' Charlotte dumped her shoes and briefcase before heading to the kitchen. 'Though I'd rather have a hot chocolate at this time of night.'

'Make mine a double,' Makayla called out, knowing that even the smoothness of decadent chocolate wouldn't help her sleep tonight.

Her head was a spinning whirl of 'what ifs' and 'maybes' that no amount of alcohol or chocolate could dull.

'Here you go, a Charlie special with extra marshmallows.' Charlotte handed her a mug and sank into the armchair opposite.

'Charlie? I thought you hated being called that.'

'I do.' Charlotte wrinkled her nose. 'Not only is my new boss a sadistic prick who gets off by torturing me from afar with enough work for ten people, he's now taken to calling me Charlie over the phone.'

'And you put up with it?'

'I need this job.' Charlotte cradled her mug in both hands and blew on the steaming drink. 'But I promise you this. The day that the Neanderthal sets foot in the office in person is the day I accidentally on purpose drive a stake through his heart.'

Makayla laughed. 'I'd like to see that.'

'Anyway, tell me about your day and why you're out here sitting in the dark. Didn't you have a dinner date with Mr Gorgeous? I thought you'd be staying over at his place tonight.'

'Loads happened so I thought it better I sleep here tonight.'

'Uh-oh. Trouble in paradise?'

Makayla shook her head. 'Not trouble as such, more like complications.'

'Want to talk about it?' Charlotte sipped at her hot chocolate. 'I may have zero experience with men but I'm a good listener.'

Makayla didn't know where to start. So she left out the phenomenal sex-capades and the stroll down memory lane, and jumped in at the deep end.

'Hudson has used his influence in the theatre industry to get me an audition with a media mogul who needs a dancer for his latest show on Broadway.'

Charlotte almost spat her hot chocolate out. 'Really? Oh, my God, that's incredible.'

'Yeah, I know, right? I'm over the moon. Can't quite believe it, to be honest. Not that I have the gig yet, but I have a shot and that's incredible in itself.'

A frown dented Charlotte's brow. 'So what's the problem?'

Makayla cupped her hands around the mug, letting the warmth infuse her. It didn't remove the chill seeping through her bones at the thought of walking away from Hudson.

'I may have fallen for Hudson and I don't want to be in love, because it'll ruin everything I've worked so hard for. Plus I don't want to hurt him after he's been so great to me, casting me as the lead in his show here then giving me this other incredible opportunity. So I'm feeling torn between my dream and the guy, when I shouldn't be. It shouldn't be an issue. I'd usually pick the dream every time. But this is *Hudson*…argh…' She ran out of steam and slumped back in the sofa, careful not to slosh hot chocolate everywhere.

Charlotte stared at her with round eyes. 'That's some dilemma.'

'Tell me about it.' Makayla sipped at her hot chocolate. The faster she drank it, the less likelihood she'd end up wearing it if this discussion got animated. 'You're the least boy-crazy woman I know, Charlotte. You're sensible and logical and I value your unbiased opinion. So tell me what you think.'

Charlotte hesitated before placing her mug on the coffee table and resting her hands in her lap. 'Okay, but before I say anything, you know I've never had a boyfriend so maybe I'm not qualified to give any advice.' Charlotte blushed. 'I'm a sad case, I know. Still want my opinion?'

'Please. You're sensible and I need that right now.' Makayla nodded. 'You can talk me down off this ledge of my own making.'

'Well.' Charlotte blew out a breath. 'Is there a chance you can have the proverbial cake and eat it too? Get the job and the guy?'

'How? If I get the job I'll be based in New York indefinitely, which is my dream. I can't ask Hudson to wait around for me. I wouldn't do that to him.'

Charlotte frowned. 'Good point. What about a long-distance relationship?'

A flare of hope made Makayla sit up before she slumped again. 'I won't have the funds to fly back and see him once every six months and I wouldn't expect him to make all the effort, flying all that way to see me. Wouldn't be fair.' She shook her head. 'Besides, have you seen how hot he is? Could I really expect him to fend off countless women for the chance of intermittent phone sex and a face-to-face once or twice a year?'

'If he feels the same way you do, he might be interested?'

He did feel the same way and that was part of her problem. If she made it on Broadway, she didn't need the distraction of wondering if Hudson was okay with their long-distance arrangement, of how he was coping and with whom.

She'd maintained her independence until now for a reason. Nothing and no one came between her and her dream. Unfortunately, her stupid heart had betrayed her this time and she felt far more for the guy than she should.

'Sorry, sweetie, the long-distance suggestion is about as logical as I get at this time of night.' Charlotte smothered a yawn. 'Let's sleep on it and I'll let you know if I come up with anything in the morning.'

'Thanks for listening.' Mak finished off the last of her hot chocolate and stood. 'On a more practical note, you mentioned moving out a few weeks ago and our lease comes up for renewal soon. With me potentially moving, shall I inform the agent to go ahead and advertise it?'

'No. Give me a few more weeks,' Charlotte said, wrinkling her nose. 'The place I had my eye on is way more than this one and if I can't take any more of the boss's crap, I may be looking for a new job soon.'

'Okay.' Makayla hesitated, knowing her flatmate's love life was none of her business, but feeling obligated to say something. 'Don't shoot the messenger, okay? But you'll never find a boyfriend if you don't go out. Mingle. Have fun.'

'I go out,' Charlotte said, crossing her arms in classic defensive posture.

'Grocery shopping and yoga don't count.'

Charlotte poked out her tongue. 'I know you're right but I can't summon the energy to go on bad dates. And the online sites or app thing isn't my scene.' She blushed. 'I'm not into casual hook-ups.'

Makayla covered her mouth in mock horror. 'Don't tell me you want a commitment.'

This time, Charlotte blew a raspberry. 'Something like that.'

'I'll make you a deal. Whatever happens with this audition, we'll have a girls' night out end of next week. Drag Abby along too so she's not tied to that ball and chain Tanner.'

Charlotte stared at her as if she'd proposed they

trawl the streets looking for men. 'I'm not really the going-out type. I hate putting on make-up and I never have anything to wear and I don't like—'

'No excuses.' Makayla held up her hand. 'We're doing this.'

Charlotte eventually nodded. 'Fine.'

'Good.' As Makayla headed for the kitchen to rinse her mug, she paused in the doorway. 'So what would a good boyfriend entail for you? Big biceps? Big pecs? Big dick—'

The cushion Charlotte flung hit her in the head, and she laughed. 'You know, I have a feeling the right guy for you is just around the corner.'

Charlotte rolled her eyes and remained silent.

Unfortunately, Makayla had already found the right guy. She just had no idea how to hold on to him; or even if she wanted to.

CHAPTER TWENTY

HUDSON JABBED AT the punching bag over and over. Left hook. Right. Repeating the mindless exercise until sweat drenched his body and dripped into his eyes. Only then did he stop for a breather, unlacing the gloves with his teeth and tugging them off before reaching for a towel.

He swiped his face with it and draped it around his neck, taking a seat on a nearby bench while slugging water. While it quenched his thirst, it did little for the tightness in his throat. The same tightness that had plagued him since he'd blurted his feelings last night.

Even now, twenty-four hours later, he couldn't believe he'd almost told Mak he loved her. His save, 'I love…doing this,' had been lame at best. And he still had no idea if she'd bought it or not. She'd bolted so fast from the bedroom that he had an idea she hadn't.

If a woman fled after hearing that the guy she was dating loved her, it wasn't a good sign. But it had jolted him back to reality. Until that moment, he'd been living in fantasyland, thinking that Mak's enthusiasm for sex and wanting to spend time with him meant she cared.

Sadly, the only thing Mak cared about was dancing and, while he admired her for being so invested in her work, he couldn't help but resent it.

The moment he'd told her about the Broadway audition, he'd lost her.

He'd known it would happen, which was why he'd held off so long.

What sort of asshole did that make him?

After flinging his towel away, he stretched out the kinks in his neck. It did little to ease the tension bunching his shoulder muscles. He'd thought a good workout at Jim's would soothe his frustration at a seemingly untenable situation. It hadn't.

Mak was an amazing dancer, one of the best he'd ever seen. She'd land the Broadway role and leave, nothing surer. Leaving behind the chump who'd fallen for her.

He should be happy for her. He was happy for her.

If he kept mentally reciting it long enough, he might actually believe it.

'Fuck,' he muttered, his hands unconsciously clenching into fists, and he stood, ready for another workout.

However, before he could slip his gloves back on, a kid claimed the punching bag he'd been using. A teen, about fourteen, with dyed black dreadlocks caught off his face in a headband, five piercings in each ear, another in his eyebrow and two in his lip. But that wasn't what captured Hudson's attention. The surly, defiant expression on the kid's face did.

He looked exactly how Hudson had at the same age.

Angry at the world. At the injustice of having to take care of a drunk for a father. At the mother who'd turned her back on him.

He'd harboured that rage for a long time, until he'd learned the truth about his mum and why she'd stooped so low.

His anger towards his father still festered, which was why he made the obligatory visits as infrequent as possible. He did enough for the old bastard by placing him in a fancy special accommodation home for patients with alcohol-induced dementia and paying all his bills. That would have to do for his penance.

Hudson watched the kid for a while. His technique wasn't bad. Though he dropped his shoulders too often and his right hook needed some serious work.

He almost offered to help but one look at the feral gleam in the kid's eyes ensured he didn't move from the bench.

The kid wasn't interested in boxing skills. He needed a way to work off his antagonism at the world and every time he lay into that bag was another jab at whoever or whatever had driven him to this.

Hudson had been lucky. He'd had Tanner, who'd had an equally shitty father, and the two of them had bonded over it. They'd come down here often in their high school days, preferring to punch the crap out of a bag rather than some of the assholes at school.

Jim's had been his go-to place. His sanctuary. A world far from getting a call from the local pub to come take his dad home, from propping up the old man and half dragging him home, from dodging fists and beer bottles, from tolerating the kind of verbal abuse a kid should never have to listen to.

Hudson had resented his father to the point of hatred. He'd escaped to this gym and found solace in doing odd jobs around the Cross. Earning money had soon become his number one goal when he'd started working at thirteen, because money would be his way out. His ticket to a life far from Kings Cross and the putrid memories it held.

'Fuck this,' the kid yelled, jabbing at the bag so furiously the chain holding it bucked and rattled like a cut snake.

Still, Hudson didn't say anything, but when the kid reluctantly met his eyes, he saw every ounce of pent-up rage and sorrow and frustration he'd once harboured.

'Want a drink?' Hudson pulled another water bottle from his bag and held it out.

It didn't surprise him when the kid scowled and

slouched off, skulking towards the door as if he couldn't wait to get away.

He hadn't wanted to accept help back then either. Had done his damnedest to keep people at bay. Because letting anyone get close had meant opening up about his home life and divulging secrets he hadn't wanted to reveal.

Mak had been the only person he'd allowed a small glimpse into his life. He'd trusted her, even back then. Having her back in his life had been a godsend.

Ensuring it would be all the harder when she left him.

CHAPTER TWENTY-ONE

THREE NIGHTS LATER, Mak was no closer to figuring out what to do about her relationship with Hudson. Though considering the lack of quality time they'd spent together over the last seventy-two hours, maybe they didn't even have a relationship.

For some inexplicable reason, she got the feeling he'd been avoiding her.

Usually after rehearsal she'd head to his place and they'd spend the night having wild monkey sex before sleeping curled in each other's arms. But the last three nights he'd cited work at the club that would keep him busy until the wee small hours. A perfectly reasonable explanation given he'd spent fewer hours at the club during the evenings because of her but his distinct lack of concern irked.

It was like he didn't miss her at all, when all she could think about, apart from the Grober audition tomorrow, was him.

She'd pretended his cool behaviour didn't bother her. Had been the epitome of a woman fine with a casual relationship. But he'd taken it a step further to-night when he'd yelled at her for a minor slip-up dur-ing rehearsal, and she knew she had to confront him.

Something was bugging him and she needed to find out before it ruined her concentration at the most important audition of her life.

She waited until the dancers filtered out to the dressing room before barging up to Hudson, where he propped against the bar in the corner, making notes.

'Can I talk to you for a second?'

He didn't look up and held up a finger. 'Let me finish this.'

She bit back her first retort: that it looked like he'd already finished them.

He took a full five minutes to finish scrawling and she used the time to do a few cool-down stretches while casting him surreptitious glances.

When he finally looked up and placed his clip-board down, a deep frown slashed his brow. 'You wanted to talk?'

'Is everything okay?'

Dumbass question, considering the frown and compressed lips.

'Last-minute glitches that need ironing out before opening night.' He tapped his pen against his notes. 'I should've known things wouldn't continue to un-fold without a hitch.'

'Anything I can do to help?'

'Just dance your ass off on Sunday night,' he said, the frown easing slightly. 'I've been a grouchy prick and I'm sorry.'

'You don't have to apologise. Your work's important to you. I get that.'

Relieved that his funk had actually been about work and not her, she continued, 'I've got my audition for Reg tomorrow.'

'Has that come around already?' He pinched the bridge of his nose. 'Shit. I feel like I've lost days with all this work. I'm swamped.' He shook his head, as if to clear it. 'Are you ready or is that a stupid question?'

'I'm ready.'

And she meant it. She'd researched the Broadway show until her eyes ached from staring at a computer screen. In a way, not spending time with Hudson the last few days had been a godsend. She shouldn't have been so angsty about it.

'Good luck—' His cell phone rang and he fished it out of his pocket. He glanced at the screen, expression inscrutable. 'I have to take this.'

Ignoring the niggle in her gut that insisted his standoffish behaviour was more than work, she said, 'Sure, I'll go get changed and pop back in to say bye.'

He nodded absent-mindedly, already turning away to take the call. She believed in hard work but Hudson was taking it to extremes at the moment as that niggle turned into something more and she knew her acceptance of his work excuse was foolish.

He managed the hottest nightclub in Sydney. Stood to reason he'd be busy all the time, yet he'd managed to juggle hours just fine when they'd first started their hot and heavy affair. So what had happened over the last few days to change things?

Ever since their stroll down memory lane in Kings Cross he'd been distant, a palpable coolness between them.

She didn't get it.

Annoyed that she was letting her mulling ruin her concentration when she should be focussed on the all-important audition tomorrow, she grabbed her workout bag and headed for the dressing room.

However, as she neared the open door leading into the dressing room, she heard her name being mentioned so she paused.

The dance world was rife with backstage gossip. She'd lived with it ever since she'd started out in this business. Her mum had warned her about it early on, when she'd realised nothing or nobody could sway Makayla from following her dream.

For the most part, she ignored it. Bitchy backstabbing wasn't her thing. But as she heard one of the male dancers call her a snooty bitch, she edged closer to the doorway. Eavesdropping wasn't her style either but she didn't want anything jeopardising Hudson's show, considering he had to make it fly.

'Did you hear the way he yelled at Miss Bossy Boots today? About time the big guy ripped those sex blinkers from his eyes and took her down a notch or two.'

Bossy Boots? As lead dancer she had the authority to discuss moves with her fellow dancers. Did that make her bossy? She'd wear it.

But sex blinkers? Her blood chilled. If they thought Hudson wore sex blinkers where she was concerned...how did they know? Hell. She'd made it clear to Hudson at the start that no one could find out about them for this very reason.

'Probably the only way she scored lead dancer,' a higher-pitched voice piped up. 'Sleeping with the boss is a sure-fire way to score the top job, even if you're an average performer.'

If her blood had frozen a few moments ago, it positively boiled now. Her secret was out and had resulted in exactly what she'd hoped to avoid. Innuendo.

And average? That was a low blow. She might not have an ego the size of the Opera House but she knew she was a damn sight better than average.

'You sure she's sleeping with him?' A third voice, a baritone of one of the other male dancers, chimed in. 'They don't appear all that close at rehearsals.'

The woman snickered. 'Are you blind? The way they look at each other when they think no one's looking is positively sickening. They're definitely bumping uglies.'

'Gross,' the baritone said. 'Doesn't mean she got the lead that way.'

'You're dumb as well as having two left feet,' the other guy said. 'I know for a fact my friend Sha auditioned for the lead and didn't even end up alongside us in the chorus, so the redhead definitely got her shot by bonking the boss.'

'You're wrong,' the baritone insisted. 'She's amazing. I've worked in stage shows all around Australia, as well as London and Paris, and I haven't seen a lead dancer as good as her.'

Makayla had to clamp down on the urge to barge in there and kiss the guy.

'You're all just jealous so, instead of moaning and bitching, why don't you all pull your fingers out and step up?' He paused and Makayla held her breath, wondering what her knight in shining armour would say next. 'I love dancing but I hate this industry because of moronic, narrow-minded idiots like all of you.'

Makayla wanted to applaud so badly she curled her fingers into fists to refrain.

Silence followed her defender's proclamation, before the woman finally spoke. 'You're right. I'm jealous as hell she's so damn good. She makes every routine look effortless and I hate her for that.'

The guy whose friend Sha missed out on being

cast in the show said, 'I still think she shagged the boss to get the role.'

Makayla didn't wait around to hear any more.

She had to confront Hudson and discover why he'd opened his big mouth.

That was when realisation hit. Was that why he'd been avoiding her the last few days? Was he feeling guilty for letting slip their secret? Had it been a mistake or had he hoped to rattle her into admitting they had more than a casual thing and had moved into serious relationship territory?

If so, he was in for a rude shock.

She wouldn't be pushed into anything, least of all a relationship that could derail her lifelong plans.

CHAPTER TWENTY-TWO

HUDSON SLIPPED HIS cell back into his pocket and stared aimlessly at the vacated stage.

He hated confrontation and would do anything to avoid it. Even as a kid he'd hide under his bed when he heard his father stumble in, bumping into walls and swearing vociferously, to avoid the inevitable skirmish that would take place.

At school, he'd used words rather than fists to work off his frustrations, and had taught Tanner to do the same.

Working odd jobs in Kings Cross as a teen had taught him the best life lesson to avoid confrontation: know how to read people. He'd been honest, savvy and dedicated to getting a job done, three qualities most people admired.

He saw those qualities in Mak and his admiration for her knew no bounds.

Now he had to be the one to tear her dream down.

'Fuck,' he muttered, dragging his hand through his hair.

Reg Grober had called, doing him the courtesy of letting him know first that the producer in New York had already filled the dance slot. Which meant Mak would be getting a call from Reg's casting agency soon.

He'd asked Reg to give him half an hour before the agency called, as he wanted to be the one to tell her. He felt bad enough about how he'd been treating her the last few days, it seemed only right.

Because establishing emotional distance between them before their impending break-up was a hell of a lot easier in theory than in practice. It had killed him, watching her walk out of rehearsal each evening, knowing he'd chosen to let her go rather than take her home to his bed and ravish her.

But he'd had to do it, had to put himself through the torture of weaning himself off her rather than going cold turkey when she left.

Now, he felt stupid. Her audition had fallen through, which meant she wouldn't be jetting off to New York soon. She'd be disappointed but he couldn't help but feel relieved.

Mak would be sticking around. And that meant… what?

They could continue deepening their relationship, only for her to eventually leave anyway?

They could maintain the status quo, both ignoring the obvious—that they were in way deeper than they thought?

They could pretend that being emotionally invested in a relationship that had no future wasn't the dumbest thing either of them had ever done?

Before he could mentally rehearse a way of letting her down gently, Mak stormed into the room and slammed the door shut behind her.

'Why did you do it?' She stalked towards him, her hands balled into fists and resting on her hips. 'Do you have any idea how this undermines me?'

Confused, Hudson stared at five-ten of angry woman advancing on him. Had the agency already rung her and she thought he'd had something to do with the audition being cancelled? If so, it revealed what she really thought of him and it wasn't good.

'Look, I had nothing to do with—'

'Don't make this worse by lying,' she said through gritted teeth. 'Do you think I'm an idiot? How else would they have found out?'

Okay, so this wasn't about the audition. It didn't make him feel any better considering she now stood close enough to jab him in the chest, fury radiating off her, making the fine hairs at her temples stand out as if she'd stuck her finger in a power socket.

'You knew when we started up that I didn't want people to know about us. You knew!' Her chest heaved as she sucked in breaths to calm her anger. He shouldn't have been turned on, but he was. It made him feel even worse. 'Now they're saying exactly what I thought they'd say if they found out—

that the only way I got the lead role was by sleeping with the boss.'

'Mak—'

'Why can't guys ever keep their big mouths shut?'

He'd been about to placate her but that jibe, lumping him with the rest of the guys she'd been with, stung.

'I didn't say a word to anyone about us,' he said, sounding lethally calm when in fact he wanted to yell at her for not trusting him enough. 'I wouldn't do that to you and it'd be nice if you thought I was a good guy who wouldn't betray you like that.'

Some of her anger deflated as her shoulders sagged. 'It mightn't have been intentional. You might've been swapping locker-room talk with Tanner and maybe someone overheard—'

'I didn't do this, Mak.'

Shit, if she was pissed at him about this, wait until he delivered the really bad news.

He could couch it in fancy terms, try to let her down gently, but he was seriously annoyed she thought he was a prick who'd talk about their relationship to others when she'd specifically asked him not to.

He'd give it to her straight.

'While you're hell-bent on blaming me for stuff I didn't do, I've got more bad news.'

Her lips compressed into a thin, unimpressed line as she glared at him in condemnation. Her frosty silence spoke volumes. Sadly, it reminded him of the last time they'd had a major blowout five years earlier, when he'd hurled vile accusations at her and she'd done nothing but stand there and take it.

He'd wanted her to defend herself, to tell him he was wrong in assuming she'd chosen a life that could only end in pain. But she'd clammed up, staring at him with such hatred he'd had no option but to leave.

He hoped this time it wouldn't mean the end of them too.

'That call I just took? Reg Grober doing me the courtesy of letting me know that the audition for the Broadway show is off. The producer in New York found someone.'

Mak's jaw dropped and she stared at him in disbelief. 'What the hell?'

'It's showbiz. It happens.' He shrugged, knowing he'd made a major mistake when she blanched and took a step back.

'It *happens*?' she mimicked, her eyes spitting so much fire he should've been fried on the spot. 'Could you be any more dismissive of my dream?'

'I feel bad for you but you'd be used to disappointment in the industry—'

'Shut the fuck up!' Disgust twisted her features as she strode towards the door, leaving him gobsmacked.

He'd expected disappointment.

He hadn't expected this level of rage.

Like she blamed him somehow.

When she stopped at the door and placed her palms against it, bracing, with her head hanging, he wanted to go to her.

He didn't.

Because he'd seen this kind of irrational anger before, when the seething person needed a scapegoat. He'd done it often enough with his dad in the past to know he wouldn't put up with it again, even from the woman he loved.

So he stood there. Watching. Waiting. Knowing without a shadow of a doubt that when she turned around and spoke, they'd be over.

CHAPTER TWENTY-THREE

MAKAYLA'S CHEST BURNED with the effort of holding back tears. She'd come in here spoiling for a fight, wanting to hurt Hudson as much as he'd hurt her by revealing their secret.

Then he'd gone and denied it, his honesty evident in his guileless eyes, and she'd felt like the biggest bitch in the world.

Until he'd lumped more crap on her and while she leaned against the door, trying to reassemble her wits, she couldn't deny the one prominent thought front and centre in her head.

That he didn't seem to care her dream had been shattered.

In fact, that aggravating shrug indicated complete nonchalance. A real 'shit happens' moment. And the anger she'd struggled to contain bubbled up again, swamping her in wave after wave of rage until she shook with it.

Spinning back around, she tried to calm herself. Failed. Deep down she knew that until she purged her innermost, insidious thoughts, she'd feel this crappy for a while.

'You're happy about this, aren't you?' She took small, measured steps towards him until they were two feet apart. Within slugging distance, not the best thought at a time like this. 'I get to stay in Sydney and we continue this thing between us. Is that it?'

'You're disappointed, I get it. But don't shoot the messenger.' His expression grim, he held up his hands. Yeah, like that would calm her. 'The agency would've called you direct about cancelling but because I put your name forward to Reg personally, he did me the courtesy of calling first. And I asked him to give me half an hour so I could tell you myself.'

'I suppose I should be grateful for that,' she said, sounding childish and churlish and hating herself for it. 'But whichever way you dress this up, whoever delivers the news, it's still the same. It sucks.'

This time when he shrugged, she had to use every ounce of self-control not to knock him on his ass.

'There'll be other opportunities. Other auditions—'

'For Broadway? Unlikely.' She shook her head, wishing he understood how momentous this had been for her. 'You think I'm being irrational and over the top but this is my life. Don't you get that?'

He didn't make a move to comfort her. Didn't move a muscle. He just stood there, way too calm, way too controlled. Like a freaking robot.

'I get it.'

When he finally spoke, his low lethal tone raised goosebumps on her arms.

'I get that losing out on this one audition has sent you into such a tailspin you seem to be blaming me for it. I get that the thought of sticking around and having a relationship with me is seemingly abhorrent to you.' His tone didn't change but his eyes…his eyes turned a glacial blue that sent a shiver through her. 'I get that maybe I was just a means to an end for you. That you used me to get the big break you've always wanted. That I mean nothing to you.'

He flung the hurtful accusations in her face clearly and concisely, each hitting home like a poison-tipped dart.

She hadn't used him.

Had she?

This was Hudson, the guy she'd fantasised about as a teen. The guy who'd stood by her. The guy who'd left because of his own demons.

Ironic, that this time she'd be the one to end things between them. Not as payback, but as a way of assuming the control she didn't have last time.

She'd still hurt. A thousand times worse this time, considering she'd fallen for him. But at least she wouldn't be left feeling as if he'd never given her a chance.

This time, they'd taken that chance.

And failed.

'If you truly believe all that BS you just spouted

at me, you're delusional. I don't know what happened here tonight. I don't know if the audition being cancelled was fate or you using any means possible to keep me around or just more of my crappy luck, but I'm done waiting for my big break.' She tapped her chest. '*I'm* going to make it happen.'

Bitterness bracketed his mouth. 'You're still accusing me of being underhanded to maintain our status quo?' He barked out a laugh devoid of amusement. 'You really think I'm a shit, don't you?'

She almost reached for him then, the bewilderment tinged with hurt on his face was that heart wrenching.

But she couldn't back down now. She had to follow through.

She was done depending on others, particularly Hudson, for her happiness.

'Once your show is done, I'm heading to New York.' She squared her shoulders, the idea sounding less ludicrous articulated out loud. 'I'm going to make it on my own, without help from anyone.'

Shock made his pupils dilate, eclipsing all that beautiful blue she'd miss so much. 'So that's it? You're just going to head to the States with no job, no work permit and limited funds?' Scepticism pinched his mouth. 'How are you going to survive 'til you land your big break?'

He stared fixedly at some point over her shoulder, unable to meet her eyes, and in that moment she knew what had him so angsty. She just knew, deep down in that part of her that could never turn back time and change her decision.

Not that she would. She'd stripped that one night to honour her mum, to thank her for the many years of sacrifice, to give her the send-off she deserved.

Hudson knew that now yet he still didn't trust her enough. He didn't believe in her, that she could survive without spiralling into some seedy way of life he obviously abhorred.

She tapped her bottom lip, pretending to think, before snapping her fingers. 'I know. If I can't make ends meet I can always take off my clothes for money. Or even better, become an escort. Or something equally nefarious that you seem to think I'm one step away from.'

'Don't be ridiculous,' he snapped, but the spots of high colour on his cheekbones belied his denial. 'I'm just worried about you—'

'I'm a big girl. I can take care of myself.' Hurting all the way to her soul, she made a grand show of glancing at her watch. 'Better head home and start making travel plans. I'll see you at final rehearsal tomorrow.'

She wanted him to say something, anything, to make her stay.

She wanted some kind of sign that they weren't over, that there was the faintest hope they could still make this work somehow.

She wanted it all: Broadway, stardom, him.

Sadly, Makayla had learned a long time ago that what she wanted and what she got were poles apart.

Her heart broke anew as Hudson just stood there, radiating disapproval, a frown creasing his brow, as he watched her back towards the door, where she spun around and marched through it, head held high.

CHAPTER TWENTY-FOUR

As if Hudson's shitty week couldn't get any worse, he'd received a call from his father's special accommodation facility first thing this morning, asking him to come in. The nurse hadn't specified the problem exactly but had forcefully suggested he pay a visit today.

This after the blow-up with Mak last night and a maximum of ninety minutes' sleep when he'd finally made it home from work at four a.m.

He'd thought discovering her naked on stage that night years ago had been bad. It had nothing on the way they'd imploded last night.

The way she'd confronted him, not giving him a chance to explain, thinking the worst of him…he'd had that a lot growing up. Teachers not believing in him because of his home life. Friends judging him for not having a good enough home to invite them over to hang out. Bosses not trusting him because nobody trusted anyone in the Cross, until he proved himself many times over.

That lack of belief drove him to be the best. To show the world that no matter what hardships he faced as a kid, nothing or nobody could keep him down. He prided himself on his work ethic, his dependability, his honesty.

Apparently, it all meant jack to Mak.

He'd been wise to distance himself this week, to re-erect emotional barriers. Their relationship had ended as he'd expected. Well, not quite what he'd expected. He'd envisaged them staying friends. Good friends. The kind of friends who chatted regularly and did video conferencing and even hopped on a plane to New York if the impulse hit.

Who was he kidding? He'd hoped they could've been a hell of a lot more than friends but that had been shot to shit.

He was better off without her.

Then why did he feel so goddamn bad?

Pulling into the parking lot of the special accommodation home, he killed the engine. It usually took him a few moments of gaining composure before he could face his father. It was the same every time he visited. Too much had happened between them, too many bad memories, to forget.

He'd tried. Had gone through a rough patch when he'd hit eighteen and gone in search of his mum. What he'd learned had driven him to drink, spending night after night drowning his sorrows in a bottle. Until he'd taken one look in the mirror, seen the resemblance to dear old dad and snapped out of it, switching to OJ without the vodka.

He'd confronted his father with the truth. Had blamed him for everything. Predictably, his old man hadn't given a shit. Had called his mother every name under the sun and accused her of driving him to drink.

Hudson knew better.

He knew the real culprit in his disastrous upbringing and it sure as hell wasn't his mother.

Taking a deep breath, he blew it out, counted to ten and opened the car door. The first thing to hit him was the sea air. Tangy. Stringent. The second thing was the views. The endless expanse of Sydney Harbour, a perfect cerulean today, dotted with sailboats and yachts, with mansions scattering north shore in the distance.

Though his father didn't deserve it he'd chosen one of the nicest accommodations in the city and paid the exorbitant rates for the privilege. Tanner accused him of being a soft touch with a core of marshmallow and his friend was probably right. But the moment he'd set foot in this place after checking out six other dementia homes, he'd known this was the right one.

Maybe it was sentimentality, maybe it was guilt, or maybe it was a futile wish he could've done something like this for his mum; whatever it was, he'd handed over the hefty entry fee for his father and worked his ass off to keep paying the bills.

If there was such a thing as karma he'd be in line for a whole heap of good stuff coming his way. Though if that were the case, his relationship with Mak would've worked out.

Swiping a hand over his face, he slammed the car door, stabbed at the remote to lock it and strode towards the front doors. Perfectly manicured lawns flanked the terracotta-bricked path, wide enough to fit two wheelchairs side by side. Flower beds filled with a riot of colour edged the garden, with towering eucalypts casting shade over the lawns.

The entire scene screamed peaceful and he absorbed as much of the ambience as he could before the upcoming confrontation. He needed it, because his obligatory visits to his father only went two ways. His father having lucid moments where he'd berate him for locking him away in this 'jail' or a bad day, where the dementia would make him ramble, alternating between angry and recalcitrant. Exactly how he'd been as a mean drunk.

Hudson didn't visit often. He felt he'd paid his dues by keeping his father at home for as long as he had and now, with this luxury accommodation. But being summoned by the nurses couldn't be a good thing and he braced himself for what he'd find.

Squaring his shoulders, he strode up the front steps and the glass doors slid open soundlessly. The faintest waft of lavender filled the foyer, probably filtered through the air conditioning ducts to calm the residents. A gleaming mahogany front desk, reminiscent of a five-star hotel, ran the length of the foyer, with huge floral arrangements strategically placed at either end.

The place definitely had a hotel feel; until he stepped through the electronically locked doors and realised his father's mind had deteriorated to the point he had to be confined.

Fixing a smile on his face, he approached the front desk. 'Hudson Watt to see Wiley Watt, my father.'

He didn't recognise the forty-something receptionist. Then again, considering his infrequent visits, it wasn't unusual.

She smiled and pointed at the locked door. 'Go right ahead. I'll buzz you in.'

When he had his hand on the handle, she said, 'You have the same eyes as Wiley.'

Blurry and nasty? He hoped not. He managed a terse nod and pushed open the door when it buzzed.

The lavender scent was stronger here, as if the cleaners were trying to drown out the smells of antiseptic and old people. It made his nose twitch.

The nurses' station stood just inside the door, a central rotund area that resembled a high-tech spaceship. Its positioning gave the nurses full view of every room and every corridor leading to the rec rooms, the grounds and the dining area. Perfect for occupants with a tendency to wander.

He recognised several of the nurses, particularly the younger ones who never failed to flirt with him. But his heart wasn't in it today so he offered them a grim smile before turning his attention to the matron who'd called him.

'Thanks for coming, Hudson.' She folded her arms, a defensive posture that wasn't a good sign.

'How's Wiley?'

He never called him Dad any more. Wiley Watt didn't deserve the title.

'He's been asking for you a lot lately. That's why I called.' She paused, as if searching for the right words. 'He's due for his annual check-up and we'll wait to see what the doctor says, but the dementia seems to be worsening. Most of his ramblings centre on you and a woman I assume is your mother, Kim? It makes him very upset. To the point he cries.'

Hudson's heart turned over. Bit late for dear old dad to grow a conscience. 'Is he lucid today?'

She nodded. 'It's one of his better days, which is why I thought you should come in and have a chat to him. See if he can make peace with whatever is bugging him so he'll be more subdued on other days?'

She didn't need to spell it out. His dad must've been saying some pretty revealing, damning stuff during his demented ramblings and the nurses thought that talking to him might ease the guilt. As if. Wiley Watt would need a year's worth of confessionals to bring some semblance of peace.

'I'll talk to him,' he said, sounding like he'd rather have a root canal. 'Thanks for letting me know.'

The nurse hesitated, before briefly touching his arm. 'I've worked in dementia wards for twenty-six years and it's rare to see people exhibit the level of regret your father is showing because they can't usually process emotions for events in the past, particularly when alcohol is the precipitating cause of the dementia. So give him a chance, okay?'

Hudson couldn't promise anything so remained silent.

The nurse sighed, her lack of judgement appreciated. 'He's in his room.'

'Thanks.'

Nothing his father could say would change the devastation of the past but if it made the nurses' jobs easier he'd listen to whatever the old man had to say.

The ten steps from the nurses' station to his father's room always seemed to take an eternity, as if his feet refused to move and dragged across the pristine carpet.

He knocked at the door, waited the obligatory five seconds, before opening it and entering. He'd learned early on during his visits that his father never answered his door and if he waited for him to open it he'd be here all day.

Wiley sat in a recliner armchair next to a large

window, sunlight streaming through and warming him like a cat, bald head gleaming. For someone who'd imbibed enough alcohol in his lifetime to pickle his liver and his brain, he didn't look too bad. Wrinkles criss-crossed his face, set in a perpetual dour expression, but he maintained a good bodyweight. He appeared fit for his seventy-eight years. If not for the dementia, Wiley would still probably be drinking himself to sleep every day.

Like every other visit, Wiley ignored him until Hudson sat in a chair opposite him. 'Hey.'

'What are you doing here?' The same guttural tone, almost a snarl, that Hudson had endured every day growing up.

'Came to see how you're doing.'

'I'm locked away in a loony bin full of stinking old fools, how do you think I'm doing?'

So he was having a good day. Completely lucid. Hudson didn't know if that boded well or not.

'This is a good place. You're well looked after,' he said, wishing he could rattle the selfish old goat and make him understand exactly how hard he had to work to pay the bills.

'You still working odd jobs at the Cross?'

Wiley's question came out of left field. In all the years he'd been here he'd never asked anything about Hudson's job, let alone the jobs he'd worked as a teen to keep food on the table.

'No, I manage a nightclub now. And I'm involved in theatre.'

Wiley screwed up his nose and snorted. 'Pansy-ass occupations, if you ask me.'

'I didn't.'

Hudson waited, curious to see what else his father would say and more than a little hopeful he'd reveal more about his mother.

He'd never forget the day he'd found her. Far too late.

It had haunted him ever since.

He'd wanted to know more about the mother he remembered as a toddler, the mother who'd cuddled him every chance she could, the mother who'd smelled like exotic frangipanis, the mother who'd tell him bedtime stories and tuck him in every night.

That was the woman he wanted to remember, not the woman lying in a grimy bedsit with a needle sticking out of her arm.

'Your mother wanted you to be a lawyer.'

Hudson startled. As if Wiley had read his mind, he'd mentioned his mum.

'Bloodsucking leeches, the lot of 'em, but would've paid well.' Wiley ran a hand over his head, smoothing back non-existent hair. 'She was dating one when we met. But couldn't resist my charms so we got hitched three months later.'

Hudson couldn't imagine his father having a single charming bone in his selfish body but he remained silent.

'I've been thinking a lot about her lately. When I'm not...' Wiley made loopy circles at his temple. 'Hate how I can't bloody remember my own name half the time.'

Another first, Wiley admitting he had a problem with his memory.

'Docs say the alcohol did it.' Wiley shook his head, having the guts to look guilty for once. 'Looks like the alcohol did a lot of things to screw up my life back then.'

His father didn't deserve an ounce of pity but for a moment, Hudson felt something close to it. 'You could've stopped at any time.'

How many times had he tipped bottles down the sink in the hope his dad would stop drinking? How many times had he heard Wiley's empty promises that he wouldn't touch another drop of the demon drink? How many times had he propped him up on the way home from the pub despite Wiley saying he'd only popped in for lemonade?

Empty promises to match his empty life since his mum had left him to be raised by a mean prick.

'I only drank to stop the pain here.' Wiley thumped a fist over his heart. 'Kim broke it when she left.'

He lowered his hand, shaking slightly. 'My fault. I drove her away. Was never good enough for her, made her do terrible things for the money then hated her for it…'

Hudson knew his mother had turned to prostitution to survive. The woman who'd owned the bed-sit had told him more than he'd wanted to know and then some when he'd tracked down his mum in Melbourne and found her dead.

But never in his worst nightmares had he suspected Wiley had made her do it while they were married.

'What did you make her do?' He spoke with lethal precision, using every ounce of self-control not to pummel this shell of a man who'd never done a single thing to earn the title of father.

'I was working full time as a mechanic when we met. We got married fast, had you nine months later so she gave up her teaching degree. But I couldn't cope with a baby, was a lousy father.' Wiley coughed and Hudson waited. He hadn't known any of this.

From the time he was old enough to understand anything, his father hadn't worked. He'd sat around the house, drinking, a belligerent man who'd scared the bejesus out of him. His mum had been the one to go out and work, mainly nights. Those had been the pits, when he'd be left with an angry man he barely knew who'd yell at him to stay in his room and not come out.

Some nights he'd gone to bed hungry, wishing his mum would suddenly appear like a guardian angel.

But he'd be asleep by the time she came home and he'd fling himself into her arms first thing in the morning, not breathing a word of how terrified he was of his father.

'I couldn't work with a hangover so after you were a few months old I lost my job. That's when things got tough.' Wiley glared at him as if it were his fault. 'Kim had no qualifications so she took whatever jobs she could. Check-out chick. Cleaner. Waitress. It still wasn't enough.'

Sorrow made Wiley's eyelids droop and for a moment Hudson thought he'd fallen asleep.

'A friend told me how much she could make in the strip clubs, taking her clothes off. I encouraged Kim to do it because we needed the money desperately.' Wiley's upper lip curled in disgust and Hudson didn't know if it was at the thought of Kim stripping or at himself for pushing her into it. 'It took the pressure off. The money was a godsend. But I couldn't look at her the same way.'

Wiley blinked rapidly, and Hudson hoped to God he wouldn't start crying. What he was hearing made him sick to his stomach. He didn't want to cope with crocodile tears too.

'Made the mistake of going to a club to watch one night. And that was the end of it for me. I snapped.' Wiley pressed his fingertips to his eyes. Hudson resisted the urge to do the same. 'Said I couldn't come near her again. That what we had was over. Drove her away deliberately with day after day of abuse.' Wiley waved his arm around. 'And ended up here because of it, a lonely old man losing his mind.'

Impotent rage simmered in Hudson's gut, a slow-burning anger he'd harboured against his father for years. The old bastard deserved it, considering he'd driven his mother away because of something he'd pushed her into doing in the first place.

But no one had held a gun to his mum's head once she'd established distance. She could've found another job, could've come for him and taken him away from his drunkard, pathetic excuse for a father.

Instead, she'd followed the money and taken the step from stripping to prostitution. And she hadn't looked back. Hadn't called him. Hadn't come for him.

The kicker? He could identify with what his father had felt the night he'd seen Kim stripping, because he'd felt the same way when he'd seen Mak naked on stage. It had changed everything between them. He'd been angry too and he'd taken it out on her, driving a wedge between their friendship for years.

The only way he'd found his way back to her was once he'd learned the truth about her motivations. That was where he differed from Wiley. He'd known Kim's motivations but he'd lashed out anyway. Bastard.

'Why are you telling me all this now?'

Wiley slumped further into the chair, as if he was

trying to disappear into it. 'Because I was a shit husband and a shit father and I don't want to go to my grave without telling you the truth.'

'That you were a mean-spirited drunk who pushed my mother away and left me being the primary caregiver for you?'

Wiley shrugged, as if the years of Hudson's sacrifice and hard work meant little.

'Been having a lot of dreams lately. Nightmares. Past blending into the present, that kind of thing.' Wiley plucked at a thread in the seam of his corduroys. 'Just felt like I had to tell someone.'

'Lucky me,' Hudson muttered. He'd heard enough. He felt pity for his father, for the shell of a man he'd become. But he couldn't forgive him. The time for absolution had long passed.

'What are you doing here? Get out of my room!' Wiley bellowed, pushing to his feet with difficulty and brandishing a non-existent cane. 'I don't let strangers into my room. Nurse!'

Hudson stood and headed for the door, relieved to leave. The switch from lucid to confusion happened like this sometimes, so quickly he didn't have time to come up with a way to placate his irate dad.

'Get out, I said.' His father's face turned puce, the familiar colour of anger Hudson recognised well from the old days. 'Get out!'

Hudson did exactly that, without a backward glance.

CHAPTER TWENTY-FIVE

MAKAYLA LOVED THE thrill of opening night. The anticipation of performing in front of a crowd. The culmination of many hours of rehearsal. The smell of make-up and hairspray mingling with the sweat of nerves. The excited chatter of performers about to strut their stuff. She'd been doing this for years and it never got old.

But this opening night didn't hold her enthralled like others.

Because once this opening night concluded, she only had another nine shows at Embue until she left her old life behind and embarked on her new one.

She'd had three days to scrounge together the money to book flights, organise travel documents and find short-term accommodation. She'd been lucky, using a contact in the industry to gain a working permit and scoring a room in a brownstone shared by four other wannabe dancers. So once her commitment at Embue was done, she'd be leaving.

She should be ecstatic.

So why the lethargy that wouldn't quit?

She'd managed to get through the remaining rehearsals by feigning complete indifference towards Hudson and he'd done the same, treating her with a frosty politeness that made her yearn for their old warmth.

But their friendship was ruined along with any chance they might have had at maintaining something more. She should've been relieved. It would've been a struggle, doing the long-distance thing. Yet seeing Hudson the past three days and not being able to tease or laugh or smile at him had been torture.

Her fingers had itched to run through his artfully mussed dark blond hair. Her eyes had automatically sought his, searching for some kind of emotion in that unique indigo blue. Her body had yearned to be close to him, to feel the heat, the spark that never failed to ignite her in a way that would never be replicated by any other man.

That was another thing. Now that she'd had phenomenally great sex, how could she ever settle for anything less? The whole situation was beyond annoying. Maybe the first thing she did when she landed in the States was find the hottest American she could and shag him senseless?

Yeah, and if it were that easy, she would've been having great sex for years. Instead, the hotties were too egotistical and lazy in bed, while the nice guys with a modicum of talent didn't do it for her outside the bedroom.

Hudson had been the best of both worlds. Worlds that had well and truly collided and imploded.

'Damn it,' she muttered, the outer corner of her fake eyelashes slipping a tad as she tried to glue it.

Mulling about the past wasn't conducive to kicking ass on stage and she wanted to do a good job if it killed her. She had to prove to Hudson that their break up didn't affect her at all. Even if her hands shook and her legs wobbled at the thought of dancing on stage in front of him.

Last time he'd seen her on stage that hadn't involved rehearsals it hadn't ended well. The thing was, that night haunted her more than it must've ever bugged him.

She'd moved past the shame but she'd never been able to shake the deep-seated belief that there might've been another way to get the money she'd needed for her mum's funeral.

A sharp knock sounded at the door before Hudson stuck his head around it. 'Ready?'

She nodded, not willing to answer when her voice might quiver as badly as her insides.

He paused, as if wanting to say something else, before half shrugging. 'On stage in ten.'

When he left, she exhaled a breath she hadn't been aware she'd been holding. Ten minutes to pull herself together.

And nail this performance.

She went through her routine pre-performance stretches and, after a final glance in the mirror, made her way backstage with a minute to spare. The other dancers milled around, going through their individual pre-performance superstitions. Some touched the curtains. Some tucked a lucky talisman into a secure place. Some did deep breathing, eyes closed.

Makayla had never believed in luck. She made her own. Starting now.

As Hudson did the intro and the curtain rose, she strutted onto the stage for the opening number.

And stumbled.

It hadn't happened once in rehearsals and it momentarily threw her. Thankfully, the other dancers were out on stage quickly, doing their own spins and pirouettes and shimmies.

Makayla had faced other minor mishaps on stage before. All part of the biz. But for some reason, she didn't recover from that initial stumble and for the next forty minutes, she struggled.

Missed steps by a beat. Felt stiff and uncoordinated. Lacked her usual joy for dance. And it must've showed. She only risked a glance at Hudson in the wings once and his stony expression told her everything she already knew.

She stank.

Mortified, she managed the finale before limping off stage, her Achilles aching as much as her pride.

She went through the routine of backslapping fel-low dancers and feigning enthusiasm, all the while wishing she could sink into the floor. After that pa-thetic performance, she would've cemented what they already suspected: that the only way she'd got the lead role was by sleeping with the boss. Ugh.

Slipping away from the mini celebration as quickly as possible, she headed for her dressing room. The sooner she got the hell out of here, the better.

She'd planned on rubbing Hudson's nose in it, tri-umphant in her professionalism. Instead, she'd let her earlier musings derail her and had put in the worst performance of her entire career.

Not waiting to remove her make-up or change out of costume, she slipped on an overcoat, grabbed her bag and made a run for it.

CHAPTER TWENTY-SIX

HUDSON WATCHED THE dancers mill about backstage. He should be mingling out front of the house, where enthusiastic patrons raved about the show while spending big at the bar.

But he couldn't tear his eyes away from Mak.

She looked…broken.

As if all the spirit had drained out of her.

Sure, she'd given a lacklustre performance but only an industry expert could tell. The audience had still applauded every move and clapped madly at the end when she'd taken the final bow.

But she'd been seriously rattled after that initial stumble and hadn't recovered. It surprised him, because she'd been flawless at rehearsals.

Unless…he'd never seen her perform in a show on stage. Was she one of those dancers who nailed the previews but couldn't translate it on the big stage?

He'd seen it before, actors who memorised entire scripts but couldn't enunciate a word in front of a crowd. Singers who performed in pubs but lost their pitch when they got their big break.

Was Mak a choker when it really counted?

He hated to think it. Followed by another worrying thought. If tonight's performance was anything to go by, how did she expect to make it on Broadway?

She'd be wasting her time, going from audition to audition, her funds dwindling. What would she do then?

The memory of her stripping naked on stage popped into his head. Fuck. Would she return to that in the US? Or like his mum, desperate for cash, much worse?

He knew nothing about her financial situation beyond what she'd told him: that she had a flatmate because her part-time job at Le Miel couldn't cover the bills alone. She might have savings but if so, why hadn't she chosen to head to the States before now…? Damn.

He watched her slip away from the dancers, was about to follow her, when a hand landed on his shoulder.

'Good work, bozo.' Tanner squeezed his shoulder, then released him. 'You may be onto something with these live dance shows.'

'Thanks.' Hudson's gaze didn't leave Mak, wishing she'd glance over her shoulder so he could signal to her to wait for him.

'If you pack the crowd in like this over the next

two weeks, I may need to think about making this a permanent gig.' Tanner slapped him on the back. 'And give you a raise.'

Another back slap and Tanner was gone, leaving Hudson craning his neck looking for Mak. She'd vanished.

Cursing under his breath, he headed for her dressing room, bypassing the dancers who'd waylay him. He should be with them, congratulating and encouraging. Yet all he could think about was getting to Mak.

The desperate edge to his urgency scared him. For someone who'd ended their relationship without a backward glance, he sure was concerned about her. In fact, it was more than concern. It was an ache in his gut that screamed...fear.

The abject failure he'd seen on Mak's face terrified him.

He didn't want her feeling like that. He wanted to pick her up and cradle her and tell her how frigging fantastic she was.

He wouldn't put her down or push her away when she needed him most.

He wasn't his father.

In that moment, he realised something else. He didn't want to be alone like Wiley either. He didn't want to live with regrets or end up by himself in some old-age home because he hadn't taken a chance on love.

He wouldn't hold Mak back but he wouldn't let her go either.

He'd fight.

Make a stand.

As he should have that night he'd seen her strip and given up on her.

Who knew, dear old dad had done him a favour, revealing the truth about what happened with his mum.

Wiley had been a quitter.

Luckily, Hudson was nothing like his father.

CHAPTER TWENTY-SEVEN

MAKAYLA HAD ALMOST made it to her car in the staff underground parking lot when Hudson burst out of a side door.

Damn it, the one person she'd hoped to avoid. She could pretend she hadn't seen him and get into her car as fast as humanly possible, but that would be poor form considering he'd given her this job at a time she'd needed it most.

She waited until he got closer, feigning nonchalance by leaning against the open driver's door. 'Is there a problem?'

'You tell me,' he said, sounding frantic, his words clipped, his voice just above a growl. 'It's usual to have a debrief after the first performance but you bolted out of there.'

'I'm exhausted.'

The lie slipped easily from her lips and she threw her bag onto the back seat in an effort to hasten her exit. 'Can we do the debrief tomorrow?'

'No.'

He took a step closer, invading her personal space in a way she would've loved last week. Now, not so much. The tantalising fragrance of his crisp after-shave reminded her of how he smelled delicious, all over, and how much she was missing out on by not having him in her life any more.

'Hudson, I'm not in the mood—'

'What happened in there?' He jerked a thumb over his shoulder towards the club. As if she needed the clarification. She knew exactly what he was talking about. 'Not that the audience noticed, but I did.'

Hating that she'd need to have the conversation she'd hoped to avoid, she shrugged. 'You of all people know it's been a big week. Plenty of upheaval.' She tapped her head. 'All the crap up here affected my performance tonight. It won't happen again.'

His eyes narrowed. 'So that's all it was? Opening night nerves? Over-analysing?'

She hadn't been talking about the dancing and he knew it. But she was all for wrapping this up as soon as possible and leaving.

'I've never danced the lead role before. And I'm ashamed to say it rattled me tonight. That's it.'

'Are you sure?'

Another step forward, bringing him within touching distance, and she had to curl her fingers into her palms to stop from doing just that.

'Because as I recall, most of that *upheaval* had to do with you and me. And you having to travel to the other side of the world to avoid having the kind of conversation we're about to have.'

A nervous fluttering started deep in Makayla's belly and wouldn't let up. She didn't want to have any conversations with Hudson, least of all ones involving the two of them.

'I'm heading overseas to work,' she said, enunciating each word with precision. 'And unlike what you implied, I won't be lying on my back with my legs spread to do it.'

'Don't be crass.'

'You're the one who seems to think I'm capable of it.'

To her horror, all the emotion she'd managed to subdue in front of him for the last few days bubbled up and lodged in her throat, making her nauseous.

'I have to go.' She slipped into her car and tried to slam the door shut.

He wouldn't budge. 'Hudson, I mean it—'

'I'm not letting you go,' he ground out. 'I've made that mistake several times now but never again.'

She gaped at him, letting the implications of his words sink in, totally missing her chance to shut the door and drive away when he moved around to the passenger side and slid into the seat next to her.

'Do you want to have this conversation here or somewhere more comfortable?'

Makayla didn't reply. For the simple reason she didn't know what to say. But whatever he had to say, she didn't want to be twisted like a pretzel in her tiny car, eyeing him while he divulged whatever declaration he had to make.

Her heart thudded out of control as she managed to start the engine and steer the car out onto the road.

'Where are we going?'

She shot him a sideways glance. 'You'll find out.'

Thankfully, he didn't say anything, content to let her drive. Then again, he'd said enough.

'I'm not letting you go...never again.'

What the hell did he mean by that?

She couldn't take him to her place, in case Charlotte was home. And she felt foolish driving to his apartment after the way things had ended between them. So she settled for her favourite spot when she wanted to get away from life.

Fifteen minutes later, she'd parked in secluded bushland on top of a cliff, with magnificent views of the harbour.

'This is my favourite go-to place and if you tell anyone it's here I'll have to kill you,' she said, finally breaking the silence.

'It's beautiful.' He swivelled his body to face her, moonlight illuminating the chiselled planes of his cheeks, his jaw. 'It's perfect.'

'For what?'

'Starting the rest of our lives.'

He pronounced it like a *fait accompli* as once

again she struggled to gain control of her galloping heart.

'I think I've missed something,' she said, her voice sounding way too quivery. 'We're over and I'm heading to New York. What part of that screams a long-lasting relationship to you?'

'The part where I love you and have been too proud or too stupid to tell you.' He clasped her hand where it rested on her gearshift. 'The part where I tell you why I freak out every time I think of you trying to make it on your own.' He lifted her hand to his lips and brushed a feather-light kiss across the back of it. 'The part where I tell you I'll do whatever it takes to be with you. Quit my job. Follow you to New York. To the ends of the bloody earth if needs be, to ensure we're together.'

The blood drained from Makayla's head, making her woozy. Nothing about this evening made sense, starting with her crappy performance and culminating in this surreal moment, where the guy she'd fallen for was vowing to follow her to maintain their relationship.

'I'm having a hard time computing this,' she admitted, confusion making her brain hurt. 'I just don't get it.'

'I visited my father yesterday. Learned a few things that helped me put things in perspective.' He threaded his fingers through hers and held on tight, as if he'd never let go. 'I don't want any secrets between us. You need to know everything before we go any further.'

'Okay,' she said, the gravity in his tone making her wonder what deep, dark secret he had to reveal and how it would impact them.

'That night I saw you strip and I freaked out? It wasn't only because I'd worked around Kings Cross and seen women on a slippery slope.' He half turned and stared out of the window. 'It's because it happened to my mum. We had no money, stripping paid well, so she ended up in that profession. I learned yesterday my dad virtually pushed her into it then despised her for it, making it untenable for her to stay around so she left. I was six at the time. I lost my mum and it devastated me. When I saw you stripping, I didn't want to lose you too.'

Shocked, she sucked in a breath. Poor Hudson. No wonder he'd had a coronary when he'd seen her that night.

'When I was sixteen, I wanted to find Mum and I traced her to Melbourne. Took the train down there. Followed a bunch of leads and finally found her.' He swallowed and locked gazes with her, the agony in his eyes making her chest ache. 'Dead. In a bedsit, from a drug overdose. She'd been prostituting to support her habit—'

His voice broke, and she leaned across the console to wrap her arms around him. How had they been best friends and she'd known nothing of this?

Of the kind of heartache that shaped a young man and made him fear anything remotely resembling an emotional commitment?

'I never told anyone,' he murmured, clinging to her, before gently easing back. 'But I'm sorry I let all that affect our friendship back then and how I treated you when I heard you were heading to New York.'

'It's okay, I get it now.'

And she did. Hudson wasn't the narrow-minded, overbearing, possessive prick she'd assumed. He was a guy scarred by his past and concerned for her welfare because of it.

'But I'm not going to earn money that way ever again. It's a promise I made to myself after that one night.' Her nose crinkled like she'd smelled something bad. 'I couldn't handle it and I wouldn't do it for anyone else but Mum. So you can rest assured I won't fall into disrepute in New York so you don't have to follow me there—'

'I do.' He reached for both her hands and held them. 'I love you. I want to be with you. And I've wasted enough years we could've been together by my own misconceptions.'

The heaviness that had weighed her down during her performance tonight lifted. 'That's twice you've said you love me. Must be real.'

'And you haven't said it once.' A glimmer of a smile played about his mouth. 'Does that mean you don't feel the same way?'

'Don't be an idiot, of course I love you.' She slipped a hand from his to thump him on the chest. 'I love you so much. There's a difference between not giving up my independence and dreams for any man, and giving up the man of my dreams.'

'Poetic,' he said, a moment before he claimed her mouth in a sizzling kiss that branded her as his. Or maybe it was the other way around.

Their tongues tangled, sinuous and hot, as he moved his lips over hers in that commanding way she loved.

He groaned into her mouth, his hands finding her breasts. She arched into him. Wanting him to touch her everywhere. She'd missed him, missed this. This way of making her feel like she was the only woman in the world for him. After his honest declaration, maybe she was.

He tried to get closer to her and thunked his head on the car roof. 'Damn, not enough room,' he said with a rueful grin.

Her body throbbed with wanting him and her panties were soaked. No way were they leaving here without getting the happy ending they both wanted.

'There's always the back seat?' She quirked an eyebrow in a saucy invitation, and he laughed.

'You're serious?'

'Unless you want to wait 'til we get back to your place—'

'Back seat it is,' he said, already clambering over the console with a few bumps, curses and grunts.

She all but tumbled into his lap in her haste to follow, and they laughed in a tangle of limbs.

'How many times have you brought a boy up here to make out in the back seat?'

'As of now, only one.' She settled herself on his lap, anticipation making her crazy for him.

'So I'm your one and only? I like the sound of that.'

He flicked his thumbs across her nipples, rigid beneath the leotard she hadn't changed out of in her haste to escape the club.

She moaned, and he fastened his mouth where his thumb had been a moment ago, giving a sharp nip that made her grab his head and hold on.

As his teeth continued to torture her nipples to the point of exquisite pleasure, she heard him unzip. Heard the rip of foil. Felt his fingers pull aside her panties.

Then finally, finally, he was inside her. Hard and thick and perfect.

His mouth released her nipple, only to claim her lips again, his tongue mimicking the demanding thrusts of his cock below.

Bracing her arms against the back seat, she rode him with abandon. Pumping up and down as if she'd never get enough. Every slide making her muscles tense. Every thrust bringing release closer.

The car filled with murmured pleas for satisfaction. Naughty demands. Each and every word bringing her closer to tumbling into the dazzling abyss she craved with his every touch.

Soon their frantic panting was the only sound in the car, the fogged windows enclosing them in their own private pleasure cave. Then he touched her clit, circling it, and she couldn't hold back any longer. Her orgasm crashed over her in a cataclysmic wave, making her see stars in the darkness.

Hudson grabbed her waist, anchoring her in a world where she floated; weightless, boneless, mindless with pleasure.

He thrust upward one last time before groaning her name, so raw, so guttural; she'd never heard anything so beautiful.

Crushing her to him, he didn't move, didn't speak.

No words were necessary.

They'd said all that needed to be said.

Hudson loved her. She loved him.

He wanted to foster her dream, not tear it down.

And they'd just sealed their love in the best way possible.

How the hell did she get so lucky?

EPILOGUE

AFTER THE ROUSING send-off Tanner had hosted for them at Embue last night, Hudson hadn't expected the gang to turn up at the airport to farewell them.

But Tanner, Abby and Charlotte had fronted up twenty-four hours later, in the wee small hours, to share a final drink.

'Here's to Mak taking Broadway by storm.' Tanner raised a beer. 'And to my putz of a friend not hanging on to her coat-tails like some dweeb.'

'I'll drink to that.' Mak clinked her champagne flute against Tanner's beer and winked at Hudson. 'Don't worry, darling, I'm fine with you tagging along for the ride.'

Hudson shot Abby a sympathetic look. 'I have no idea how you put up with this idiot.'

'It's a tough job, but somebody's got to do it.' Abby leaned her head against Tanner's shoulder, totally smitten, batting her eyelashes at Hudson's friend who dropped a kiss on the tip of her nose.

'Sickening,' Hudson muttered, unable to hide a

goofy grin as he locked gazes with Tanner and he saw the same starstruck gleam reflected in his.

They'd been through so much growing up in Kings Cross. Had survived the tough streets and tougher fathers. Now look how far they'd come. Abby and Mak were beautiful, intelligent and talented in their respective fields, and they adored them.

'How did schmucks like us get so lucky?' Tanner asked, reading his mind.

'No idea, but I'm eternally frigging grateful.' Hudson clinked his beer against Tanner's, counting his blessings daily that he had a woman like Mak in his life.

'If I'd known this would be one giant love-fest, I never would've tagged along,' Charlotte said, poking her tongue out. 'I'm happy for you guys, but you make me sick.'

'Aww, honey.' Mak slipped an arm around her friend's waist. 'You'll meet someone soon.'

'Yeah, and I'll be sitting alongside the pilot flying your plane too.' Charlotte rolled her eyes. 'No offence, Hudson and Tanner, but men are the pits.'

Hating Charlotte's morose expression, Hudson proposed a toast. 'To Charlotte. A wonderful woman who needs to find some bozo like us to rip the blinkers from his eyes.'

'To Charlotte.' They chorused in unison, and Hudson was relieved when she mouthed 'thank you' at him.

Mak tapped her bottom lip, making Hudson hard

in an instant. With a little luck and a lot of manoeu-
vring in a tight space, he might get to join the mile-
high club shortly.

'You know, Char, I predict you'll have some hottie wrapped around your finger by the time we come
back for a visit in six months.' Mak nudged Abby. 'I'm
counting on you to help her find said hottie, okay?'

'Poor you,' Charlotte said to Abby. 'Hasn't happened in twenty-six years, can't see it happening in
six months.'

Abby glared at Mak. 'Don't put that kind of pressure on her.'

Hudson bit back a laugh. What Abby really meant
was, 'Don't put that kind of pressure on me.'

Mak grinned and blew Abby a kiss. 'I'm going
to miss you.'

'You're going to miss my pastries, more like it.'
Abby sounded curt, but Hudson saw the glint of tears
in her eyes.

Great. Just what he needed when he wanted to
whisk his girlfriend away: three blubbering women.

Intent on circumventing any potential water-
works, he raised his beer again. 'To us. Following
dreams and following our hearts.'

They echoed his toast, and as Abby, Tanner and
Charlotte engaged in a heated debate about online
dating sites and their validity for finding long-lasting
happiness, Hudson leaned into Mak.

'Ready to embrace your future?'

'With you, always.' She snuggled into his side, warm and loving, where she belonged.

This amazing woman wasn't the only one ready to embrace the future. He had no idea what it might bring but as long as he had Mak, he was ready to face it, head-on.

* * * * *

COMING SOON!

We really hope you enjoyed reading this book. If you're looking for more romance, be sure to head to the shops when new books are available on

Thursday
26th July

To see which titles are coming soon, please visit
millsandboon.co.uk

LET'S TALK

Romance

For exclusive extracts, competitions
and special offers, find us online:

 facebook.com/millsandboon

 @millsandboonuk

 @millsandboon

Or get in touch on 0844 844 1351*

For all the latest titles coming soon, visit
millsandboon.co.uk/nextmonth

*Calls cost 7p per minute plus your phone company's price per minute access charg